The Best
AMERICAN
ESSAYS
2016

GUEST EDITORS OF
THE BEST AMERICAN ESSAYS

The Best AMERICAN ESSAYS® 2016

Edited and with an Introduction
by JONATHAN FRANZEN

Robert Atwan, Series Editor

A Mariner Original
HOUGHTON MIFFLIN HARCOURT
BOSTON • NEW YORK

www.hmhco.com

ISSN 0888-3742
ISBN 978-0-544-81210-9

Printed in the United States of America
DOC 10 9 8 7 6 5 4 3 2
4500636803

Contents

Foreword

ONE OF THE MOST INTRIGUING —and puzzling—comments I've encountered on the art of the essay comes from one of America's foremost essayists, Ralph Waldo Emerson. After the remarkable Elizabeth Peabody showed her good friend Emerson an essay written by her future brother-in-law, Nathaniel Hawthorne, Emerson "complained that there was no inside in it." Though he never wrote an essay on the essay—most of his remarks on craft and composition are scattered throughout his journals and recorded conversations—Emerson did know plenty about essays and essay-writing. What could he have meant by an essay having "no inside"?

Hawthorne had published the essay Emerson complained about, "Foot-prints on the Sea-shore," in 1838. A personal, meditative essay (easily found online) that recounts an afternoon spent in near-solitude at a sandy stretch of beach near his home in Salem, Massachusetts, "Foot-prints" was like nothing Emerson ever wrote or would write. A more accomplished essayist than usually acknowledged, Hawthorne, borrowing from his illustrious predecessor Washington Irving, called the essay a "sketch." Hawthorne published many sketches, intermingling them with his "tales" and making no distinction between fiction and nonfiction when he collected them in various volumes. With its neoclassical language (perhaps he's having a bit of fun calling caught fish "scaly prey") and private musings mixed with erotic suggestions stimulated by his characteristic voyeurism, "Foot-prints" is about as far from Emerson as an essay can get.

But how is Hawthorne's essay lacking an "inside"? I don't think

Emerson (he and Hawthorne shared no warmth) is complaining
here about mere surfaces, superficiality. What I think Emerson
finds missing is an interiority, an inner dynamic of creative conflict. Hawthorne seems too evasively comfortable in his little private excursion to the seashore. There seems to be little at stake or
at risk emotionally or intellectually. Unlike Emerson's own essays,
Hawthorne's "Foot-prints" contains no centripetal force. Its movement does not seek a center, a vital "inside." Or so I suppose Emerson thought when he enigmatically criticized Hawthorne's essay.

It's not a long way from "Foot-prints on the Sea-shore" to "Once
More to the Lake." These are both satisfying essays in their way,
but Emerson favored a different kinetics, one that—as it turned
out—had little influence on future essayists in the way that his
literary hero Montaigne indisputedly did. Both essayists are wholly
attracted to Pyrrhonism (from the ancient Greek philosopher Pyr-
rho, who allegedly maintained that nothing can be known with
certainty). But Montaigne's stance of "Que sais-je?" (What do I
know?) represented a skepticism immersed in his presence and
personality—which centuries later still come alive on the page. In
nearly all of Emerson's writing we do not encounter an engaging
personality. We know his thoughts and style of thinking, but we
rarely get a glimpse of the man himself. Montaigne's essays are his
memoir; Emerson's essays, with their chilly impersonality, might
be considered almost an anti-memoir. Disappointed readers will
always ask the same question: "Where's Waldo?"

Emerson was preoccupied with sentences. As biographer Robert
D. Richardson observes in his succinct book on Emerson's creative
process, *First We Read, Then We Write*, Emerson spoke of writing
only in terms of sentences, not in terms of the essay. But the art of
the sentence was not achieved without great struggle. Richardson
cites one of Emerson's letters to his friend Thomas Carlyle: "Here
I sit and read and write with very little system and as far as regards
composition with the most fragmentary result: paragraphs incom-
pressible, each sentence an infinitely repellent particle." This isn't
what one would expect to find in a student's guide to composition,
but Richardson's admirable book is as close as anyone can come to
workshopping the essay with Ralph Waldo Emerson.

Coherence wasn't one of Emerson's compositional goals. He
famously wrote that "consistency is the hobgoblin of little minds."
Richardson expands on this by citing the comments of a Williams

College student, Charles Woodbury, a young man Emerson be-
friended in his sixties and often spoke to about writing, life, and
ideas. "Neither concern yourself about consistency," he once said.
"The moment you putty and plaster your expressions to make
them hang together, you have begun a weakening process . . . If
you must be contradictory, let it be clean and sharp as the two
blades of scissors meet."

He was intellectually suspicious of many conventional rhetorical
techniques, which he saw as obstructions to original thought. He
dismisses skeletons, outlines, and scaffolding as creative interfer-
ences. He dislikes classifications and categorizations. In his journal
he admits that many left his lectures "puzzled." As an orator and
one of the most prominent lecturers of his time, he had a devotion to eloquence, but it was not the rhetorical brand of eloquence
many expected. Rhetoric comes from the outside and is something
we tend to impose on our thoughts. Emerson's eloquence sought
the unsystematic inside: spontaneity, surprise, magic. As a writer
and thinker, he was more interested in the spark than the fire.

Yeats memorably said, "Out of the quarrel with others we make
rhetoric, out of the quarrel with ourselves we make poetry." Emerson aspired to the poetry that originates from that quarrel with
ourselves. At the core of the essays we find a remarkable self-opposition that seems to be an abundant source of creativity. A mind
in process, he knew, is rarely rhetorically persuasive. Toward the
conclusion of one of his finest essays, "Circles," he writes,

> Let me remind the reader that I am only an experimenter. Do not set
> the least value on what I do, or the least discredit on what I do not, as
> if I pretended to settle any thing as true or false. I unsettle all things.
> No facts are to me sacred; none are profane; I simply experiment, an
> endless seeker with no Past at my back.

Trigger warning: Emerson's essays are not "safe spaces." Not even
for himself.

And Emerson is not for everyone. For many readers, all that
can be seen is the outside—the lofty exhortations, the bewilder-
ing transitions, the poetically expressed abstractions. But unless
we read him with keen attention to the Wittgensteinian struggle
with language going on "inside" the essay, we miss the literary and
intellectual exhilaration. There was some fun had at Emerson's ex-
pense a few years ago when someone discovered the English phi-

losopher John Stuart Mill's surprising comments in his copy of the essays. Mill was not impressed and apparently enjoyed annotating the margins with "nonsense," "fudge," "stupid," "pooh," "trash," "sentimental," "superficial," and "very stupid."

A preeminent logician and hardheaded Utilitarian, Mill, a stickler for precision, was clearly no Concord Transcendentalist. Yet despite his marginal barbs, the two thinkers had something important in common: they shared—along with Montaigne—a passion for free and open discussion and a rare mental capacity for self-opposition. In the chapter "Of the Liberty of Thought and Discussion" in his classic argument *On Liberty,* Mill demands a level of tolerance and respect for opposing opinions that would seem humanly out of reach at any time, and especially so in our current climate of polarized intolerance. For Mill, like Emerson, nothing was truly settled, and he proposed an all but impossible moral obligation on individual thought: "We can never be sure that the opinion we are attempting to stifle is a false opinion; and, if we were sure, stifling it would be an evil still." He believed that "all silencing of discussion is an assumption of infallibility," and he maintained what to him represented a crucial distinction: there is "the greatest difference," he wrote, "between presuming an opinion to be true, because, with every opportunity for contesting it, it has not been refuted, and assuming its truth for the purpose of not permitting its refutation."

Emerson, as I read him, would certainly agree with Mill's receptivity to contrary opinions, whether they are debated in a public arena or deep within ourselves. And perhaps that simply shows how irrelevant he is today.

The Best American Essays features a selection of the year's outstanding essays—essays of literary achievement that show an awareness of craft and forcefulness of thought. Hundreds of essays are gathered annually from a wide assortment of national and regional publications. These essays are then screened, and approximately 100 are turned over to a distinguished guest editor, who may add a few personal discoveries and who makes the final selection. The list of notable essays appearing in the back of the book is drawn from a final comprehensive list that includes not only all the essays submitted to the guest editor but also many that were not submitted.

To qualify for the volume, the essay must be a work of respectable literary quality, intended as a fully developed, independent essay (not an excerpt) on a subject of general interest (not specialized scholarship), originally written in English (or translated by the author) for publication in an American periodical during the calendar year. Note that abridgements and excerpts taken from longer works and published in magazines do not qualify for the series, but if considered significant they will appear in the list of notable essays in the back of the volume. Today's essay is a highly flexible and shifting form, however, so these criteria are not carved in stone.

Magazine editors who want to be sure their contributors will be considered each year should submit issues or subscriptions to

The Best American Essays
Houghton Mifflin Harcourt
222 Berkeley St., #11
Boston, MA 02116

Writers and editors are welcome to submit published essays from any American periodical for consideration; unpublished work does not qualify for the series and cannot be reviewed or evaluated. Also ineligible are essays that have been published in book form—such as a contribution to a collection—but have never appeared in a periodical. All submissions must be directly from the publication and not in manuscript or printout format. Editors of online magazines and literary bloggers should not assume that appropriate work will be seen; they are invited to submit printed copies of the essays to the address above. Please note that, owing to the increasing number of submissions from online sources, material that does not include a full citation (name of publication, date of publication, and author contact information) will no longer be considered.

I'd like to dedicate this thirty-first volume in the series to the great essayist, neurologist, and scientist Dr. Oliver Sacks, who died after a brave struggle with cancer on August 30, 2015, in New York City at the age of eighty-two. He wrote brilliantly right up to the end, and we are pleased to once again include one of his essays in this series, though, sadly, one of his last.

As always, I'm indebted to Nicole Angeloro for her keen editorial skills and uncanny ability to keep the annual express train running smoothly and on schedule. A special thanks to other publishing people with Houghton Mifflin Harcourt—Liz Duvall, Carla Gray, and Megan Wilson. I'm extremely grateful to Jonathan Franzen for agreeing to serve as guest editor and for contributing an introduction that is a must-read for anyone interested in the art of the essay. What he says about the essayist's difficult embrace of risk and honesty can be felt throughout this exceptionally diverse and often emotionally turbulent collection.

R.A.

Introduction

IF AN ESSAY is something *essayed*—something hazarded, not definitive, not authoritative; something ventured on the basis of the author's personal experience and subjectivity—we might seem to be living in an essayistic golden age. Which party you went to on Friday night, who you saw there, and how you felt about it afterward: the presumption of social media is that even the tiniest subjective micronarrative is worthy not only of private notation, as in a diary, but of sharing with other people. Bloggers, both pro and amateur, operate on a similar presumption. Traditionally hard news reporting, in places like *The New York Times,* has softened up to allow the *I,* with its voice and opinions and impressions, to take the front-page spotlight. Book reviewers (who nowadays are basically all amateurs, since almost none of them earn a living wage) feel less and less constrained to discuss novels with any kind of objectivity; it didn't use to matter if Raskolnikov and Lily Bart were likable, but the question of "likability," with its implicit privileging of the reviewer's personal feelings, is now a key element of critical judgment. And literary fiction is looking more and more like essay. Some of the most influential novels of recent years, by Ben Lerner and Rachel Cusk and Karl Ove Knausgård, take the method of self-conscious first-person testimony to a new level. Their more extreme admirers will tell you that imagination and invention are outmoded contrivances; that to inhabit the subjectivity of a character unlike the author is an act of appropriation, even colonialism; that the only authentic and politically defensible mode of narrative is autobiography.

And yet the personal essay itself—the formal apparatus developed by Montaigne and advanced by Emerson and Woolf and Baldwin—is in eclipse. Many large-circulation American magazines, including *The New Yorker,* have all but ceased to publish pure essays. The form persists mainly in smaller publications that collectively have fewer readers than Adele has Twitter followers. Is the essay becoming an endangered species? Or is it a species that has so fully invaded the larger culture that it no longer needs its original niche?

A personal and subjective micronarrative: the few lessons I've learned about writing essays were given by my editor at *The New Yorker,* Henry Finder. I first came to Henry, in 1994, as a would-be journalist in pressing need of money. Largely through dumb luck, I produced a publishable story about the U.S. Postal Service, and then, through native incompetence, I wrote an unpublishable piece about the Sierra Club. This was the point at which Henry suggested that I might have some aptitude as an essayist. I heard him to be saying, "since you're obviously a crap journalist," and denied that I had any such aptitude. I'd been raised with a midwestern horror of yakking too much about myself, and I had an additional prejudice, derived from certain wrongheaded ideas about novel-writing, against the *stating* of things that could more rewardingly be *depicted.* But I still needed money, and so I kept calling Henry for book review assignments. On one of these calls, he asked me if I had any interest in the tobacco industry—the subject of a major new history by Richard Kluger. I quickly said, "Cigarettes are the last thing in the world I want to write about." To this, Henry even more quickly replied, "*Therefore* you must write about them."

This was my first lesson from Henry, and it remains the most important one. After smoking throughout my twenties, I'd succeeded in quitting for two years in my early thirties. But when I was assigned the post-office piece and became terrified of picking up the phone and introducing myself as a *New Yorker* journalist, I'd taken up the habit again. In the years since then, I'd managed to think of myself as a nonsmoker, or at least as a person so firmly resolved to quit again that I might as well already have been a nonsmoker, even as I continued to smoke. My state of mind was like a quantum wave function in which I could be totally a smoker but also totally not a smoker, so long as I never took measure of myself.

And it was instantly clear to me that writing about cigarettes would force me to take my measure. This is what essays do.

There was also the problem of my mother, whose father had died of lung cancer and who was militantly anti-tobacco. I'd concealed my habit from her for more than fifteen years. One reason I needed to preserve my indeterminacy as a smoker/nonsmoker was that I didn't enjoy lying to her. As soon as I could succeed in quitting again, permanently, the wave function would collapse and I would be, 100 percent, the nonsmoker I'd always represented myself to be—but only if I didn't first come out, in print, as a smoker.

Henry had been a twentysomething wunderkind when Tina Brown hired him at *The New Yorker*. He had a distinctive tight-chested manner of speaking, a kind of hyper-articulate mumble, like prose acutely well edited but barely legible. I was awed by his intelligence and erudition and had quickly come to live in fear of disappointing him. His passionate emphasis in "*Therefore* you must write about them"—he was the only speaker I knew who could get away with the stressed initial "*Therefore*" and the imperative "must" —allowed me to hope that I'd registered in his consciousness in some small way, and that he cared about my development as a writer.

And so I went to work on the essay, every day combusting half a dozen Merit Ultra Lights in front of a box fan in my living room window, and handed in the only thing I ever wrote for Henry that didn't need his editing. I don't remember how my mother got her hands on the essay or how she conveyed to me her deep sense of betrayal, whether by letter or in a phone call, but I do remember that she then didn't communicate with me for six weeks—by a wide margin the longest she ever went silent on me. It was exactly as I'd feared. But when she got over it and began sending me letters again, I felt seen by her, seen for what I was, in a way I'd never felt before. It wasn't just that my "real" self had been concealed from her; it was as if there hadn't really been a self to see.

Kierkegaard, in *Either/Or*, makes fun of the "busy man" for whom busyness is a way of avoiding an honest self-reckoning. You might wake up in the night and realize that you're lonely in your marriage, or that you need to think about what your carbon footprint is doing to the planet, but the next day you have a million little things to do, and the day after that you have another million things. As long as there's no end of little things, you never have to stop and confront the bigger questions. Writing or reading an essay isn't the only way to stop and ask yourself who you really are and what your life might mean, but it is one good way. And if you consider how laughably unbusy Kierkegaard's Copenhagen was compared to our own age, those subjective tweets and blog posts don't seem so essayistic. They seem more like a means of avoiding what a real essay might force on us. We spend our days reading, on screens, stuff we'd never bother reading in a printed book, and bitch about how busy we are.

I quit cigarettes for the second time in 1997. And then, in 2002, for the final time. And then, in 2003, for the last and final time —unless you count the smokeless nicotine that's coursing through my bloodstream as I write this. Attempting to write an honest essay doesn't alter the multiplicity of my selves; I'm still simultaneously a reptile-brained addict, a worrier about my health, an eternal teenager, a self-medicating depressive. What changes, if I take the time to stop and measure, is that my multiselved identity acquires *substance*.

One of the mysteries of literature is that personal substance, as perceived by both the writer and the reader, is situated outside the body of either of them, on some kind of page. How can I feel realer to myself in a thing I'm writing than I do inside my body? How can I feel closer to another person when I'm reading her words than I do when I'm sitting next to her? The answer, in part, is that both writing and reading demand full attentiveness. But it surely also has to do with the kind of *ordering* that is possible only on the page.

Here I might mention two other lessons I learned from Henry Finder. One was "Every essay, even a think piece, tells a story." The other was "There are only two ways to organize material: 'Like goes with like' and 'This followed that.'" These precepts may seem self-evident, but any grader of high school or college essays can tell you that they aren't. To me it was especially not evident that a think piece should follow the rules of drama. And yet: Doesn't a good argument begin by positing some difficult problem? And doesn't it then propose an escape from the problem through some bold proposition, and set up obstacles in the form of objections and counterarguments, and finally, through a series of reversals, take us to an unforeseen but satisfying conclusion?

If you accept Henry's premise that a successful prose piece consists of material arranged in the form of a story, and if you share my own conviction that our identities consist of the stories we tell about ourselves ("I am the person who was born in the Midwest and defected to the Northeast; I am the person who married young and later defected from the marriage"), it makes sense that we should get a strong hit of personal substance from the labor of writing and the pleasure of reading. When I'm alone in the woods or having dinner with a friend, I'm overwhelmed by the quantity and specificity of sensory data coming at me from random stimuli. The act of writing subtracts almost everything, leaving only the alphabet and punctuation marks, and progresses toward nonrandomness. Sometimes the work consists of distilling a familiar story and discovering, in the process, which seemingly essential elements can be omitted and which new elements unexpectedly need to be added. Sometimes—especially in the case of an argument— a completely new story is called for. The discipline of fashioning a compelling narrative can crystallize thoughts and feelings that you only dimly knew you had in you. The default organizing principle for the essayist, therefore, is "This followed that." Every essay in this volume, with the exception of Ela Harrison's love letter to the art of translation, tells a chronologically ordered story, advances a sequential argument ("This follows *from* that"), or both.

Henry's other organizing principle, "Like goes with like," comes in both basic and expert versions. The basic version holds that when you're looking at a mass of material that doesn't lend itself to storytelling, you should sort it into categories, grouping similar elements together; again, this may sound self-evident, but the selecting of categories often leads to fruitful insights, as in Richard M. Lange's investigation of why merely witnessing a violent death is traumatic. In the expert version of the principle, the grouping of like with like becomes the very engine of the essay's meaning. Two beautiful examples are Jill Sisson Quinn's "Big Night," which turns on the *alikeness* of studying salamanders and entering an adoption lottery, and Justin Phillip Reed's "Killing Like They Do in the Movies," which reads the history of American lynchings through the eerie lens of Hollywood horror flicks.

My main criterion in selecting this year's essays was whether an author had taken a risk. There exist other modes of essay, lyrical modes, free-associative modes, political modes, and I admit to excluding some fine instances of them simply because they didn't satisfy my taste for intensity. In the essays I did choose, risk itself comes in different forms. There's the perennial risk of upsetting family and friends by writing about them or revealing secrets to them. There's the professional risk that Laura Kipnis took in publishing "Sexual Paranoia Strikes Academe." There's the risk of advancing a potentially controversial theory of anti-Semitism or post-combat stress; the risk of being called a bad person for sleeping with married men or for severing contact with a parent; the risk of looking beyond racial identity at a moment when #BlackLives Matter is focusing national attention on it. There is, finally, the risk I feel most grateful to a writer for taking: shame. As Arthur Miller once said, "The best work that anybody ever writes is on the verge of embarrassing him, always." The writer has to be like the firefighter, whose job, while everyone else is fleeing the flames, is to run straight into them. Your material feels too hot, too shameful, to even think about? *Therefore* you must write about it.

Shame, in digital media, occurs most frequently as a transitive verb, an action you inflict on someone else. As a noun — a thing you might fear experiencing yourself — it tends to remain carefully hidden. Social media, in particular, are celebrated by their advocates for enabling the construction of personas through which the user can "safely" experiment with different aspects of his or her personality. But most of these personas are self-flattering in one way or another, cooler or cockier or handsomer than the real person behind them, and the Internet is structured to create communities of the intensely like-minded. Although the virtual world may look from a distance like a free-for-all of essayistic self-exposure, it actually functions more like a system of *avoiding* the potentially shameful self.

What distinguishes the essay from most of the writing that occurs within this system isn't the presumption that your private story is of interest to strangers. The difference is that the essayist's experiments aren't safe. Risk is implicit from the minute you decide to write "an essay" rather than something casual, fragmentary, impromptu. The sheer act of carefully crafting a story raises the stakes. And the rigors of craft — the demands of form, the solitary sustained engagement with twenty-six letters and some punctuation marks — have the terrible power to reveal where you've been lying to yourself and what you haven't properly thought through. The rigors of craft give you substance. And then, instead of sharing with a closed circle of friends or with a community safely known to be like-minded, you submit the finished written thing to an audience of readers who may or may not be sympathetic. To publish an honest essay is, always, to risk shame. But the reward, if you're lucky enough to get it, is connection with a grateful stranger. The essay as a species may be verging on endangered, but a mediated world of buried shames has greater need of it than ever.

JONATHAN FRANZEN

The Best
AMERICAN
ESSAYS
2016

FRANCISCO CANTÚ

Bajadas

FROM *Ploughshares*

ba·ja·da *noun*
1: a steep curved descending road or trail
2: an alluvial plain formed at the base of a mountain by the coalescing of several alluvial fans

    —Origin 1865–70, Americanism: from the Spanish feminine
    past participle of *bajar:* to descend

20 December

SANTIAGO QUIT THE academy yesterday. We were on our way
into town when I heard the news, speeding across the cold and
brittle grasslands of New Mexico. Morales must have told me, or
maybe it was Hart. I called Santiago as soon as I found out. You
don't have to quit, I told him, you can still finish, you should stay. I
can't, he said, it's not the work for me. I have to go back to Puerto
Rico; I have to be with my family. I wished him luck and told him I
was sorry to see him go. He thanked me and said to finish for the
both of us, and I promised that I would.

Of all my classmates, it was Santiago I most wanted to see graduate. He marched out of step, his gear was a mess, he couldn't
handle his weapon, and it took him over fifteen minutes to run the
mile and a half. But he tried harder than any of us. He sweated the
most, yelled the loudest. He was thirty-eight, an accountant from
Puerto Rico, a husband and a father. Yesterday he left the firing
range with a pocket full of live rounds, and the instructors ordered
him to sing "I'm a Little Teapot" in front of the class. He didn't
know the song, so they suggested "God Bless America." He belted

out the chorus at the top of his lungs, his chest heaving after each line. We laughed, all of us, at his thick accent, at the misremembered verses, at his voice, off-key and quaking.

In town, over drinks, Hart went on about the winters in Detroit. I can't go back there, he said, not like Santiago. Fuck that. He asked Morales and me about winter in Arizona. Morales laughed. You don't have to worry about snow where we're going, *vato*, that's for sure. Hart thought it sounded nice. Nice? I asked. Just wait until the summer. Have you ever felt 115 degrees? Hell no, he said. Well, I told him, we'll be out in the heat, fetching dead bodies from the desert. Who the fuck walks in the desert when it's 115? he asked. I drank my way through another beer and went rambling on about how everyone used to cross in the city, in San Diego and El Paso, until they shut it all down in the '90s with fences and newly hired Border Patrol agents like us. If they sealed the cities, they thought, people wouldn't risk crossing in the mountains and the deserts. But they were wrong, I said, and now we're the ones who get to deal with it. Morales looked at me, his eyes dark and buried beneath his brow. I'm sorry, I told them, I can't help it—I studied this shit in school.

On our way back to the academy, I sat in the backseat of Morales's truck. In the front, Morales told Hart about growing up on the border in Douglas, about uncles and cousins on the south side, and I sat with my head against the cold glass of the window, staring at the darkened plain, slipping in and out of sleep.

3 *January*

Last week my mother flew in from Arizona to see me, because —she said—we've never missed a Christmas together. She picked me up at the academy on Christmas Eve and we drove through the straw-colored hills, leaving behind the trembling Chihuahuan grasslands as we climbed into the evergreen mountains of southern New Mexico. We stayed the night in a two-room cabin, warm and bright with pinewood. We set up a miniature tree on the living room table, decorating it with tiny glass bulbs. Then, wrapped in blankets, we laughed and drank eggnog and brandy until the conversation deteriorated into discussion of my impending work.

Look, my mother said, I spent most of my adult life working

for the government as a park ranger, so don't take this the wrong way—but don't you think it's below you, earning a degree just to become a border cop? Look, I said, I spent four years away from home, studying this place through facts, policy, and history. I'm tired of reading. I want to exist outside, to know the reality of this border, day in and day out. Are you crazy? she said. You grew up with me, living in deserts and national parks. We've never been far from the border. Sure, I said, but I don't truly understand the landscape, I don't know how to handle myself in the face of ugliness or danger. My mother balked. There are ways to learn that don't place you at risk, she said, ways that let you help people. I fumed. I can still help people, I told her—I speak Spanish, I've lived in Mexico, I've been to the places where people are coming from. And don't worry, I told her, I won't place myself at risk—I'm not too proud to back away from danger.

Good, she said. We hugged, and she told me she was happy I'd soon be back home in Arizona, closer to her. Before bed we each opened a single present, as we have done every Christmas Eve since I can remember.

In the morning we ate brunch at the town's historic hotel, feasting on pot roast by a crackling fire. Afterward we climbed the stairs to a narrow lookout tower where people crowded and huddled together in jackets, walking in slow circles to take in the view. Below us an expanse of sunlit plain stretched westward from the base of the mountain. I watched as the landscape shifted under the winter light. Behind me, my mother placed her hand on my shoulder and pointed to a cloud of gypsum sand in the distance, impossibly small, swirling across the basin desert.

24 *February*

We caught our first dope load today, only our second day after arriving at the station from the academy. We were east of the port of entry when the sensor hit at Sykes trail. At the trailhead, Cole, our supervisor, found foot sign for eight and had us pile out of the vehicles. For four miles we made our way toward the mountains following toe digs and kicked-over rocks. Cole went in front and called us up one by one to watch us cut sign. We found the first bundle discarded among the boulders at the base of the pass. We spread out to comb the hillsides and after about ten minutes we had recovered two backpacks filled with food and clothes and four more fifty-pound bundles wrapped in sugar sacks spray-painted black. Cole had us dump the packs, and I watched as several of my classmates ripped and tore at the clothing, scattering it among the tangled branches of mesquite and paloverde. In one of the backpacks I found a laminated prayer card depicting Saint Jude, a tongue of flames hovering above his head. Morales found a pack of cigarettes and sat smoking on a rock as others laughed loudly and stepped on a heap of food. Nearby, Hart giggled and shouted to us as he pissed on a pile of ransacked belongings. As we hiked with the bundles back to our vehicles, the February sun grew low in the sky and cast a warm light over the desert. At the edge of the trail, in the pink shade of a paloverde, a desert tortoise raised itself up on its front legs to watch us pass.

2 April

Tonight we stood for hours in the darkness along the pole line. After we had tired of the cold and the buzzing of the power lines, Cole had us lay a spike strip across the dirt road and return to wait in our vehicles parked in a nearby wash. We sat with the engines on and the heat blasting, and after a few minutes of silence, Morales asked Cole why some of the agents at the station called him "Black Death." He laughed and pulled a can of Copenhagen from his shirt pocket. You have to be careful, he said, the Indians out here, when they're drunk and walking at night between the villages, they fall asleep on the fucking road. He packed the can as he spoke, swinging his right arm and thumping his forefinger across the lid. When it's cold out, he explained, the asphalt holds warmth from the sun, even at night. A few years ago I was working the midnight shift, driving down IR-9, and I saw this fucking Indian asleep in the middle of the road. I stopped the truck and woke his ass up. His brother was there with him, sleeping in the bushes. They were drunk as hell. Cole pinched a wad of dip into his mouth. His lower lip bulged, catching the green light from the control panel. I gave the guys a ride into the next village, he said, dropped them off at their cousin's place. Told them not to sleep on the goddamn road. Cole grabbed an empty Pepsi cup from the center console and spit. Maybe nine or ten months later, he continued, same fucking spot, I ran over the guy, killed him right there. Same fucking guy, asleep on the damn road. I never even saw him. After that they started calling me Black Death. Cole laughed and spat into his cup and a few of us laughed with him, not knowing exactly what kind of laugh it was.

Just after midnight, a blacked-out truck roared across the spikes and three of its tires went. We tore after it, speeding blindly through a cloud of dust until we realized the vehicle had turned. We doubled back to where the tire sign left the road and followed it until we found the truck abandoned at the foot of a hill. In the back of the truck we found two marijuana bundles and a .22 rifle. Cole sent us to scour the hillside with our flashlights, but we only found one other bundle. It's a fucking gimme load, Cole said. I asked what he meant. It's a goddamn distraction, that's what. They're waiting us out. But my classmates and I didn't care, we were high from the chase. We drove the truck into a wash until it became stuck, and slashed the unpopped tire, leaving it there with the lights on and the engine running. On the way back to the station, I asked Cole what would happen to the truck. He told me he'd call the tribal police to seize the vehicle, but I knew he wouldn't. Even if he did, they wouldn't come for it, they wouldn't want the paperwork either. They too would leave it here to be ransacked, picked over, and lit on fire—evidence of a swirling disorder.

4 April

After sundown Cole sent Morales up a hill near the highway with a thermal reconnaissance camera. Let me borrow your beanie, *vato*, he said to me, it's cold out. I handed it to him and stayed inside the vehicle, waiting with the others. An hour later he spotted a group of ten just east of mile marker five. We rushed out of the car and set out on foot as he guided us in on the radio, but by the time we reached the group, they had already scattered. We found them one by one, huddled in the brush and curled up around the trunks of paloverde trees and cholla cactus. Not one of them ran. We made them take off their shoelaces and empty their backpacks, and we walked all ten of them single file back to the road. For a while I walked next to an older man who told me they were all from Michoacán. It's beautiful there, I said. Yes, he replied, but there's no work. You've been to Michoacán? he asked. I told him I had. Then you must have seen what it is to live in Mexico, he said. And now you see what it is like for us at the border. *Pues sí,* I said, we're out here every day. For a while we walked silently next to each other and then, after several minutes, he sighed deeply. *Hay mucha desesperación,* he told me, almost whispering. I tried to look at his face, but it was too dark.

At the station I processed the man for deportation, and he asked me after I had taken his fingerprints if there was any work at the station for him. You don't understand, I said, you've just got to wait here until the bus comes. They'll take you to Tucson and then to Nogales and then you'll be back in Mexico. I understand, he assured me, I just want to know if there is something I can do while I wait, something to help. I can take out the trash or clean out the cells. I want to show you that I'm here to work, that I'm not a bad person, that I'm not here to bring in drugs, I'm not here to do anything illegal. I want to work. I looked at him. I know that, I said.

7 *April*

Sunday night Cole showed us the layup spot where he had almost been run over by smugglers. He led us to a wide wash full of old blankets and discarded clothes and pieces of twine and empty cans of tuna and crushed water bottles. We climbed out of the wash and walked to a nearby cactus, a tall and sprawling chain-fruit cholla, and Cole asked if any of us had hand sanitizer. Someone tossed him a small bottle and he emptied the gel on the black trunk of the cactus. Cole asked for a lighter, and with it he lit the gel and stepped back to watch the flames crawl up the trunk, crackling and popping as they engulfed the plant's spiny arms. In the light from the fire, Cole packed his can of dip and took a pinch into his mouth. His bottom lip shone taut and smooth, his shaved black skin reflecting the flames. He spit into the fire and the rest of us stood with him in a circle around the cholla as it burned, laughing loudly, taking pictures and video with our phones, watching as thick smoke billowed into the night, filling the air with the burnt smell of tar and resin, like freshly laid asphalt.

9 April

Cole was ahead scouting the trail in the darkness when he radioed about the mountain lion. Come with your sidearms drawn, he said. We figured he was full of shit. We had been talking loudly, walking with our flashlights on—surely a mountain lion would shy away. We continued down the trail until the ground leveled off, and it was then that a grave hiss issued up from the darkness beside us, a sound like hot wind escaping the depths of the earth. Holy fucking shit, we said. We drew our sidearms and shuffled down the path back to back, casting light in all directions around us. In that moment I felt a profound and immediate fear—not of the danger posed to us by the animal, but rather of the idea that it would show itself to us, so many men armed and heedless, that it would be shot down and lit on fire and left here beside the trail, another relic of a desert unspooling.

7 June

There are days when I feel I am becoming good at what I do. And then I wonder, what does it mean to be good at this? I wonder sometimes how I might explain certain things, the sense in what we do when they run from us, scattering into the brush, leaving behind their water jugs and their backpacks full of food and clothes, how to explain what we do when we discover their layup spots stocked with water and stashed rations. Of course, what you do depends on who you're with, depends on what kind of agent you are, what kind of agent you want to become, but it's true that we slash their bottles and drain their water into the dry earth, that we dump their backpacks and pile their food and clothes to be crushed and pissed on and stepped over, strewn across the desert and set ablaze, and Christ, it sounds terrible, and maybe it is, but the idea is that when they come out from their hiding places, when they regroup and return to find their stockpiles ransacked and stripped, they'll realize then their situation, that they're fucked, that it's hopeless to continue on, and they'll quit right then and there, they'll save themselves, they'll struggle toward the nearest highway or dirt road to flag down some passing agent or they'll head for the nearest parched village to knock on someone's door, someone who will give them food and water and call us to take them in—that's the idea, the sense in it all. But still I have nightmares, visions of them staggering through the desert, men from Michoacán, from places I've known, men lost and wandering without food or water, dying slowly as they look for some road, some village, some way out. In my dreams I seek them, searching in vain until finally I am met by their bodies lying facedown on the ground before me, dead and stinking on the desert floor, human waypoints in a vast and smoldering expanse.

23 June

Last month we were released from the training unit and dispersed into rotating shifts to work under journeymen agents. For the past week I've been partnered with Mortenson, a four-year veteran and the Mormon son of a Salt Lake City cop. This morning, at dawn, we sat together in the port of entry and watched from the camera room as two men and a woman cut a hole in the pedestrian fence. Mortenson and I bolted from the room and ran to the site of the breach, rounding the corner just in time to see the two men already scrambling back through the hole to Mexico. The woman stood motionless beside the fence, too scared to run. As Mortenson inspected the breach, the girl wept, telling me it was her birthday, that she was turning twenty-three, and she pleaded for me to let her go, swearing she would never cross again. Mortenson turned and took a long look at the woman and then laughed. I booked her last week, he said.

She spoke hurriedly to us as we walked back to the port of entry, and while Mortenson went inside to gather our things, I stood with her in the parking lot. She told me she was from Guadalajara, that she had some problems there, that she had already tried four times to cross. She swore to me that she would stay in Mexico for good this time, that she would finally go back to finish music school. *Te lo juro,* she said. She looked at me and smiled. Someday I'm going to be a singer, you know. I believe it, I said, smiling back. She told me that she thought I was nice, and before Mortenson returned from the port, she snuck her counterfeit green card into my hand, telling me she didn't want to get in trouble if they found it on her at the processing center. When Mortenson came back, we helped her into the patrol vehicle and drove north toward the station, laughing and applauding as she sang to us from the backseat. She's going to be a singer, I told Mortenson. The woman beamed. She already is, he said.

27 July

Last night, finally allowed to patrol on my own, I sat watching storms roll across the moonlit desert. There were three of them: the first due south in Mexico; the second in the east, creeping down from the mountains; the third hovering just behind me, close enough for me to feel smatterings of rain and gusts of warm wind. In the distance, hot lightning appeared like a line of neon, illuminating the desert in a shuddering white light.

30 July

Agents found Martin Ubalde de la Vega and his three companions on the bombing range ten miles west of the highway. At the time of rescue, the four men had been in the desert for six days and had wandered in the July heat for more than forty-eight hours without food or water. By the time they were found, one of the men had already met his death. Of the survivors, one was quickly treated and discharged from the hospital, while another remained in intensive care, recently awoken from a coma, unable to remember his own name. When I arrived at the hospital asking for the third survivor, nurses explained that he was recovering from kidney failure and they guided me to his room, where he lay hidden like a dark stone in white sheets.

I had been charged with watching over de la Vega until his condition was stable, at which point I would transport him to the station to be processed for deportation. I settled in a chair next to him, and after several moments of silence, I asked him to tell me about himself. He answered timidly, as if unsure of what to say or even how to speak. He began by apologizing for his Spanish, explaining that he only knew what they had taught him in school. He told me he came from the jungles of Guerrero, that in his village they spoke Mixtec and farmed the green earth. He was the father of seven children, he said, five girls and two boys. His eldest daughter lived in California and he had crossed the border with plans to go there, to live with her and find work.

We spent the following hours watching *telenovelas* and occasionally de la Vega would turn to ask me about the women in America, wondering if they were like the ones on TV. Then, smiling, he began to tell me about his youngest daughter, still in Mexico. She's just turned eighteen, he said. You could marry her.

Later that afternoon de la Vega was cleared for release. The nurse brought in his belongings—a pair of blue jeans and sneakers with holes worn through the soles. I asked what had happened to his shirt. I don't know, he told me. I looked at the nurse and she shrugged, telling me he had come that way. We've got no clothes here, she added, only hospital gowns. As we exited the building, I imagined de la Vega's embarrassment, the fear he must have at remaining bare-chested as he was to be ferried through alien territory, booked and transferred between government processing centers and bused to the border to enter his country alone and half naked.

At the patrol vehicle, I placed de la Vega in the passenger seat and popped the trunk. At the back of the cruiser, I undid my gun belt, unbuttoned my uniform shirt, and removed my white V-neck. Then I reassembled my uniform and returned to the passenger door and offered de la Vega my undershirt. Before leaving town, I asked de la Vega if he was hungry. You should eat something now, I told him, at the station there's only juice and crackers. De la Vega agreed and I asked what he was hungry for. What do Americans eat? he asked. I laughed. Here we eat mostly Mexican food. He looked at me unbelievingly. But we also eat hamburgers, I said. As we pulled into the drive-through window at McDonald's, de la Vega told me he didn't have any money. *Yo te invito,* I said.

As we drove south along the open highway, I tuned in to a Mexican radio station and we listened to the sounds of *norteño* as de la Vega finished his meal. After he had eaten, de la Vega sat silently next to me, watching the passing desert. Then, quietly, as if whispering to me or to someone else, he began to speak of the rains in Guerrero, about the wet and green jungle, and I wondered if he could have ever been made to imagine a place like this—a place where one of his companions would meet his death and another would be made to forget his own name, a landscape where the earth still burned with volcanic heat.

4 August

This evening as I cut for sign along the border road, I watched a Sonoran coachwhip snake try to find its way into Mexico through the pedestrian fence. The animal slithered along the length of the mesh looking for a way south, hitting its head against the rusted metal again and again until finally I guided it over to the wide opening of a wash grate. After the snake made its way across the adjacent road, I stood for a while looking through the mesh, staring at the undulating tracks it left in the dirt.

7 August

Yesterday on the border road a woman on the south side of the pedestrian fence flagged me down as I passed. I stopped my vehicle and went over to her. With panic in her voice she asked me if I knew about her son—he had crossed days ago, she said, or maybe it was a week ago, she wasn't sure. She hadn't heard anything from him, no one had, and she didn't know if he had been caught or if he was lost somewhere in the desert or if he was even still alive. *Estamos desesperados,* she told me, her voice quivering, with one hand clawing at her chest and the other pressed trembling against the border fence. I don't remember what I told her, if I took down the man's name or if I gave her the phone number to some faraway office or remote hotline, but I remember thinking later about de la Vega, about his dead and delirious companions, about all the questions I should have asked the woman. I arrived home that evening and threw my gun belt and uniform across the couch, standing alone in my cavernous living room. I called my mother. I'm safe, I told her, I'm at home.

29 August

At the end of the night, Mortenson called me into the processing room and asked me to translate for two girls who had just been brought in, nine- and ten-year-old sisters who were picked up with two women at the checkpoint. He told me to ask them basic questions: Where is your mother? In California. Who are the women who brought you here? Friends. Where are you from? Sinaloa. The girls peppered me with nervous questions in return: When could they go home? Where were the women who drove them, when were they coming back? Could they call their mother? I tried to explain things to them, but they were too young, too bewildered, too distraught at being surrounded by men in uniform. One of the agents brought the girls a bag of Skittles, but even then they couldn't smile, they couldn't say thank you, they just stood there, looking at the candy with horror.

After the girls were placed in a holding cell, I told Mortenson I had to leave. My shift's over, I said. He told me they still needed to interview the women who were picked up with the girls and asked me to stay and translate. I can't help anymore, I told him, I have to go home. As I drove away from the station, I tried not to think of the girls and my hands shook at the wheel. I wanted to call my mother, but it was too late, it was the middle of the night.

30 August

Last night I dreamed I was grinding my teeth out, spitting the crumbled pieces into my palms and holding them in my cupped hands, searching for someone to show them to, someone who could see what was happening.

12 September

Morales was the first to hear him, screaming in the distance from one of the spider roads. He hiked for a mile or two and found the kid lying on the ground, hysterical. For more than twenty-four hours he had been lost in a vast mesquite thicket. The coyote who left him there told him he was holding back the group and handed him half a liter of water, pointing to some hills in the distance, telling him to walk at them until he found a road. When I arrived with the water, the kid was on the ground next to Morales, lurching in the shade and crying like a child. The kid was fat—his pants hung from his ass and his fly was half open, his zipper broken, his shirt hanging loosely from his shoulders, inside out and torn and soaked in sweat. Morales looked at me and smiled and then turned to the kid. Your water's here, *Gordo.* I kneeled next to him and handed him the gallon jug. He took a sip and began to pant and groan. Drink more, I said, but drink slowly. I can't, he moaned, I'm going to die. No you're not, I told him, you're still sweating.

After the kid drank some water, we helped him up and tried walking him through the thicket toward the road. He lagged and staggered, crying out behind us. *Ay oficial,* he would moan, *no puedo.* As we crouched and barged through tangled branches, I slowly became overwhelmed by his panic until finally we broke out of the thicket and spotted the dirt road. You see the trucks, *Gordo?* Can you make it that far? Maybe we should just leave you here, *no puedes, verdad?*

On the ride back to the station, the kid regained some composure. He was nineteen years old, he told me, and had planned to go to Oregon to sell heroin, *un puño a la vez.* You can make a lot of money that way, he told me. For several minutes the kid was silent. You know, he finally said, I really thought I was going to die in that thicket. I prayed to God that I would get out, I prayed to the Virgin and to all the saints, to every saint I could think of. It's strange, he said, I've never done that before. I've never believed in God.

30 September

Today I went to the hospital to see Morales. He was in a motorcycle accident two weeks ago and wasn't wearing his helmet. For a while we had been hearing at the station that he might not make it. I was too afraid to see him a week ago when he was in a coma, and I was afraid, still, to see him a few days later after he had come out of it, when he would wake up cursing and pulling his tubes out, when he still didn't recognize anybody. When I finally saw him, I was surprised how thin he was, how frail. He had bruises under his deep-set eyes, a feeding tube in his nose, an IV line in his arm, and a huge gash across the left side of his skull where half his hair had been shaved off. *Ey vato,* he said to me quietly. I smiled at him. I like your haircut, I said. As Morales spoke to me he seemed far away, his eyes scanning the room as if searching for some landmark, something to suggest the nature of the place he had come to. His childhood friend from Douglas was there. He told me Morales couldn't see out of his left eye but that doctors thought the sight would come back eventually. His mother and father were there too, speaking quietly to each other in Spanish. A little while after I arrived, Cole and Hart came, and as they stood talking at his bedside, I could see a wet glaze in Cole's eyes. I excused myself from the room, telling everyone I'd come back, but I didn't.

13 October

Last week I took the border road out to the lava flow, driving for more than an hour across rocky hills and long valleys. The earth became darker as I neared the flow, devoid of plants and cactus. To the south a pale band of sand dunes underlined the base of a nameless cordillera, shifting at the horizon in shades of purple and dark clay. I drove across the lava flow and looked over black rocks glistening as if wet under the afternoon sun, rocks pockmarked from a time when the earth melted and simmered between erupting volcanoes, a molten crust cracking and shifting as it cooled.

25 December

At midnight on Christmas Eve, just before the end of my shift, I heard gunshots ring out in Mexico. I stopped my vehicle at the top of a small hill and stood on the roof to watch the sparkling of fireworks along the southern horizon. After returning home, I woke my mother, who had come to visit for the holiday, her eyes bleary with worry and sleep. We sat in my empty living room in the night-weary hours of the morning, drinking eggnog and stringing popcorn around an artificial tree. My mother asked about my shift. It was fine, I said. She asked me if I liked my work, if I was learning what I wanted. It's not something to like, I said, it's not a classroom. It's a job, and I'm getting used to it, and I'm getting good at it. I can make sense of what that means later.

You know, my mother said, it's not just your safety I worry about. I know how the soul can be placed at hazard fighting impossible battles. I spent my whole career working for the government, slowly losing a sense of purpose even though I remained close to the outdoors, close to my passion. I don't want that for you.

I cut her off—I didn't want to tell about my dreams of dead bodies, about the fires burning in the desert, about my hands shaking at the wheel. Mom, I said, let's open a present.

30 December

Tonight the scope truck spotted a group of twenty just north of the line. The operator said they were moving slowly, that it looked as if there might be women and children in the group. He guided us in, and we quickly located their sign and then lost it again across a stretch of hard-packed desert pavement. We split up and combed the hillside, hunting for toe digs and kicked-over rocks. On the walk back to the car, I became furious. There were supposed to be twenty of them, they were supposed to be slow, but still I couldn't catch up, I couldn't stay on the sign, I couldn't even get close enough to hear them in the distance, and so now they remained out there in the desert: men, women, and children, entire families invisible and unheard, and I was powerless to help them, powerless to keep them from straying through the night and the cold.

Girl

FROM *Guernica*

Hair

THE YEAR IS 1990. The place is San Francisco, the Castro. It is Halloween night. I am in my friend John's bathroom, alone in front of the mirror, wearing a black turtleneck and leggings. My face glows back at me from the light of twelve 100-watt bulbs.

In high school I learned to do makeup for theater. I did fake mustaches and eyelashes then, bruises, wounds, tattoos. I remember always being tempted then to do what I have just done now, and always stopping, always thinking I would do it later.

This is that day.

My face, in the makeup I have just applied, is a success. My high cheekbones, large slanting eyes, wide mouth, small chin, and rounded jaw have been restrung in base, powder, eyeliner, lipstick, eyebrow pencil. With these tools I have built another face on top of my own, unrecognizable, and yet I am already adjusting to it; somehow I have always known how to put this face together. My hands do not shake, but move with the slow assurance of routine.

I am smiling.

I pick up the black eyeliner pencil and go back to the outer corners of my eyes, drawing slashes there, and, licking the edges of my fingers, I pull the lines out into sharp black points — the wings of crows, not their feet.

I have nine moles on my face, all obscured by base and powder. I choose one on my upper lip, to the right, where everyone inserts a beauty mark. I have one already, it feels like a prophecy. I dot it with the pencil.

I pick up the lipstick and open my mouth in an O. I have always loved unscrewing lipsticks, and as the shining nub appears I feel a charge. I apply the color, Mauve Frost, then reapply, and with that my face shimmers—a white sky, the mole a black planet, the eyes its ringed big sisters. I press my lips down against each other and feel the color spread anywhere it hasn't gone yet.

The wig is shoulder-length blond hair, artificial—Dynel doll hair, like Barbie's, which is why I choose it. The cap shows how cheap the wig is, so I cut a headband out of a T-shirt sleeve and make it into a fall.

The wig I put on last. Without it, you can see my man's hairline, receding faintly into a widow's peak. You can see my dark hair, you can tell I'm not a blond woman or a white one, or even a woman. It is a Valkyrie's headpiece, and I gel it to hold it into place. The static it generates pulls the hairs out into the air one by one. In an hour I will have a faint halo of frizz. Blue sparks will fly from me when I touch people.

John knocks on the door. "Girl!" he says through the door. "Aren't you ready yet?" He is already finished, dressed in a sweater and black miniskirt, his black banged wig tied up with a pink bow. He has highlighted his cheekbones with rouge, which I forgo. He is wearing high heels; I have on combat boots. I decided to wear sensible shoes, but John wears "fuck me" pumps, the heels three inches high. This is my first time. It is Halloween tonight in the Castro and we are both trying to pass, to be "real," only we are imitating very different women.

What kind of girl am I? With the wig in place, I understand that it is possible I am in drag not just as a girl but as a white girl. Or as someone trying to pass as a white girl.

"Come in!" I yell back. John appears over my shoulder in the mirror, a cheerleader gone wrong, the girl who sits on the back of the rebel's motorcycle. His brows rise all the way up.

"Jesus Mother of God," he says. "Girl, you're beautiful. I don't believe it."

"Believe it," I say, looking into his eyes.

I tilt my head back and carefully toss my hair over my right shoulder in the way I have seen my younger sister do. I realize I know one more thing about her than I did before—what it feels like to do this and why you would. It's like your own little thunder-clap.

"Scared of you," John says. "You're flawless."

"So are you," I say. "Where's Fred?" Fred is my newest boyfriend, and I have been unsure if I should do this with him, but here we are.

"Are you okay?" Fred asks, as if something has gone wrong in the bathroom. "Oh my God, you are beautiful." He steps into the doorway, dazed. He still looks like himself, a skinny white boy with big ears and long eyelashes, his dark hair all of an inch long. He hasn't gotten dressed yet.

He is really spellbound, though, in a way he hasn't been before this. I have never had this effect on a man, never transfixed him so thoroughly, and I wonder what I might be able to make him do now that I could not before. "Honey," he says, his voice full of wonder. He walks closer, slowly, his head hung, looking up at me. I feel my smile rise from somewhere old in me, maybe older than me; I know this scene, I have seen this scene a thousand times and never thought I would be in it; this is the scene where the beautiful girl receives her man's adoration and I am that girl.

In this moment the confusion of my whole life has receded. No one will ask me if I am white or Asian. No one will ask me if I am a man or a woman. No one will ask me why I love men. For a moment I want Fred to stay a man all night. There is nothing brave in this: any man and woman can walk together, in love and unharassed in this country, in this world—and for a moment I just want to be his overly made-up girlfriend all night. I want him to be my quiet, strong man. I want to hold his hand all night and have it be only that; not political, not dangerous, just that. I want the ancient reassurances legislated for by centuries by mobs.

He puts his arms around me and I tip my head back. "Wow," he says. "Even up close."

"Ever kissed a girl?" I ask.

"No," he says, and laughs.

"Now's your chance," I say, and he leans in, kissing me slowly through his smile.

My Country

I am half white, half Korean, or, to be more specific, Scotch-Irish, Irish, Welsh, Korean, Chinese, Mongolian. It is a regular topic, my whole life, this question of what I am. People are always telling me, like my first San Francisco hairdresser.

"Girl, you are mixed, aren't you? But you can pass," he said, as if this were a good thing.

"Pass as what?" I asked.

"White. You look white."

When people use the word *passing* in talking about race, they only ever mean one thing, but I still make them say it. He told me he was Filipino. "You could be one of us," he said. "But you're not."

Yes. I *could be,* but I am not. I am used to this feeling.

As a child in Korea, living in my grandfather's house, I was not to play in the street by myself: Amerasian children had no rights there generally, as usually no one knew who their father was, and they could be bought and sold as help or prostitutes, or both. No one would check to see if I was any different from the others.

"One day everyone will look like you," people say to me, all the time. I am a citizen of a nation that has only ever existed in the future, a nation where nationalism dies of confusion. And so I cringe when someone tells me I am a "fine mix," that it "worked well"; what if it hadn't?

After I read Eduardo Galeano's stories in *Memory of Fire,* I mostly remember the mulatto ex-slaves in Haiti, obliterated when the French recaptured the island, the *mestiza* Argentinean courtesans —hated both by the white women for daring to put on wigs as fine as theirs, and by the Chilote slaves, who think the courtesans put on airs when they do so. The book is supposed to be a lyric history of the Americas, but it read more like a history of racial mixing.

I found in it a pattern for the history of half-breeds hidden in every culture: historically, we are allowed neither the privileges of the ruling class nor the community of those who are ruled. To each side that disowns us, we represent everything the other does not have. We survive only if we are valued, and we are valued only for strength, or beauty, sometimes for intelligence or cunning. As I read these stories of who survives and who does not, I know that I have survived in all of these ways and that these are the only ways I have survived so far.

This beauty I find when I put on drag, then: it is made up of these talismans of power, a balancing act of the self-hatreds of at least two cultures, an act I've engaged in my whole life, here on the fulcrum I make of my face. That night, I find I want this beauty

to last because it seems more powerful than any beauty I've had
before. Being pretty like this is stronger than any drug I've ever
tried.

But in my blond hair, I ask myself, Are you really passing? Or is
it just the dark, the night, people seeing what they want to see?

And what exactly are you passing as? And is that what we are
really doing here?

Each time I pass that night it is a victory over these doubts, a hit
off the pipe. This hair is all mermaid's gold, and like anyone in a
fairy tale I want it to be real when I wake up.

Angels

John and I are patient as we make Fred up. His eyelids flutter as
we try to line and shadow them, he talks while we try to put on his
lipstick. He feels this will liberate him, and tells us, repeats, how
much he would never have done this before. I realize he means
before me.

"Close your eyes," I tell him. He closes them. I feel like his big
sister. I dust the puff ball with translucent powder and hold it in
front of his face. I take a big breath and blow it toward him. A
cloud surrounds him and settles lightly across his skin. The sheen
of the base is gone, replaced by powder smoothness. He giggles.

John pulls the wig down from behind him and twists it into
place. He comes around beside me and we look at Fred carefully
for fixable flaws. There are none. Fred opens his eyes. "Well?"

"Definitely the smart sister. Kate Jackson," John says and turns
toward me, smiling. "I'm the pretty one, the femmy one. Farrah.
Which one are you, girl?"

I shake my head and pull the lapels of my leather trench coat. I
don't feel like any of Charlie's Angels and I know I don't look like
one. I look more like a lost member of the *Faster, Pussycat! Kill! Kill!*
gang. Like if Tura Satana had a child with the blond sidekick. Or
just took her hair out for a ride one day.

"You're the mean sister," John says, with a laugh. "The one that
makes you cry and breaks all your dolls."

Outside John's apartment Eighteenth Street is full of cars, their
headlights like footlights for the sidewalk stage in the early night.
I can see my hair flashing around me in the dark as it catches the

light. Doing drag on Halloween night in the Castro is an amateur, but high-level, competitive sport. Participating means doing drag in front of people who do drag on just about every other day of the year, and some of these people are my friends. I am most nervous at the thought of seeing them. I want to measure up.

According to the paper the next day, 400,000 people will come into the Castro tonight to see us. They will all try to drive down this street, and many will succeed. Some will have baseball bats, beer bottles, guns. Some of them hate drag queens, trans women, gender queers. They will tell you they want their girls to be girls. If they pick you up and find out the truth they will beat and maybe kill you. Being good at a blow job is a survival skill for some of my friends for this very reason—though men are unpredictable at best.

"Most men, when they find out you have a dick, well, hon, they roll right over." This is something a drag-queen friend tells me early on in my life here. "Turns out their whole lives, all they ever wanted was to get fucked and they never had the nerve to ask for it."

I think about this a lot. I find I think about it right now, on the street, in my new look.

John, Fred, and I walk out in front of the stopped cars. They are full of people I will never see again. John swivels on his heels, pivoting as he walks, smiling and waving. He knows he is why they are here from the suburbs, that he is what they have come to see. I smile at a boy behind a steering wheel who catches my eye. He honks and yells, all excitement. I twirl my hair and keep walking, strutting. In the second grade, the boys would stop me in the hall to tell me I walked like a girl, my hips switching, and as I cross this street and feel the cars full of people watching me, for the first time I really let myself walk as I have always felt my hips want to. I have always walked this way, but I have never walked this way like this.

The yelling continues from the car, and the boy's friends lean out the window, shouting for me. John is laughing. "Shit, girl, you better be careful. I'm going to keep my eye on you." Fred is walking quietly ahead of us. From behind, in his camouflage jacket, he looks like a man with long hair. His legs move from his thin hips in straight lines, he bobs as he steps, and the wig hair bounces gently at his shoulders. He has always walked like this also, I can see this, and here is a difference between us. I don't want him to be hurt tonight, however that happens—either for not being enough of a girl or for being too much, not enough of a boy.

The catcalls from the cars make me feel strong at first. Isn't beauty strong? I'd always thought beauty was strength and so I wanted to be beautiful. Those cheers on the street are like a weightlifter's bench-press record. The blond hair is like a flag, and all around me in the night are teams. But with each shout I am more aware of the edge, how the excitement could turn into violence, blood, bruises, death.

We arrive at Café Flore, a few blocks from John's apartment. We run into Danny Nicoletta, a photographer friend. He sees us and does not recognize me. I see him every day at this café, I have posed for him on other occasions. He has no idea who I am. I wave at him and as he looks at me, I feel him examine the frosted blond thing in front of him. I toss my hair—I already love the way this feels, to punctuate arrivals, announcements, a change of mood with your hair.

"Hi Danny," I say finally.

He screams.

"Oh my God, you look exactly like this girl who used to babysit for me," he says. He takes out his camera and snaps photos of me in the middle of the crowded café, and the flash is like a little kiss each time it hits my retinas.

We leave the café and I move through the Halloween night, glowing, as if all of the headlights and flashes have been stored inside me. I pause to peer into store windows, to catch a glimpse of myself. I stop to let people take my picture, and wave if they yell. I dance with friends to music playing from the tower of speakers by a stage set up outside the café. A parade of what look to be heavily muscled prom queens in glistening gowns and baubles pours out into the street from one of the gyms nearby. They glow beneath the stage lights, their shoulders and chests shaved smooth, their pectorals suitable for cleavage. They titter and coo at the people lining the streets, affecting the manner of easily shocked women, or they strut, waving the wave of queens. As they come by, they appraise us with a glance and then move on.

This power I feel tonight, I understand now—this is what it means when we say "queen."

Girl

My fascination with makeup started young. I remember the first time I wore lipstick in public. I was seven, eight years old at the time, with my mother at the Jordan Marsh makeup counter at the Maine Mall in South Portland, Maine. We were Christmas shopping, I think—it was winter, at least—and she was there trying on samples.

My mother is a beauty, from a family of Maine farmers who are almost all tall, long-waisted, thin, and pretty, the men and the women. Her eyes are Atlantic Ocean blue. She has a pragmatic streak, from being a farmer's daughter, that typically rules her, but she also loves fashion and glamour—when she was younger, she wore simple but chic clothes she often accessorized with cocktail rings, knee-high black leather boots, white sunglasses with black frames.

I had a secret from my mom, or at least I thought I did: I would go into her bathroom and try on her makeup, looking at myself in the mirror. I spent hours in front of my mother's bathroom mirror, rearranging my facial expressions—my face at rest looked unresolved to me, in between one thing and another. I would sometimes stare at my face and imagine it was either more white or more Asian. But makeup I understood; I had watched the change that came over my mother when she put on makeup and I wanted it for myself. So while she was busy at the makeup counter, I reached up for one of the lipsticks, applied it, and then turned to her with a smile.

I thought it would surprise her, make her happy. I am sure the reddish orange color looked clownish, even frightening, on my little face.

"Alexander," was all she said, stepping off the chair at the Clinique counter and sweeping me up. She pulled my ski mask over my head and led me out of the department store to the car, like I had stolen something. We drove home in silence, and once there, she washed the lipstick off my face and warned me to never do that again.

She was angry, upset, she felt betrayed by me. There was a line, and I had thought I could go back and forth across it, but it seemed I could not.

Until I could. Until I did.

I was not just mistaken for a member of other races, as a child. I was also often mistaken for a girl. What a beautiful little girl you have, people used to say to my mother at the grocery store when I was six, seven, eight. She had let my hair grow long.

I'm a boy, I would say each time. And they would turn red, or stammer an apology, or say, His hair is so long, and I would feel as if I had done something wrong, or she had.

I have been trying to convince people for so long that I am a real boy, it is a relief to stop—to run in the other direction.

Before Halloween night, I thought I knew some things about being a woman. I'd had women teachers, read women writers, women were my best friends growing up. But that night was a glimpse into a universe beside my own. Drag is its own world of experience—a theater of being female more than a reality. It isn't like being trans either—it isn't, the more I think about it, like anything except what it is: costumes, illusion, a spell you cast on others and on yourself. But girl, girl is something else.

My friends in San Francisco at this time, we all call each other "girl," except for the ones who think they are too butch for such nellying, though we call them "girl" maybe most of all. My women friends call each other "girl" too, and they say it sometimes like they are a little surprised at how much they like it. This, for me, began in meetings for ACT UP and Queer Nation, a little word that moved in on us all back then. When we say it, the word is like a stone we pass one to the other: the stone thrown at all of us. And the more we catch it and pass it, it seems like the less it can hurt us, the more we know who our new family is now. Who knows us, and who doesn't. It is something like a bullet turned into something like a badge of pride.

Later that night we go to a club, Club Uranus. John and Fred have removed their wigs and makeup. I have decided not to. Fred was uncomfortable—a wig is hot—and John wanted to get laid by a man as a man. I wasn't ready to let go. As we walked there, we passed heterosexual couples on the street. I walked with Fred, holding his arm, and noted the passing men who treated me like a woman—and the women who did also. Only one person let on that they saw through me—a man at a stoplight who leaned out his car window to shout, "Hey, Lola! Come back here, baby! I love you!"

My friend Darren is there, a thin blond boy done up as Marie Antoinette in hair nearly a foot tall and a professional costume rental dress, hoopskirts and all. On his feet, combat boots also. He raises his skirts periodically to show he is wearing nothing underneath.

Soon I am on the go-go stage by the bar. On my back, riding me, is a skinny white boy in a thong made out of duct tape, his body shaved. We are both sweating, the lights a crown of wet bright heat. The music is loud and very fast, and I roll my head like a lion, whipping the wig around for the cool air this lets in. People squeeze by the stage, staring and ignoring us alternately.

I see very little, but I soon spot Fred, who raises his hand and gives me a little wave from where he is standing. I want to tell him I know the boy on my back, and that it isn't anything he needs to worry about, but he seems to understand this. I wonder if he is jealous, but I tell myself he is not, that he knew what he was getting into with me—when we met, he mentioned the other stages he had seen me on around town. Tonight is one of those nights when I am growing, changing quickly, without warning, into new shapes and configurations, and I don't know where this all goes.

I feel more at home than I ever have in that moment, not in San Francisco, not on earth, but in myself. I am on the other side of something and I don't know what it is. I wait to find out.

Real

I am proud for years of the way I looked real that night. I remember the men who thought I was a real woman, the straight guys in the cars whooping at me and their expressions when I said, "Thanks, guys," my voice my voice, and the change that rippled over their faces.

You wanted me, I wanted to say. You might still want me.

Real is good. Real is what you want. No one does drag to be a real woman, though. Drag is not the same as that. Drag knows it is different. But if you can pass as real, when it comes to drag, that is its own gold medal.

I'm also very aware of how that night was the first night I felt comfortable with my face. It makes me wary, even confused. I can feel the longing for the power I had. I jones for it like it's cocaine.

The little boy I used to be, in the mirror making faces, he was happy. But the process took so much work. I can't do that every day, though I know women who do. And that isn't the answer to my unhappiness, and I know it.

When my friend Danny gives me a photo from that night, I see something I didn't notice at the time. I look a little like my mom. I had put on my glasses for him—a joke about "girls who wear glasses"—and in that one picture, I see it all—the dark edges of my real hair sticking out, the cheapness of the wig, the smooth face, finally confident.

I send a copy to my sister and write, *This is what I would look like if I was your big sister.*

I can't skip what I need to do to love this face by making it over. I can't chase after the power I felt that night, the fleeting sense of finally belonging to the status quo, by making myself into something that looks like the something they want. Being real means being at home in this face, just as it is when I wake up.

I am not the person who appeared for the first time that night. I am the one only I saw, the one I had rejected until then, the one I needed to see, and didn't see until I had taken nearly everything about him away. His face is not half this or half that, it is all something else.

Sometimes you don't know who you are until you put on a mask.

A few months after Halloween, a friend borrows my wig. He has begun performing in drag on a regular basis. I have not. I bring it into the bookstore where we both work and pass it off to him. It looks like a burned-out thing, what's left in the wick of a candle after a long night.

I go to see my friend perform in the wig—he has turned it into the ponytail of a titanic hair sculpture, made from three separate wigs. He is beautiful beneath its impossible size, a hoopskirted vision, his face whited out, a beauty mark on his lip. Who was the first blond to dot a beauty mark on her upper lip? How far back in time do we have to go? It is like some spirit in the wig has moved on, into him.

He never gives me the wig back, and I don't ask for it back—it was never really mine.

CHARLES COMEY

Against Honeymoons

FROM *The Point*

MY WIFE IS seated in a beach chair. She peers over her book and sees me approaching some seals hauled up on the sand. There are only a little over a thousand of these Hawaiian monk seals in existence. When they are discovered on beaches, volunteers rope off an area around them to form a zone where they can rest undisturbed.

So my transgression of one of these knee-high boundary ropes draws the attention of everyone who has been standing at the edge of the rope watching the seals. Hauled up, they look like smooth brown boulders lying on the sand. They don't move. All spectators, wife included, hold their breath as I continue to bear down on the group. When I get very close—just a couple of steps away —the nearest seal heaves its head back. Its nose is suddenly drawn directly upwards. It lets out a double "*haauwll . . . haauwll*" that is Jabba-like: a wheezy barking that vibrates in the air in a way that communicates girth.

My wife's favorite part of our honeymoon is this moment: my shoulders-up posture of mortal fear, stunned sandaled foot stuck out momentarily in midstride; then the acrobatic leap-pivot of redirection that looks like I have bounced off of something springy. To the spectators, until then incredulous at the edge of the rope, I am pardoned. Not a rule-flouting asshole after all. Just oblivious. Or, more precisely, *actually that oblivious*. As it lays its head back on the ground, the seal makes a sound like the last of the water gurgling down a drain. Then a hard, sand-scattering sniff. I retreat at a pace slowed so as not to recall prey in flight. A tall woman with short blond hair smiles at me commiseratingly as I cross back over the very bright and obvious orange rope. Maybe it has unconsciously struck some of the spectators as an image of all our trespassing on the island.

Probably there are lots of different ways to be distracted. You can be distracted because you are elsewhere, like if I had been walking on the beach but really, in my mind, I was having a conversation with my sister or something. Then there are various ways of being in a "state of distraction," where the mind can't get a grip on anything, e.g., kids with ADHD. Then there is the way in which I was distracted on the beach. This was different. I wasn't thinking about anything else. I was in paradise, with no responsibilities whatsoever, but my mind was like that of someone with stage fright: attention bent back on itself, focus jammed up and cresting like the big storm-heaved Hawaiian breakers. In some sense I think I saw the seals.

I was on my honeymoon. The strange and tricky thing about a honeymoon is that even while it's happening, it's already lived as a story. We sit inside it saying, "We will have been here."

The honeymoon as we know it, the postnuptial trip for two, hasn't been around all that long. In the nineteenth century there was something called a "bridal tour," where newlyweds would travel, sometimes accompanied by friends and family, to visit relatives who hadn't been able to attend the wedding. The bridal tour made sense when a marriage was much more about social ties and the joining of two families than it is now: the pair journeyed not as tourists but as a tour. At the turn of the century couples began to adapt the bridal tour to make it a private pleasure trip instead. In *Marriage, a History* Stephanie Coontz talks about the transition from bridal tour to honeymoon as part of a larger revolution in the form of family life in general: the increasing interiority and privacy of the family unit, as well as marriage becoming obsessively all about the two individuals and their bond.

It's easy to understand why, for the first half of the twentieth century, the honeymoon was so appealing. Until relatively recently a marriage came after courtship: after semipublic calls to an eligible girl, usually in her living room. The honeymoon provided some much needed one-on-one time. Naturally, in its privacy, this was also the time to cleave, carnally, finally, to one's new spouse. In fact at first the honeymoon was a bit scandalous for this reason,

because of the attention it drew to the bridal bed. But as the twentieth century softened in its attitude toward sexuality that turned
around. To my grandparents' generation, the thundering of Niagara Falls was a trope for newlywed sex, and going to Niagara was
about giving in to an irresistible force of nature. (Thus the rhym-
ing of "Viagra," which is meant to draw on that association.)

Which is to say that it used to be pretty clear what the honeymoon was about: it was the space the couple took to begin new
intimacies. This is still the lingering idea that the "honeymoon"
evokes, still how the trip is sold. The advertisement has the couple
at their beachside balcony. A glass of wine is drooping in her hand,
and her eyes say something like "at last." The trouble is that in our
own time an actual honeymoon has little to do with an "at last"
anymore. For almost all of us it is silly to go on a honeymoon for
privacy. The couple plots their trip to a remote island where they
will at last stare uninterrupted into each other's eyes, but they do
the plotting alone around their kitchen table.

The guidebook's cover had a picture of Kauai from above on it.
I don't know why a Kauai guidebook would have anything else.
Kauai is, in my opinion, irresistibly appealing from that angle.
From above, Kauai looks like a fat oyster with a barnacle in the
middle. The barnacle is a volcano. Its natural attractions are appointed evenly to its shores: the huge canyons in the west; the long
sunny southern coast (where we would be staying); the more populated "Coconut Coast" in the east, with its rivers and waterfalls;
the sharp, serrated ridgelines around Hanalei in the north, with
perfectly flat fields at their feet running out to deep beaches.

The perfection of Kauai's roundness is fully comprehended
when you open up the guidebook and look at the road map on
the inside cover. There is a perimeter road, but it cannot connect
through the rugged Na Pali coastline in the northwest. So the island is round, but you cannot go 'round it, and unless you are
exploring it by boat it might as well be long and skinny.

We arrived at our hotel at 1:00 a.m. The lobby was part of an
enormous hall with an open-air atrium in the middle of it, which
housed (if that's the word) a tiny jungle. As we checked in, we
could see parrots perched sleepily on the boughs of the trees, and,
looking through the trees, all the way out to the audible surf. As
I remember it, we woke up noonish the next day. We slept late

because of jet lag, but also because it was so dark outside. Where I come from, when the rain starts it sprinkles and spits. Here, as I stepped out our door, the first raindrop fell from the sky and made a wet spot on my shirt the size of my thumb. A half hour later we were walking by the lobby and tropical rain teemed into the atrium like nothing I've ever seen. It was awesome, but the awe was like what one would feel at watching the ocean finally invited indoors. It set off some hardwired anxiety about flooding.

Swimming in the rain through the turns and lobes of the fern-girded "lagoons" of the resort; a manmade waterfall rumbling on your head, cocooning you concussively in a membrane of water; sitting in the 100-plus-degree hot tub while cold rain makes little iridescent crowns on the water like the surface is simmering and steaming—that is really neat. But you can only do so much of it. In fact I think that one's body can only handle so much of it. We went to a place that the resort called a library—really a bar—and played checkers with wrinkled fingers.

The next day, with the rain not letting up, all paradise-specific plans were pretty much kaput. I thought maybe we could visit the nearby botanic gardens—this seemed rain-compatible—but on the phone the gardener informed me that the entry road had just washed away in an avalanche. Then this same guy, unprovoked, told me that if we were thinking of snorkeling at some point, this kind of intense rain would make the shallow snorkelable waters muddy (this being the sort of place where the material from the road had ended up), which are the conditions in which sharks mistakenly bite people. Then he added, as if in consolation, "The nice thing is it never rains this hard." The rain did abate for an hour that afternoon. We found a small sandy gap between the jagged volcanic rocks on Shipwreck Beach outside our hotel and carefully boogie boarded among them. Until, that is, a Hawaiian family showed up with their own boogie boards, and the matriarch almost ran me over with a stony face that said "I don't see you."

I won't pretend to be one of these people who likes the rain, at least not day after day. Glancing at the useless guidebook on the nightstand, the stubs of paper poking out marking what we were supposed to be doing, it felt a bit like the plot of a really depressing *National Lampoon* movie with only one joke in it. But my purpose here is not to complain about the rain. In fact the impetus for writing this is that, on reflection, those were our best days.

Something awfully dear had been paid by pocketbook and planet to get us all the way out here just to be rained on. But now I see that the rain, while it lasted, had protected us. I was irritated but more or less sound of mind.

On the third day my wife and I sort of decided to just carry on like it wasn't raining. We walked from the hotel up onto a bluff. From here we could see a solitary monk seal somersaulting in a pool among the wave-lapped rocks below. We were about to head back (we were getting soaked) when we noticed a path—or more like a weblike network of paths—through the sandy pine groves that grew along the lithified cliff. We wandered through these until eventually they converged on a trail that took us through the old burial ground of the kings of the island. We got lucky and the rain lightened to a drizzle. Looking out over the ocean, the clouds were a lumpy but unpunctured, untouched low sheet below which even lower, closer clouds were marauding. Then the sheet was pulled back and the sun shone. That's the moment when I really remember it taking over: the seemingly inexplicable anxiety about my trip. I remember that up there, with a king's vista of the gray Pacific, something in me had turned the wrong way. I was witnessing beauty, I knew, but the beauty was just making me watch the churning clouds, worried about losing our pocket of good weather. This was the quiet beginning of my real botheredness regarding "experiences." We walked along the cliff until it dropped down to a remote beach. Fog opened and closed the landscape to us.

My sense is that a lot of people actually have a hard time traveling for leisure. There are some people, of course, who fail to really "get away" because they can't leave something behind. The classic image would be the honeymooner apologizing as she ducks into a room to take another call from work. When she isn't on the phone you can catch her staring into space.

Solutions to being elsewhere are, it seems to me, pretty straightforward under most circumstances. Shut off the phone. Then time is on your side. My distraction, by contrast, was a bit more insidious. It seemed to feed on the objectively good experiences of the trip itself. It wasn't that I couldn't see my perfect macadamia-crusted mahi-mahi because my thoughts were elsewhere; to speak truthfully I could see my mahi-mahi very clearly. But it was like I aimed my fork at the fish but kept accidentally skewering something else—my future reminiscence of it. I wasn't elsewhere, but I seemed to inhabit a time other than the present. I wanted to be, as we say, "present." But my problem with presence seemed to be capable of feeding on my own awareness of it. "Just relax," I would tell myself. "Well, I can't relax when I'm anxious about relaxing," I would (accurately) reflect, and so forth as new and seemingly more nuanced forms of self-correction recommended themselves seductively as a solution to the problem they were creating.

The latter part of our trip contained some dry weather. On the first dry day, the sunny one, we went to the beach, and I nearly trod on the flipper of an endangered seal, as reported. On the second we went for a hike. The name of the mountain, the "Sleeping Giant," seemed auspicious. I thought that hiking would be exhausting enough to cut off oxygen to my new second self. A walk, Thoreau says somewhere, returns us to our senses.

The path up the Sleeping Giant had turned to black volcanic mud from the rain: wet and smooth and sticky like potter's slip. It made a sucking *fup* with each step up, then, on stepping down, tiny pip-popping noises as more mud oozed out and accumulated around the sides of our shoes. As we neared the top, another couple came down the path. I have no complaints about making such a clichéd choice of venue. But there is a strange feeling when one comes around a corner and stands face to face with what are obviously other honeymooners. Few times in my life have I felt so powerfully the idea of alternate selves. She had straight blond hair. He had jeans on and was hiking in Chacos, with a minimal backpack and a bottle of water in his hand. This is when we would have exchanged exclamations on the incredible mud. But they passed us in silence down the canyon path.

Who knows what their story was. I thought I saw in them the same sort of ingrown distraction I had. This was speculation of course. But there was, in fact, a striking speechlessness to everyone we encountered on our honeymoon once the rain stopped. When it was raining we would talk about the weather. (I've never understood why people make fun of talking about the weather. It is of perennial consequence and thus never not interesting.) But once the weather was clear no one wanted to say anything to each other.

As I said, the honeymoon as we know it, the trip, hasn't been around very long. It's pretty much a twentieth-century phenomenon. The term *honeymoon,* however, is much older. It used to refer more generally to the sweetness of the earliest days of a marriage. Some people think that the word comes from a tradition in some European cultures in which mead (fermented honey) was drunk by the new couple for the first moon of marriage. Mead was supposed to be an aphrodisiac. This etymology is cute but probably not accurate.

The OED doesn't mention mead. Instead it points out that in early recorded uses of the term, the *moon* in *honeymoon* refers to the fact that no sooner is the moon full than it begins to wane. The lexicographer Richard Huloet writes in 1552: "Hony mone, a terme proverbially applied to such as be newe maried, whiche wyll not fall out at the fyrste, but the one loveth the other at the beginnynge excedyngly, the likelyhode of theyr exceadynge love appearing to aswage, ye which time the vulgar people cal the hony mone." Thomas Blount in 1656 is more explicit on the lunar metaphor: "Hony-moon, applyed to those marryed persons that love well at first, and decline in affection afterwards; it is hony now, but it will change as the Moon." So back in the day, to say of a couple that they were in their "honeymoon" wasn't sentimental but diagnostic, like saying someone is on a shopper's high. Perhaps it was a bit more wistful than that, but the point was jocular chiding of the couple (and the species).

It is tempting to call the sixteenth- and seventeenth-century use of the word *honeymoon* cynical, but if you think about it that might be a bit anachronistic. It wasn't cynical to draw attention to the fact that "exceeding love" was going to fade from a new marriage, because back then love was not an ideal of married life. The institution had other priorities, for which the vagaries of love could be a problem. For the ruling and propertied classes, marriage was about connections and the control of inheritance. For the lower classes it was about these things too, as well as a partnership for day-to-day labor. And it was an association pleasing to God. It wasn't until the Enlightenment that people began to believe that personal love and marriage were somehow essentially bound up together—that one would, in an ideal life, "marry for love." And it was much, much later than that that we got to where we are now, the other extreme, when a loveless marriage is a monstrosity.

Some people think that once love fully infiltrates the institution, this will mean the dissolution of marriage itself, which (it will someday occur to us) will have surrendered its logic and purpose. Maybe. But the general idea of promising oneself to lifelong companionship with another person has proven to be less frail than conservatives have proclaimed year after year. Marriage in the West has outlived some seemingly vital parts of the order it upheld, e.g., the loss of the laws and cultural norms around "illegitimate" children. It survived women working outside the home. By all appearances it will survive gay marriage. Certainly the gay marriage movement underscores the continued power of the institution, given that the movement is driven by the desire of an excluded group to take part in it. What is clear, however, is that marriage isn't what it used to be. Something has changed at its core. And as love is increasingly thought of as its center and its condition, the rites, roles, and laws of marriage have been transforming as well.

An instructive example is the wedding. At many weddings, vows are spoken that date to the eleventh century. After the love revolution, however, what those words are doing is not the same. It used to be that two individuals walked into the church one day and walked out of it with a new relationship, new responsibilities, new rules, effected in the public vow. Whatever its other ethical dimensions, the wedding was on the model of a contract, and could be prosecuted like one.

When love becomes the basis of marriage, however, the vows take on a different kind of significance. They become the declaration, the lived representation, of the ardor that the two people feel for each other. This change has been accelerating in the last fifty years, when many premarital couples start to live together and basically have mini-marriages. The words commemorate and crown the bond; they do not bind. This commemoration is not nothing. The "I do" marks and makes memorial a mutual devotion that already has a life of its own but that otherwise sprawls in a messy and often unspoken way across a lifelong loving companionship. But a representation is a radically different sort of thing for a ceremony to be, and a very different experience.

I believe that the honeymoon has had a similar recent history. In the twentieth century the honeymoon was for intimacy and initiation. In the last couple of generations, it lost this more direct function. Now intimacy and initiation take place in the first months of, as we put it in our maximally understated and sweetly simple way, "being with" someone.

What happens when the honeymoon loses its function? Does it just become a vacation with a special name? That's basically how I approached it (not really thinking one thing or another about it). I thought it was a good excuse to go somewhere warm in December. We were, as everyone else we know is, exhausted. I vaguely figured that if twenty-first-century honeymooners don't fall into each other's arms anymore, well, then they collapse on the bed side by side. It sounded nice. But my experience was that that's not quite the honeymoon's mood either. Instead the honeymoon has gone the way of weddings and a lot of other traditional things: what was once performative becomes commemorative.

This memory-making—that this is to be a representative good time, that the cameras are rolling, as it were—can make you do all sorts of idiotic things on your honeymoon. I was seriously considering making some sort of stand against a whole Hawaiian family, one on six (what would this even have looked like?), because they had stolen my boogie-boarding spot. I stood in the shallows, with a foamy wave sucking at my calves, scheming how to seize the day.

The worst of it, though, is the nasty pathology of presence. The honeymooner wants, above all, to be present. But he wants to be that way so that he *can have been that way* on his honeymoon. The result, in my experience anyway, is the opposite of that intended: each moment slips through his fingers; everything is always already over.

In its own way, the wedding too is lived to be looked back upon. But for the wedding this has an intrinsic nobility. The wedding is an experience that is to be fulfilled through time. Importantly, in the case of a wedding, the self-consciousness that marks the ceremony, the sweaty palms and anxiety and audience and all, is a match for the deliberateness of being married—the work, the will, that is poured into it and makes its inner life, perhaps in the twenty-first century more than ever. In contrast to this, the contemporary "honeymoon" has no place to put self-consciousness. It has plenty of portent, but the portent has no path to development in one's life. The honeymoon confusedly tries to commemorate something sensual and spontaneous—the honeyed early times of marriage. The idea, vaguely, is not to fulfill its memories but just to relive them, to reminisce. The result is a minor disgrace of the mind.

*

As we descend the Sleeping Giant we can hear the crowing of Kauai's feral roosters. Kauai is full of wild chickens. They live in the woods. They are all colors: gray; black-and-white speckled; green; orange with a rust-brown hood; a skinny drab brown one who looks like a mother who has no time to take care of herself, with ten chicks, beaks down, pecking, peeping, taking up a sidewalk. They stand on the posts of chain-link fences. They dart in and out of the fluorescent square of light under an awning. The guidebook had mentioned these. The chickens were brought over by the original Hawaiians in their double-hulled sailing canoes on their 2,500-mile colonial voyage from the South Pacific in the fourth century. (The big mystery with these colonists being where they thought they were going.) With no predators—for example, there are no snakes on the islands—the chickens thrive.

When we get back to our car at the bottom of the climb, a rooster with an electric blue-green body and a gray tail is standing in the crook of a U-shaped tree branch. He goes "cock-a-doodle-doo," then hops off and struts away into the lush understory. The honeymooner can't hear it. The end stage of honeymoon sickness is when *A-MA-ZING*—itself the most numb of exclamations—is mouthed by your face.

PAUL CRENSHAW

Names

FROM *Hobart*

KELLER WAS KILLER and Weaver was Weiner and Penn was Penis or just a dick. Benavidez was Bean Burrito and Ellenberger was Hamburger and Alarid got called asshole more than his real name. Hoteling was Hot Ding-a-ling. Ramirez was Rape-kit. I was Crankshaft or Cumshot or Cocksucker, depending on who was doing the calling, whether my fellow soldiers or the drill sergeants who stalked the halls of Basic Training scowling behind mirrored shades, their boot steps ricocheting like rifles.

Crawford got called Crotchface. Rhea became Gonorrhea after Talley(whacker) scrawled the gonor in front of Rhea, though with a name like Rhea it was only a matter of time before someone put the gonor in front. Clapp was too easy and so no one even bothered changing his name, only put "the" in front of Clapp, and Syphers couldn't escape syphilis any more than any of us could escape Fort Sill where we found ourselves in the summer of 1990. Sackett was Sackbreath and Swallows got asked what he swallowed more times than I care to count, though we all laughed every time, exhausted as we were from long hours and little sleep and hard training, our eyes red and bones tired and some fear lingering deep inside that made us think such jokes were funny.

Nguyen we just called Gook. Ten Bears became Ten Bears Fucking. Black we called White and White we called Black and Green we called Baby-shit and Brown was just Shit. Bevilacqua was Aqua Velva, which was getting off pretty light as far as names went so sometimes we called him Bologna or Ballsack.

Leaks had a leaky dick, and Lebowitz was a lesbian, to which he would proclaim loudly that he was indeed a lesbian, trapped

in a man's body, another lame joke that we all laughed at because
there was nothing else to do, no other way to get through the
long days than to laugh and name each other dicks and diseases
and dysfunctions. At eighteen we were barely grown boys wield-
ing weapons of war while bombs went off in our little part of the
world and the ground shook beneath us. Our drill sergeants were
constantly calling us cocks and cunts, threatening us with physical violence. We were scared all the time—of our drill sergeants,
of the base where we had been sent to train, of the future—and
to keep the fear from flying out we flung bravado at one another
in our choice of words. We were all dysfunctional, we thought,
for we were told so by the drill sergeants all the time, from the
first long days when we arrived at Fort Sill and cried sometimes
in this harsh new place, through the hot afternoons of drill and
ceremony, marching in big round wheels under the summer sun,
all the called commands a way to discipline us, make us move as
one unit instead of fifty different men, like the naming was to
break us down so we could pull closer together; through Basic Rifle Marksmanship and the hand grenade course and the bayonet
course where we stabbed dummies of Russian soldiers; through
med-training where we learned to treat sucking chest wounds and
splint broken limbs and administer antidotes for anthrax and sarin
and mustard gas; through morning eight-mile runs and evening
mail call and even through the too-short nights. We could shoot
and fire and knock out hundreds of push-ups but were constantly
derided, a strategy meant to demean us but also demand that we
rise above such degradation.

I'll say we did. That a man can get used to being called dick-
head or dumbfuck or some other designation, to be named by his
nationality or upbringing, some physical attribute like Aaronson's
Dicknose or Biobaku's almost blue skin. Twenty-five years later I
laugh at being called Crankshaft and Cumshot. Benavidez's big
belly did seem to hold a lot of burritos, and when we graduated
and were waiting to be released for the last time, some of us to go
to college and some of us to war, we shook hands hard. I'll miss
you, Motherfucker, we said, and other words that only made sense
in light of living with fifty men for months at a time, hearing farts
and of football and girls they'd fucked, all the things men say to
make themselves sound stronger.

Perhaps we were scared of letting one another know how we

felt so we hid everything behind a screen. Perhaps all our words are only screens for what we might say if we were better people or perhaps we only use words that fit what world we find ourselves in. Our voices were hoarse from yelling all the time, making us sound much older than we were, and we had to shave every morning now, look at ourselves in the mirror and see the men we might become.

In our final days of training, as we wound down toward release and finally began to relax a little, Saddam Hussein invaded Kuwait and we were all called together so the drill sergeants could tell us we were going to war. We stood there in stunned silence until someone—Talleywhacker, maybe, or Hot Ding-a-ling, said we'd fuck that fucking towel-headed sandnigger right in the fucking asshole is what we would do, and we all cheered with our hoarse voices standing there in our young boots.

But later that night after lights out, as we lay on our bunks in the darkness, we had no words to contain how we felt. The silence stood around us like stones. We could hear bombs off in the distant part of the base, as if the war had already come. The windows rattled softly in their panes. There were no jokes, no called names. Only a hundred quiet conversations, Alarid or Benavidez or Talley whispering across the big bay dorm, "Hey Crenshaw, hey man, are you scared?"

JAQUIRA DÍAZ

Ordinary Girls

FROM *The Kenyon Review*

WE STARTED TALKING about dying long before the first woman jumped. What our parents would do once we were gone. What Mr. Nuñez, the assistant principal at Nautilus Middle School, would say about us on the morning announcements, how many of our friends would cry right there on the spot. The songs they would dedicate to us on Power 96 so that all of Miami Beach could mourn us—Boyz II Men's "It's So Hard to Say Goodbye to Yesterday," DRS's "Gangsta Lean." Who would go to our funerals—boys who'd broken our hearts, boys whose hearts we'd broken.

She was a French woman, the first jumper, that's what people said. She didn't live in Southgate Towers—Papi's high-rise apartment complex, where he also worked as a security guard—but her boyfriend did. According to the boyfriend's neighbors, they'd been having problems—she drank a lot, he drank a lot, they fought. That night, the neighbors told Papi, she'd been banging on the door for a while, calling the boyfriend's name when he wouldn't open. My father was in the security booth outside the lobby when he started getting calls from some of the Southgate residents. They thought they'd heard a crash, something falling from the sky, the air-conditioning unit on the roof maybe. Or maybe someone had flung something heavy off their balcony. Nobody had expected it to be a person, least of all my father.

Our planning started way before the French woman jumped, during a four-month stint living with my mother in Normandy Isle, across the street from Normandy Park. One day after school, Boogie and I were on the swings, rocking back and forth, digging our sneakers into the dirt and kicking off. We talked about how we'd do it, imagined we could make it look like a tragic accident. We'd get hit by a Metro bus while crossing the street, which would be easy since nobody expected a girl to just step in front of a bus in the middle of the afternoon. The park would be alive with people —ballers on the courts, kids on the merry-go-round, boys riding their bikes on the sidewalk, hood rats on the corner waiting for who knows what. We'd smoke one last stolen cigarette, flick the butt before we jumped the fence out of the park. Then we'd take care of it, the business of dying.

Some girls took sleeping pills and then called 911, or slit their wrists the wrong way and waited to be found in the bathtub. But we didn't want to be like those ordinary girls. We wanted to be throttled, mangled, thrown. We wanted the violence. We wanted something we could never come back from.

Ordinary girls didn't drive their parents' cars off the Fifth Street Bridge into Biscayne Bay, or jump off the back of a pickup in the middle of I-95, or set themselves on fire. Ordinary girls didn't fall from the sky.

We spent most afternoons that way, in the park, smoking my mother's cigarettes, drinking her beer. Sometimes we paid the neighborhood *tecatos* to get us bottles of strawberry Cisco, or Mad Dog 20/20, or St. Ides Special Brew. Occasionally Kilo, my boy-friend, and his cousin Papo would show up with a bag of Krypto and smoke us out. We'd lie on the bunk beds, listen to DJ Laz's power mix, and laugh our asses off. Until the effect wore off and we were ourselves again—reckless, and unafraid, and pissed off at our parents for not caring that we spent most of our time on the streets or drunk or high, for being deadbeats and scutterheads. But it wasn't just our parents. We were pissed off at the whole fuck-ing world—our teachers, the principal, the school security, the DARE cop. All those people, they just didn't get that there was no way in hell we could care about homework, or getting to school on time—or at all—when our parents were on drugs or getting stabbed, and we were getting arrested or jumped or worse. Only three months before, Mikey, Kilo's best friend, had been killed in a drive-by shooting.

One Saturday morning, after a long night of drinking and smok-ing out on the beach, the four of us walked back to Normandy Isle in a haze. It was so early the sky was still gray and the Metro buses had just started running. The sidewalk along Normandy Drive was secluded except for the four of us. For a while we just walked, sand in our sneakers, our mouths dry, my hair frizzy from the beach air, Kilo holding my hand, Papo and Boogie holding hands in front of us, the four of us marching down Normandy Drive, laughing and fucking up all the lyrics to Slick Rick's "La Di Da Di." It was our thing—pretending we were beach bums, that nothing could touch us, that life would always be like this. Carefree and limitless and full of music. We didn't yet know that Miami Beach wouldn't always be ours, that even in a few years when we were all gone, we would still, always, lay claim to it, that we would never truly belong anywhere else.

We had just gotten to Normandy Park when we spotted this kid riding his bike across the street. He was dark-skinned, with hair shaved close to the scalp, wearing a wifebeater and baggy jean shorts. I knew him from the neighborhood. Everybody called him Bambi. He was older than us, out of high school already, but he looked young.

When I glanced at Kilo, his face had changed, turned the color of paper. His lips were pressed together, and I could see the vein in his temple throbbing like it did when he was fighting with his mom, or when he was about to throw down. We all stopped in the middle of the sidewalk, and Kilo let go of my hand, pulled out his pack of Newports, and lit one. He took a long drag, then rubbed at his eye with the back of his hand.

"Y'all know that guy?" Kilo asked.

"That's Bambi," I said.

"Doesn't he look just like Mikey?" Kilo asked, but nobody said a word.

Back in my room, the four of us piled up on the bunk beds. Kilo and I sat side by side on the bottom bunk, our backs against the wall, and Boogie and Papo fell asleep on the top. After a while, Kilo leaned over and laid his head on my lap, the vein in his temple still throbbing. I put my hand on his head, listened to him breathing, and after a while I noticed he had tears in his eyes. I wiped them away with my thumb, but they kept coming. He wrapped his arms around my waist awkwardly like he needed to hold on to something but didn't know how. This was not the Kilo I knew.

The Kilo I knew threw up gang signs and wore baggy jeans and wifebeaters and high-top Air Jordans. He was tattooed and foul-mouthed and crazy. He looked at people hard, laughed loudly, talked back to everybody, played streetball, and dunked on half the guys in Normandy Park. The Kilo I knew smoked blunts, drank Olde English 800 by the quart, talked dirty, cracked his knuckles, sucker-punched a guy twice his size, tagged all over the back of the Metro bus, got kicked out of school.

We were like that for a long time, Kilo crying into my lap, holding me, and me not able to say a single word. While I hated seeing him that way, the truth is it also made dying seem like more of an option. And I realized that that was exactly what I wanted—a love like that. I wanted somebody who loved me so much my death would break her.

The first time, I was eleven.

I was living with Mami in South Beach. She'd been diagnosed with paranoid schizophrenia three years before and was on a cocktail of antipsychotics and anxiety medications. She was also using cocaine. Our nights together were unpredictable. Sometimes my mother slept for sixteen hours straight. Sometimes she paced around the apartment talking to herself, laughing, screaming at me for doing God knows what. Sometimes she threw plates across the room, or threatened to burn me with a hot iron, or gave me a full-blown ass-whipping. I was five-feet-six by the time I was eleven, four inches taller than my mother, something she loved to remind me of as she was kicking my ass—the bigger I got, the bigger my beat-down had to be. Eventually I started hitting her back. We came to blows regularly.

That weekend I was alone with my mother. She was manic, talking to herself, screaming at me, insisting that I'd stolen a pair of her heels. She searched the entire apartment, turning over cushions, upending tables, emptying all the drawers onto the floor, pulling hangers out of the closets. When she didn't find her shoes, she made me search, standing behind me as I opened and closed and opened and closed drawers, as I turned over mattresses and emptied out the bathroom cabinets. I did this over and over, and every time I didn't find the pair of heels, she'd slap the back of my head, harder each time. Until I refused to search anymore.

I knew what it would mean, to defy my mother, but I did it anyway. I turned to her, balled my hands into fists, took a step back, and said, "I didn't take your goddamned shoes." I turned to leave, and that's when I felt the whack on the back of my head—hard, much harder than before—and then a shower of blows.

She beat me until I fell, and after I fell, and stopped only when she was good and ready.

Afterward she put on multiple layers of makeup, slipped into a slinky silver dress, found a substitute pair of heels, and announced that she was going dancing.

I was still on the floor when she walked out the door, couldn't have gotten up even if I'd wanted to.

I got up a few hours later and took my mother's pills, all of them—antipsychotics, sleeping pills, anxiety pills. I washed them down with half a bottle of Dawn dishwashing liquid. I'd heard the stories about toddlers who'd gotten poisoned with Drano, or detergent, or bleach, but all we had was Dawn. If we'd had any Drano or bleach, I would've downed that too. I was determined to die.

Later I sat in the living room, waited for my mother to come home.

When she found me, I was on my knees on the kitchen floor, throwing up blue.

I don't remember falling asleep, or making my way from the living room to the kitchen, or being on my knees.

There is the faint memory of riding in the ambulance, sitting up on the stretcher, someone's hand pressing hard against my chest, shaking me, bringing me back from wherever I was.

There is a woman's voice: *What is your name? Open your eyes. What did you take? Don't fall asleep.*

There I am sinking, sinking. Then I'm gagging, a tube up my nostril, down my throat. *Don't fight it. Don't cough. Swallow.*

There is chaos, the shuffle of people all around me, moving me, prodding me, holding me up until I'm throwing up charcoal into a plastic container.

There I am: stomach thrusting against the back of my throat until my eyeballs are almost bursting until there's charcoal vomit splattered down the front of my T-shirt until there's nothing left inside me and I realize I'm in a hospital and I'm in a hospital bed and there is my mother and there is my father and there I am. I am eleven and I am alive.

*

I used to imagine that the French woman knew something about pain, about planning. That she had tried before, as a child, as a teenager. That she sat in her bedroom and listened to whatever was on the radio, wrote poems about darkness, dreamed of jumping off bridges and arsenic cocktails and death by electrocution. Because she was no ordinary girl.

I'd like to think that someone loved her—before she jumped, and after—even if she didn't know it.

Or maybe she did.

That Halloween we decided to throw a party. We spent the night at Kilo's and woke up around 2:00 p.m., crusty-eyed and cotton-mouthed and ready for trouble. I called up my aunt Titi, who lived a short walk from Kilo's neighborhood—and smoked weed all day every day—and told her we needed a place for a party. An hour later we were at her apartment on Harding Avenue, smoking her Krypto and listening to her '80s freestyle. We called everyone we knew with the details. Bring your own weed, we told them, and wear a costume.

Whenever somebody's mom would ask about a chaperone, we put Titi on the phone. She gave them her address and phone number, said *please* and *thank you,* laughed easily. She was every teenage hoodlum's dream, my aunt. Like an older best friend who would cover for you, go to court with you when you didn't want your parents to find out you got caught stealing at Woolworth's or the bodega around the corner, who acted like a teenager even though she was in her twenties. She partied with us, smoked us out, then took us to the movies or skinny-dipping on South Beach. She taught us not just how to fight but how to fight *dirty,* to bite the soft spots on the neck and inner thigh, to pull off earrings and hair weaves, to use anything as a weapon: pens and pencils, keys, a sock full of nickels, Master combination locks.

That night Boogie and I dressed up as toddlers, parting our hair into pigtails, dotting our faces with eyeliner freckles, baby-blue pacifiers hanging from the gold chains around our necks. We wore Mickey Mouse and Pooh Bear pajamas, sucked on Charms Blow Pops, drank malt liquor out of baby bottles. The apartment filled up with our friends from Nautilus, Kilo's friends from the barrio, Titi's weedhead friends. We sat in a circle on the living room floor and passed around a Dutch, blasting House of Pain

on Titi's stereo, until Kilo and I got bored of watching everybody
jump around and stole a dozen eggs from her kitchen.

Outside, we climbed onto the hood of somebody's old Chevy
Caprice and flung eggs at trick-or-treaters, some old scutterhead
stumbling down the street, a guy in a pickup. Afterward, when all
the eggs were splattered down Seventy-Seventh and Harding, we
jumped off the car, Kilo all sweaty, the malt liquor in my baby bottle already warm. Kilo lit two cigarettes, handed me one. I slurred
a faded version of Lil' Suzy's "Take Me in Your Arms," and we
started slow-dancing right there on the sidewalk, Kilo breathing
smoke into my neck—danced in the yard next to Titi's apartment
building and collapsed onto the grass. Then we lay there, side by
side, laughing and laughing at nothing, at everything. Everybody
else seemed so far away, even though we lay there listening to their
coming and going, the building's front door opening, closing,
footsteps scurrying across the lawn, our friends coming over to
say, "You got grass all up in your pigtails," and, "I think they passed
out," and, "The hell you doing down there?"

When Boogie and Papo came over, one of them kicked my
sneaker. Then Papo said, "Think they'll notice if I piss in their
mouths?"

"I'll fuck you up," Kilo said.

"You dead?" Boogie asked, giggling.

"My eyes are open," I said.

"Don't mean you can't be dead," Boogie said.

I didn't look over at Kilo, but I could hear him breathing beside
me. He wasn't laughing like the rest of us. I wouldn't realize it
until much later, after the Krypto and the Olde English had worn
off, after that miserable fall with my mother, after going back to
my father's house, after Kilo had cheated with a girl from the barrio and gotten her pregnant and named the baby Mikey, like he
hoped this Mikey would be the one to save him. After hating her
for stealing him from me, after stealing him back years later, even
if only for a little while, after the two of us, trying to be those same
two kids we'd been, got drunk at the beach on a Saturday night,
snorted an eight ball in just a couple hours, after he watched me
take one bump of scutter after another and told me to *Slow down,
ma* and *Watch out, baby girl, go easy, that's how motherfuckers OD* and I
told him that that was exactly how I wanted to go and that it would
be the best way to die and that nobody would miss me anyway, af-

ter he snatched the baggie from me, took my face in his hands, his breath rank like stale cigarettes and Hennessy, and said *Don't ever let me hear you say that shit again* and *I don't wanna lose you* and after I let him hug me and thought about the two of us lying in the grass that Halloween when we were only thirteen and fourteen, how we were just kids but seemed so much older, already so tired, so damn tired it was like we'd been fighting a war. That's when it would hit me, that Kilo wasn't that different from me, that maybe back then he'd also been dreaming about dying. Maybe it was seeing his homeboy shot down right in front of him and having to look in the mirror every day, face himself, accept that he was still here, still alive, Mikey's memory like a ghost that was always calling.

But that Halloween, the two of us on the grass, all I knew was that I felt nothing and everything all at once. Boogie and Papo lingered for a while, joking, smoking, laughing, and I didn't even notice when they sneaked back to the party. I couldn't tell how long we lay there—could've been minutes, could've been hours—but I sat up when we almost got trampled by a pack of kids running wild through the yard toward Titi's building. There were like six or seven of them, boys and girls we went to school with, sprinting, pushing each other out of the way, calling out, "Move!" and "Run!" and "Go-go-go-go-go!"

Later, in the middle of Titi's living room, with the music turned down and their eyes wide, everybody listening and holding their breaths, they would tell a story about how they'd been hanging on the corner of Seventy-Seventh and Harding. How a couple of them had been sitting on the hood of a car, while Kilo and I were passed out in the yard or pretending to be dead or whatever it was we were doing. How some guys in a pickup had pulled up right next to them, how the passenger had rolled down the window, pulled out a gun, and asked which one of them had thrown the eggs. And while I stood there, the spinning in my head already fading, the dancing and the laughing and Kilo's face against my neck already like a dream I was sure to forget, I wouldn't feel guilty for egging those guys, and I wouldn't feel bad that my friends almost got shot because of us. I would resent them for being that close to death. I would imagine, like something out of a movie, the truck pulling up, the slow opening of the tinted window, moonlight reflecting on the glass, then the barrel of the gun, like a promise.

*

I walked into the school counselor's office one afternoon, on a whim. I told myself it was because I had a math test during fifth period that I hadn't bothered to study for, that I didn't want to see Ms. Jones's face in front of the class as she handed out the test, how she'd be staring at me as I took one and passed it back. Truth was I couldn't care less. Every time Ms. Jones called me to her desk and asked, her voice almost a whisper, why I hadn't turned in any homework that week or the week before that, or why I never brought books to school, I just shrugged, rolled my eyes. The last three times, she'd threatened to send me to the principal's office if it happened again. Next day, same shit. I'd walk up to her desk again, cross my arms, say, "My bad," and act like it was the first time in my life I'd ever heard of books or homework. Eventually Ms. Jones gave up, like I knew she would.

I didn't know what I'd say when I walked into Ms. Gold's office. She was known in most cliques as the counselor for the losers, druggies, troublemakers, kids who got suspended, kids who fought or brought knives to school, kids who flunked so much they were already too old for Nautilus—kids whose parents were drunks or junkies, or whose parents beat them, homeless kids, bullied kids, kids with eating disorders, or brain disorders, or anger problems. So naturally, when I showed up at her door, she knew *exactly* who I was.

"Come on in, Jaqui," she said, her voice hoarse, like she smoked a few packs a day. "Have a seat." She ran her hand through her long mane of orange hair, and I noticed her fingernails were long as hell and painted gold. She dressed like she was a young woman —ivory pencil skirt, short-sleeved blouse, black high heels—and smelled like floral perfume. She was an attractive woman and wore lots of makeup, but up close, you could tell how old she really was. Older than my mother. Probably a grandmother. This made me like her right away.

I stepped inside the small office and sat in the nearest seat. It was bigger than I'd imagined, with a few chairs set up in a circle. I wondered how she knew my name and if there would be other people coming.

"I've been wondering when you'd show up," she said, sitting at her desk chair. She leaned over and opened a drawer, rummaged through some files, then pulled one out. "I was going to get you out of class if you didn't make it over to me soon."

I tried not to look surprised. "For real?"

She smiled at me a long time, looking me over, studying me. Then, finally, she said, "I know all about you."

I doubted that she knew *all* about me, but at the same time, I was afraid of what she did know, and how. "Like what?"

She opened the file and put on her reading glasses, flipped through the pages quickly. "Well," she said, "I know you've been suspended quite a few times." She observed me from behind her reading glasses.

"Okay," I said, not surprised to find that everything she thought she knew she'd read from my school records.

She kept going, not taking her eyes off me. "I know you've been in a number of fights, in and out of school, that you ran away from home a year ago and the police picked you up two weeks later, that you were arrested last month for aggravated battery, and you have a hearing coming up." She took her glasses off and waited.

I took a deep breath but said nothing.

"I know you're *angry*," she said, really emphasizing the word *angry*, "but what I don't know is why."

I shrugged and looked down at my sneakers, suddenly feeling like I'd made a mistake, like I'd rather be faking my way through Ms. Jones's math test than sitting there being questioned.

"So why don't you tell me," she said, closing the file without even looking at it.

"I don't know," I said.

She nodded. "Why don't you tell me about your situation at home?"

I had no idea what she meant by "situation," but I just shrugged again, rolled my eyes like I'd done so many times with Ms. Jones. "What do you wanna know?"

"Let's start with what brought you here."

I considered telling her that I'd just wanted to get out of class, but somehow I didn't think she'd like that. I crossed my legs, uncrossed them. "Sometimes I live with my father," I said, "and sometimes I live with my mother."

"So they share custody."

I shook my head no. "I just go whenever I want."

"Where are you living now?"

"Mostly with my mother. But sometimes I don't sleep there."

"So where do you sleep?"

"Friends' houses, boyfriend's house, the beach."

"The beach?" she said, raising her eyebrows.

It could've been her expression, the way her face contorted into something I read as disbelief, then anger, then pity, even though she was supposed to be the counselor for all the school's fuckups, so she was supposed to be the woman who'd heard it all, seen it all. Or could've been something else—that I'd admitted this for the first time, confessed it to someone other than my delinquent friends, even though it wasn't really anything, nothing compared to what still needed confessing. That once, last year, I stood in front of the mirror in my father's bathroom with a box cutter, determined to slit my wrists, but then couldn't do it, and instead I carved up my upper arm so deep it left a scar. That sometimes I saw myself climbing up on the concrete balcony in my father's high-rise building, saw myself sitting on the edge, leaning forward, letting the pull of gravity take me. That even though I didn't like to think about it, I found myself catching feelings for girls, that sometimes when I was around Boogie the swelling in my chest and throat was like a bomb that was ready to explode.

But I couldn't say any of this. I didn't know why. But right then, sitting in Ms. Gold's office, the last place I'd expected to be even an hour before, I started to cry.

The second time was that winter. Holiday break. My mother was off her meds, and we'd been fighting for three days straight. We screamed at each other because there was no food in the house. Because my music was too loud. Because, my mother claimed, there had been a woman in the apartment going through her things and I'd been the one to let her in. Mami always had these stories—a woman who came into our living room and moved all the furniture while we slept, a man who kept looking in our windows at 2:00 a.m., people sending her messages through the television or the radio, a fat guy who came in and ate all our food while my mother stood in the kitchen, paralyzed with fear.

That morning my mother woke me before sunrise as she paced around the apartment talking to herself, refusing to take her pills or let me sleep. I covered my head with my pillow, and she pulled it off, started shaking me. I needed to get up, she said, help her check all the windows so nobody could get in the house. I turned over, my back to her.

She shook me again, yelled, "I said get up!"

"Fine!" I said. "I'm up." I'd already learned that when my mother was like this, I had no choice but to do what she ordered. So I ran around the apartment checking all the windows—the living room, her bedroom, my bedroom. I made sure the deadbolt on the front door was locked, then got back into bed.

Ten minutes later my mother burst into my room, insisting that I'd left the windows open again. But this time I didn't get up. I was awake but refused to indulge her. She yelled. I yelled back. She threatened. I threatened back. Then she left.

She came back with a steak knife, pointed it at me like it was a sword.

"Who are you?" she asked.

I jerked up and hit my head on the wooden beam of the top bunk. "What the fuck are you doing?" I jumped out of bed and on instinct grabbed my pillow, the closest thing I could use as a shield.

"Tell me who you are," she said, "because you are not my daughter."

I should've cried, begged her to stop, to put the knife down. I should've apologized and told her I loved her. But I didn't.

"Are you serious?" I asked. "I never wanted to be your daughter! You're not my mother. You're a crazy fucking crackhead!"

She stood there for a while without saying a word.

I kept my eye on the knife, gripping the pillow with both hands.

"You are small," she said finally, "like a fly. You are so small I could squash you. You are nobody. You are nothing."

I didn't believe what my mother said—not at first. I took it the same way I always took her rambling—everything she said was nonsense. But after she turned back for her room, left me standing there with the pillow in my hands, everything quiet except for the sound of my own breathing, something changed. It was like a switch that got flipped and everything that happened after was mechanical.

Dropping the pillow on the bed, the beeline for the kitchen for a glass of water from the tap, a car horn blaring across the street somewhere.

My mother rushing to the living room window, peeking through the blinds.

The bottles of my mother's prescriptions on the counter, untouched for weeks.

My mother running back into her bedroom, slamming the door shut.

The first pill, a drink of water. The second pill, another drink. The third, fourth, fifth, another drink.

My mother coming back out of her bedroom, pacing back and forth. Bedroom, living room, bedroom.

Another pill, another drink. Bedroom, living room. Another pill and another and another.

The car horn again.

The way my mother walked past me so many times but never once turned to look at me, to see me killing myself again and again.

The wanting, more than anything else, to sleep.

My mother saying, "You are small."

My mother saying, "You are nobody."

My mother saying, "You are nothing."

The second time, I swallowed all my mother's pills, locked myself in my room, didn't sit to wait until she found me. The second time, I slid a dresser in front of the bedroom door to keep my mother out. The second time, I woke sick to my stomach, stumbled out of bed but couldn't get the dresser out of the way in time to make it to the bathroom, so I threw up all over the carpet in my bedroom. The second time, I woke to find that, again, I had not died.

In my bedroom, spewing a foul white foam that I assumed was my mother's pills, and then the Kentucky Fried Chicken that Kilo had brought over late last night—blowing chunks of chicken and mashed potatoes and macaroni and cheese—I was sure that if I didn't die of a prescription drug overdose, then the retching would kill me. I bent over the mess on the carpet and the vomiting turned to dry heaving.

It took me a few minutes to straighten up, to push the dresser out of the way, to wash my face and brush my teeth, to get my sneakers on and my hair in a ponytail, to stuff some of my things in my backpack and go.

I walked past Normandy Park, feeling jittery and weak, headed toward the Circle-K, where I bought a small bottle of Gatorade and got some change for the pay phone. Outside, I sipped some of the Gatorade, then picked up the phone, my hands shaking. And then

I threw up again, just liquid this time, left the receiver dangling, and bent over right there on the spot.

Again it took me a minute to get myself together. Then I finally made the call. I put two quarters in the phone and dialed my father. The line rang four or five times before Papi picked up.

"Hello," he said, but not like a question, more like he was annoyed at whoever was calling. I was surprised by the sound of his voice, which I hadn't heard in months—not since I ran away to my mother's house. His voice stirred something inside me, and I couldn't believe how much I missed him, how much I *needed* him. I wanted to ask him for help. I wanted to tell him everything that happened since I left, ask him to come and get me, take me home. But he'd let me down so many times, and I'd let *him* down so many times, I was sure it was the only thing we would ever do—let each other down.

"Hello?" he said again.

But I couldn't do it. So I hung up.

I stood there for a long time, feeling tired and weak and so sick. I considered just going back to my mother's, getting back in bed, letting myself drift off. But I wasn't sure if the pills could still work, if my body had absorbed some of them before I threw up, if there was still a chance I could die.

I picked up the receiver again, but this time I called Kilo.

Twenty minutes later, Kilo's dad picked me up in front of my mom's building. He was driving his station wagon, Papo riding shotgun, and Kilo in the back. I got in, dropped my backpack on the floor, and thanked them for picking me up.

"Where to?" Kilo's dad asked.

I gave him my father's address in South Beach, and he made a right out of my mom's complex.

In the backseat, Kilo held my hand. I hadn't told him that my mother had pulled a knife on me, or that just hours before, I'd swallowed her pills and gone to bed, that I woke up vomiting, surprised to still be alive. All I'd said on the phone was that I was sick and needed a ride to my father's.

I leaned my head on his shoulder, and he put his arm around me. In the front, Papo and Kilo's dad were talking about the Miami Dolphins, Joe Robbie Stadium, what they planned to do this winter. When I called Kilo for a ride, I'd already known that I'd be leaving Normandy Isle for good, that there was no way in hell I'd ever go back with my mother, not if I could help it. I knew that my leaving would mean I wouldn't see Kilo, Boogie, and Papo every day, and maybe I wouldn't be able to stay out all night or hang in the streets whenever I wanted, that we could easily drift apart. But I was so tired.

Kilo leaned over, kissed me on the cheek, then whispered something in my ear that I couldn't make out. I told myself that he said, "I love you," even though I knew it wasn't true, but for now I needed it to be.

I spent most of the ride to South Beach thinking of our time as if it were already in the past. How Kilo and I danced at the Nautilus Middle School Halloween dance, all sweaty and breathless and crazy. How once Papo introduced me to his neighbor as his sister-in-law, and afterward he always called me *Sis*. How we walked all over the place—the four of us shooting the shit from Seventy-First and Collins to Normandy Isle to Bay Harbor, even at three, four in the morning. How Boogie and I sat on a bench by the courts in Normandy Park, knocking back a quart, pretending we were grown and watching the pickup game. How Kilo and Papo acted like they were super-fly streetballers when really they were just okay. How in Kilo's room the walls were all tagged up with spray paint and Sharpie, covered in bad graffiti, his homeboys' names, their neighborhoods, and on the bedroom door, the largest piece: RIP MIKEY. How once I got so pissed that my name wasn't written anywhere, I took his Sharpie and wrote JAQUI N BOOGIE on the wall next to his bed, then drew a heart around it. How he came when I called. How maybe he saved my life and didn't even know it.

By January we would barely see each other. By Valentine's Day, Kilo would already be with the girl who'd become the mother of his baby.

When I got out of the car in front of my father's apartment complex, the air was too warm for winter. Even for December in Miami Beach. I strapped on my backpack, watched the station wagon as it drove off, headed north. They would drive past North Beach, past Seventy-First and Collins, then make a left toward Crespi Park. I would go into the lobby of the south tower, take the elevator up to my father's apartment on the eighth floor, where my *abuela* would greet me with a hot meal and *café con leche,* always ready to forgive me for stealing her cigarettes, for running away, for getting arrested so many times.

A few days after going back home, I would have a dream. I'd be on the roof of the north tower, standing close to the edge, my arms extended like wings. I would be looking down at Biscayne Bay and across at the Venetian Islands, and then I would jump, and before I hit the ground, I would be flying, flying. The dream would come back every couple of months, and always I would fly before hitting concrete.

A couple of years after the French woman jumped, another woman—Papi's friend—would fling herself off one of the balconies. The south tower this time. She would hit the side of the building, then the roof of the pool maintenance storage shed, then the ground. She would fall fifteen stories. And she would live.

IRINA DUMITRESCU

My Father and The Wine

FROM *The Yale Review*

> The making of wine binds me to my ancestors who were tough-
> sinewed peasants and whose feet were rooted in the earth.
> —Angelo Pellegrini, *The Unprejudiced Palate*

NOW AND THEN I click a link to find out what the hipsters are
up to. The hipsters are raising chickens and slaughtering them at
home, I read; the hipsters are distilling hooch. This is trendy and
far out and probably how we should all live, despite being smelly
and arduous. No doubt they have it right, the hipsters, and if they
are fermenting cheese and spritzing meat into sausage casings in
Brooklyn, then surely we will soon follow them in the lesser me-
tropolises. But the romance of do-it-yourself is tainted for me. I cannot muster up the enthusiasm to kill my own rabbit and pickle it.
There is a droning voice in my head that says, You do this because
you never had to. You do it because you do not know the humiliation and occasional physical danger of an immigrant father who
held on to his past using food. You do this because the ethics of
the undertaking are clear to you, and you don't—yet—understand
the exquisite liberation of food that comes from a supermarket.

First, and last, and every time, above all things, was The Wine.
It was never just wine, it was always The Wine, that year's massive
household production, the gravitational pull of which none of us
could escape. This is not because my father came from the country. He was a city boy par excellence, but he could remember days
when Bucharest had dirtier hands, or at least cleaner dirt on its
hands. He used to tell me with a grin how when he was a child,

chickens were always bought alive. The housewives would go out to the street with a knife and flag down a passing man to kill the bird they wanted to cook for dinner. Businessmen who wanted to display their machismo refused the knife and wrung the chicken's neck barehanded. This was the old Bucharest, when my father's father still had his sausage factory, when salami still hung in their attic to cure and my father was responsible for tending to it. It was when my grandfather still made his own wine.

After we had moved through two new countries and multiple apartments in each, after we had finally settled in a house in the blandest cookie-cutter suburbs we could find, my father started to talk about making wine. Enough moving around and you'll want to reach for a bit of what was good back home. Enough moving around and you'll want to drink, I suppose. The decision to start making wine was helped along by the fact that alcohol sales are controlled by a government monopoly in Ontario, the LCBO, leading to small selection and high prices for a liquid as essential to Romanians as milk is to white-bread North American families. My father saw this as the oppressive fruit of Canadian puritanism, and he set about staging his own private revolution. In this, he had the help of "the Italians," purveyors of everything needed by the suburban vintner with Old World sensibilities: massive bottles, special corks to let the gas out, industrial quantities of grapes, and the facilities for turning them into must. I was in my early teens at this point, still excited by the enterprise and even a little proud. As my father studied the chemistry of winemaking with the assiduousness of the university professor he had once been, I designed wine labels on the computer with the title CASA DUMITRESCU, and struggled to align a sheet of sticky labels in our dot-matrix printer so that the graphic would come out right. It was not very good wine, though back then I couldn't tell, but it was ours and it was cheap. My father calculated the cost per liter to two dollars, a magnificent savings to our family over retail wine, and clearly a wise financial move.

A fifty-gallon barrel cut in two will provide two excellent stomping vats. The heftier children and maiden aunts with heavy bottoms will be delighted to do the treading to the accompaniment of a tarantella or lively Irish jig.

Soon enough, our own Casa Dumitrescu became more crowded, as my surviving three grandparents came over from Romania and moved in with us. My grandfather was aged and absent by then, but I still remember him making sausage once, his trembling hands struggling to work the sturdy old meat grinder. My father became more ambitious in his winemaking, deciding that the Italians were good for grapes but that he did not trust their pulping machines not to adulterate his must with traces of other varietals. He went to Price Club, the daddy of Costco and perennial favorite of immigrant families in search of a deal, and bought a giant gray plastic garbage bin. This he carefully washed out, set up in our garage, and filled with muscat grapes. And then, for days on end, my two grandmothers and I stood around this bin and squeezed grapes. With our bare hands. I do not know if you have any experience of making must in this way, but muscats are tough, tight little berries, and you have to strain to crush every last one, and each bunch of grapes made our hands ache even more. My grandmothers and I tried to work out how we might get one of us into the garbage bin to apply feet to our common problem, but it was narrow and had two wheels at the bottom, and hopping in seemed an unsafe, if tempting, proposition. So we squeezed on into the night, tired but not thinking to question my father's imperative. This was, after all, The Wine.

At some point it occurred to my father that the price-gouging, racketeering deviousness of the Ontario government was not limited to wine; a greater injustice was also being perpetrated. A typical Romanian meal begins with plum brandy, Țuică in Romanian, or *slivovitz* as it is more widely known in Eastern Europe. Now, while fine wines could be had at extortionate prices, Țuică was hard to come by at all in the LCBO stores, and even when available, it was inevitably industrially produced and tasteless. The situation has improved over the years, but if you wanted a decent Țuică in the nineties, you had to smuggle it back from Romania, nonchalantly lying to the customs officer at Pearson Airport and hoping she did not discover the four quarts of hard liquor in plastic bottles and various massive country salamis and cheeses nestled among, and stinking up, your clothing.

But my father, an engineer who had designed a bridge to go over the Danube and paper-light satellites that went into space, and who, even more breathtakingly, had failed two terminally stupid students with parents high up in the Communist Party— failed them not once, not twice, but three times, until the dean took the exams out of his hands to protect him from his own probity—my father was not going to be frustrated in his basic, Romanian male desire for plum brandy at dinner. My father could design a joint for the Canadarm and a wind tunnel for testing airplanes. My father could assemble Ikea furniture efficiently and without error. My father sure as hell could put together his own still.

Now here was more treacherous territory, for while Ontarians were allowed to make wine and beer to their hearts' content, hooch was another matter. You couldn't just have a bunch of grandmas and a teenage girl making it in open daylight. This was closed-garage-door business. The garbage bins multiplied. Now there were some for fermenting plums, some that held a mix of fruit from our own backyard, and just to make any foray into the garage as confusing as possible, a few with enough pickled cabbage and cauliflower to keep a Transylvanian village free of scurvy for a winter. A metal boiler appeared from somewhere, as did a large plastic bucket and some copper tubing. And a spout. My father explained to me the physics of the thing (he was always so good at teaching what he wanted to teach): how the alcohol would be first to vaporize in the boiler due to its lower boiling point, how it would travel up through the copper tubing he had painstakingly coiled and, upon reaching the bucket filled with cold water, would condense and drip out of the spout into a waiting bottle.

The experiment was a success. After his first year of lonely distillation, my father's friends began fermenting plums in their homes too. Groups of them gathered in our garage in the evening, in the hazy yellow light of the one bulb hanging from the ceiling, and took turns boiling their own Țuică in his still. They smoked and talked for hours, watching single drops emerge from the spout. It took ages to fill a bottle, and they probably consumed the liquor much faster than they made it. But even then I suspected the true draw was the solitude of the process, the absence of nagging wives, children, and elderly parents, the heavy fumes of hot alcohol, the trancelike peace of drip, drip, drip.

*

> In many regions, blackbirds, sparrows, catbirds, robins, and larks
> are purely destructive and a menace to crops. People now and
> then complain that their cherries, raspberries, strawberries, or
> blueberries are entirely eaten by the birds.

Making liquor happened also to be an ecologically responsible
hobby, as my father insisted on using the sparse fruit that grew in
our yard for experimental blends: a few cherries produced by our
insect-decimated trees, some bruised strawberries I had painstakingly planted and tended, the riotous bounty of a raspberry bush
that grew beyond our expectations. And then there was the grape-
vine. Our dining room opened out onto a tiled patio covered by
a wooden trellis. My father planted grapevines at the base of the
posts that held up the sides of this trellis, and after a while, with
a bit of care and nudging and wires to guide them in the right
direction, the vines worked their way up the posts and over the
wood slats. Their leaves grew large and gave cool shade in the summer. They even grew fruit. But the berries never really ripened;
the grapes disappeared or fell to the ground still hard, a source of
unending frustration to my father. We found out that the culprit
was a raccoon that liked to clamber all over our trellis, disturbing
the delicate grapes. Thus began the feud between one, or perhaps
more, Upper Canadian raccoon and an East European professor
of engineering, and if you have ever had any dealings with raccoons you probably already know who won.

My father began by hanging bells from the trellis, hoping to
scare the beast away with noise. Raccoons are not frightened by
the tinkling of bells. Then he bought a foul-tasting substance that
he painted around the bottoms of the posts, so as to prevent the
raccoon from climbing up them. But the trellis was attached to the
roof, so the raccoon could reach the vine that way. Clearly it was
time for more extreme measures. My father went to Price Club
and bought two weapons, a plastic pellet rifle and a pellet pistol.
These he placed on the dining room table, so that if he happened
to hear or see a raccoon he could quickly grab a firearm on his
way out. When we protested, he insisted he did not want to kill the
raccoon, simply to scare it away from the grapes, which had, after
all, been destined for greater things. After a few weeks of having
two plastic guns lying ready on our table as if we were the Hatfields
expecting a visit from the McCoys, my mother put her foot down
and made him take them back to the store.

Things were at a standstill when I came back from school one day to find my father covered in blood. Covered in blood, and angry. The story went like this. He had been in the kitchen chopping onions with a large chef's knife when he heard a rustling on the patio. He rushed out of the house, knife still in hand, and there it was: the raccoon. He looked at the animal. It stared right back at him, unfazed. Exactly what happened next is unclear, but there seems to have been a skirmish. My father lunged at the raccoon with his knife, and at the last the animal moved out of the way. The knife tip stuck in the wooden post, the blade broke off from the handle, but my father's hand kept going in its trajectory along the blade. The raccoon escaped unharmed. My father never tried to salvage any of the grapes again.

This was the way things worked in the logic of do-it-yourself. What began as an eminently practical proposition would soon get out of hand. Always, behind the inanities of our everyday existence there were two unassailable arguments: it was cheaper to do things this way, and it was authentically Romanian, part of our identity. I found it easy to argue against the first. Few normal families buy at retail the amount of wine we produced in a year, so it was hard to be convinced of the great savings involved. We would have simply drunk less, and had fewer authentically Romanian family fights in the middle of dinner, if our wine had cost ten dollars a liter instead of two. But the nod to tradition was harder to counteract because it spoke to something I felt too. True, I longed to eat out in restaurants and use ready-made salad dressings, as native Canadian families did. Still, even then I could tell there were dishes in our cuisine that were better than anything Canada had to offer, and that they were worth extra effort, a bit of sweat, a few burns and cuts. There was an element of community in it too, because you made massive amounts of food and drink partly so you could serve it to other Romanians at parties. Even in a huge city like Toronto, with its thousands of immigrants, there were few Romanian restaurants, and no good ones. If we wanted the food of home we had to make it or have friends who made it. Ideally, everybody prepared his or her own version, and the evenings after a gathering could be spent in fruitful discussion about whose recipe for cabbage rolls was best, whose cooking had too much Hungarian influence, which live-in grandmother was the most gifted baker, whose wine was never going to be as good as my father's.

I think this feeling of diasporic togetherness is part of why my father got involved with the lambs. He had a younger coworker who ran a farm north of Toronto, an Italian, and therefore automatically a kindred soul. More important, he raised sheep. The succulent memory of a party where a bunch of Romanians set up a spit in their yard and roasted a lamb on it must have gotten to my father because he set about coordinating a mass purchase of lambs for the coming Easter. Fourteen families were in: each would buy half a lamb, and my father would organize it all with his Italian engineer-cum-farmer friend. The deal got messy, for predictable reasons. There were seven lambs ordered for fourteen families, but every family wanted the front part. It was not unusual at that time to hear my father furiously slamming the telephone down and yelling, "I told them at the start, *they* have to decide who gets the ass and who gets the head!"

I was able to maintain a bemused distance from it all until one afternoon when the doorbell rang persistently. I opened the door to see my impatient father, who thrust a large black garbage bag in my arms and said, "Clear some space in the fridge and put this in there." It took me a moment to realize what was happening, but as my arms felt the round contours of a small body through the plastic bag I understood this was one of the lambs, our lamb. Fighting back tears, and as quickly as possible, I shoved bottles and Tupperware aside in the largest part of our fridge, folded in the animal as best I could, and leaned against the door to press it shut. To this day, I can't remember if we got the ass or the head.

Still, after all the drama of his various projects, nobody could have guessed it would be yogurt that would nearly do us all in. Yogurt is a tricky issue: I have inherited some of my father's madness on this point. Since leaving our house in the Toronto suburbs I have moved through five cities in the United States and Germany. In each new home I must spend an enormous amount of energy finding an acceptable yogurt, not too sweet, not bland, not adulterated by bananas or vanilla or cappuccino goji berries, or whatever other abomination is currently being used to sell yogurt to people who do not actually like yogurt. Then I try to find the largest possible container sold of that yogurt, so as never to be without. When I lived in Dallas and was addicted to a Bulgarian-style yogurt made by, appropriately, an aerospace engineer in Austin, I had to fight the urge to buy the gallon-sized jars despite living alone. So I understand my father, understand that once he had found the "Balkan style" yogurt that was closest in taste to what we knew from back home, he didn't want to have to buy a fresh container every day.

The normal thing to do in this circumstance would be to purchase a yogurt maker, but making yogurt in miniature cups would not do it for us; it was not really the point of the exercise. Romanians do not serve food in miniature cups. Modest, individual portions are basically inimical to our culture as a whole. Again, my father carefully explained the process to me: how a cup of starter yogurt would provide enough culture for a gallon of milk, that it was important to keep it warm, but not too hot, over many hours. Instead of a little electric machine, my father used a large pot which he wrapped in towels to keep it cozy overnight after it had been heated on the stove. The resulting yogurt was watery and lacked the firm tartness I loved about our chosen brand, but my father was convinced we would save an enormous amount of money by never having to buy yogurt again. And really, it was the least objectionable of his undertakings: it didn't involve guns or illegal distilling or the transport of dead lambs. Until, that is, I woke up one night to the smell of something burning. The entire house was dark with smoke, and our fire alarm had not sounded. It turned out that my father had forgotten to turn the stove off, and despite the electric element giving off such a small amount of heat, eventually the contents of the pot began to burn, badly. After that, yogurt was something we got at the store, though years later my father did give me a yogurt machine with six little cups that he had found on sale somewhere. I haven't had the courage to use it yet.

When, a year or so later, he managed to burn up the kitchen properly, the ample bounty of Casa Dumitrescu came in handy. It was a simple grease fire that began when he left some onions he was frying to answer the phone, but it destroyed a good deal of our cabinetry before he managed to put it out. My mother was at home to receive the assessor from the insurance company a few weeks later, and since it was lunchtime and his presence in our house made him a kind of guest, she offered him a bowl of soup. He accepted, and, I imagine, warmed and comforted by both soup and the empathetic smiles of my understanding mother, told her his story. He was Polish and was going through a heartbreaking divorce. My mother quite naturally poured him a glass of the house wine, and they continued talking. Afternoon turned into evening, and my father came home from work. Knowing well the therapeutic properties of Țuică and assuming that the poor insurance man hadn't had anything so good since leaving his native Poland, my father pulled out a bottle and started filling little glasses. I think the assessment lasted until about 10:00 p.m. My parents soon had an entirely new kitchen.

> Every fall I make wine for the family dinner table and for the good friends who cross my threshold. These have learned to enjoy it as any European. They praise its quality and drain their glasses like true sons of Bacchus. If they do not make it themselves, it is because I dispense it so freely, frequently bringing it to their table when I dine with them.

The kitchen remodel was a high point, but as the years passed The Wine became more and more of a burden on our family. Even when money was tight there was never a question of sitting out a year of wine production. The economic rationale for it was, after all, unbeatable, or, rather, none of us had the emotional energy to challenge my father on something so clearly central to his life. I grew embarrassed at the gallon-sized jug that was always at the foot of our table, envied my friends whose parents bought wine in decent, normal-sized bottles. My father probably knew more about the different varieties of wine than any of them, but *we*, his family, didn't. For us there was no Bordeaux or Côtes du Rhône or Merlot, there was only the special blend of Casa Dumitrescu, always changing in composition, always tasting the same. Part of my father's goal in making wine was to revive our Romanian heritage in Canada, a place that never really felt like home to him. Unfortunately, what he kept alive for us was the familiar feeling of life under communism, where you could only ever have one brand of any product and daren't complain about it lest the big man who ran things get sour.

This is not to say that there were not still occasional moments of pride, even as my father and I went from being tight accomplices in my early teens to arguing almost constantly as I approached twenty. My small residential college at the University of Toronto lived off stuffy Anglophile pretension and a measure of worldly sophistication, and I discovered to my surprise that I could impress the provost or an influential alumnus with an exotic bottle of homemade Țuică. As more time passed, I also cared less what other people thought. Somewhere at the core of my father's obsession was a set of values that still feel true to me: that wine is just a beverage that goes with food, neither demon nor fetish; that local stores should not determine the limits of your culinary pleasure; that there is a warm joy in giving people food you made yourself, even if it is simple. Especially if it is simple. That gardening and cooking and fermenting and decanting can give you, if not a home, then at least a feeling that you belong to yourself even if you're not sure who exactly you are anymore.

As trendy as immigrant foodways and home canning and novels by ethnic women with "spice" in the title are nowadays, the dream of authenticity in food is old romance. When I discovered Angelo Pellegrini's *The Unprejudiced Palate,* originally published in 1948, it seemed I had found my father's script and bible. No wonder my father loved the Italians so! Pellegrini, who left hunger-ravaged Italy and settled in the bountiful Northwest, waxes poetic on the spiritual value of tending a small vegetable garden, the joys of serving guests out of your own cellar, and the sheer deliciousness of fresh ingredients, put together simply but with a measure of peasant cunning. His book is a paean to immigrant wisdom, pungent and coarse though it might seem from the outside. Even in the 1940s, he notes, I read with some guilt, how the second generation grumbles about the unappealing, unhygienic food practices of their Old World parents. And yet Pellegrini is also uncannily like me, a child immigrant who grew into the language of his new home, becoming a professor of English literature. Although his mother did a great deal of the cooking, his father is Pellegrini's model and authority, the one who taught him how to think about food and, naturally, how to make wine. Like Pellegrini, I could write a chapter on "The Things My Fathers Used to Do," but while the émigré Italian paid attention and followed in their footsteps, I strayed.

I left for graduate school in the wake of one of our family's uglier moments. That summer my father's get-rich scheme was to buy fixer-upper houses, renovate them, and resell them at a profit, none of these activities fitting into what one might call his skill set. My mother was unwilling to risk their life savings on this business venture, and he presented her with an ultimatum: compliance or divorce. In the middle of this, he and I had our worst fight, so furious that when the power went out all over the eastern seaboard I was sure that my anger had blown out the lights. We had patched things up into cold civility by the time my parents drove with me down to New England. At that point he had also dropped the idea of buying property and with it, quietly, the threat of divorce. But my mother had not forgotten, and she had her own thoughts about a marriage that could be traded in for a run-down house. She made her mind up when, having said their good-byes to me and set out on the highway, the first thing my father asked was, "So when are we going to start making The Wine?"

Years later, a family friend confessed to my mother how much he had dreaded coming over for dinner. You see, when someone makes their own wine, you can't simply drink it when it's served to you. You have to comment on it. You have to discuss its qualities, how well it turned out this year, how successful this particular blend of grapes was. Basically, you have to act like you're at a wine tasting and it's the pinnacle of sophistication to detect the fine nuances distinguishing Casa Dumitrescu 1998 from Casa Dumitrescu 1997. A failure of hospitality of this magnitude is the stuff Greek tragedies are made of, but its core is innocent, a natural imbalance of interest and passion. Here is what no one admits in their gleeful reports on the year of planting their own vegetables, baking their own bread, and brewing coca-cola with self-harvested cane sugar and homegrown cocaine: some undertakings require absolute, unyielding dedication, and not every member of the family or community can match it. Oh, it's one thing to go berry picking with the kids on a farm and make a pot of jam at the end of the day. But if you are pickling tomatoes because you miss a taste from your childhood, you have to try to get it right, which means you have to do a lot of pickling. It also means the people around you will have to eat a lot of sour tomatoes while you work out the recipe.

Wine is even more demanding, requiring copious equipment, knowledge, and most of all time. It has to be tended, observed, cared for. You have to judge the fermentation, know when to rack it to another bottle, siphoning it away from its sediment. It is intimate too, in the various demands it makes on the body of its maker: my father labored to lift bottles and bruise grapes, and he always racked wine the old-fashioned, unsanitary way, by sucking on one end of a hose and placing it in the fresh bottle, allowing the pressure to drive the wine into its new receptacle. The liquid that a proud vintner puts on the table is the fruit of months of planning, mixing, crushing, washing, testing, tasting, pouring, and smelling, but all the guest knows is that he is drinking mediocre wine. The wine was my father's second child, one whose faults he couldn't see.

The deep irony of the years that followed the divorce was that my father's liquors improved. His wine was now more than palatable, and his Țuică was the real thing, a pleasure to start a meal with. We had all put in time, but he stuck it through. It took a long while for us to be able to talk to each other after our fight and my parents' subsequent split, and even then our encounters were awkward, veins of hurt pulsing under the surface. But it helped that all we ever did, on those tense holiday visits, was eat and drink together. On the worst days, food and alcohol were social lubricants, keeping mouths from talking too much, giving the illusion of celebration and togetherness around a table. On the better days, it was easy to enjoy a good plum brandy, to appreciate it honestly, to see him enjoy the compliment. He would send me off with several bottles to take home with me, some pure Țuică, some experiments he had colored with tea, flavored with fruit, or aged in a bourbon wood barrel. I didn't know what to do with that much hard liquor, but inevitably something would come up—an exam passed, a dissertation submitted, another move to yet another new city—and the Țuică I found in my stores provided the punctuation.

We do not speak anymore, my father and I. The decision was his. When I went to pack my things for my most recent move, now so far from Toronto that I'm almost back where I started, I found one more plastic bottle of Țuică. It was full, and it would clearly be the last I would ever have from his hands. I decided not to put it in the container with all my other belongings, wrapping it instead in a plastic bag and hiding it in my luggage; it was perfectly legal, but it felt illicit. This is also an authentic Romanian gesture, one I performed instinctively. One of my parents' friends escaped from Romania in the 1980s by hiding on a train, leaving his family behind but tightly grasping, under his jacket, two bottles of exquisite wine from the vineyard where he had worked. He opened one bottle with great pomp on his twenty-fifth wedding anniversary, and told his guests he was saving the second for his elder daughter's wedding, which he did not live to see. I did not wait so long. The bottle of Țuică was a little crushed by the time it reached my new home, looking as if it might crack the moment I tried to unscrew the cap. But it held, and to celebrate the start of our new life, I poured a generous amount into espresso cups for me and my husband. I expected the fresh, clean punch-in-the-face of all-natural, homemade plum brandy, but that is not what I tasted in the cup. This bottle, it turned out, was one of my father's experiments, an infusion with orange peels that had taken on a powerful bitter note over the years. It was undrinkable.

> They will want to suck at the siphon hose and taste whatever you taste. They will laugh and smack their lips and assure you that the wine is very good. When you leave the cellar they will insist on carrying the bottle to the dinner table . . . And as they cling tightly to the bottle, with all the elaborate care of which little ones are capable on such occasions, you may possibly glimpse a comforting symbol—the child drawing closer to the father.

ELA HARRISON

My Heart Lies Between
"The Fleet" and "All the Ships"

FROM *The Georgia Review*

FOR THE PAST several years, my friends have known it as "my translating job that I love." When asked for specifics, I start by saying I'm employed as a translator for a Dutch publishing house, preparing an English version of an Ancient Greek–Italian dictionary. At this point, the person's eyes may glaze over ("She said *Ancient Greek!*"). Or I see the wheels start to spin—*Dutch . . . English . . . Ancient Greek . . . Italian . . . translating—a dictionary?* Or *Dictionaries usually involve one, or at most two, languages. Not three.* Or *Ancient Greek is a dead language—why does it need a new dictionary?*

How can I explain the allure of rapid passage from one word to the next—one world to the next—as I work word by word through an amassed list so long I can perceive no horizon? Sometimes, whole dictionary pages, 7-by-10-inch, two columns per side, fine print, are filled with compounds based on a single concept or word: *recently wealthy (nouveau riche); fresh from war; of recent appearance; freshly killed* (twice, from two different words for "kill"); *recently grown; freshly poured.* Then I encounter, perhaps, a couple words having to do with even numbers, whose base is a sound-alike of the word for "recent"—and next maybe on into the "bread" words, another sound-alike: *To give bread, giver of bread, bread seller, bread basket, piece of bread, bakery, to be a baker, pertaining to a baker, baker . . .*

Conversely, sometimes each successive entry is a leap of worlds. A word for a poisonous plant will be followed by a verb that, in its different manifestations, can mean *to raise* or *to rise,* and can also refer to the sun, a sail, or growth into adulthood. Every time I save one such entry and move along to the next, I enter a new sphere of thought and sound.

To gather and explicate all the words of a dead language is to build on the work of others. I can't go to the newspapers or listen to how things are said on the radio, can't assay a sample of Internet verbiage or pull words out of current bestsellers. A comprehensive alpha-through-omega requires a grand scavenger hunt through the best literary sources—Homer, Plato, the New Testament, the historians and dramatists and orators of centuries past—as well as the mass of texts engraved on stone or written on papyrus, to say nothing of official and private documents, letters, graffiti, tombstones.

Greek words carved on rocks, penned on papyrus carbonized by volcanic eruption, or wrapped around a mummy are still unearthed every year. Once the words are gathered—and literally cleaned up by archaeologists and others—they must be presented in snippets of sentences showing off their most flattering profiles if they are to make useful dictionary entries. The size of the lexicon is immense, what with all the objects and concepts that need words and descriptors, along with the great propensity of Greek to bud adjectives off nouns and verbs, to derive nouns and verbs out of adjectives, to form adverbs out of past tenses of verbs, to borrow words from other languages, and to make up new ones completely. Alpha alone—the letter with the greatest number of entries by far—comprises 406 pages in three columns of tiny print, with up to fifty entries per page depending on the length of the individual entries.

Here is another dimension of my wonder: as I move from one entry to the next, I am not only shifting sound and thought gears, I'm skipping across centuries and social strata. For example, I may encounter a series of words with essentially the same meaning, but that were each spoken in a different epoch, when one or another suffix was mostly used. One comes from the most highbrow style of classical Athens; another is a colloquial form found only in texts from Egypt; another is not attested later than the *Iliad*, and yet another not earlier than Saint Luke.

Four-hundred-plus pages of alpha sounds like a fat wad of print, and it is . . . and there are twenty-two other letters to traverse. But I'm not working on a paper page. These myriads of words are filed in a database I access over the Internet, sitting thousands of miles away from where the language was spoken at a time when the fastest computer was the human brain with an abacus. Five other translators are also at work (over the duration of the project there were a total of ten), none of whom I've met, and all of whom are located in different states or countries. We are totally dependent on electronic hardware and optic fibers, web browsers, online databases, and specialized software. The voluminous physical book with its light-gauge pages is our anchor, the bridge between the high-tech practicalities of our work and this language that so far precedes high technology—although, in an ironic twist I enjoy, it was to supply so much of the high-tech lexicon.

Paper page . . . web page . . . The Greek words I'm dealing with were written on scrolls of goatskin that were rolled up rather than turned, or they were scrawled on scraps of pottery, or carved on a wall or pillar, or brushed onto papyrus with a reed pen. Of course, many other words of Ancient Greek were never written down; instead, they were spoken in some remote area where writing was unknown, and they disappeared when no one used them anymore. As I do my small part to preserve these survivors, this "dead language," in a novel nonphysical context, I wonder about those disembodied words echoing in some word-Neverland. That I am working with Italian as well as English pushes the *echoiness* of words closer to the front of my mind. What I'm doing, essentially, is overwriting the Italian translations of Professor Franco Montanari's dictionary. The Italian gives me a template and a structure for a given lemma (dictionary entry), but I'm expected to rely on my expertise in Greek at least as much, especially when it comes to translating the snippets of example passages. I'm more apt to notice metaphorical resonances in languages other than my native one—even in other dialects of English—whereas in my native idiom I take such connections for granted, unreflectingly. For instance, the jump from *paper* page to *web* page is easy, but what about *screen*? I never think about computer screens as having a metaphorical relationship to anything else, but when I go into Italian I'm acutely conscious that *schermo* is also a curtain, a veil, even a shield. The Modern Greek word for (computer) screen is—with allowance for change in pronunciation—exactly the word for the veil that in the language of Homeric epic would shroud a modest young woman—and suddenly, working with these three languages, I am aware of the delicate balance of hiding and self-revelation I'm granted by the (screen of) computer and Internet—of the connection, even, between *revelation* and *veil* in my own language.

The most comprehensive Ancient Greek–English dictionary was last updated in 1996 and reflects the state of knowledge of Ancient Greek in 1940. Montanari's Ancient Greek–Italian dictionary was first published in 1995, and expanded and updated in 2004. The third edition came out in 2013, while we were in the later stages of our translation based on the second edition. In other words, this Ancient Greek–Italian dictionary is far more up-to-date than the most complete existing Ancient Greek–English dictionary, and with electronic technology, it's easier to keep current (revise an entry, or add a new one to the database)—which slows its obsolescence, or even perhaps renders the obsolescence obsolete. The end result of this project will be a unidirectional dictionary translating all known words of Ancient Greek into English, but the whispers of Italian are in the very bones of our creation.

The beneficiaries of the project are few. Such a comprehensive dictionary would overwhelm a beginner, and whatever the number of beginning students of Ancient Greek—a small crowd no doubt —only a small percentage will become the sorts of experts who would use such an exhaustive volume. But for those few practitioners it will crucially include even obscure and elusive words, thereby validating such words' existence, and it will give comprehensive histories of the usages of more common words. This new dictionary will verify an unexpected meaning for a supposedly familiar word, and it will show how the meaning of a word has changed over the 1,500-year period of Greek the dictionary covers.

Covering this span of the language's life would be like creating a dictionary for English spanning back to before the Normans arrived in the British Isles and began creating the zesty amalgam of Germanic and Romance that makes the vocabulary of English so expressive and easily added to. There are old, pre-Greek words in Ancient Greek too, marked by their peculiar forms, like *erebinthos,* a chickpea, which shares the *-inthos* ending with place-names like Corinth, showing the great age of that settlement, showing how ancient is the cultivation of chickpeas—of which, in reality, no variety exists in the wild.

I'm aware of how oddly my excitement about words of arcane provenance and about the metaphorical nether parts of our own words might come across in casual conversation with a friend in the grocery line, but—for me at least, and I can't be *that* rare—these are valuable areas of research. To canvass and explicate the full instrument of a language is to make it alive despite its no longer being spoken, is to capture the vigor of the words and the kind of people who used them: beautiful words; words for objects we have never seen; names for tools we dig up and try to identify; names of aphrodisiac plants gone extinct; words for concepts and metaphors we have never thought of, and some that we also use, coincidentally, in unconscious imitation. For example, the Greeks too used grains of sand on the beach as proverbial for innumerable multitudes, but we probably created the same metaphor independently of them. I can easily say why I am doing this work.

At the big-picture level, I marvel at the juxtapositions the project presents to me: I work thousands of miles from where the language was spoken between 3,000 and 1,500 years ago; in order to have the required comprehensive list of words, I'm going via Italian into English; alphabetical order is essential and yet arbitrary. At the nearer level, I'm excited—my appetite is stimulated—by the choice snippets of classical literature presenting the context of a given word. I remember a cited play or poem, and in a little room in the back of my head I relive some of its story. I strive to provide the most elegant translation of a disembodied snippet, approving or censuring the Italian translation as I match efforts with it and aim to surpass its example. At the microscopic level, every word of Ancient Greek—how it sounds (or how it might have sounded, since of course we don't know for sure), and how its set of meanings overlaps or fails to overlap with English and Italian—creates for me an understanding of other ways to approach the world, and thus re-creates my own worldview over and over. As unreal as the physical symbols of words behind the veil of my computer screen may seem, as unreal as may seem words we don't know how to pronounce and that refer to unknown objects, I feel these words and symbols connecting me to a fierce, distant reality of which I would otherwise have no conception.

In truth, I'm addicted to the work. Every time I promise myself I'll take a break when I've finished ten more entries, or turn my attention to one of my other jobs, or go stretch my body, I take on ten more. I mark my time against a constantly unrolling arc of words, and the arc is coruscated with tangents and arbitrary transitions, just like my own experience of time and behavior. But the arc is solidified and anchored in the rote movements of my fingers and eyes. Stepping back from my own compulsion, I watch in fascination as I become a grand funnel into which Greek and Italian are poured, and out of which comes English. I like to say I'm a *trivium*—a three-way crossroads. Instead of two roads intersecting, touching one another and then diverging again like the letter *X,* the two roads of Greek and Italian intersect, touch one another, and become a single, new road—English out of Italian and Ancient Greek—like the letter *Y.* This letter exemplifies the *process* of creating the *product,* the English version, which exists in real time. I trace it over and over, enact it for each word—different product, same process—with every entry I translate.

The scale of this dictionary is so grand that when I'm in there working lemma by lemma (literally, *leaving,* from the Greek; the technical term for "dictionary entry"), it's like being on the ground of the "flat" earth. I can't see the curving arc. But my snail-like, step-by-step momentum charts the route of my own life. When I enter the private room of each entry in the database, for a moment I have the word and its lemma to myself. Eventually I will leave the room by hitting SAVE. Or else it's a much briefer visit —the entry merely redirects the reader to another entry, and the abbreviation "v." is automatically translated to "see"—and I exit via the BACK button. These series of finger-clicks that get me in or out, this rhythm, the way whole sequences of words are sometimes so similar—all could contribute to monotony or rote behavior, to one word blurring into the next. But what happens in the middle is what matters. There are moments of anarchy when I type a nonsensical joke-definition containing a bad pun or doggerelesque alliteration, or when my fingers are misaligned by one key and *for* comes out as *got* or *order* as *iesewe* or *one* as *ibe.* Scary moments in the privacy of the lemma's room. I correct the mischief quickly and move on. No one will ever know—but haven't we all, at one time or another, wanted to be in charge of what words get to mean or say?

During this series of middles, of visits, life continues outside. I might be about to leave for an appointment, or the library whose Wi-Fi I'm using might be about to close. My bladder's demands might finally be unignorable; I'm drumming my knees. Someone might call on the phone, or come up and start talking to me. I might continue to translate while giving them some of my attention. Sometimes I catch myself making strange monsters like *desiderable* when overwriting Italian with English.

At home, I can't see the output of my oil heater unless the sun is hitting a shadowless spot on the hardwood floor, yet the heat spreads to my body nonetheless; just so, something in the essence of each lemma, and in the process of looking at it and changing it, kindles my body. Just as I seek and revel in heat, I crave and go after this connection with words. I have marked hours of sleepless nights in mania, grappling with my teeming self from one word to the next. I have stretched out hours of fasting, one word to the next, avoiding food for yet more drip-drip moments of sustenance I find in language, even though these are uneven.

Sometimes the satisfaction is just a matter of transcribing someone's name and noting that it *is* a name. Sometimes a name is an ambivalent descriptor, hinting at word-stories: strongman Ajax, constantly referred to as "son of Telamon"—why was his father called Telamon, i.e., *baldric, strong belt*? Common nouns smuggle in stories as well. The Ancient Greek word *halcyon* means "kingfisher" —in English too that's what *halcyon* still means, underneath it all —but in Italian *alcione* means "seagull." Look more closely, and the Greek *hal-* is "salt (sea)" and *kyon* is "the one who incubates." Kingfishers were thought to hatch their young at sea; perhaps the Italians thought seagulls did so too.

Sometimes a highly complex word, or a preposition with multiple meanings, takes up a whole three-column dictionary page, or even more; its "private room" on my screen requires scrolling and scrolling no matter how big my monitor and is rich with illustrative quotations from hundreds of years' worth of evolution of the word that showcase its action. I'm a thrill-seeker for these voyages of definition but feel warmed even by the less interesting or less expansive tasks such as one-to-one explications of word and object: "pole," "an unknown plant," "a type of meter," "to sell," "wrasse" (a type of fish). Yes, these short entries teach me about the world too.

The editor in chief for the project metes out access to the database a few hundred entries at a time. I don't always realize I've run out until it is the middle of the night in the Netherlands, or, worse, Friday night. When I need to wait for him to send more, the rest of my day is blankly empty—although there's always plenty else I should be doing. I can't imagine what my life will be like without this series of words and their demands—their juxtapositions with one another like jostling elbows, reinforcing, undermining—their stories, their vistas, continually unfolding before me. The passage from one word to another has served as a lifeline at times when my experience outside of the dictionary was a battle: the next word always draws me on. Diving in is what I do when I receive more entries, but perhaps even more accurately, a new cache causes language and story to dive into me.

A good dictionary entry will disambiguate a word with examples in context, and it will indicate the ways the word's set of meanings does and does not correspond to the meanings of similar words in the target language. *Pen* means something very different in a school than it does on a farm. Diverting a stream is an activity different from diverting someone's attention, although their similarity might give you the insight that attention is like a stream. And what is a *sake*, a *dint*, or *rather*? Except in the very simplest word-object or word-action correspondences, a good dictionary doesn't simply line up two columns of words, one for each language shaking hands across a table, representing a common intent, because that's not how language works. Not every language will use the same word for diverting both streams and attention. English-speakers keep *prana, chi, karma*—or *amok, kamikaze,* and the like—because English lacks native words for those concepts, requiring a phrase instead, and so we borrow the Eastern words as a shortcut.

As I make crosses of Ancient Greek and English, ostensibly I'm overwriting and translating from the Italian, which disappears in this process. But like all the translators on this project, I'm a classical scholar, not an Italianist, and I think this is as it should be. When I read poetry translated by a poet who relies on the translations of others and is unacquainted with the original language, I always miss a certain depth and rootedness, no matter how good this new version is *as poetry* (and as much as I love, for instance, Coleman Barks's renditions of Rumi). The same intimacy with the original should go for dictionary entries, where the task must be to choose the best word of English to correspond with the Greek, no matter what Italian word has been supplied—that is, to translate the phrases quoted to illustrate the use of the word *in full representation of the Greek.* An Italianist might not be able to look at the abbreviated author's name attached to a quoted phrase and immediately know whether the snippet came from comedy or tragedy or history, philosophy or epic, Stoic or Christian texts, and thereby adjust the tone of the translation accordingly. She or he probably wouldn't know that shields at the time of the Homeric poems were made of layers of beaten leather, or that the dative case can sometimes express agency, would have no basis for visualizing the complex mechanisms of Greek door bolts or grasping the many nuances of the infinitive and how it can be put into English. To create a translation that brings words vividly to life for the dictionary user, I have to know both how the words exist within the Greek (participating in its grammar) and what sort of world the words describe (how they interact with its objects).

Yet the Italian is also essential. For each lemma, the stage directions are in Italian—*passive voice; in a positive sense; and; or; philosophical; never found in prose; frequently metaphorical*—the kinds of information that clarify the many different uses and sorts of words. And of course there are many words of Ancient Greek that I do not know, that I must learn from the Italian lexicographer. As large as my working vocabulary of English itself may be—and I do need a huge vocabulary in English for my intent to translate the Greek in a manner simultaneously faithful to its letter and spirit *and* producing idiomatic and beautiful English—I probably do not know half the words in the Oxford English Dictionary and, proportionately, even fewer Greek words. I rely on the original, Italian work for identification of plants, unusual animals, pieces of equipment, obscure characters, and a plethora beyond my imagination of concepts, epithets, and ways to do things to people.

I'd never heard nor thought of a whip for torture made with flails of small knucklebones, or the sorts of human interactions that would make use of such. A special scraping tool called a *strigil* was used to cleanse the oiled body, in lieu of bathing, and I imagine how hard it would have been to take showers with so much less available water, how to organize a city of coexisting bodies with no plumbing. An adjective that means "lacking in extension," i.e., tiny, can also mean "immeasurable" or "infinite." An adjective that can really refer only to days and other measures of time means "favorable to conception of boys." Words for plants are often also words for birds: I think of the gaudy orange-and-blue bird of paradise flowers, and of butterflies and bees, and recognize my own multiple associations of flying creatures and flowers. The bird of paradise struggles to raise its orange wing-petals in a damp London yard; carrion butterflies bloom on rotting fruit in Thailand; a shimmering blue bird settles on a cluster of yellow umbelliferous flowers on a parched hillside in Athens one cicada-shimmering afternoon.

The stylized, larger-than-life sculpture of the ancient Greeks and their scantly surviving portraiture give us no kind of photographic impression of anyone's face in which to descry a likeness to one of our grandparents or colleagues. Documentaries and movies based on classical literature or myth deal in stereotypes —bearded men with long hair, women in flowing robes, keening music in the background—mysterious a cappella women's voices, a lute plucked in minor modes. These representations—the ancient Greeks' own and our culture's—enforce a sense of remoteness between us-now and them-then. They convey beauty and loss, beyond our ken both; they convey the notion that the characters in the myths, even the histories, are themselves conscious of their ancientry and the transience of their own world and culture.

The language too is so distant—even from Modern Greek. We don't know for sure how the sounds were pronounced, but we do know, based on study of Greek metrics, on comparison with related languages, and on the testimony of scholars such as Dionysius of Halicarnassus, that until 200 BCE or even later, the accentual system was based on pitch, not stress—more like Thai or Vietnamese than the familiar European languages, or than Greek itself from that time on. (By the time the Alexandrians introduced written diacritics to indicate pitch changes, in the second century BCE, the requisite distinctions of vowel length were collapsing and the stress accent taking over.) But that flowerlike bird, those birdlike flowers—these connect me to people who interacted with the world in the same ways that I do. The delicious word *isthmus* refers to a neck of land, and the Greeks knew the same somatic metaphor; an isthmus could be a human neck too. These were people who inhabited a world I recognize. I begin to see and hear myself in the bits and pieces of their lives that surface through the words they used. Their storied Echo and Narcissus offer two different kinds of reflection—sound reflecting sound as it hits a solid object, image reflecting image. Narcissus became a flower; Echo haunts rocky places like an unseen bird.

As a writer, I find my energy frequently turns outward from the poem or essay I'm composing to imagining how what I'm saying may transfer to readers—whether it conveys something of import, whether it will move spirits. This impulse is certainly present too as I take care of the translation of each dictionary entry, sometimes adjusting two or three times before submitting it. I consider carefully whether the context in which a word had been uttered (if said context is available) would better merit a translation of "laudable" or of "worth praising." I hope I will have enabled a reader of Ancient Greek to puzzle out the sentence she or he is stuck on because I translated a word "divert" and not "deviate," as it also could have been. Is it better to say "the cavalry" or "all the horsemen" in a given context? Or in another, "one who has absolute power" or "plenipotentiary"?

Words are the world; my here and now is words. I am unable to cry when someone dies until I'm hit by the memory of how he pronounced *used,* or how she said *criminy* when she spilled her tea. When my mother reads a recipe aloud sotto voce, it doesn't conjure the finished food item—I'm only struck again by her pronunciation of *crush* as *crash* and of *batter* as *butter,* her still not distinguishing *a* and *u* after all these years speaking English—and her being bemused by the oddness of the word *treacle.*

Life is words. It is Heraclitus's pun on *bios* as life versus the *bios* that, differently accented, means the death-dealing blow. It is that *life* is an anagram of *file,* which can be a spice mix, an abrasive tool, a row of people or objects, or a place where words can be collocated on a computer or in a paper folder. *Car* is a yellow Matchbox toy with flappy doors, but *automobile* brings to mind insurance companies and roadside assistance, backup. I feel emotion stir when I'm choosing whether to say *word list* or *lexicon, catalogue* or *litany.* My heart is in the choice between *the fleet* and *all the ships.*

When I say that last, I'm thinking of Sappho's sixteenth fragment. The poem opens "Some say an army of horse and some say infantry / and some a fleet of ships is the most beautiful thing / on the black earth, but I say it is / whatever each one loves." An army of ships, a collectivity of ships, a fleet. In Sappho, the "army of ships" is one of three different kinds of army, neatly collocated with cavalry and infantry. If I say "fleet," I tend to think of something military, with that punny flavor of swiftness special to English. If I say "all the ships," I see sails in different shapes, ships with high-polished wood and boats with flaking paint; I review in my mind all the names for floating vessels in Greek and English, and I savor their sounds and images. These lip-smacks of words, their savors, the snatches of poetry they evoke—they feed my heart as well as my brain.

As I work, embodied, in time, I am never conscious of the dictionary *as a whole*, as a book, as an entity out in the world. I work on it in fragments, I translate cutouts and pieces. I might translate hundreds of words in a day and barely cover a half-dozen pages of the tome. No one will *read* this dictionary. People will consult it, looking up separate entries in separate places, based on the logic of the sentence they are trying to puzzle out. That logic is every bit as logical (or illogical) as the alphabetic sequence that is the filing system of all these words. The arc of alpha through omega vanishes in the use of the thing. The initial letter of the word that enrolls in its proper place on the grand arc is arbitrary, and so is its meaning, without good explication. People will read what they can find about a word fragmented from the other words that give it life, or brought to life in a fragment of poetry out of its own context. Who was demanding a ransom, and did they receive it? Why is a *clepsydra*, the ancient hourglass, etymologically a "thief of water"?

In a good afternoon I do the equivalent of four print-dictionary pages and come out as exhausted as the priestess of Delphi after her prophetic trance. I worked on alpha for months. I should point out, though, that before getting into alpha I had already translated pi (which is almost as long), and theta, zeta, and iota, and after I finished alpha I mopped up mu. My translating these letters out of alphabetical order didn't matter a whit—an eloquent demonstration of the arbitrariness of the arc to which I'm anchored.

Some words change meaning significantly over time; some words mean different things in different places. (In British English, an eraser is called a "rubber," and British visitors to the U.S. learn to their embarrassment that's not what the word means here. Or, if you're an American-English-speaker, try saying "fanny pack" over in the U.K., and expect embarrassed sniggers or derisive snorts of laughter.) Many Greek words have multiple meanings, so that across the contexts of space, time, and speakers a word can have a spectrum of senses that includes opposites. I always pause with these opposites—they seem to want to teach me something: that blessings and curses share the same bed, can come from the same mouth with the same word; that the boundaries of *learn* and *teach* are fuzzy, as are those of *borrow* and *lend*.

An array of different font styles and background colors differentiates the aforementioned stage directions, just as you'd expect in a reference dictionary. On the computer, these different colors and formats are built on xml code, a fact I can repeat but, not being a tech-head, can tell very little more about. On the other hand, I can now fix code using xml tags. In the little editing panel that is my theater of activities, it's easy to ride roughshod over underlying code and squish it. Hitting UNDO usually leaves you worse off than before you made the mistake. Furthermore, English and Italian do not order words in the same way, and sometimes a piece of the Italian I'm overwriting is superfluous, or (more often) I need to add something to the English version. I want to make the most elegant possible English translation of the Greek word with no vestige of Italian idiom; if I don't want to contort my English, I must manipulate code.

When I was a graduate student at Stanford, sophomores referred to my ilk as "fuzzies"—I'm a computer user in the same way that I'm a car user. I can lift up the hood but know little more than how to check and replace fluids. But now that I've learned to "view source code" and tidy it up, and now that I'm free to order the components as seems best, I find myself spending even longer on each entry, making sure that every comma and abbreviation is tagged correctly. The job has been an arc of learning for me, and someone who went before me doubtless went through a similar arc preparing the database I work on, building the Ancient Greek–Italian entries for me to convert. When I flag mistakes, I think of all the inconsistencies in my own translating: how I overlooked errors of code I had not yet known how to see when I started out, or my potentially ambiguous translations of Greek's many predicative adjectives. Then I multiply this by the cohort of translators living in different countries and continents, all doubtless making different decisions on these matters. This dictionary will not have pure, seamless skin with perfect surface tension. Even after we proofread it keenly and closely, suturing some of the idiosyncratic choices of different translators, seams and inconsistencies will split and spill.

I worked on words beginning *anti-* for over a week—hundreds of them—finally running out and into words beginning *antl-*. Just about any verb, and many nouns too, can have an *anti-* version. I've seen permutations of meaning and nuance produced by this prefix ranging from *mutual* to *reciprocal* to *turn-taking* to *corresponding* to *facing* to *opposite* to *against,* so that the word from which our *antiphonal* comes can be used to mean either "harmonious" or "discordant." As a user of English, I am sometimes fussy about redundancy. "Also . . . as well" is a pet peeve. Why say "return back" when *back* is an intrinsic part of the meaning of *return?* But as I go through various words prefixed *anti-* in ways that at first seem redundant, I realize how nuanced a single word can be. "To resound back" sounds redundant, but prefixed with *anti-,* the Greek verb *to resound* can mean simply "to resound back," or "to resound in response to something," or "to sing in responsion"—two choirs singing in call and response—I have to admit this is not redundancy. And how beautiful the Italian for "resound"—*rimbombare.* Echo and Narcissus again, a mirror maze of *anti*phony across millennia and miles, where I keep finding reflected my own thoughts and images.

When I pick myself up and dust myself off from the *anti-* ride, the *antl-* words are waiting. This seems an unlikely and cumbersome mouthful of sounds—but of course, that's an English-speaker's perspective. We have only *antler* and its derivatives, and *antlia,* a pure Greek word you've likely never seen used. But even in this comprehensive dictionary, Greek has only eleven entries so beginning, as opposed to seventeen whole pages of the preceding *anti-* sequence, and we move on to the richer tribe of *antr-.*

Ancient Greek—and Italian too—use different forms of one and the same verb to indicate, for example, that a person is dressing *someone else* or is dressing *him- or herself,* or that a general is *gathering his army* versus *the army is gathering;* English grammar says *dress* or *gather* and lets the context and pronouns show this difference. Translating terms for weights and measures, let alone concepts from the theoretical physics of the era, is educated guesswork, and it exemplifies the bizarreness of the enterprise of finding words in twenty-first-century English—or Italian—to fit with words from a world, a people, a set of concepts and cultural practices, of 2,000 years ago. Their rules and attire for boxing and wrestling were different from ours. Their religious practices, superstitions, and metaphors were very different—although, like us, these people *shook off* sleep and used *grains of sand on a beach* to evoke a countless multitude. Other metaphorical extensions are at a remove from us. We can understand what it means to have a lobe missing in an organ of the body, but we don't have an adjective *lobeless*. And if we did have that adjective, it would probably mean nothing more than "lacking a lobe," whereas in Greek it means "inauspicious." Unlike the Greeks, we don't use the condition of sacrificed animals' organs to predict the outcome of an intended project, so for us a missing lobe in an ox's liver doesn't spell defeat in an intended battle. And then there are metaphors that may be beyond us. We can understand the phrase "to wipe one's head with a sword" in its literal meaning, just as we can understand the concept of "lobeless." But why is this phrase used to mean "to exonerate oneself, declare oneself innocent (of a sacrilegious crime)"? The Greeks saw the grains of sand innumerable as do we, but words and phrases such as these remind me of how differently (and of what else) they also saw.

In the crossing from Ancient Greek to a modern language, not everything *transmits*. Given my obsession with arcs of crossing and their beginnings and endings, it's no surprise that this is only one of several arcs that preoccupy me as I work. The dictionary itself, in its finished book form, appears as a grand trajectory—exemplifies the concept of "trajectory." Alpha through omega and A through Z are bywords for inclusive comprehensiveness, with each letter containing its own alphabet of words. But no one reads a dictionary that way: if a person has more than one word to consult, these words are likely in quite different places in the dictionary, the ordering of the words being altogether arbitrary relative to their meanings. There may be sequences of words related to one another by a common prefix, just as in life there may be a stretch of days that seem alike, but then the list continues to something completely different, and the order of the letters does nothing to warn us of the change.

Embodied, moving through time, I translate in fragments: a one-, two-, or three-word translation (*hair, down, foliage*); an indication of whether *hair* refers to what grows on a person's head or what grows on the branches of trees; a short quotation from ancient comedy punning on the two meanings. There are slots into which each of these explications needs to be typed—physical as well as mental movement. Although the meat and sinew and aqueous humors of my body have no knowledge of the layouts of computer keyboards, my eyes and fingers know where the letters are and produce words and punctuated sentences because the keyboard is there, making patterns that would be mere meaningless tattoos were there nothing resting on my lap. My mind controls my body, but I do not know how.

The fingers on my right hand constantly press the arrow keys to move between these slots or slide the mouse to jump from one to the next; my left pinkie constantly tucks under to reach the SHIFT key, to coordinate with my right pinkie on the right-arrow key to highlight a whole word or passage that needs overwriting. The elephantine dictionary project is an abstract conception, but I am a body in a chair, moving my fingers, tapping keys, and making things appear and disappear on the screen in front of me. I am moving my hands in repetitive ways at awkward angles, doing physical work in real time. Yet the cobblestone arch of arbitrary and unimportant and disused words is often more real to me than bodily sensations, or even than interactions with other human beings.

This work with words, this anchoring sequence of arbitrariness, this paradox of orderings and numberings and xml codings and nerve impulses and bodily sensations—this is where I feel my heart most alive. By way of this practice, this immersion in words and the sculpting of reflections or responsions between and among the other languages and English, my feelings are astir when I'm choosing whether to say "word list," "lexicon," "catalogue," or "litany." Then, a richening, a rightness, comes when I hit on "corpus," for the compendium of words *is* a corpus—a body—mirroring and shaping my own. Words are the most perfect index and teacher of what it is to be a human being.

Everyone who speaks is choosing words, juxtaposing words, invoking words and their special flavors and resonances—not always the same ones for the same speakers—regardless of how aware each speaker may be of making choices. A body settles into its most comfortable postures, just as a corpus of language features commoner words, more readily available to choose, at different times and places. The isthmus is a neck of land and the neck of a body. Words map my animal body onto the world I inhabit. Words confirm that I am a microcosm of what surrounds me; they are the air through which I see myself reflected in my landscape, the ether through which whatever I send out into the world will echo back to me.

SEBASTIAN JUNGER

The Bonds of Battle

FROM *Vanity Fair*

THE FIRST TIME I experienced what I now understand to be post-traumatic stress disorder, I was in a subway station in New York City, where I live. It was almost a year before the attacks of 9/11, and I'd just come back from two months in Afghanistan with Ahmad Shah Massoud, the leader of the Northern Alliance. I was on assignment to write a profile of Massoud, who fought a desperate resistance against the Taliban until they assassinated him two days before 9/11. At one point during my trip we were on a frontline position that his forces had just taken over from the Taliban, and the inevitable counterattack started with an hour-long rocket barrage. All we could do was curl up in the trenches and hope. I felt deranged for days afterward, as if I'd lived through the end of the world.

By the time I got home, though, I wasn't thinking about that or any of the other horrific things we'd seen; I mentally buried all of it until one day, a few months later, when I went into the subway at rush hour to catch the C train downtown. Suddenly I found myself backed up against a metal support column, absolutely convinced I was going to die. There were too many people on the platform, the trains were coming into the station too fast, the lights were too bright, the world was too loud. I couldn't quite explain what was wrong, but I was far more scared than I'd ever been in Afghanistan.

I stood there with my back to the column until I couldn't take it anymore, and then I sprinted for the exit and walked home. I had no idea that what I'd just experienced had anything to do with combat; I just thought I was going crazy. For the next several months I kept having panic attacks whenever I was in a small place with too many people—airplanes, ski gondolas, crowded bars. Gradually the incidents stopped, and I didn't think about them again until I found myself talking to a woman at a picnic who worked as a psychotherapist. She asked whether I'd been affected by my war experiences, and I said no, I didn't think so. But for some reason I described my puzzling panic attack in the subway. "That's called post-traumatic stress disorder," she said. "You'll be hearing a lot more about that in the next few years."

I had classic short-term (acute) PTSD. From an evolutionary perspective, it's exactly the response you want to have when your life is in danger: you want to be vigilant, you want to react to strange noises, you want to sleep lightly and wake easily, you want to have flashbacks that remind you of the danger, and you want to be, by turns, anxious and depressed. Anxiety keeps you ready to fight, and depression keeps you from being too active and putting yourself at greater risk. This is a universal human adaptation to danger that is common to other mammals as well. It may be unpleasant, but it's preferable to getting eaten. (Because PTSD is so adaptive, many have begun leaving the word *disorder* out of the term to avoid stigmatizing a basically healthy reaction.)

Because PTSD is a natural response to danger, it's almost unavoidable in the short term and mostly self-correcting in the long term. Only about 20 percent of people exposed to trauma react with long-term (chronic) PTSD. Rape is one of the most psychologically devastating things that can happen to a person, for example—far more traumatizing than most military deployments—and according to a 1992 study published in the *Journal of Traumatic Stress*, 94 percent of rape survivors exhibit signs of extreme trauma immediately afterward. And yet nine months later 47 percent of rape survivors have recovered enough to resume living normal lives.

Combat is generally less traumatic than rape but harder to recover from. The reason, strangely, is that the trauma of combat is interwoven with other, positive experiences that become difficult to separate from the harm. "Treating combat veterans is different from treating rape victims, because rape victims don't have this idea that some aspects of their experience are worth retaining," says Dr. Rachel Yehuda, a professor of psychiatry and neuroscience and director of traumatic-stress studies at Mount Sinai Hospital in

New York. Yehuda has studied PTSD in a wide range of people, including combat veterans and Holocaust survivors. "For most people in combat, their experiences range from the best to the worst of times," Yehuda adds. "It's the most important thing someone has ever done—especially since these people are so young when they go in—and it's probably the first time they're ever free, completely, of their societal constraints. They're going to miss being entrenched in this very important and defining world."

Oddly, one of the most traumatic events for soldiers is witnessing harm to other people—even to the enemy. In a survey done after the first Gulf War by David Marlowe, an expert in stress-related disorders working with the Department of Defense, combat veterans reported that killing an enemy soldier—or even witnessing one getting killed—was more distressing than being wounded oneself. But the very worst experience, by a significant margin, was having a friend die. In war after war, army after army, losing a buddy is considered to be the most distressing thing that can possibly happen. It serves as a trigger for psychological breakdown on the battlefield and readjustment difficulties after the soldier has returned home.

Terrible as such experiences are, however, roughly 80 percent of people exposed to them eventually recover, according to a 2008 study in the *Journal of Behavioral Medicine*. If one considers the extreme hardship and violence of our prehistory, it makes sense that humans are able to sustain enormous psychic damage and continue functioning; otherwise our species would have died out long ago. "It is possible that our common generalized anxiety disorders are the evolutionary legacy of a world in which mild recurring fear was adaptive," writes anthropologist and neuroscientist Melvin Konner, in a collection called *Understanding Trauma*. "Stress is the essence of evolution by natural selection and close to the essence of life itself."

A 2007 analysis from the Institute of Medicine and the National Research Council found that statistically, people who fail to overcome trauma tend to be people who are already burdened by psychological issues—either because they inherited them or because they suffered trauma or abuse as children. According to a 2003 study on high-risk twins and combat-related PTSD, if you fought in Vietnam and your twin brother did not—but suffers from psychiatric disorders—you are more likely to get PTSD after your deployment. If you experienced the death of a loved one, or even weren't held enough as a child, you are up to seven times more likely to develop the kinds of anxiety disorders that can contribute to PTSD, according to a 1989 study in the *British Journal of Psychiatry*. And according to statistics published in the *Journal of Consulting and Clinical Psychology* in 2000, if you have an educational deficit, if you are female, if you have a low IQ, or if you were abused as a child, you are at an elevated risk of developing PTSD. These factors are nearly as predictive of PTSD as the severity of the trauma itself.

Suicide by combat veterans is often seen as an extreme expression of PTSD, but currently there is no statistical relationship between suicide and combat, according to a study published in April in the *Journal of the American Medical Association Psychiatry*. Combat veterans are no more likely to kill themselves than veterans who were never under fire. The much-discussed estimated figure of twenty-two vets a day committing suicide is deceptive: it was only in 2008, for the first time in decades, that the U.S. Army veteran suicide rate, though enormously tragic, surpassed the civilian rate in America. And even so, the majority of veterans who kill themselves are over the age of fifty. Generally speaking, the more time that passes after a trauma, the less likely a suicide is to have anything to do with it, according to many studies. Among younger vets, deployment to Iraq or Afghanistan *lowers* the incidence of suicide because soldiers with obvious mental-health issues are less likely to be deployed with their units, according to an analysis published in *Annals of Epidemiology* in 2015. The most accurate predictor of post-deployment suicide, as it turns out, isn't combat or repeated deployments or losing a buddy but suicide attempts *before* deployment. The single most effective action the U.S. military could take to reduce veteran suicide would be to screen for preexisting mental disorders.

It seems intuitively obvious that combat is connected to psychological trauma, but the relationship is a complicated one. Many soldiers go through horrific experiences but fare better than others who experienced danger only briefly, or not at all. Unmanned-drone pilots, for instance—who watch their missiles kill human beings by remote camera—have been calculated as having the same PTSD rates as pilots who fly actual combat missions in war zones, according to a 2013 analysis published in the *Medical Surveillance Monthly Report*. And even among regular infantry, danger and psychological breakdown during combat are not necessarily connected. During the 1973 Yom Kippur War, when Israel was invaded simultaneously by Egypt and Syria, rear-base troops in the Israeli military had psychological breakdowns at three times the rate of elite frontline troops, relative to their casualties. And during the air campaign of the first Gulf War, more than 80 percent of psychiatric casualties in the U.S. Army's VII Corps came from support units that took almost no incoming fire, according to a 1992 study on army stress casualties.

Conversely, American airborne and other highly trained units in World War II had some of the lowest rates of psychiatric casualties of the entire military, relative to their number of wounded. A sense of helplessness is deeply traumatic to people, but high levels of training seem to counteract that so effectively that elite soldiers are psychologically insulated from even extreme risk. Part of the reason, it has been found, is that elite soldiers have higher-than-average levels of an amino acid called neuropeptide-Y, which acts as a chemical buffer against hormones that are secreted by the endocrine system during times of high stress. In one 1968 study, published in the *Archive of General Psychiatry*, Special Forces soldiers in Vietnam had levels of the stress hormone cortisol go down before an anticipated attack, while less experienced combatants saw their levels go up.

Shell Shock

All this is new science, however. For most of the nation's history, psychological effects of combat trauma have been variously attributed to neuroses, shell shock, or simple cowardice. When men have failed to obey orders due to trauma they have been beaten, imprisoned, "treated" with electroshock therapy, or simply shot as a warning to others. (For British troops, cowardice was a capital crime until 1930.) It was not until after the Vietnam War that the American Psychiatric Association listed combat trauma as an official diagnosis. Tens of thousands of vets were struggling with "Post-Vietnam Syndrome"—nightmares, insomnia, addiction, paranoia

—and their struggle could no longer be written off to weakness or personal failings. Obviously, these problems could also affect war reporters, cops, firefighters, or anyone else subjected to trauma. In 1980, the APA finally included post-traumatic stress disorder in the third edition of the *Diagnostic and Statistical Manual of Mental Disorders.*

Thirty-five years after acknowledging the problem in its current form, the American military now has the highest PTSD rate in its history—and probably in the world. Horrific experiences are unfortunately universal, but long-term impairment from them is not, and despite billions of dollars spent on treatment, half of our Iraq and Afghanistan veterans have applied for permanent disability. Of those veterans treated, roughly a third have been diagnosed with PTSD. Since only about 10 percent of our armed forces actually see combat, the majority of vets claiming to suffer from PTSD seem to have been affected by something other than direct exposure to danger.

This is not a new phenomenon: decade after decade and war after war, American combat deaths have dropped steadily while trauma and disability claims have continued to rise. They are in an almost inverse relationship with each other. Soldiers in Vietnam suffered roughly one-quarter the casualty rate of troops in World War II, for example, but filed for disability at a rate that was nearly 50 percent higher, according to a 2013 report in the *Journal of Anxiety Disorders.* It's tempting to attribute this disparity to the toxic reception they had at home, but that doesn't seem to be the case. Today's vets claim three times the number of disabilities that Vietnam vets did despite a generally warm reception back home and a casualty rate that, thank God, is roughly one-third what it was in Vietnam. Today most disability claims are for hearing loss, tinnitus, and PTSD—the latter two of which can be exaggerated or faked. Even the first Gulf War—which lasted only a hundred hours—produced nearly twice the disability rates of World War II. Clearly, there is a feedback loop of disability claims, compensation, and more disability claims that cannot go on forever.

Part of the problem is bureaucratic: in an effort to speed up access to benefits, in 2010 the Veterans Administration declared that soldiers no longer have to cite a specific incident—a firefight, a roadside bomb—in order to be eligible for disability compensation. He or she simply has to report being impaired in daily life. As a result, PTSD claims have reportedly risen 60 percent to 150,000 a year. Clearly this has produced a system that is vulnerable to abuse and bureaucratic error. A recent investigation by the VA's Office of Inspector General found that the higher a veteran's PTSD disability rating, the more treatment he or she tends to seek until achieving a rating of 100 percent, at which point treatment visits drop by 82 percent and many vets quit completely. In theory, the most traumatized people should be seeking more help, not less. It's hard to avoid the conclusion that some vets are getting treatment simply to raise their disability rating.

In addition to being an enormous waste of taxpayer money, such fraud, intentional or not, does real harm to the vets who truly need help. One Veterans Administration counselor I spoke with described having to physically protect someone in a PTSD support group because some other vets wanted to beat him up for faking his trauma. This counselor, who asked to remain anonymous, said that many combat veterans actively avoid the VA because they worry about losing their temper around patients who are milking the system. "It's the real deals—the guys who have seen the most —that this tends to bother," this counselor told me.

The majority of traumatized vets are *not* faking their symptoms, however. They return from wars that are safer than those their fathers and grandfathers fought, and yet far greater numbers of them wind up alienated and depressed. This is true even for people who didn't experience combat. In other words, the problem doesn't seem to be trauma on the battlefield so much as reentry into society. Anthropological research from around the world shows that recovery from war is heavily influenced by the society one returns to, and there are societies that make that process relatively easy. Ethnographic studies on hunter-gatherer societies rarely turn up evidence of chronic PTSD among their warriors, for example, and oral histories of Native American warfare consistently fail to mention psychological trauma. Anthropologists and oral historians weren't expressly looking for PTSD, but the high frequency of warfare in these groups makes the scarcity of any mention of it revealing. Even the Israeli military—with mandatory national service and two generations of intermittent warfare—has by some measures a PTSD rate as low as 1 percent.

If we weed out the malingerers on the one hand and the deeply traumatized on the other, we are still left with enormous numbers of veterans who had utterly ordinary wartime experiences and yet feel dangerously alienated back home. Clinically speaking, such alienation is not the same thing as PTSD, but both seem to result from military service abroad, so it's understandable that vets and even clinicians are prone to conflating them. Either way, it makes one wonder exactly what it is about modern society that is so mortally dispiriting to come home to.

Soldier's Creed

Any discussion of PTSD and its associated sense of alienation in society must address the fact that many soldiers find themselves missing the war after it's over. That troubling fact can be found in written accounts from war after war, country after country, century after century. Awkward as it is to say, part of the trauma of war seems to be giving it up. There are ancient human behaviors in war—loyalty, inter-reliance, cooperation—that typify good soldiering and can't be easily found in modern society. This can produce a kind of nostalgia for the hard times that even civilians are susceptible to: after World War II, many Londoners claimed to miss the communal underground living that characterized life during the Blitz (despite the fact that more than 40,000 civilians lost their lives). And the war that is missed doesn't even have to be a shooting war: "I am a survivor of the AIDS epidemic," a man wrote on the comment board of an online talk I gave about war. "Now that AIDS is no longer a death sentence, I must admit that I miss those days of extreme brotherhood . . . which led to deep emotions and understandings that are above anything I have felt since the plague years."

What all these people seem to miss isn't danger or loss, per se, but the closeness and cooperation that danger and loss often engender. Humans evolved to survive in extremely harsh environments, and our capacity for cooperation and sharing clearly helped us do that. Structurally, a band of hunter-gatherers and a platoon in combat are almost exactly the same: in each case, the group numbers between thirty and fifty individuals, they sleep in a common area, they conduct patrols, they are completely reliant on one another for support, comfort, and defense, and they share a group identity that most would risk their lives for. Personal interest is subsumed into group interest because personal survival is not possible without group survival. From an evolutionary perspective, it's not at all surprising that many soldiers respond to combat in positive ways and miss it when it's gone.

There are obvious psychological stresses on a person in a group, but there may be even greater stresses on a person in isolation. Most higher primates, including humans, are intensely social, and there are few examples of individuals surviving outside of a group. A modern soldier returning from combat goes from the kind of close-knit situation that humans evolved for into a society where most people work outside the home, children are educated by strangers, families are isolated from wider communities, personal gain almost completely eclipses collective good, and people sleep alone or with a partner. Even if he or she is in a family, that is not the same as belonging to a large, self-sufficient group that shares and experiences almost everything collectively. Whatever the technological advances of modern society—and they're nearly miraculous—the individual lifestyles that those technologies spawn may be deeply brutalizing to the human spirit.

"You'll have to be prepared to say that we are not a good society—that we are an *antihuman* society," anthropologist Sharon Abramowitz warned when I tried this theory out on her. Abramowitz was in Ivory Coast during the start of the civil war there in 2002 and experienced firsthand the extremely close bonds created by hardship and danger. "We are not good to each other. Our tribalism is about an extremely narrow group of people: our children, our spouse, maybe our parents. Our society is alienating, technical, cold, and mystifying. Our fundamental desire as human beings is to be close to others, and our society does not allow for that."

This is an old problem, and today's vets are not the first Americans to balk at coming home. A source of continual embarrassment along the American frontier—from the late 1600s until the end of the Indian Wars, in the 1890s—was a phenomenon known as "the White Indians." The term referred to white settlers who were kidnapped by Indians—or simply ran off to them—and became so enamored of that life that they refused to leave. According to many writers of the time, including Benjamin Franklin, the reverse never happened: Indians never ran off to join white society. And if a peace treaty required that a tribe give up their adopted members, these members would often have to be put under guard and returned home by force. Inevitably, many would escape to rejoin their Indian families. "Thousands of Europeans are Indians, and we have no examples of even one of those aborigines having from choice become European," wrote a French-born writer in America named Michel-Guillaume-Saint-Jean de Crèvecoeur in an essay published in 1782.

One could say that combat vets are the White Indians of today, and that they miss the war because it was, finally, an experience of human closeness that they can't easily find back home. Not the closeness of family, which is rare enough, but the closeness of community and tribe. The kind of closeness that gets endlessly venerated in Hollywood movies but only actually shows up in contemporary society when something goes wrong—when tornados obliterate towns or planes are flown into skyscrapers. Those events briefly give us a reason to act communally, and most of us do. "There is something to be said for using risk to forge social bonds," Abramowitz pointed out. "Having something to fight for, and fight through, is a good and important thing."

Certainly the society we have created is hard on us by virtually every metric that we use to measure human happiness. This problem may disproportionately affect people, like soldiers, who are making a radical transition back home.

It is incredibly hard to measure and quantify the human experience, but some studies have found that many people in certain modern societies self-report high levels of happiness. And yet numerous cross-cultural studies show that as affluence and urbanization rise in a given society, so do rates of depression, suicide, and schizophrenia (along with health issues such as obesity and diabetes). People in wealthy countries suffer unipolar depression at more than double the rate that they do in poor countries, according to a study by the World Health Organization, and people in countries with large income disparities—like the United States —run a much higher risk of developing mood disorders at some point in their lives. A 2006 cross-cultural study of women focusing on depression and modernization compared depression rates in rural and urban Nigeria and rural and urban North America, and found that women in rural areas of both countries were far less likely to get depressed than urban women. And urban American women—the most affluent demographic of the study—were the *most* likely to succumb to depression.

In America, the more assimilated a person is into contemporary society, the more likely he or she is to develop depression in his or her lifetime. According to a 2004 study in *The Journal of Nervous and Mental Disease,* Mexicans born in the United States are highly assimilated into American culture and have much higher rates of depression than Mexicans born in Mexico. By contrast, Amish communities have an exceedingly low rate of reported depression because, in part, it is theorized, they have completely resisted modernization. They won't even drive cars. "The economic and marketing forces of modern society have engineered an environment promoting decisions that maximize consumption at the long-term cost of well-being," one survey of these studies, from the *Journal of Affective Disorders* in 2012, concluded. "In effect, humans have dragged a body with a long hominid history into an overfed, malnourished, sedentary, sunlight-deficient, sleep-deprived, competitive, inequitable and socially-isolating environment with dire consequences."

For more than half a million years, our recent hominid ancestors lived nomadic lives of extreme duress on the plains of East Africa, but the advent of agriculture changed that about 10,000 years ago. That is only 400 generations—not enough to adapt, genetically, to the changes in diet and society that ensued. Privately worked land and the accumulation of capital made humans less oriented toward group welfare, and the Industrial Revolution pushed society further in that direction. No one knows how the so-called Information Age will affect us, but there's a good chance that home technology and the Internet will only intensify our drift toward solipsism and alienation.

Meanwhile, many of the behaviors that had high survival value in our evolutionary past, like problem-solving, cooperation, and intergroup competition, are still rewarded by bumps of dopamine and other hormones into our system. Those hormones serve to reinforce whatever behavior it was that produced those hormones in the first place. Group affiliation and cooperation were clearly adaptive because in many animals, including humans, they trigger a surge in levels of a neuropeptide called oxytocin. Not only does oxytocin create a glow of well-being in people, it promotes greater levels of trust and bonding, which unite them further still. Hominids that were rewarded with oxytocin for cooperating with one another must have out-fought, out-hunted, and out-bred the ones that didn't. Those are the hominids that modern humans are descended from.

According to one study published in *Science* in June 2010, this feedback loop of oxytocin and group loyalty creates an expectation that members will "self-sacrifice to contribute to in-group welfare." There may be no better description of a soldier's ethos than that sentence. One of the most noticeable things about life in the military is that you are virtually never alone: day after day, month after month, you are close enough to speak to, if not touch, a dozen or more people. You eat together, sleep together, laugh together, suffer together. That level of intimacy duplicates our evolutionary past very closely and must create a nearly continual oxytocin reward system.

Hero's Welcome

When soldiers return to modern society, they must go through —among other adjustments—a terrific oxytocin withdrawal. The chronic isolation of modern society begins in childhood and continues our entire lives. Infants in hunter-gatherer societies are carried by their mothers as much as 50 to 90 percent of the time, often in wraps that keep them strapped to the mother's back so that her hands are free. That roughly corresponds to carrying rates among other primates, according to primatologist and psychologist Harriet J. Smith. One can get an idea of how desperately important touch is to primates from a landmark experiment conducted in the 1950s by a psychologist and primatologist named Harry Harlow. Baby rhesus monkeys were separated from their mothers and presented with the choice of two kinds of surrogates: a cuddly mother made out of terry cloth or an uninviting mother made out of wire mesh. The wire-mesh mother, however, had a nipple that would dispense warm milk. The babies invariably took their nourishment quickly in order to rush back and cling to the terry-cloth mother, which had enough softness to provide the illusion of affection. But even that isn't enough for psychological health: in a separate experiment, more than 75 percent of female baby rhesus monkeys raised with terry-cloth mothers—as opposed to real ones—grew up to be abusive and neglectful to their own young.

In the 1970s, American mothers maintained skin-to-skin contact with their nine-month-old babies as little as 16 percent of the time, which is a level of contact that traditional societies would probably consider a form of child abuse. Also unthinkable would be the common practice of making young children sleep by themselves in their own room. In two American studies of middle-class families during the 1980s, 85 percent of young children slept alone—a figure that rose to 95 percent among families considered "well-educated." Northern European societies, including America, are the only ones in history to make very young children sleep alone in such numbers. The isolation is thought to trigger fears that make many children bond intensely with stuffed animals for reassurance. Only in Northern European societies do children go through the well-known developmental stage of bonding with stuffed animals; elsewhere, children get their sense of safety from the adults sleeping near them.

More broadly, in most human societies, almost nobody sleeps alone. Sleeping in family groups of one sort or another has been the norm throughout human history and is still commonplace in most of the world. Again, Northern European societies are among the few where people sleep alone or with a partner in a private room. When I was with American soldiers at a remote outpost in Afghanistan, we slept in narrow plywood huts where I could reach out and touch three other men from where I slept. They snored, they talked, they got up in the middle of the night to use the piss tubes, but we felt safe because we were in a group. The Taliban attacked the position regularly, and the most determined attacks often came at dawn. Another unit in a nearby valley was almost overrun and took 50 percent casualties in just such an attack. And yet I slept better surrounded by those noisy, snoring men than I ever did camping alone in the woods of New England.

Many soldiers will tell you that one of the hardest things about coming home is learning to sleep without the security of a group of heavily armed men around them. In that sense, being in a war

zone with your platoon feels safer than being in an American suburb by yourself. I know a vet who felt so threatened at home that
he would get up in the middle of the night to build fighting positions out of the living room furniture. This is a radically different
experience from what warriors in other societies go through, such
as the Yanomami, of the Orinoco and Amazon Basins, who go to
war with their entire age cohort and return to face, together, whatever the psychological consequences may be. As one anthropologist pointed out to me, trauma is usually a group experience, so
trauma recovery should be a group experience as well. But in our
society it's not.

"Our whole approach to mental health has been hijacked by
pharmaceutical logic," I was told by Gary Barker, an anthropologist whose group, Promundo, is dedicated to understanding and
preventing violence. "PTSD is a crisis of connection and disrup-
tion, not an illness that you carry within you."

This individualizing of mental health is not just an American
problem, or a veteran problem; it affects everybody. A British anthropologist named Bill West told me that the extreme poverty of
the 1930s and the collective trauma of the Blitz served to unify an
entire generation of English people. "I link the experience of the
Blitz to voting in the Labour Party in 1945, and the establishing
of the National Health Service and a strong welfare state," he said.
"Those policies were supported well into the sixties by all political
parties. That kind of cultural cohesiveness, along with Christianity, was very helpful after the war. It's an open question whether
people's problems are located in the individual. If enough people
in society are sick, you have to wonder whether it isn't actually society that's sick."

Ideally, we would compare hunter-gatherer society to post-indus-
trial society to see which one copes better with PTSD. When the
Sioux, Cheyenne, and Arapaho fighters returned to their camps
after annihilating Custer and his regiment at Little Bighorn, for
example, were they traumatized and alienated by the experience
—or did they fit right back into society? There is no way to know
for sure, but less direct comparisons can still illuminate how cohesiveness affects trauma. In experiments with lab rats, for example,
a subject that is traumatized—but not injured—after an attack by
a larger rat usually recovers within forty-eight hours *unless it is kept*

in isolation, according to data published in 2005 in *Neuroscience & Biobehavioral Reviews.* The ones that are kept apart from other rats are the only ones that develop long-term traumatic symptoms. And a study of risk factors for PTSD in humans closely mirrored those results. In a 2000 study in the *Journal of Consulting and Clinical Psychology,* "lack of social support" was found to be around two times more reliable at predicting who got PTSD and who didn't than the severity of the trauma itself. You could be mildly traumatized, in other words—on a par with, say, an ordinary rear-base deployment to Afghanistan—and experience long-term PTSD simply because of a lack of social support back home.

Anthropologist and psychiatrist Brandon Kohrt found a similar phenomenon in the villages of southern Nepal, where a civil war has been rumbling for years. Kohrt explained to me that there are two kinds of villages there: exclusively Hindu ones, which are extremely stratified, and mixed Buddhist/Hindu ones, which are far more open and cohesive. He said that child soldiers, both male and female, who go back to Hindu villages can remain traumatized for years, while those from mixed-religion villages tended to recover very quickly. "PTSD is a disorder of recovery, and if treatment only focuses on identifying symptoms, it pathologizes and alienates vets," according to Kohrt. "But if the focus is on family and community, it puts them in a situation of collective healing."

Israel is arguably the only modern country that retains a sufficient sense of community to mitigate the effects of combat on a mass scale. Despite decades of intermittent war, the Israel Defense Forces have a PTSD rate as low as 1 percent. Two of the foremost reasons have to do with national military service and the proximity of the combat—the war is virtually on their doorstep. "Being in the military is something that most people have done," I was told by Dr. Arieh Shalev, who has devoted the last twenty years to studying PTSD. "Those who come back from combat are reintegrated into a society where those experiences are very well understood. We did a study of seventeen-year-olds who had lost their father in the military, compared to those who had lost their fathers to accidents. The ones whose fathers died in combat did much better than those whose fathers hadn't."

According to Shalev, the closer the public is to the actual combat, the better the war will be understood and the less difficulty soldiers will have when they come home. The Israelis are benefiting from what could be called the shared public meaning of a war. Such public meaning—which would often occur in more communal, tribal societies—seems to help soldiers even in a fully modern society such as Israel. It is probably not generated by empty, reflexive phrases—such as "Thank you for your service"—that many Americans feel compelled to offer soldiers and vets. If anything, those comments only serve to underline the enormous chasm between military and civilian society in this country.

Another Israeli researcher, Reuven Gal, found that the perceived legitimacy of a war was more important to soldiers' general morale than was the combat readiness of the unit they were in. And that legitimacy, in turn, was a function of the war's physical distance from the homeland: "The Israeli soldiers who were abruptly mobilized and thrown into dreadful battles in the middle of Yom Kippur Day in 1973 had no doubts about the legitimacy of the war," Gal wrote in the *Journal of Applied Psychology* in 1986. "Many of those soldiers who were fighting in the Golan Heights against the flood of Syrian tanks needed only to look behind their shoulders to see their homes and remind themselves that they were fighting for their very survival."

In that sense the Israelis are far more like the Sioux, Cheyenne, and Arapaho at Little Bighorn than they are like us. America's distance from her enemies means that her wars have generally been fought far away from her population centers, and as a result those wars have been harder to explain and justify than Israel's have been. The people who will bear the psychic cost of that ambiguity will, of course, be the soldiers.

A Bright Shining Lie

"I talked to my mom only one time from Mars," a Vietnam vet named Gregory Gomez told me about the physical and spiritual distance between his home and the war zone. Gomez is a pureblooded Apache who grew up in West Texas. He says his grandfather was arrested and executed by Texas Rangers in 1915 because they wanted his land; they strung him from a tree limb, cut off his genitals, and stuffed them in his mouth. Consequently, Gomez felt no allegiance to the U.S. government, but he volunteered for service in Vietnam anyway. "Most of us Indian guys who went to Vietnam went because we were warriors," Gomez told me. "I did not fight for this country. I fought for Mother Earth. I wanted to experience combat. I wanted to know how I'd do."

Gomez was in a Marine Corps Force Recon unit, one of the most elite designations in the U.S. military. He was part of a four-man team that would insert by helicopter into enemy territory north of the DMZ and stay for two weeks at a time. They had no medic and no backup and didn't even dare eat C rations, because, Gomez said, they were afraid their body odor would give them away. They ate Vietnamese food and watched enemy soldiers pass just yards away in the dense jungle. "Everyone who has lived through something like that has lived through trauma, and you can never go back," he told me. "You are seventeen or eighteen or nineteen and you just hit that wall. You become very old men."

American Indians, proportionally, have provided more soldiers to America's wars than almost any other ethnic group in this country. They are also the product of an ancient and vibrant warring culture that takes great pains to protect the warrior from society, and vice versa. Although those traditions have obviously broken down since the end of the Indian Wars, there may be something to be learned from the principles upon which they stand. When Gomez came home he essentially isolated himself for more than a decade. He didn't drink, and he lived a normal life except that occasionally he'd go to the corner store to get a soda and would wind up in Oklahoma or East Texas without any idea how he got there.

He finally started seeing a therapist at the VA as well as undergoing traditional Indian rituals. It was a combination that seemed to work. In the 1980s he underwent an extremely painful ceremony called the Sun Dance. At the start of the ceremony, the dancers have wooden skewers driven through the skin of their chests. Leather thongs are tied to the skewers and then attached to the top of a tall pole at the center of the dance ground. To a steady drumbeat, the dancers move in a circle while leaning back on the leather thongs until, after many hours, the skewers finally tear free. "I dance back and I throw my arms and yell and I can see the ropes and the piercing sticks like in slow motion, flying from my chest towards the grandfather's tree," Gomez told me about the experience. "And I had this incredible feeling of euphoria and strength, like I could do anything. That's when the healing takes place. That's when life changes take place."

America is a largely de-ritualized society that obviously can't just borrow from another society to heal its psychic wounds. But the spirit of community healing and empowerment that forms the basis of these ceremonies is certainly one that might be converted to a secular modern society. The shocking disconnect for veterans isn't so much that civilians don't know what they went through —it's unrealistic to expect anyone to fully understand another person's experience—but that what they went through doesn't seem relevant back home. Given the profound alienation that afflicts modern society, when combat vets say that they want to go back to war, they may be having an entirely healthy response to the perceived emptiness of modern life.

One way to change this dynamic might be to emulate the Israelis and mandate national service (with a military or combat option). We could also emulate the Nepalese and try to have communities better integrate people of different ethnic and religious groups. Finally, we could emulate many tribal societies—including the Apache—by getting rid of parades and replacing them with some form of homecoming ceremony. An almost universal component of these ceremonies is the dramatic retelling of combat experiences to the warrior's community. We could achieve that on Veterans Day by making every town and city hall in the country available to veterans who want to speak publicly about the war. The vapid phrase "I support the troops" would then mean actually showing up at your town hall every Veterans Day to hear these people out. Some vets will be angry, some will be proud, and some will be crying so hard they can't speak. But a community ceremony like that would finally return the experience of war to our entire nation, rather than just leaving it to the people who fought.

It might also begin to reassemble a society that has been spiritually cannibalizing itself for generations. We keep wondering how to save the vets, but the real question is how to save ourselves. If we do that, the vets will be fine. If we don't, it won't matter anyway.

LAURA KIPNIS

Sexual Paranoia

FROM *The Chronicle Review*

YOU HAVE TO feel a little sorry these days for professors married to their former students. They used to be respectable citizens —leaders in their fields, department chairs, maybe even a dean or two—and now they're abusers of power *avant la lettre*. I suspect you can barely throw a stone on most campuses around the country without hitting a few of these neo-miscreants. Who knows what coercions they deployed back in the day to corral those students into submission; at least that's the fear evinced by today's new campus dating policies. And think how their kids must feel! A friend of mine is the offspring of such a coupling—does she look at her father a little differently now, I wonder.

It's been barely a year since the Great Prohibition took effect in my own workplace. Before that, students and professors could date whomever we wanted; the next day we were off-limits to one another—*verboten, traife,* dangerous (and perhaps therefore all the more alluring).

Of course, the residues of the wild old days are everywhere. On my campus, several such "mixed" couples leap to mind, including female professors wed to former students. Not to mention the legions who've dated a graduate student or two in their day—plenty of female professors in that category too; in fact, I'm one of them. Don't ask for details. It's one of those things it now behooves one to be reticent about, lest you be branded a predator.

Forgive my slightly mocking tone. I suppose I'm out of step with the new realities because I came of age in a different time, under a different version of feminism, minus the layers of prohibition and sexual terror surrounding the unequal-power dilemmas of today.

When I was in college, hooking up with professors was more or less part of the curriculum. Admittedly, I went to an art school, and mine was the lucky generation that came of age in that too-brief interregnum after the sexual revolution and before AIDS turned sex into a crime scene replete with perpetrators and victims—back when sex, even when not so great or when people got their feelings hurt, fell under the category of life experience. It's not that I didn't make my share of mistakes, or act stupidly and inchoately, but it was embarrassing, not traumatizing.

As Jane Gallop recalls in *Feminist Accused of Sexual Harassment* (1997), her own generational *cri de coeur,* sleeping with professors made her feel cocky, not taken advantage of. She admits to seducing more than one of them as a grad student—she wanted to see them naked, she says, like other men. Lots of smart, ambitious women were doing the same thing, according to her, because it was a way to experience your own power.

But somehow power seemed a lot less powerful back then. The gulf between students and faculty wasn't a shark-filled moat; a misstep wasn't fatal. We partied together, drank and got high together, slept together. The teachers may have been older and more accomplished, but you didn't feel they could take advantage of you because of it. How would they?

Which isn't to say that teacher-student relations were guaranteed to turn out well, but then what percentage of romances do? No doubt there were jealousies, sometimes things didn't go the way you wanted—which was probably good training for the rest of life. It was also an excellent education in not taking power too seriously, and I suspect the less seriously you take it, the more strategies you have for contending with it.

It's the fiction of the all-powerful professor embedded in the new campus codes that appalls me. And the kowtowing to the fiction—kowtowing wrapped in a vaguely feminist air of rectitude. If this is feminism, it's feminism hijacked by melodrama. The melodramatic imagination's obsession with helpless victims and powerful predators is what's shaping the conversation of the moment, to the detriment of those whose interests are supposedly being protected, namely, students. The result? Students' sense of vulnerability is skyrocketing.

I've done what I can to adapt myself to the new paradigm. Around a decade ago, as colleges began instituting new "offensive environment" guidelines, I appointed myself the task of actually reading my university's sexual-harassment handbook, which I'd thus far avoided doing. I was pleased to learn that our guidelines were less prohibitive than those of the more draconian new codes. You were permitted to date students; you just weren't supposed to harass them into it. I could live with that.

However, we were warned in two separate places that inappropriate humor violates university policy. I'd always thought inappropriateness was pretty much the definition of humor—I believe Freud would agree. Why all this delicacy? Students were being encouraged to regard themselves as such exquisitely sensitive creatures that an errant classroom remark could impede their education, as such hothouse flowers that an unfunny joke was likely to create lasting trauma.

Knowing my own propensity for unfunny jokes, and given that telling one could now land you, the unfunny prof, on the carpet or even the national news, I decided to put my name down for one of the voluntary harassment workshops on my campus, hoping that my good citizenship might be noticed and applauded by the relevant university powers.

At the appointed hour, things kicked off with a "sexual-harassment pretest." This was administered by an earnest midfifties psychologist I'll call David and an earnest young woman with a master's in social work I'll call Beth. The pretest consisted of a long list of true-false questions such as "If I make sexual comments to someone and that person doesn't ask me to stop, then I guess that my behavior is probably welcome."

Despite the painful dumbness of these questions and the fading of afternoon into evening, a roomful of people with advanced degrees seemed grimly determined to shut up and play along, probably aided by a collective wish to be sprung by cocktail hour. That is, until we were handed a printed list of "guidelines." Number one on the list was "Do not make unwanted sexual advances."

Someone demanded querulously from the back, "But how do you know they're unwanted until you try?" (Okay, it was me.) David seemed oddly flustered by the question and began frantically jangling the change in his pants pocket.

"Do you really want me to answer that?" he finally responded, trying to make a joke out of it. I did want him to answer, because it's something I'd been wondering—How are you supposed to know in advance? Do people wear their desires emblazoned on their foreheads?—but I didn't want to be seen by my colleagues as a troublemaker. There was an awkward pause while David stared me down. Another person piped up helpfully, "What about smoldering glances?"

Everyone laughed, but David's coin-jangling was becoming more pronounced. A theater professor spoke up, guiltily admitting to having complimented a student on her hairstyle that very afternoon (one of the "Do Nots" involved not commenting on students' appearance), but as a gay male, he wondered whether *not* to have complimented her would have been grounds for offense. He mimicked the female student, tossing her mane around in a "Notice my hair" manner, and people began shouting suggestions about other dumb pretest scenarios for him to perform, like sexual-harassment charades. Rebellion was in the air. The man sitting next to me, an ethnographer who studied street gangs, whispered, "They've lost control of the room." David was jangling his change so frantically that it was hard to keep your eyes off his groin.

I recalled a long-forgotten pop-psychology guide to body language that identified change-jangling as an unconscious masturbation substitute. If the leader of our sexual-harassment workshop was engaging in public masturbatory-like behavior, seizing his private pleasure in the midst of the very institutional mechanism designed to clamp such delinquent urges, what hope for the rest of us?

Let's face it: other people's sexuality is often just weird and creepy. Sex is leaky and anxiety-ridden; intelligent people can be oblivious about it. Of course the gulf between desire and knowledge has long been a tragicomic staple. Consider some notable treatments of the student-professor hookup theme—J. M. Coetzee's *Disgrace;* Francine Prose's *Blue Angel;* Jonathan Franzen's *The Corrections*—in which learning has an inverse relation to self-knowledge, professors are emblems of sexual stupidity, and such disasters ensue that it's hard not to read them as cautionary tales about the disastrous effects of intellect on practical intelligence.

The implementers of the new campus codes seemed awfully optimistic about rectifying the condition, I thought to myself.

*

The optimism continues, outpaced only by all the new prohibitions and behavior codes required to sustain it. According to the latest version of our campus policy, "differences in institutional power and the inherent risk of coercion are so great" between teachers and students that no romance, dating, or sexual relationships will be permitted, even between students and professors from different departments. (Relations between graduate students and professors aren't outright banned, but are "problematic" and must be reported if you're in the same department.) Yale and other places had already instituted similar policies; Harvard jumped on board last month, though it's a sign of the incoherence surrounding these issues that the second sentence of the *New York Times* story on Harvard reads: "The move comes as the Obama administration investigates the handling of accusations of sexual assault at dozens of colleges, including Harvard." As everyone knows, the accusations in the news have been about students assaulting other students, not students dating professors.

Of course, the codes themselves also shape the narratives and emotional climate of professor-student interactions. An undergraduate sued my own university, alleging that a philosophy professor had engaged in "unwelcome and inappropriate sexual advances" and that the university punished him insufficiently for it. The details that emerged in news reports and legal papers were murky and contested, and the suit was eventually thrown out of court.

In brief: The two had gone to an art exhibit together—an outing initiated by the student—and then to some other exhibits and bars. She says he bought her alcohol and forced her to drink, so much that by the end of the evening she was going in and out of consciousness. He says she drank of her own volition. (She was under legal drinking age; he says he thought she was twenty-two.) She says he made various sexual insinuations, and that she wanted him to drive her home (they'd driven in his car); he says she insisted on sleeping over at his place. She says she woke up in his bed with his arms around her, and that he groped her. He denies making advances and says she made advances, which he deflected. He says they slept on top of the covers, clothed. Neither says they had sex. He says she sent friendly texts in the days after and wanted to meet. She says she attempted suicide two days later, now has PTSD, and has had to take medical leave.

The aftermath has been a score of back-and-forth lawsuits. After trying to get a financial settlement from the professor, the student filed a Title IX suit against the university: she wants her tuition reimbursed, compensation for emotional distress, and other damages. Because the professor wasn't terminated, when she runs into him it triggers her PTSD, she says. (The university claims that it appropriately sanctioned the professor, denying him a raise and a named chair.) She's also suing the professor for gender violence. He sued the university for gender discrimination (he says he wasn't allowed to present evidence disproving the student's allegations) —this suit was thrown out; so was the student's lawsuit against the university. The professor sued, for defamation, various colleagues, administrators, and a former grad student whom, according to his complaint, he had previously dated; a judge dismissed those suits this month. He sued local media outlets for using the word *rape* as a synonym for sexual assault—a complaint thrown out by a different judge who said rape was an accurate enough summary of the charges, even though the assault was confined to fondling, which the professor denies occurred. (This professor isn't someone I know or have met, by the way.)

What a mess. And what a slippery slope, from alleged fondler to rapist. But here's the real problem with these charges: this is melodrama. I'm quite sure that professors can be sleazebags. I'm less sure that any professor can force an unwilling student to drink, especially to the point of passing out. With what power? What sorts of repercussions can there possibly be if the student refuses?

Indeed, these are precisely the sorts of situations already covered by existing sexual-harassment codes, so if students think that professors have such unlimited powers that they can compel someone to drink or retaliate if she doesn't, then these students have been very badly educated about the nature and limits of institutional power.

In fact, it's just as likely that a student can derail a professor's career these days as the other way around, which is pretty much what happened in the case of the accused philosophy professor.

To a cultural critic, the representation of emotion in all these documents plays to the gallery. The student charges that she "suffered and will continue to suffer humiliation, mental and emotional anguish, anxiety, and distress." As I read through the complaint, it struck me that the lawsuit and our new consensual-relations code share a common set of tropes, and a certain narrative inevitability. In both, students and professors are stock characters in a predetermined story. According to the code, students are putty in the hands of all-powerful professors. According to the lawsuit, the student was virtually a rag doll, taken advantage of by a skillful predator who scripted a drunken evening of galleries and bars, all for the opportunity of some groping.

Everywhere on campuses today you find scholars whose work elaborates sophisticated models of power and agency. It would be hard to overstate the influence, across disciplines, of Michel Foucault, whose signature idea was that power has no permanent address or valence. Yet our workplaces themselves are promulgating the crudest version of top-down power imaginable, recasting the professoriate as Snidely Whiplashes twirling our mustaches and students as helpless damsels tied to railroad tracks. Students lack volition and independent desires of their own; professors are would-be coercers with dastardly plans to corrupt the innocent.

Even the language these policies come packaged in seems designed for maximum stupefaction, with students eager to add their voices to the din. Shortly after the new policy went into effect on my campus, we all received a long email from the Title IX Coordinating Committee. This was in the midst of student protests about the continued employment of the accused philosophy professor: 100 or so students, mouths taped shut (by themselves), had marched on the dean's office. (A planned sit-in of the professor's class went awry when he preemptively canceled it.) The committee was responding to a student-government petition demanding that "survivors" be informed about the outcomes of sexual-harassment investigations. The petition also demanded that the new policies be amended to include possible termination of faculty members who violate its provisions.

There was more, but my eye was struck by the word *survivor,* which was repeated several times. Wouldn't the proper term be *accuser*? How can someone be referred to as a survivor before a finding on the accusation—assuming we don't want to predetermine the guilt of the accused, that is. At the risk of sounding like some bow-tied neocon columnist, this is also a horrifying perversion of the language by people who should know better. Are you seriously telling me, I wanted to ask the Title IX Committee, that the same term now encompasses both someone allegedly groped by a professor and my great-aunt, who lived through the Nazi death camps? I emailed an inquiry to this effect to the university's general counsel, one of the email's signatories, but got no reply.

For the record, I strongly believe that bona fide harassers should be chemically castrated, stripped of their property, and hung up by their thumbs in the nearest public square. Let no one think I'm soft on harassment. But I also believe that the myths and fantasies about power perpetuated in these new codes are leaving our students disabled when it comes to the ordinary interpersonal tangles and erotic confusions that pretty much everyone has to deal with at some point in life, because that's simply part of the human condition.

In the post–Title IX landscape, sexual panic rules. Slippery slopes abound. Gropers become rapists and accusers become survivors, opening the door for another panicky conflation: teacher-student sex and incest. Recall that it was incest victims who earlier popularized the use of the term *survivor*, previously reserved for those who'd survived the Holocaust. The migration of the term itself is telling, exposing the core anxiety about teacher-student romances: that there's a whiff of perversity about such couples, notwithstanding all the venerable married ones.

These are anxious times for officialdom, and students too are increasingly afflicted with the condition—after all, anxiety is contagious. Around the time the "survivor" email arrived, something happened that I'd never experienced in many decades of teaching, which was that two students—one male, one female—in two classes informed me, separately, that they were unable to watch assigned films because they "triggered" something for them. I was baffled by the congruence until the following week, when the *Times* ran a story titled "Trauma Warnings Move from the Internet to the Ivory Tower," and the word *trigger* was suddenly all over the news.

I didn't press the two students on the nature of these triggers. I knew them both pretty well from previous classes, and they'd always seemed well adjusted enough, so I couldn't help wondering. One of the films dealt with fascism and bigotry: the triggeree was a minority student, though not the minority targeted in the film. Still, I could see what might be upsetting. In the other case, the connection between the student and the film was obscure: no overlapping identity categories, and though there was some sexual content in the film, it wasn't particularly explicit. We exchanged emails about whether she should sit out the discussion too; I proposed that she attend and leave if it got uncomfortable. I was trying to be empathetic, though I was also convinced that I was impeding her education rather than contributing to it.

I teach in a film program. We're supposed to be instilling critical skills in our students (at least that's how I see it), even those who aspire to churn out formulaic dreck for Hollywood. Which is how I framed it to my student: if she hoped for a career in the industry, getting more critical distance on material she found upsetting would seem advisable, given the nature of even mainstream media. I had an image of her in a meeting with a bunch of execs, telling them that she couldn't watch one of the company's films because it was a trigger for her. She agreed this could be a problem, and sat in on the discussion with no discernible ill effects.

But what do we expect will become of students, successfully cocooned from uncomfortable feelings, once they leave the sanctuary of academe for the boorish badlands of real life? What becomes of students so committed to their own vulnerability, conditioned to imagine they have no agency, and protected from unequal power arrangements in romantic life? I can't help asking, because there's a distressing little fact about the discomfort of vulnerability, which is that it's pretty much a daily experience in the world, and every sentient being has to learn how to somehow negotiate the consequences and fallout, or go through life flummoxed at every turn.

Here's a story that brought the point home for me. I was talking to a woman who'd just published her first book. She was around thirty, a friend of a friend. The book had started at a major trade press, then ended up published by a different press, and I was curious why. She alluded to problems with her first editor. I pressed for details, and out they came in a rush.

Her editor had developed a sort of obsession with her, constantly calling, taking her out for fancy meals, and eventually confessing his love. Meanwhile, he wasn't reading the chapters she gave him; in fact, he was doing barely any work on the manuscript at all. She wasn't really into him, though she admitted that if she'd been more attracted to him, it might have been another story. But for him it was escalating. He wanted to leave his wife for her! There were kids too, a bunch of them. Still no feedback on the chapters.

Meanwhile he was Skyping her in his underwear from hotel rooms and complaining about his marriage, and she was letting it go on because she felt that her fate was in his hands. Nothing really happened between them—well, maybe a bit of fumbling, but she kept him at a distance. The thing was that she didn't want to rebuff him too bluntly because she was worried about the fate of her book—worried he'd reject the manuscript, she'd have to pay back the advance, and she'd never get it published anywhere else.

I'd actually once met this guy—he'd edited a friend's book (badly). He was sort of a nebbish, hard to see as threatening. "Did you talk to your agent?" I asked the woman. I was playing the situation out in my mind, wondering what I'd do. No, she hadn't talked to her agent, for various reasons, including fears that she'd led the would-be paramour on and that her book wasn't any good.

Suddenly the editor left for a job at another press, and the publisher called the contract, demanding a final manuscript, which was overdue and nowhere near finished. In despair, the author finally confessed the situation to our mutual friend, another writer, who employed the backbone-stiffening phrase "sexual harassment" and insisted that the woman get her agent involved. Which she did, and the agent negotiated an exit deal with the publisher by explaining what had taken place. The author was let out of the contract and got to take the book to another press.

What struck me most, hearing the story, was how incapacitated this woman had felt, despite her advanced degree and accomplishments. The reason, I think, was that she imagined she was the only vulnerable one in the situation. But look at the editor: he was married, with a midlevel job in the scandal-averse world of corporate publishing. It simply wasn't the case that he had all the power in the situation or nothing to lose. He may have been an occluded jerk, but he was also a fairly human-sized one.

So that's an example of a real-world situation, postgraduation. Somehow I don't see the publishing industry instituting codes banning unhappily married editors from going goopy over authors, though even with such a ban, will any set of regulations ever prevent affective misunderstandings and erotic crossed signals, compounded by power differentials, compounded further by subjective levels of vulnerability?

The question, then, is what kind of education prepares people to deal with the inevitably messy gray areas of life? Personally I'd start by promoting a less vulnerable sense of self than the one our new campus codes are peddling. Maybe I see it this way because I wasn't educated to think that holders of institutional power were quite so fearsome, nor did the institutions themselves seem so mighty. Of course, they didn't aspire to reach quite as deeply into our lives back then. What no one's much saying about the efflorescence of these new policies is the degree to which they expand the power of the institutions themselves. As for those of us employed by them, what power we have is fairly contingent, especially lately. Get real: what's more powerful—a professor who crosses the line, or the shaming capabilities of social media?

For myself, I don't much want to date students these days, but it's not like I don't understand the appeal. Recently I was at a book party, and a much younger man, an assistant professor, started a conversation. He reminded me that we'd met a decade or so ago, when he was a grad student—we'd been at some sort of event and sat next to each other. He said he thought we'd been flirting. In fact, he was sure we'd been flirting. I searched my memory. He wasn't in it, though I didn't doubt his recollection; I've been known to flirt. He couldn't believe I didn't remember him. I apologized. He pretended to be miffed. I pretended to be regretful. I asked him about his work. He told me about it, in a charming way. Wait a second, I thought, was he flirting with me now? As an aging biological female, and all too aware of what that means in our culture, I was skeptical. On the heels of doubt came a surge of joy: "Still got it," crowed some perverse inner imp in silent congratulation, jackbooting the reality principle into assent. My psyche broke out the champagne, and all of us were in a far better mood for the rest of the evening.

Intergenerational desire has always been a dilemma as well as an occasion for mutual fascination. Whether or not it's a brilliant move, plenty of professors I know, male and female, have hooked up with students, though informal evidence suggests that female professors do it less, and rarely with undergraduates. (The gender asymmetries here would require a dozen more articles to explicate.) Some of these professors act well, some are jerks, and it would benefit students to learn the identifying marks of the latter breed early on, because postcollegiate life is full of them. I propose a round of mandatory workshops on this useful topic for all students, beginning immediately.

But here's another way to look at it: the *longue durée*. Societies keep reformulating the kinds of cautionary stories they tell about intergenerational erotics and the catastrophes that result, starting with Oedipus. The details vary; so do the kinds of catastrophes prophesied—once it was plagues and crop failure, these days it's psychological trauma. Even over the past half century, the story keeps getting reconfigured. In the preceding era, the Freudian version reigned: Children universally desire their parents, such desires meet up with social prohibitions—the incest taboo—and become repressed. Neurosis ensues.

These days the desire persists, but what's shifted is the direction of the arrows. Now it's parents—or their surrogates, teachers —who do all the desiring; children are conveniently returned to innocence. So long to childhood sexuality, the most irksome part of the Freudian story. So too with the new campus dating codes, which also excise student desire from the story, extending the presumption of the innocent child well into his or her collegiate career. Except that students aren't children.

Among the problems with treating students like children is that they become increasingly childlike in response. *The New York Times Magazine* recently reported on the tangled story of a twenty-one-year-old former Stanford undergraduate suing a twenty-nine-year-old tech entrepreneur she'd dated for a year. He'd been a mentor in a business class she was enrolled in, though they'd met long before. They traveled together and spent time with each other's families. Marriage was discussed. After they broke up, she charged that their consensual relationship had actually been psychological kidnapping, and that she'd been raped every time they'd had sex. She seems to regard herself as a helpless child in a woman's body. She demanded that Stanford investigate and is bringing a civil suit against the guy—this despite the fact that her own mother had introduced the couple, approved the relationship every step of the way, and been in more or less constant contact with the suitor.

No doubt some twenty-one-year-olds are fragile and emotionally immature (helicopter parenting probably plays a role), but is this now to be our normative conception of personhood? A twenty-one-year-old incapable of consent? A certain brand of radical feminist—the late Andrea Dworkin, for one—held that women's consent was meaningless in the context of patriarchy, but Dworkin was generally considered an extremist. She'd have been gratified to hear that her convictions had finally gone mainstream, not merely driving campus policy but also shaping the basic social narratives of love and romance in our time.

It used to be said of many enclaves in academe that they were old-boys clubs and testosterone-fueled, no doubt still true of certain disciplines. Thanks to institutional feminism's successes, some tides have turned, meaning that menopausal women now occupy more positions of administrative power, edging out at least some of the old boys and bringing a different hormonal style—a more delibidinalized one, perhaps—to bear on policy decisions. And so the pendulum swings, overshooting the middle ground by a hundred miles or so.

The feminism I identified with as a student stressed independence and resilience. In the intervening years, the climate of sanctimony about student vulnerability has grown too thick to penetrate; no one dares question it lest you're labeled antifeminist. Or worse, a sex criminal. I asked someone on our Faculty Senate if there'd been any pushback when the administration presented the new consensual-relations policy (though by then it was a fait accompli—the senate's role was "advisory").

"I don't quite know how to characterize the willingness of my supposed feminist colleagues to hand over the rights of faculty —women as well as men—to administrators and attorneys in the name of protection from unwanted sexual advances," he said. "I suppose the word would be *zeal*." His own view was that the existing sexual-harassment policy already protected students from coercion and a hostile environment; the new rules infantilized students and presumed the guilt of professors. When I asked if I could quote him, he begged for anonymity, fearing vilification from his colleagues.

These are things you're not supposed to say on campuses now. But let's be frank. To begin with, if colleges and universities around the country were in any way serious about policies to prevent sexual assaults, the path is obvious: don't ban teacher-student romance, ban fraternities. And if we want to limit the potential for sexual favoritism—another rationale often proffered for the new policies—then let's include the institutionalized sexual favoritism of spousal hiring, with trailing spouses getting ranks and perks based on whom they're sleeping with rather than CVs alone, and brought in at salaries often dwarfing those of senior and more accomplished colleagues who didn't have the foresight to couple more advantageously.

Lastly: the new codes sweeping American campuses aren't just a striking abridgment of everyone's freedom, they're also intellectually embarrassing. Sexual paranoia reigns; students are trauma cases waiting to happen. If you wanted to produce a pacified, cowering citizenry, this would be the method. And in that sense, we're all the victims.

JORDAN KISNER

Thin Places

FROM *n+1*

THE ELECTRODE IS the width of angel-hair pasta. A surgeon
has threaded it through one of the four dime-sized holes in the
patient's skull, and it is advancing into her one millimeter at a
time, controlled by a small knob that another surgeon is turning
and turning with great concentration.

This morning a nurse shaved off the patient's hair, and the surgeon drilled these holes around the crown of her head, two in
her temples and two in the back. Then he fastened a metal brace
the size of a dog cage around her head to hold the wires steady as
they enter her brain. Surrounding the patient, the brace, and the
doctor is a giant O-shaped machine the color of tangerine sherbet,
which is taking live images inside her head. The patient is awake.

First the electrode passes through the part of the brain closest
to the bone, the part of her that knows the names of things and
left from right. Then it bores down through the part of her that
knows how to draw, the part that recognizes her mother's face and
remembers what she said to the nurse when he asked about the
birthmark on her temple. Down through the part of her that likes
sex and the part that knows how to talk. Down almost to the deepest part of the brain, the stem, which is responsible for her breath
and her heart. This movement, from outside the patient's body
through the opening in her skull and into the core of her brain, is
called transversal.

The transversal has been plotted carefully. The path of the needle is precise to the millimeter, avoiding important veins and arter-
ies as well as nerve clusters better left untouched. The destination
is Area 24, also known as the ventral anterior cingulate. Hers is suf-

fering from either underdevelopment or hyperactivity, depending on which doctor is explaining it. The electrode will stay inside her to deliver electric currents to Area 24 for the next several years, or possibly forever.

The patient finds herself strapped to a gurney with wide belts, naked under her paper gown, because this morning, like every morning, she thought, 117 times, "I am going to kill a stranger." A pacifist by nature and in her politics, she finds this thought sickening and goes to great lengths to ensure that it doesn't come true. An elaborate protocol has arisen: every time the thought "I am going to kill a stranger" pops into her mind she jerks her head hard and declares silently, "I am a peaceful person, I am a peaceful person, I am a peaceful person." This quells the panic that rises—*Is* she peaceful? What if she killed someone by accident? What if she flew into a sudden rage? What if she is, at heart, monstrous?—and works like penance: three peaceful thoughts for every murderous one keeps the balance tipped in the right direction. This becomes more difficult when the thoughts come quickly. The number of times she thinks "I am going to kill a stranger" has to be prime or the thought's power increases, so she'll restart the cycle as many times as necessary to bring the count to a prime number. A twenty-minute reprieve is as much as she hopes for in a day.

She has thrown out all her knives, scissors, heavy blunt objects, needles, and sharp pens. She stopped driving a long time ago. She never stands near train tracks or close to people on the sidewalk, just in case something were to come over her and she were to push someone into traffic. Despite being shy, she feels compelled to introduce herself to almost everyone she sees. Once she meets them, they are no longer strangers and therefore no longer in danger of her. This became exhausting—and alarming to the strangers—so a few years ago she stopped leaving her house altogether. Now she lives in terror of what she might do to deliverymen.

Over the years doctors have prescribed nine medications in various combinations, as well as talk therapy, exposure therapy, cognitive behavioral therapy, and electroconvulsive shock therapy, all with meager results. Her case is, to use their terminology, "intractable." She had to sign all manner of paperwork formally acknowledging this, attesting, for example, that she knows what the word *intractable* means, before she could find herself in this room with Frankensteinian screws in her temples, counting the ceiling tiles. She consented to everything without hesitation.

The first electrode's transversal produces soft, whooshy noises from the monitor in the corner. These noises are her brain waves, tracked by the exploratory electrode, which will forge the correct path before the doctor inserts the permanent electrode. His target is two and a half or three millimeters wide. Once he's reached it, he will remove the exploratory electrode and thread in the one that will be wired to a battery pack sewn in under her collarbone. It will pulse electricity into Area 24 at a constant rhythm for several years, until the battery dies and needs to be changed. She has to be awake during the insertion so that she can tell them what it feels like.

The patient is not altogether articulate about what it feels like. She has been strapped down to prevent her from bolting or fighting or trying to tear the metal cage off her head. This is both terrifying and comforting, as the thoughts are coming in inexorable waves now and she is grateful for anything that will help her keep them from coming true. This is a familiar scene: the afflicted tied down while being ministered to by some credentialed man in a robe carrying an instrument. It used to be books and crucifixes. There used to be prayer and incantation. Now there are only the muted sounds of her brainwaves, the rhythmic beeps and clicks of the vitals monitor, and the voice of the doctor as he murmurs to her through her thought torrent. He sounds calm.

The goal is to alter her experience of reality "with minimal side effects." No one has been able to tell her whether or why this will work. Only a few dozen people have ever had this treatment for a psychological condition, and so every new patient is an experiment. Initially, doctors hypothesized that the electricity would curb overactive neurons; now they suspect it may actually stimulate neurons, or change the types of information neural pathways can transmit, but they're not sure, just as they're unsure precisely where in her brain to place the electrodes for best results. They are learning as they go; once this is all over, her experience will be another data point.

What the doctors do know is what the anterior cingulate cortex does, generally speaking. It houses consciousness, in the existential sense, and emotional pain. It regulates motivation, impulse control, and the anticipation of both delight and catastrophe. Francis Crick proposed it as the center of free will. It's also responsible, in part, for the human capacity for empathy.

There are, naturally, a number of things that could go wrong. Possible but unlikely: hemorrhage, brain damage, stroke, seizure, infection, death. Possible but slightly more likely: memory "problems," trouble speaking, depression, and mania. These latter risks have an aftertaste of irony. The electrode might turn her from a person who speaks compulsively to strangers to a person who cannot speak well at all; it may transform her mind from one reduced to four obsessive thoughts to one hyperexpansive with mania. She wonders what it would be like to go from having one mind to another and then remembers she has already done that.

The doctor in the paper bonnet interrupts this line of thinking to announce that they're ready to begin testing voltages. The electrode has arrived at what they think will be the right place, and now it is time to see what happens to her mind when they turn it on.

She closes her eyes and waits.

This procedure is called deep brain stimulation (DBS). The patient described above is a composite of people I've met, people I've read about, and people whose surgeries I've seen in videos. She is fashioned after the few dozen patients who have undergone DBS to treat severe obsessive-compulsive disorder, an experimental application now in clinical trials at Mount Sinai Hospital in New York, Brown University, the University of Rochester, and a handful of other medical centers. Her symptoms aren't so much fictional as typical: thousands of people are crippled by fears of hurting others. It is shocking how many have thrown out their knives.

Deep brain stimulation has been used for years to diminish tremors in people with Parkinson's disease, but it's experimental and controversial as a treatment for psychiatric disorders.* Only a few OCD patients have undergone it (roughly two dozen so far in the current, FDA-approved study, and no more than a hundred

---

* Nevertheless, it's being researched with enthusiasm as a possible alternative to the neurosurgical protocol that preceded it, ablation, in which targeted parts of the brain circuitry are burned by lasers until permanently "neutralized." Deep brain stimulation, for all its echoes of dystopian sci-fi, has the benefit of being adjustable and, for the most part, reversible.

in the U.S. total), and like many historical attempts to alter the mind, it seems halfway magical because no one really understands its mechanisms. Obsessive-compulsive disorder is not like Parkinson's disease—the symptoms aren't visible and physical (trembling hands) so much as experiential and behavioral—so neurosurgery-as-treatment becomes more existential in its implications. Compounding this is the fact that, neurochemically, obsessive-compulsive disorder bears a conspicuous resemblance to falling in love. Scientists have scanned the brains of the pathologically obsessive and held them up next to brain scans of the love-struck, and the images turned colors in the same places. Doctors drew blood and found the same chemical imbalances—namely, a serotonin deficit. The philosophical distinction between deactivating a part of someone's brain and deactivating some part of their mind or self begins to blur.

I've done months of research about deep brain stimulation—reviewing articles, deciphering studies, interviewing physicians, scrolling through procedure videos on YouTube—for no special reason other than what you might call—ahem—a persistent curiosity. While reading the literature, it's easy to think in clinical abstractions, but then I watched a video of an older woman undergoing the procedure and was struck by the way her voice was muffled by the nest of equipment. The doctors kept having to ask her to speak up during the adjustment phase, when she was supposed to be reporting changes in her psychological state. "I said I almost just laughed," she repeated, gazing at the equipment before her with an expression of wonder. "I haven't laughed in . . . a very long time." The doctor nodded dispassionately. "Can you describe that for us?"

It seems important to cling to the concrete, to remember that illness is not a metaphor or a study but a phenomenon unfolding in (and on) real bodies in real rooms. Its qualia, the crinkly paper hospital gown and metallic adrenaline taste, the mutable and inexpressible shades of pain, demand articulation because they matter. We work so hard at telling others *what it is like* to be sick in whichever particular way we are sick; we are reassured to hear that our particulars fit within larger known narratives of illness. With sickness as with anything else, communicating what it is like so others can know, or understanding others in precisely the way they wish we could, is next to impossible. We try anyway.

Admittedly, most OCD patients are not like my imagined girl. Usually, the disease is damaging but not devastating in a relationship-ruining, inpatient-care, life-disintegrating way. It is considered a less challenging diagnosis than, for example, bipolar disorder, schizophrenia, or any of the personality disorders.* It is "neurosis," not "psychosis," "mental illness" as opposed to "insanity." The existence of the DBS study, though, and the interest it draws from patients and practitioners alike, subtly undermines this differentiation. Extreme treatment reflects the disease's extreme power to cripple. Neurologically, OCD seems to act on similar parts of the brain as schizophrenia; experientially, both diseases are marked by foreign-seeming intrusions on the mind. Both patients are overcome with thoughts, images, and impulses that are, to use the clinical word, ego-dystonic: they feel alien to and in conflict with the self. They feel other. In obsessive-compulsive patients, these thoughts tend to be violent or violating, obscene, immoral, or some other shade of horrifying.

What distinguishes obsessive-compulsive patients from schizophrenic patients is their ability to live inside a paradox: the thoughts hijacking their minds feel urgently not "theirs," but the thoughts are nevertheless something going on in their own minds and bodies. These thoughts are alien, but they have not been planted by aliens. In the medical community, this is known as "insight."

Having insight is not enough to make the thoughts go away. A little while ago, I was talking to a writer who has to touch things —all the slats on the staircase, all the poles as he walks down the street. He knows this doesn't make sense. Sometimes, though not terribly often, he has to go back home to make sure that he didn't leave a cigarette burning, even when he can remember perfectly well that he didn't. He only has to do this when alone. When he's with people, he doesn't have to touch anything.

He told me that since childhood he's been fascinated with the idea that everyone is God. I asked him what he meant, and he said

---

* It's worth noting, though, that OCD has something like a 91 percent lifetime comorbidity with other Axis-1 diseases, most commonly depression, generalized anxiety disorder, panic disorder, addiction, and anorexia/bulimia. In a study published in 2008, three-quarters of OCD patients from a clinical sample met the criteria for lifetime mood disorders, nearly 40 percent were unable to work because of psychopathologies, and 14 percent were on disability specifically for OCD. In light of these numbers, a diagnosis of OCD is plenty grim.

that he had a suspicion that God was everywhere and everyone, and all our souls are the same soul, God's soul, but we're just walking around in different meat suits. That's how he said it: "We're all stuck in our own meat suits."

I suddenly felt very aware of how different he and I look—his height and beard and age, his ruddiness, his tie; my stringy arms, bitten nails, and freckles. He is older than I am, and bigger, and embodied in a sort of ragged, robust way that I am not. At first I couldn't quite tell whether he was fucking with me when he leaned in and looked into my brown eyes with his blue ones and said, "What I'm saying is that maybe we're all the same, we just don't know it because we're separated into our own bodies," but then I decided that he was not fucking with me and was serious, at least partly, about this hypothetical.

And part of me was thinking, *Get a grip.*

Another part was thinking, *Well, exactly.*

Which did not signal that I was on board with the meat-suit theory per se, only that I was not surprised, even a little, to discover another person with OCD who'd been worrying his whole life about the distinctions and correspondences between himself and other people, and between himself and God. You don't have to have OCD or any mental illness to have concerns like this, but the urgency of locating the boundaries of the self, the distinction between what is inside and outside, you and not-you, becomes particularly acute when your mind seems a little too permeable.

Obsession was initially a term of warfare. In Latin, *obsessio* indicated the first phase of a siege on a city, when the city was surrounded on all sides but its citadel remained intact. *Obsessio* was followed by *possessio*, when the attacker breached the walls and took the city from the inside. In *Obsession: A History*, Lennard Davis explains the way these two words were adapted to explain demonic possession in the third century: "In the case of *obsession*, that person was aware of being besieged by the devil since the demon did not have complete control, had not entered the city of the soul, and the victim could therefore attempt to resist." Demonology was, for many centuries thereafter, the only language available for explaining obsession and other insanities. Obsession was understood as a torment of the soul and, often, a spiritual punishment. The cure was exorcism.

This went on for more than a thousand years, until some Protestant churches began to retreat from the idea of possession (piqued at the way the Catholic Church had, per Davis, "the inside track on exorcisms"). In 1731, the English Parliament repealed laws banning witchcraft, which had been the most common grounds for exorcism. Modern medicine was in its nascent stages, and as it developed it annexed mental affliction, recategorizing madness as a physical rather than a spiritual problem. The demonological model was replaced by the medical model. Scientists discovered the nervous system and, with it, "nerves," and the possibility of a physiological source of mental states.* Davis notes, "The nerves are the physical link to the mental—they are dissectible, discernible, and physical, yet their effects are metaphysical, symbolic, and affective."

In the same era, roughly the late seventeenth to early eighteenth century, the notion of "partial madness" emerged to accommodate people who were mentally ill but tethered enough to reality to recognize their illness or sane enough to function within society. One could be "a conscious 'I' who is watching an obsessed self instead of a deranged and unconscious self dwelling in a lunatic." Sanity went from a binary category (sane/insane) to a triad: you could be lucid, a lunatic, or a neurotic. The "monomaniacs," as obsessives came to be known, were the stars of this new formulation. The monomaniac tended to be high functioning and highly thought of. Davis writes, "A certain cachet developed, a notion of being fashionable, in having one of these partial, intermittent conditions." Neurosis was constructed as intrinsic to character, but as a possible asset. It was a sign of advancement, complexity, genius, cosmopolitanism, and, so to speak, *heightened sensibilities*.†

---

* In the seventeenth and early eighteenth centuries, nerves were thought of primarily as connective tissues in musculature. It wasn't until later in the eighteenth century that the nervous system was understood to have any relationship with emotion. With this switch came the association of the word *nerves* with anxiety, nervousness, hysteria, and other "morbid affections," an evolution to which we owe dubious thanks for the nervous Nellie, Jane Austen's exquisitely irritating Mrs. Bennett (who won't stop mewling, "My poor nerves!"), fashionable neuroses, and Woody Allen.

† The particular metaphors that arose around neurosis, or "nervous diseases," are suspiciously similar to the metaphors that, in *Illness as Metaphor*, Susan Sontag argued were associated with tuberculosis in the nineteenth century: nobility of soul, creativity, Romantic melancholy, et cetera. Sontag was unimpressed with this

Such was the case with Sigmund Freud's most famous obsessive. The Rat Man, as Freud nicknamed him to protect his identity, was clever and charming, a successful professional man who was nevertheless ruled by disturbing fantasies of rodents attacking his father and fiancée. Freud, writing in 1909, took a therapeutic approach to the Rat Man that became typical for a time: the man's problems were purely issues of the psyche. His obsessions stemmed from the fact that he'd been punished for masturbating as a child, and had formed as a defense mechanism against the anger, aggression, and anxiety he felt in his adult relationships. The cure: analysis.

A hundred years later, we don't think of the mind as something that can be entered, invaded, or deciphered so much as something that can be altered and adjusted. The mind is less the point, actually—Freud's methods have become passé. Now we talk about the brain, which is not parametric in that our metaphors for it do not indicate that the brain has parameters that can be violated. Insanity is now more biological than spiritual. "Mental illness" is no longer a breach of the self but a neurochemical event happening to—but separate from—the self. Like hypertension, it happens in our cells, and we swallow pills to get rid of it.*

This is more or less how grown-ups talked about what was wrong with me for several years after I was diagnosed with OCD at thirteen. I was, clinically, a nervous wreck, and many of my fears were about the transformation of my own mind. Was I insane? Was I doomed? Was this who I really was? Therapists and my parents were ready with reassurances that what was happening was only an accident of serotonin, a mysterious but correctable "imbalance" no more essential to who I was than a flu or a sunburn. I balked at taking medication, worried it would change who I was. "You

---

equation: "My point is that illness is *not* a metaphor," she wrote, "and that the most truthful way of regarding illness—and the healthiest way of being ill—is one most purified of, most resistant to, metaphoric thinking. Yet it is hardly possible to take up one's residence in the kingdom of the ill unprejudiced by the lurid metaphors with which it has been landscaped." Later in the book, she lambasted the modern impulse to psychologize disease, declaring psychology a "sublimated spiritualism" with such sneering conviction that Denis Donoghue, reviewing the book for the *New York Times*, was emboldened to declare her mind "powerful rather than subtle," a critique it might have been entertaining to witness Sontag read in the paper.

* Incidentally, since the dawn of psychotropic medications, the incidence of OCD in the general population has jumped from 0.005 percent to 3 percent.

have an illness, and this is just medicine to correct that illness," I was told. "It's like having diabetes. You wouldn't refuse insulin because your body's 'authentic' state is to have diabetes." In the end, I couldn't take the panic attacks, so I took the Prozac and, with it, this narrative of what was happening. It worked. The pills made my hands shake, but my mind was transformed back, more or less, to the healthy, stable state I remembered.

When I was seventeen, not long after weaning myself off Prozac, I relapsed. It happened sort of slowly. The thoughts came back, but at first I could fend them off. I blew past them with the buoyancy of a teenager whose life was going well. I was a few months away from leaving for what seemed like the most exciting college in the world, and I had my first boyfriend. Gradually, though, I stopped being able to ignore the thoughts. They came too quickly, and one day they seemed to bring real danger with them. Something darkly magical began to happen: I would gaze out at sunny days, beach days, Southern California sunsets, and feel the sidewalks begin to warp. The sky was cloudless, but something was terribly wrong. This feeling would steal an hour one day, and then I'd be myself again. The next day, two hours. As weeks passed, the sinister entered, and sick fear took over.

At the time I worked as a barista for a local breakfast-and-lunch place on the beach, pulling espresso and pouring green-tea lattes in an eight-by-eight-foot alcove off the restaurant's kitchen. A wall obstructed my view of the line cooks, so I spent my shifts in isolation, handing cup after cup out a window the size of a cereal box to a man named Fernando who ate toast with whipped cream for breakfast. I'd be pouring cappuccinos and humming in my little wall-hole and then suddenly, as if from nowhere, a terrifying sentence would appear in my mind. Then another. Then a dozen. Panic attacks rolled in hourly. I began taping poems to the espresso machine to memorize, figuring that if I had to entertain thoughts that weren't mine I might at least try to make them beautiful. I knew what was happening, but knowledge didn't help. Diagnostic categories, the language of treatment—they weren't enough. My teenage hair started to gray; my hands shook at the machine. I was growing desperate. One afternoon, I stepped into the back alley behind the restaurant, dialed my therapist, and told her that I thought I might not survive it.

I was understudying Juliet that summer for a local production

of *Romeo and Juliet,* which meant sitting in on rehearsals and learning the lines and blocking. This should have been fun and exciting—and it was some days, particularly when the handsome blue-
eyed actor playing Romeo made a point of flirting with me. (The
regular Juliet was sleeping with Mercutio.) But most days it felt
like something was very, very wrong. People often describe the way
your body senses instinctually that you're in the presence of a so-
ciopath or in physical danger. The feeling can be confusing at first,
because your body is telling you something that your rational mind
doesn't yet know. *Why do I feel so unsettled and skin-crawly when she's
so nice? This party is so fun; why do I feel like I have to get out of here?*
I spent benign afternoons in rehearsal forcing myself not to bolt
from the room. The theater, the restaurant, my bedroom—every
place seemed menacing and uncanny. I spent hours in complex,
circuitous rationalizations and self-assurances that boiled down to,
in endless repetition: "But nothing's wrong, but nothing's wrong,
but nothing's wrong."

Of course, something was wrong. The imminent danger was my
misfiring sense of imminent danger, the revelation that the stabil-
ity and habitability of the world can change as the mind changes.
Minds are not reliably stable or habitable. They are subject to radical and sometimes horrible transformation. This is a danger of the
world that is, as I was discovering, intangible but absolutely real.

Juliet has a monologue in the fourth act, spoken alone in her
bedroom as she prepares to take a potion that will plunge her
into a sleep so profound she'll appear dead. She and Romeo have
agreed that she'll drink this potion, and once she's been mourned
and entombed in the family mausoleum he'll come to wake her,
and they'll sneak out of Verona under cover of night and begin
their life together. She's resolved, even impatient, to go through
with the plan and reunite with Romeo, but as she uncorks the vial,
a thought occurs to her. "What if it be a poison, which the friar
subtly hath minister'd to have me dead?" Fairly quickly she dis-
penses with this anxiety (the friar is a holy man and a trustworthy
friend), but another pops up to fill its place: What if she wakes
up before Romeo arrives? What if she suffocates in the tomb?
Her nervousness takes on a tinge of panic. What if, worse yet, she
wakes too early but does *not* suffocate, and is left alone in the vault
"where, for these many hundred years, the bones of all my buried ancestors are packed: where bloody Tybalt lies festering in his

shroud?" Then she strikes on the most frightening thought: what if she, surrounded by bodies and smells and "shrieks like mandrakes torn out of the earth, that living mortals, hearing them, run mad," is so overwhelmed that she loses her mind? Will I "madly play with my forefathers' joints," she wonders,

> And pluck the mangled Tybalt from his shroud?
> And, in this rage, with some great kinsman's bone,
> As with a club, dash out my desperate brains?
> O, look! Methinks I see my cousin's ghost
> Seeking out Romeo—

Quickly, she is hallucinating with panic. The loss of her own mind, imagined in the grotesque vision of herself fondling dead bodies in the dark, is made real by her own terror. The figure of Tybalt rises before her to kill Romeo. Desperate to make Tybalt—and the vision—stop, she seizes the potion bottle and, in a gesture that's not a little suicidal, swallows it all. She collapses. End scene.

I dreaded this monologue, but I memorized it, made notes on it, even diagrammed it. I was convinced that the young woman playing Juliet, beautiful as she was in the balcony scene, failed to capture this movement from nervousness to wild, unhinged fear. But I also hoped I'd never have to perform the scene myself. It felt too close. Acting demands letting go of the self in a way that is usually considered self-destructive or pathological in real life; acting demands that you make way for other selves.

But then there's the trick of coming back, of reconstructing the boundaries between your mind and your character's mind. Sometimes this is hard to do. There are characters you don't want to play because you know they'll be frightening to expand into or difficult to come back from.

That summer when I was feeling very much like Juliet holding the potion, the therapist would tell me, "Just know that those thoughts aren't you. That's the OCD, it's not you." It was a kind gesture—she was offering me the illness narrative that reigns now, the one that constructs very, very firm boundaries between brain and self, illness and consciousness, self and other. I clung to that for a while, the notion that the maelstrom happening in my brain was not *of* me but *outside* me, happening to me. That there was a tidy line dividing "me" from "disease," and the disease was classifiable as "other." But then it became difficult to tell whether certain thoughts should go in the me box or the disease box—where did "I want to throw a rock through the kitchen window" belong? Eventually I could no longer avoid the fact that mental illness is not like infection; there's no outside invader. And if a disease is produced in your body, in your mind, then what is it if not you?

Recently I found an image of Juliet and the potion, a film still taken from Franco Zeffirelli's 1968 rendition that is famous even though it didn't make the movie's final cut. Juliet is shown in profile, dressed in a beautiful white nightgown with long sleeves draping to her waist. Her dark hair, a little tangled, hangs loose down her back like mine did when I was seventeen. She is kneeling at what appears to be an altar but is in fact the carved headboard of her bed; what seems to be the prayer cushion is her pillow, where Romeo's head lay not long ago. We know she's no longer a virgin, but she looks virginal, like one of the saints offering herself up. Her eyes are closed in fear or love or ecstasy, head tilted back in the light that glows down on her wrists and cheekbones. Her hands are clasped at her mouth in what looks like prayer, but if you look closely you can see the vial at her lips. She's imbibing something, but what?

In a sense, what keeps an OCD patient rooted in the world of the neurotic rather than the psychotic, what tethers her to a certain agreed-on reality, the adherence to which seems to be our measure of functional sanity, is her healthy sense of the boundaries of her own ego—her ability to toggle complex and contradictory conceptions of self and other, real and not real, rational and irrational. She is obsessed, not possessed. She has insight. Most patients, though, have moments when their grip on me/not-me slips. In the medical community, this is known as magical thinking.

Obsessions often feel like the work of some cruel and sentient force equipped with its own devious logic, showering you with the exact thoughts and images you find most disturbing and devising new monstrosities as you defuse the old ones. Obsession knows you better than you know yourself. It outwits you. For this reason and others, insight is slippery even for diagnosticians. How is it defined, and how much of it is a patient supposed to have? Are lapses in insight allowed? What sort? How many? In his 1996 book, *Theoretical Approaches to Obsessive-Compulsive Disorder*, the clinical psychologist Ian Jakes writes:

The absence of reported insight cannot distinguish all obsessions from delusions ... Further difficulties ... may be raised by those patients who are classified by some diagnosticians as "partially deluded." These patients are held to have beliefs that would otherwise satisfy the criteria for delusions but do not hold these beliefs with absolute conviction ... How, then, are obsessions to be distinguished from partial delusions, and how are those cases of OCD where reported insight is absent to be distinguished from delusions?

Nearly twenty years later, these categories and definitions are still fluid: in 2013, the *DSM-5* altered OCD's diagnostic criteria to allow for patients who have only "partial insight" or, within certain parameters, lack insight altogether.

Later in this section, Jakes describes a young woman whose case was typical but challenging theoretically. He gives her only five sentences, but the portrait is complex and, in a way, complete. D.S. was twenty-nine and afraid that she might lose possession of her own thoughts, that they might travel from her head down her arms and escape through her fingertips into the world. She worried that she would leave a trail of ideas and images in her wake, clinging like residue to everything she touched. D.S. knew, for the most part, that this wasn't possible, but sometimes she wasn't sure. Her frontiers, the places where she stopped and everything and everyone else began, seemed changeful and pervious. Jakes calls this phenomenon "ego boundary confusion."

I love this young woman with anxious fingers. I wonder about her—what she looks like, where she is, whether she ever got better. If she is still living, she is forty-seven now. Her fears have such poetic overtones; they riff on common fears of contagion, which are often amplified and uncontrollable in patients with OCD. "Our bodies are not our boundaries," writes Eula Biss in *On Immunity*. "Fear of contamination rests on the belief, widespread in our culture as in others, that something can impart its essence to us on contact. We are forever polluted, as we see it, by contact with a pollutant." This notion extends past the physical realm of germ contamination and into metaphor. We worry about the "bad seed" and fear that someone's awful luck, lousy attitude, or even insanity will "rub off" on us.* At the same time, the things most precious to

* Two roommates, one family member, and a handful of acquaintances have reported to me, independently of one another, that they "caught" OCD after

us often risk—or demand—this kind of contagion. The "sacred" places of the body are the ones where membranes are exposed: our mouths, our eyes, our genitals, the places where we connect with others and make ourselves vulnerable to them.

Accordingly, it is just as common to look for membranes where there are none. We trace our fingers over the faces or bodies of people we love as if we wish we could leave unspoken thoughts and feelings behind like residue. We place our foreheads together and press gently, as if to see whether we can merge that way. We struggle toward each other out of our little meat suits.

Sometimes it works. There is a kind of love where you start to lose track of where you start and stop. It isn't typically sustainable over long periods—it can come and go—but this version of total connection, or total mutual contamination, feels in the moment like the central operating miracle of the universe. Near the end of Toni Morrison's *Beloved*, the prose breaks down in an ecstatic rush:

> I am Beloved and she is mine . . . how can I say things that are pictures I am not separate from her there is no place where I stop her face is my own and I want to be there in the place where her face is and to be looking at it too a hot thing

This is an exact description of that love. In the book, though, it is also a description of a furious, sublimated obsession, a daughter haunting the mother who killed her. It's a story about love but, just as importantly, about horror; a thwarted love so ferocious it manifests and turns its object from memory to flesh. *Beloved* is in one sense a fable about the chiaroscuro of staying half-merged to someone else, the redemptive power and the unholy danger of "not separate from."

This is one danger that the current, hyperclinical story of illness seems designed to protect us from. If we are permeable the risks

---

watching the television show *Monk*, by which they usually meant that they'd started buying hand sanitizer and color-coding their folders. These are instances of the way we subtly assume mental states can be "catching," but also examples of the way OCD has become equated with desirable perfectionism, much as it was equated with sophistication in the nineteenth century. In certain circles, it is now a form of poorly disguised self-congratulation to profess, in confessional tones, that you are "totally OCD" about your work, your house, your record collection, eating organic. Like gluten intolerance, it's an ailment that has taken on chic associations, especially to people who don't really have it.

are infinite, and it's comforting to imagine firm borders guarding our soft places. Though as Biss points out, when it comes to the body, those borders are largely imagined. For the mind, whose boundaries are literally imagined, the notion of borderlessness, of endless susceptibility to mimetic contagion, is overwhelming. But by denying it entirely, by constructing unimpeachable binaries (me/you, mind/brain, illness/self), we create an experience of the world that's soothing but radically impoverished. If the truth lies somewhere in the middle, then the trick is the mapping. The other day, I found something in an old notebook that I don't remember writing. At the end of a long list of notes I had given up and scrawled, in big letters, *Where do I start and stop, is what I want to know.*

Sometimes I imagine my fictional girl well again. Out of the hospital, electrodes safely implanted, and responding with promise. Depending on which hospital treated her, she might be sent to an outpatient group therapy called "narrative enhancement."

Dr. Philip Yanos, who developed narrative enhancement therapy, explained to me that its function is to help mentally ill patients overcome internalized stigmas about their conditions. They learn about the ways they have been taught ideas like "I can't have a normal life" or "I'm a bad person" or "There's just something wrong with me." Then they tell the stories of their lives over and over and over to one another. They talk about their lives before they got sick, and they talk about what it was like to be sick, and they talk about now. The therapist and the other patients repeat back to the patient the story she's telling, but suggest more empowering language, and then the patient tells the story again but more like the way they said it.

The goal is to help patients integrate their notions of who they were before their sicknesses with who they are now. The task is to go back and find a thread of a story that can be pulled across the hospitalization or the psychotic break or the shock therapy, from then to now, from "her" to "me." It matters what stories you tell yourself about yourself. When the integrity of the story is violated, people get stuck at the point of fracture. They might re-form themselves around the brokenness, or they might restlessly circle forever, trying to understand what broke and why. The importance of the "coherent narrative self" is paramount: without it, even if the symptoms subside, you might never move on, which is another way of saying get well.

This is the story of how my obsessive-compulsive disorder began: When I was twelve, I had a friend who was going through some major psychological disturbance. She was a new friend, because I was new that year in school, and she revealed her problems to me incrementally, each confession like a gift signifying a deeper level of intimacy. First she showed me the box of safety pins and thumbtacks. She pulled them out of her backpack while we sat knee-to-knee on the bus and told me that she used them to cut herself. Next she told me she was bulimic and suicidally depressed. Eventually she told me that there was "a thing in her head" named Ailis, and that Ailis wanted her dead. Ailis, I gathered, was something between a voice and a demon. My friend talked about Ailis all the time, as if she were a mutual acquaintance. On days when I'd been a particularly sweet or loyal friend, she would smile at me meaningfully and say, "Ailis really doesn't like you."

We looked a little alike. (Her breasts were bigger.) We enjoyed the same things. (She turned me on to theater.) Teachers sometimes mixed up our names, and I was quietly pleased at being one of a pair. When she started telling me about thumbtacks and Ailis, I was fascinated and curious and, most of all, thrilled to be brought in. This was interesting, and presented an exciting challenge: I would love her to health. She would ask, "Why doesn't it scare you to hear about these things?" and I would tell her blithely, "Because these problems are yours, not mine. You are you, and I am me." This answer seemed to annoy her, and she would change the subject.

One night we were up late talking on the phone while I babysat for the neighbors. *Vertigo*, which I'd never seen, was on TV. In the film, Kim Novak's character appears to be possessed by a ghost that is driving her to suicide. "There's a woman in my head who wants me dead," she confesses to Jimmy Stewart after trying to hurl herself off a cliff. "She talks to me all the time." Stewart, a sucker for a blonde with a dark streak, falls in love anyway. Unfortunately, he isn't able to love her to health. He takes her to a place she keeps seeing in her nightmares, an old Spanish mission on the coast, hoping to convince her that she can overcome her fears and exorcise the ghost, but she breaks away from him, dashes up the bell tower, and jumps to her death. This moment at the film's halfway point marks a shift in focus from her possession to his obsession: her madness transfers to him. Unable to let her go, he is ruined by her.

It was during the bell-tower scene—Can this possibly be true? This is how I remember it—as Novak dashed up the steps, that my friend asked me again why I was never frightened by her confessions. I repeated my usual answer—you are you, and I am me—and she replied, "You never think you're going to be one of these people, like me, until you are one." Suddenly something came open inside me, and I knew she was right. I hung up the phone and had my first panic attack.

It's uncanny how closely Novak's confession ("There's a woman in my head who wants me dead. She talks to me all the time") matches my friend's description of Ailis as I remember it, and how closely Ailis and Novak's homicidal ghost resemble each other. The synchronicity unnerves me, particularly because I had 100 percent forgotten Novak's imagined woman until I watched the movie again recently. For fifteen years—years during which I carefully avoided *Vertigo*—I remembered only the bell-tower scene, her gray suit ascending the stairwell and then falling past the window.

Did I drastically conflate memories and invent all the details of Ailis in the years since that night? Had my friend seen *Vertigo*, and was it she who suggested I watch it, hoping that I'd see she was not the first person to be visited by an Ailis, perhaps even hoping that I might be visited next—and if so, *why*? I've been asking myself these questions for a while now. Neither scenario makes sense. I am sure I didn't invent Ailis, and yet the diabolical, premeditated manipulation required for the second scenario is so extreme I'd rather find it implausible. Any other possibility demands a coincidence on the level of an act of God. This is a fault in this story I can't overlook and can't heal. It just is.

I've been considering that uncanny confluence for months, but the thing I've been considering for fifteen years is the moment that came next. When my friend said, "You could be like me," and I was plunged irreversibly into a new kind of fear—what was that? In so many ways the moment marks a before and an after, but I don't really know how to talk about it. You could say it was ego boundary confusion. You could say it was mimetic contamination. You could say, maybe, that it was the beginning of real empathy.

What I will not say is that it was only a chemical reaction, because while that might be correct, it isn't true.

The summer I was seventeen and relapsing, I ran across a moment in the *Phaedrus* when Socrates theorizes that madness "is the channel by which we receive the greatest blessings . . . So, according to the evidence provided by our ancestors, madness is a nobler thing than sober sense . . . madness comes from God, whereas sober sense is merely human."

Fuck you, Socrates, I thought.

I have said in my darker moments that I would never wish this mess on anyone, even the girl I got it from. (As if that mattered.) I will probably say this again someday, my whining masquerading as largesse, and I will mean it, but it is also true that I know something I did not know before, which is that we are more expansive than we imagine. And this expansiveness is both powerful and frightening. It can ruin you to madness, or fate or God or disease or demons or whatever you call the unknowables. But it is gorgeous too. It's how the better unknowables get in. I think about being thirteen and hanging up the phone, standing frozen in the middle of the carpet in the neighbor's living room while Jimmy Stewart watched Kim Novak's body plummet to the terra-cotta and looking at him and looking at her with my friend's voice ringing in my mind and feeling like I was being cracked wide at the sternum and the top of the head at once, being opened and emptied and invaded, aware suddenly of the way poor, monomaniacal Jimmy could be me and strange, possessed Kim could be me, and my friend with that creature in her head could be me too.

The warping force of that first panic was truly horrifying. Madness is not some holy blessing; pathology is not the same as pathos. And yet that vertigo has echoes in other rooms and reckonings I've seen, other moments of being opened and emptied and invaded by another person but beautifully, of flinging or being flung wide by radical, magical ego boundary confusions and quiet acts of self-extension over breakfast.

The other morning I heard a woman on the radio describe her art, enormous conceptual installations that involve manipulations of breath and light. As she was explaining her process, this artist used a phrase I'd never heard before: "thin places." It's a Celtic concept, one that stems from an old proverb that says, "Heaven and earth are only three feet apart, but in the thin places that distance is even smaller." In thin places, the folklore goes, the barrier between the physical world and the spiritual world wears thin and becomes porous. Invisible things, like music or love or dead people or God, might become visible there, or if they don't become visible they become so present and tangible that it doesn't matter. Distinctions between you and not-you, real and unreal, worldly and otherworldly, fall away.

The original thin places were wild landscapes because the idea was born in the heaths of Connemara, a place that's so austere and ancient, so full of twists and hiding places and divots a thousand years old, that it seems somehow likely you might poke a hole through to another reality. But the radio lady said that the delight of thin places was the unpredictability of their location. You can find them someplace with magic written all over it, like Connemara or the Himalayas, but they also pop up in dive bars, bedrooms, hospital rooms. They can appear and disappear.

Because thin places involve an encounter with the ineffable they're hard to talk about. You know something has happened, some dissolution or expansion, but like most things that feel holy and a little dangerous, it just sounds weird in post-factum description. It helps to have someone with you there, someone else to feel what's happening so you can look at each other in awe. Afterward, when you are trying to explain it to other people and sounding like a New Age crank or genuinely insane, you can turn to that person and know that it was real. Or you can choose never to talk about it to anyone else and only sometimes turn to each other and say, What was that? *What was that?*

But then, the thin places I've known aren't always places, per se. Sometimes a thin place appears between people. Sometimes it happens only inside you.

"It could be said, even here, that what remains of the self / Unwinds into a vanishing light," wrote Mark Strand for his friend Joseph Brodsky after Brodsky's death. In this unwinding, the divide between Brodsky's body and spirit, and even between the two men, blurs and disappears. "None of the boundaries hold." Here, transversal takes on a quality of communion, the kind that arises when frontiers fall—a quality that seems inherent, even in the modern transversals of operating rooms where the new exorcism comes in rubber gloves and medical is miracle and knowing and nothing pass into each other and through. Before the word became the name of a medical technique, it was geometry's nod to the importance of the in-between: a transversal is the line that connects other lines. You use it to discern parallels; taking the transverse of two lines reveals whether they'll eventually touch.

After neurosurgical transversal for OCD, the improvements, if they come, will arrive with time. For patients with movement disorders the new world comes all at once, and the first sign is their hands. As the transversal proceeds, the doctors instruct them to hold out one hand and watch the tremors change. The arms start out waving crazily like hoses left unattended but then, within seconds, shudder to stillness. For the first time in years, the fingers can bend to hold a pill or a pen or just to touch lightly. Whatever possessed the muscles is gone, and while it's only electrical impulses, it really does look like a miracle. As a matter of course, the patients weep.

One woman whose name I no longer remember did something extraordinary as she cried. In the recovery room, she sat up immediately without saying a word and extended her new hand to her husband.* Improbably, it stayed obediently outstretched, quivering only a little. The room went still. The doctors and nurses stopped their work and watched as her husband quietly extended his palm toward hers. The air between them grew warm and vanished, and then everyone was weeping in the fluorescent light.

---

* The exact same gesture sets the events of *Romeo and Juliet* in motion: "palm to palm is holy palmer's kiss." A young man and woman press their hands together at a dance, and whatever happens just then transforms them. I think of the play as orchestrated around two thin places: the holy's palmer's kiss (two hands) and Juliet taking the potion (only her hand).

AMITAVA KUMAR

Pyre

FROM *Granta*

MY MOTHER DIED in Patna on January 7, 2014. We cremated
her two days later on the banks of the Ganga at Konhara Ghat near
Patna, more than 150 miles downriver from the burning ghats of
Benares, where Hindus have cremated their dead since at least
the middle of the first millennium BCE. I took notes. During the
long fourteen-hour flight to India I dealt with my sorrow by writing
in my notebook a brief obituary for a Hindi newspaper that Ma
read each morning. I was paying tribute. But once I had arrived
in Patna, my reasons for note-taking became more complicated.
Grief makes you a stranger to yourself, and I was struck by this person that I saw pierced with loss. I was taking notes so that I could
remember who I was in those days following my mother's death.

A Hindu cremation is usually held on the day of the death. In
Ma's case, there was an inevitable delay. She had wanted me to
be the one who lit her funeral pyre, but I live in New York; I had
boarded a direct flight to Delhi and then taken another plane to
Patna. It was evening on the next day by the time I reached there.
My family had tried to spare me from distress and hadn't told me
that Ma had already died; but, unknown to them, before I left
home I'd received a message on Facebook from a distant relative
offering condolences. A large crowd stood in the dark outside our
house and no one moved or spoke when I arrived. In the par-
lorlike space on the ground floor of our house, my father sat on
a sofa with other males whom I didn't immediately recognize. I
touched my father's feet and he said something about my luck in
getting a quick connecting flight from Delhi. I stepped further inside. My two sisters were sitting on a mattress next to a metal box,

their faces looking swollen; I embraced them, and when I did that the other women in the room, seated on chairs pushed against the wall, began to wail.

A white sheet and strings of marigolds covered the rectangular box, but at its foot the renting company had painted in large letters in Hindi: EST. 1967 PHONE 2219692. At first I thought the aluminum box was connected to an electrical outlet, but later I found out that the box had space along its sides that had been packed with ice. A square glass window on its cover allowed a view of Ma's face. Her head was resting on a thin yellow pillow with a red flower print. Bits of cotton had been stuffed into her nostrils.

An older cousin took me to another room and told me that the cremation would be held the next morning. I was asked if I wanted to get my head shaved at the ghat just before the ceremony or if I'd prefer to visit a barber's in the morning and be spared the sting of the winter cold. I chose the latter. There could be no cooking fire in the house till the body had been cremated, and a simple vegetarian meal was brought from a relative's house. When most of the visitors had left for the night, my elder sister, whom I call Didi, said that the casket needed to be filled with fresh ice. A widowed aunt remarked that we should remove any jewelry from Ma because otherwise the doms at the burning ghat, the men from the supposedly untouchable caste who built the pyre and were the custodians of the whole ceremony, would simply snatch it away. They didn't care, she said, and would just tear the flesh to rip off the gold. It was their right.

Ma's nose stud came off easily enough, but the earrings were a problem. Her white hair was wrapped around the stud; using a pair of scissors, I cut the hair, but the earrings seemed stuck to the skin. My younger sister struggled with one of them and I with the other. I didn't succeed, and someone else had to complete the task. At one point I found myself saying it was better to use surgical scissors right then so that we didn't have to watch Ma's ears torn by other hands. Didi said of the doms, using an English term borrowed from her medical books, "For them, it is just a *cadaver.*" I was unsettled but understood that the doms were also reflecting an understanding that was drawn from deep within Hinduism: once the spirit has departed from the body, what remains is mere matter, no different from the log of wood on which it is placed. There was maybe a lesson in this for us, that we discard our squeamishness about death, but I felt a great tenderness as I looked down at my mother in that metal box. I caressed her cheeks. They felt cold to the touch, and slightly moist, as if even in death she had kept up her habit of applying lotion. A thin line of red fluid, like betel juice, glistened between her lips.

Having touched Ma's body, I also felt I should wash my hands. I went up to her room. Over the past couple of hours there had been the comfort of shared tears, but now I was alone for the first time. In the room where I had last seen my mother alive and quite well, only a few months earlier, her walking stick was leaning against the wall. Her saris, whose smell would have been familiar to me, hung in the cupboard. Next to the bed were the two pairs of her white sneakers equipped with Velcro straps for her arthritic hands. Standing in front of the bathroom sink, it occurred to me that the bar of Pears soap in the blue plastic dish was the one that Ma had put there just before she died. My first notes in Patna were about these items, which appeared to me like memorials that I knew would soon disappear.

My sisters and I slept that night on mattresses spread on the floor around the aluminum box. On waking up after perhaps four hours of sleep, I saw that my younger sister was awake, sitting quietly with her back to the wall, looking vacant and sad. Under the light of a bulb near a side door, visible through the glass, stood a man with a scarf wrapped around his head. It took me a minute to recognize him. He was from our ancestral village in Champaran and had been a servant in our house in Patna when I was a boy. He had traveled through the night with fresh bamboo that would be used to make the bier on which, according to custom, Ma's body would be carried out of the house and put on the funeral pyre.

When the sun came out after an hour, the rosebushes in the garden were only half visible through the fog, and the fog was still there on the water when we arrived at the river around noon.

That morning, while my sisters were washing Ma's body in preparation for the funeral, my father and I went to get our heads shaved. Papa asked the barber the name of his village; it turned out that the barber's village and ours were in the same district. My father knew a politician from the barber's village. The radio was playing Hindi songs. *Zulfein teri itni ghani, dekh ke inko, yeh sochta hoon . . . Maula mere Maula mere.* The barber was a small, dark man with a limp. He was extremely polite to my father, listening quietly while he talked about inflation and the changes in the economy. At one point my father said that when he started life in Patna, he could buy a chicken for ten rupees and that now it would be difficult to get an egg for that amount.

I listened to what my father was saying with a rising sense of annoyance. I thought he was being pedantic when I wanted him to be sad—but why exactly? So that I could write down fragments of sentences in a little notebook? I began to see that Papa too was finding comfort by writing his own story of loss. There can be so much pathos in accounting. All the dumb confusion and wild fear of our lives rearranged in tidy rows in a ledger. One set of figures to indicate birth, and another set for death: the concerted attempt to repress the accidents and the pain of the period in between. Entire lives and accompanying histories of loss reduced to neat numbers. My father, with his phenomenal memory, was doing what he knew how to do best. He was saying to everyone in the room that everything had changed but the past was still connected to the present, if only through a narrative about changes in the price of eggs and chicken.

Ma's body had been taken out of the aluminum box by the time Papa and I returned home. Her fingernails and toenails were painted red. She was now draped in a pink Banarasi organza sari and a burgundy shawl with tiny silver bells and a shiny gold pattern of leaves. There were bright new bangles on her arm. Minutes before we left for the burning ghat, my father was brought into the room where Ma's adorned body lay on a stretcher on the floor. He was asked to put orange *sindoor* in the parting of Ma's hair, repeating the act he had performed on the day he married her. Papa was sobbing by now, but he was asked to repeat the gesture thrice. Then all the women in the family, many of them weeping loudly, took turns rubbing the auspicious powder in Ma's hair.

When we were in the car, driving to the Ganga for the cremation, Didi said that my mother was lucky. At her death, Ma had been dressed up in new clothes. Papa had put *sindoor* on her head, signifying that they were getting married again. Ma was going out as a bride. Had my father died first, none of this would have happened. If Ma were still living, *sindoor* would have been wiped away from her head. She would be expected to wear white. The women from the family who were now wailing would still be wailing, but if Ma were the widow, these women would have had the task of breaking all the bangles on her wrist before Papa's corpse was taken out of the house.

As I listened to my sister, I understood that even in the midst of profound grief it was necessary to find comfort. One needed solace. It was possible to hold despair at bay by imagining broken bangles and the destiny that my mother had escaped. I would have found the sight of my mother's bare arms unbearable.

I left India nearly three decades ago, and would see my mother for only a few days each year during my visits to Patna. Over the past ten or fifteen years, her health had been declining. She suffered from arthritis and the medicines she took for it had side effects, and sometimes my phone rang with news that she'd fallen asleep in the bathroom or had a seizure on the morning after she had fasted during a festival. I knew that one day the news would be worse and I would be asked to come to Patna. I was fifty years old and had never before attended a funeral. I didn't know what was more surprising, that some of the rituals were new to me or that they were exactly as I had imagined. That my mother's corpse had been dressed as a bride was new and disconcerting, and I'd have preferred a plainer look; on the other hand, the body placed on the bamboo bier, its canopy covered with an orange sheet of cotton, was a familiar daily sight on the streets of my childhood. In my notebook that night I noted that my contribution to the funeral had been limited to lighting my mother's funeral pyre. In more ways than one, the rituals of death had reminded me that I was an outsider. There were five hundred people at the *shraadh* dinner. I only knew a few of them. I wouldn't have known how to make arrangements for the food or the priests. Likewise for the *shamiana*, the community hall where the dinner was held, the notice in the newspapers about the *shraadh*, even the chairs on which the visitors sat.

There is a remarkable short story by A. K. Ramanujan called "Annayya's Anthropology" in which the Kannada protagonist, a graduate student at the University of Chicago, makes a terrible discovery while looking at a book in the library. The book is by an American anthropologist whose fieldwork had been done in India; the pictures in the book from Annayya's hometown appear familiar to him. One of the photographs illustrates a Hindu cremation, and Annayya recognizes in the crowd a cousin who owns a photography studio. This is a picture that appears to have been taken in

Annayya's own home in Mysore. The cousin, whose name is Sundararaya, is mentioned in the book's foreword. When Annayya looks more carefully at the corpse in the photograph, he sees that it is his father on the pyre. Ramanujan was making a point about the discipline of anthropology, about the ironies of our self-discoveries in the mirror of Western knowledge, but the story tugs at the immigrant's dread that distance will prevent his fulfillment of filial duty.

I had been luckier than Annayya. I had been able to speak to Didi in Patna when Ma was taken to a hospital on the night she died. On WhatsApp, on my phone, a text came from my sister later in the evening, assuring me that Ma was doing better. Then came the call about my flight timings. While the use of social media also meant that I got the news of my mother's death from a near stranger on Facebook, it was also true that technology and modern travel had made it quite easy for me to arrive in Patna in less than twenty hours to cremate my mother. During the prayer ceremonies a priest told me that the reason Hindu customs dictated a mourning period of thirteen days was that it used to take time for all the relatives to be informed and for them to travel to the home of the deceased. But this, he said, putting his hand on his ear, is the age of the mobile phone.

At the ghat, the smoke from the funeral fires mixed with the lingering fog of the winter afternoon. An advance party organized by a cousin's husband had pitched a small *shamiana* on the bank and arranged a few red plastic chairs next to it. Above the din, a tuneless *bhajan* played on a loudspeaker. In the crowd, I was led first in one direction and then another. My movements were restrained because of what I was wearing; according to custom, my body was wrapped in two pieces of unstitched cotton. My freshly shaven head was bare. I saw that Ma's body had already been put on the pyre. There was such a press of strangers, many of them beggars and curious children, that I had to ask people loudly to move back. Ma lay on heavy logs and a bed of straw, but the priest directed me to pile thinner firewood over the rest of the body. Other family members joined me, adding sticks in the shape of a tent over the corpse.

Ma's face had been left bare. Now the priest told me to put five pieces of sandalwood near my mother's mouth. Some of the *sindoor* that had been put in Ma's hair had scattered and lodged

in her eyebrows and on her eyelids. The dom who would give me
the fire had an X-shaped plaster stuck on his right cheek. He had
a dark face and his eyes were bloodshot. His head was wrapped in
a brown-and-blue muffler to protect him from the cold; he wore
jeans and a thin black jacket and he had about him an air of insou-
ciance that would have bothered my mother, but I liked him. His
presence was somehow reassuring, or real, because he was outside
the circle of our grief and yet the main doer. He was solemn, but
he certainly wasn't sober; his very casualness brought a quotidian
touch to the scene, and he accentuated this by haggling about his
payment. A maternal uncle's son stood behind me, repeating for
my benefit the priest's instructions—this cousin of mine, a few
years older than I, had cremated his son recently. The boy had
passed away after his liver stopped working, the result of an al-
lergic reaction to medicines that have reportedly been banned
outside India. The priest told me to sprinkle *gangajal* again—the
endless act of purification with what is in reality polluted water
—before the dom lit a bundle of tall straw for me. Three circles
around the pyre. Then followed the ritual that is called *mukhaagni*.
I understood suddenly why the priest had given me the five pieces
of sandalwood, the size of small Snickers bars, to put near my
mother's mouth. In that moment, while performing *mukhaagni* in-
adequately, inefficiently, even badly, in my grief and bewilderment,
the thought passed through my mind: Is this why my mother had
wanted me present at her death? *Mukhaagni*—in Sanskrit, *mukha*
is "mouth" and *agni* is "fire"—means in practice that the male who
is closest to the deceased, often the son, sometimes the father, and
in some cases, I imagine, the husband, puts fire into the mouth of
the person on the pyre.

A cremation on a riverbank in India is by its very nature public, but usually the only mourners present are men. In our case,
my sisters and other younger women from the family had accompanied Ma's body. When I turned from the pyre I saw my sisters
standing at the edge of the circle. I went to them and put my arms
around their shoulders. The flames had risen at once and they
hid Ma's body behind an orange curtain. Soon there were fewer
people standing around the pyre and the older men, my father's
friends, began to settle down on the plastic chairs at a distance of
about thirty feet from the pyre. A relative put a shawl around me.
Then the dom said that the fire was burning too quickly, meaning

that the fire would go out before the corpse had been incinerated, so a few men from our party took down a part of the *shamiana* and used it as a screen against the wind.

The fire needed to burn for three hours. Badly managed fires and, sometimes, the plain paucity of firewood—for the pyre requires at least 150 kilos of wood but often as much as 400 kilos or more—are to be blamed for the partially charred torsos flung into the Ganga. And as wood costs money—10,000 rupees in our case—the poor in particular can be insufficiently burned. The chief minister of Bihar, Jitan Ram Manjhi, a man from the formerly untouchable Musahar (or rat-eating) caste, told an audience in Patna last year that his family was so poor that when his grandfather died they just threw his body into the river.

I asked Didi why we hadn't taken Ma's body to Patna's electric crematorium, but she only said that Ma wouldn't have wanted it. Didi didn't need to say anything else. I could imagine my mother resisting the idea of being put in a metal tray where other bodies had been laid and pushed inside an oven where electric coils would reduce her to ashes. Her choice, superstitious and irrational as it might be, didn't pose a problem for us. We could afford the more expensive and customary means of disposing of the dead. Nearly 300 kilos of wood had been purchased for Ma's pyre and, in addition to that, 10 kilos of sandalwood. This was one of the many instances during those days when I recognized that we were paying for the comfort of subscribing to tradition. The electric crematorium is often the choice of the poor, costing only about 300 rupees. I learned that over 700 dead are cremated at the electric crematorium at Patna's Bans Ghat each month, and a somewhat smaller number at the more distant Gulbi Ghat electric crematorium. These numbers are only a fraction of the 3,000 cremated on traditional pyres at Bans Ghat on average each month. This despite the fact that electric cremation is also quicker, taking only forty-five minutes, except when there is a long wait due to power cuts. There can also be other delays. Back when I was in college, the corpse of a relative of mine, a sweet old lady with a fondness for betel leaf, was taken to the Patna crematorium, but the operator there said that he would be available only after he had watched that day's broadcast of the TV serial *Ramayan*. The mourners waited an extra hour.

While we sat under the *shamiana* watching the fire do its work, my younger sister, Dibu, said that she had put perfume on Ma's corpse because fragrances were something Ma liked. Dibu began to talk about how Ma used to put perfume in the new handkerchiefs that she gave away to younger female relatives who visited her. In Bihar, a Hindu woman leaving her home is given a handkerchief with a few grains of rice, a pinch of turmeric, leaves of grass, coins, and a sweet *laddu*. These items had also been put beside Ma on the pyre, and, I now learned, inside Ma's mouth my sisters had placed a gold leaf. I thought of the priest telling me each time I completed a circle around the pyre that I was to put the fire into my mother's mouth. I didn't, or couldn't. It wasn't so much that I found it odd or appalling that such a custom should exist; instead, I remember being startled that no one had cared to warn me about it. But perhaps I shouldn't have been. Death provided a normalizing context for everything that was being done. No act appeared outlandish, because it had a place in the tradition, each Sanskrit verse carrying an intonation of centuries of practice. And if there was any doubt about the efficacy of sacred rituals, everywhere around us banal homilies were being offered to make death appear less strange or devastating. The *bhajan* that had been playing on the loudspeaker all afternoon was in praise of fire. *Death, you think you have defeated us, but we sing the song of burning firewood.* Even though it was tuneless, and even tasteless, the song turned cremation into a somewhat celebratory act. It struck me that the music disavowed its own macabre nature and made everything acceptable. And now, as the fire burned lower and there was visibly less to burn, I saw that everyone, myself included, had momentarily returned to a sense of the ordinary. This feeling wouldn't last more than a few hours, but at that time I felt free from the contagion of tears. I remember complaining about the loud music. Everyone had been fasting since morning, and *pedas* from a local confectioner were taken out of paper boxes. I took a box of *pedas* to our young dom, but he refused; he didn't want anything sweet to eat. I was handed a packet of salted crackers to pass on to him. Tea was served in small plastic cups. Street dogs and goats wandered past the funeral pyres. Broken strings of marigold, fruit peels, and bits of bedding, including blankets and a pillow pulled from the fire, littered the sandy bank. One of my uncles had lost his car keys and people from our group left to look for them.

The dom had so far used a ten-foot-long bamboo to rearrange

the burning logs, but when the fire died down he poked around the burning embers with his callused fingers. I was summoned for another round of prayers and offerings to the fire. The men in my family gave directions to the dom as he scooped Ma's remains —ash and bones, including a few vertebrae, but other small bones too, white and curiously flat—into a large earthen pot. This pot was wrapped in red cloth and later that evening hung from a high branch on the mango tree outside our house. Its contents were to be immersed in the Ganga at the holy sites upriver: Benares, Prayag, and Haridwar. This was a journey my sisters and I would undertake later in the week; but that afternoon, after the pot had been filled, the rest of the half-burned wood and ash and what might have been a part of the hipbone were flung into the river while the priest chanted prayers. Flower petals, mostly marigold, had been stuffed in polythene bags which had the names of local sari shops printed on them, and at the end everyone took part in casting handfuls of bright petals on the brown waters. I took pictures. The photograph of the yellow marigold floating on the Ganga, rather than my mother's burning pyre, is what I put up on Facebook that evening.

RICHARD M. LANGE

Of Human Carnage

FROM *Catamaran*

ON MARCH 12, 2012, my girlfriend, Elizabeth, and I were driving on Costa Rica's Inter-American Highway, the major north-
south highway through the country. We were on the second-to-last
day of a three-week bird-watching trip that had included most of
the good birding spots in the northern two-thirds of the country.
That morning we had left the cabin we'd rented on Cerro de la
Muerte (the Hill of Death) and were headed to our last stop, a
small hotel in Alajuela, near the Juan Santamaría International
Airport, where we were scheduled to catch our return flight to
California the next morning.

As anyone who has done it will tell you, driving in Costa Rica
is a challenge. Roads are narrow, most streets are unmarked, and
the highways are filled with speeding big rigs. In many places, a
lone sign telling you to *ceda el paso* (yield) is your only warning that
the highway is about to narrow to a single lane for *both* directions.
Throughout our travels, we'd seen pedestrians (including unattended children) walking the narrowest of shoulders. On some
stretches there is no shoulder at all—the roadway is bounded by
steep drops or weed-choked ditches. In these places, the pedestrians and bicyclists are forced, under threat of instant death, to
maintain an extremely disciplined line along the very edge of the
asphalt.

Where Elizabeth and I were traveling, about halfway between
Cartago and San José, the two northbound lanes are divided from
the southbound lanes by a section of neighborhood. I was behind
the wheel, my eyes on the road ahead as I listened for any updates
from our rented SUV's GPS system, which spoke to us in a kindly

female voice we had affectionately dubbed Carmen Sabetodo. The afternoon commute under way, traffic was much heavier than it had been anywhere else on our trip. Cars were traveling at about sixty miles an hour, which is pretty fast for Costa Rica, as most of the roads are too narrow and winding for such a speed. On the left sat a row of small houses, their fenceless yards coming right to the edge of the highway. On the right, a steep-sided ditch lined with concrete—essentially a mammoth rain gutter—ran alongside. Across the ditch, a treeless embankment climbed thirty or so feet.

Well up ahead, on the right-hand edge of the asphalt, I saw a figure. It was a man, dressed in dark pants and a powder-blue shirt. In the first instant that I noticed him, I felt something was wrong, that he wasn't just another pedestrian walking a dangerous edge of roadway. Standing on the highway side of the concrete ditch, he seemed in a particularly precarious spot. I imagined he'd slid down the embankment accidentally and, unable to climb back up, had decided the only way out of his predicament was to cross the ditch and then, if it was possible, cross the highway. And now there he stood, weighing the feasibility of the second part of his plan. He was leaning toward the moving traffic, as though seeking the right moment to dash across. As a white SUV approached he leaned back slightly, the vehicle missing him by inches. Behind the SUV was a big-rig truck. When it reached him, he dove in front of it.

In an instant, my mind involuntarily revised its sense of what was happening. The man, it seemed, had not come to the edge of the highway by accident. He was some kind of daredevil, attempting to dive into the middle of the lane so that the truck would harmlessly pass over him, after which he would quickly scramble back into the roadside ditch before being hit by the next vehicle. I imagined a group of friends were looking on, probably from atop the embankment, and he was performing for their awe and admiration. For that fraction of a second, I was so convinced of this scenario that my brain actually formed the thought: *This is dumb! You're not going to make it!* But of course the man was not a daredevil; he was committing suicide.

When the truck's front bumper hit him, there was an explosion of pink, his body, or some part of it, bursting like a water balloon. As the truck rolled over him, he was struck by first one set of wheels, then another, then another, causing him to careen and tumble along under the chassis. The amount of time between my first noticing him and seeing his body battered under the truck was probably two seconds, too short of an interval to put into words any of my quick succession of thoughts, but when my brain finally caught up with what was happening, I gasped, "*Oh, my God!*"

Lifting my foot from the accelerator, I swerved as far to the left as I could to avoid hitting the man myself. Mindful of the heavy traffic on the road, I was trying to slow as quickly as possible, to signal to the vehicles behind me that something had happened, but not so quickly that I got rammed by an inattentive driver. My next thought was to get beyond the scene before I pulled over, to not stop until I was out of range of its gruesomeness.

As our vehicle neared the body lying in the road, I spoke forcefully to Elizabeth: "Don't look!" I think I even put a hand in front of her face. She immediately covered her eyes, which created a strange moment of solitude between myself and whatever I was about to see. I felt like a child who'd stumbled into some scary place—a spiderweb-filled basement or a dark cave—and realized he was going to face the terror alone.

There seemed no possibility the man had survived, but I wanted to assess whether or not he could be helped. My eyes found his body on the asphalt. He lay on his stomach, unmoving, his feet toward the roadside ditch. For some reason I could see his back and shoulders but not his head. Getting closer, I saw that his head was gone. A few feet farther down the road lay pieces of his shattered skull.

About a hundred yards beyond the body, the big rig was coming to a stop in the right-hand lane. I pulled in front of it and cut the engine. Hoping to spare Elizabeth any further horror, particularly the sight of the man's headless and shattered body, I gave her another firm directive: "Stay here! Do not get out of this car!"

Her face white with shock, she nodded.

I climbed out and ran back up the highway toward the truck. As I reached it my dominant thought was that I did not want to see again—or see better—what I had just seen. If someone wanted me to go beyond the truck, they would have to be armed or strong enough to physically force me. Even then, if they wanted me to look again at the pieces of the man's body, they would have to pry my eyelids open.

When I reached the driver, he was standing in front of his vehicle, talking on his cell phone. He too, I noticed, had taken up a spot that kept his truck between himself and the gore back up the road. I speak Spanish, and initially the bits of conversation I overheard made me think he was describing the accident to the police, but it eventually became clear he was talking to someone at the company he worked for—a dispatcher or possibly his boss. His eyes were pegged open, and he spoke as though in a trance—head still, mouth opening and closing robotically. When he hung up, I started to tell him it wasn't his fault, but my voice broke. I placed a hand on his shoulder; the hand, I noticed, was trembling. He said nothing, his eyes refusing to meet mine.

A school bus pulled up next to us in the left lane and stopped. A dozen girls, all about fifteen, sat in the first few rows behind the driver, all in some state of shock, many crying into cell phones. Without getting out of his seat, the bus driver opened the door and gave the truck driver some simple directions: don't move the truck, wait for the police, ask the witnesses to stay here. Despite his clear-minded directives, the bus driver was ashen, his voice rising and falling in pitch as he spoke. *"Estará bien,"* he said a few times. Then he drove his devastated passengers away.

At this point I looked back down the road, making sure I'd parked my vehicle in such a way that the bus could get around it, and saw Elizabeth. She'd gotten out of the SUV and was standing on the side of the highway, shaking and crying. I ran to her.

As I wrapped her in my arms and tried to comfort her, I noticed, across the highway, a middle-aged woman in shorts and a dark shirt who'd come out of her house to see what was happening. She waved us over. I led Elizabeth across the asphalt, and the woman, without a word, took Elizabeth by the hand and led her to a covered patio that fronted her house. I started back up the hill toward the truck but was met by a different woman, this one younger, maybe thirty or so, walking quickly toward me holding a pen and a pad of paper. She wasn't wearing any kind of uniform, but she comported herself professionally, like a medic or a police officer. She told me I needed to give a statement, that the truck driver might be in serious legal trouble if I didn't. Working to stay calm and speak in coherent Spanish, I told her that I would definitely give a statement, but I also explained that I was an American, that this was my last day in Costa Rica, that my girlfriend was upset and I didn't want to keep her here any longer than I had to.

She nodded. *"Sí. Pero dame su información."*

I carefully wrote out my name and email address, along with the name of the hotel in Alajuela where we'd be staying the night.

"*Lo vio usted?*" she asked.

"*Sí. El hombre*"—I didn't know the word for "dove," so I said "threw himself"— "*se tiro en frente del camion. No fue la culpa del camionero.*"

Concurring with my version of what had happened, she nodded and went back up the road.

At this point the son of the woman who was tending to Elizabeth emerged from the house. He was skinny, about seventeen, wearing shorts and a white T-shirt, half hopping and half walking across the lawn as he struggled to fit a pair of flip-flops on his feet. "What happened?" he asked me, in Spanish.

"A man got hit by a truck."

"Is he dead?"

I nodded.

"Are you sure?"

"*Perdio su cabeza,*" I said, miming the act of lifting my head from my shoulders.

His eyes grew wider and he tore off up the hill, his mother yelling after him to be careful.

Stepping onto the patio to check on Elizabeth, I saw she'd been given a seat at a table and was taking sips from a glass of water. I patted her back and stroked her shoulder.

"*Qué lástima,*" the mother said to me.

A minute later the son came running back, his eyes wide and face pale. His expression unequivocally conveyed the same message my brain had been shouting since I'd exited the SUV: DO NOT GO PAST THE TRUCK! "*Ohhh,*" he shuddered. "*Es malo.*" Taking his cue from the woman who'd come down the road, he found a pencil and a piece of paper and handed them to me. I again wrote out my information.

When I finished, the mother pointed to the SUV. "Is that your car?"

The SUV, I now remembered, was still parked in the right-hand lane of the highway. Its windows were open and Elizabeth's and my suitcases (which contained all of our credit cards, our passports, and most of our remaining cash) were sitting in plain view on the back seat. Before getting out and running up the road toward the truck, I'd had the thought that Elizabeth might need to move the SUV to make way for emergency vehicles, so I'd left the keys in the ignition. The backup of traffic behind the accident included taxis, buses, and other passenger-carrying vehicles that wouldn't be going anywhere for a long time, and dozens of people had decided to get out and make their way on foot. In groups of two and three, they were streaming down the highway. The mother had noticed a couple of young men standing at the open windows of the SUV, peering inside.

At this point I made a decision that I'm not proud of. I knew the right thing was to stay and wait for the police, to give an official statement and convey, in person, my conviction that the dead man had dived in front of the truck on purpose. But my stress overruled my sense of duty. The truck driver, by way of the competent woman with the notepad, had my information, and now so did the mother and her son. If anybody wanted to reach me, they could. But I wasn't hanging around any longer.

"Let's go," I said to Elizabeth.

The mother appeared to sympathize. She nodded and helped me get Elizabeth to her feet.

I walked Elizabeth back across the highway to the SUV, our approach sending the two suspicious men on their way. I put Elizabeth into the passenger seat and then hustled around to the driver's side and climbed in. Taking a deep breath, I started the engine and carefully—very, very carefully—drove away.

For weeks after the events in Costa Rica, Elizabeth had little appetite, suffered nightmares, and struggled to enjoy anything. At random unguarded moments she broke into tears. Before our trip, she had spent months completing applications to grad school —gathering letters of recommendation, slaving over her statement of purpose, devoting hundreds and hundreds of hours to studying for the general and subject-specific GRE tests—but now the whole enterprise seemed rather meaningless to her.

My own symptoms were similar but worse. Previous to the accident, my sensitivity to violence on TV or in movies was about average—I'd never been one for cartoonish horror-flick splatter, but neither was I much bothered by the "realistic" violence in films like *The Godfather* or *No Country for Old Men*. Following the accident, however, I was deeply disturbed by just about any violence. One night, on a sketch-comedy show on TV, a mannequin dressed as one of the characters was tossed into the street and run over by a car. I nearly vomited, turned off the TV, and left the room.

I was also hounded by a pervasive sense of fear. I couldn't help thinking it could have been *my* vehicle the man selected and repeatedly imagined making eye contact with him as his head dropped below the horizon of the SUV's hood. As bad as my trauma was at having simply *witnessed* his death, I couldn't imagine the pain of having been the agent of it. I was sure that on some future road I would kill someone. Aside from never getting behind the wheel again, there didn't seem to be anything I could do about this. (My fear ramped up considerably when, a few days after Elizabeth and I arrived back in California, a distraught man killed himself by jumping into traffic during the morning commute on Highway 1, less than a mile from where we live.)

But my deepest and most unrelenting symptom was a profound obsession with death itself. Before Costa Rica I had not spent much time thinking about it, but afterward I not only replayed and dwelled on the images I'd seen out there on the tropically heated asphalt, I thought about death throughout history—particularly gruesome, violent death. I imagined the accidents and calamities that must have struck ancient humans trying to bring down mastodons and rhinos with rocks and spears. I pictured hunters and gatherers being taken by tigers, wolves, and other apex predators. My mental re-creations spared no details: razor-sharp teeth and claws shredding flesh, powerful jaws crushing bone, people crying out in agony, their mouths filling with blood.

I thought too of the violence that humans have perpetrated (and continue to perpetrate) against other humans. Lines from Homer that I'd read years before kept running through my mind: "Agamemnon stabbed straight at his face as he came on in fury with the sharp spear . . . [and] the spearhead passed through this and the bone, and the inward brain was all spattered forth."[1] As an avid reader of history, I knew that from ancient times through the Dark and Middle Ages and on up to the modern era, just about every civilization has condoned, under some circumstance or another, the savaging of human bodies. The Romans fed slaves to lions. Nordic peoples broke open rib cages so lungs and other vital organs could be removed while the victims were still alive. European Christians put heretics on Catherine wheels and beat them to death with clubs. Muslims buried people up to their necks and pummeled them with rocks until their skulls were lumps of bone and meat. Here in the modern civilized West we killed people by shooting them, hanging them, or sizzling their lungs with poison gas. In addition to these "intimate" kinds of death, we killed each other by the thousands and millions during periods of mass slaughter. The American Civil War: 600,000 killed; World War I: 16 million killed; World War II: 60 million killed.[2] I thought about the genocides in Rwanda and Serbia, the wars in Iraq, Afghanistan, Libya, and Syria, and the lesser-known but no less gruesome battles in places often neglected by the Western media: Eritrea, Chad, Congo. The attendant human savagery of these conflicts — the pain and blood and suffering, the raw carnage — suddenly weighed on me as never before.

It also occurred to me that for as long as humans have been suffering gruesome deaths, other humans have been witnessing them. (Indeed, the ancient and medieval killing rituals I mention above were usually witnessed by large crowds, with audience members often encouraged to take part in the savagery.) During prehistoric times, it doesn't seem likely that anyone lived a natural life without being present while some member of his tribe, clan, or family was mauled by a bear or eaten by a puma — or speared or bludgeoned or thrown from a cliff. Shifting to more recent history, I wondered what it must have been like to survive Columbine, to have been one of the firefighters who on September 11 witnessed bodies impacting the ground from eighty-six floors above. Or to have seen friends and fellow soldiers killed in Iraq or Afghanistan. It did not surprise me to learn that, according to the U.S. Department of Veterans Affairs, 20 percent of the soldiers who've returned from fighting in those countries are suffering from post-traumatic stress disorder.[3] Other statistics are even more telling: though Iraq and Afghanistan war veterans make up far less than 1 percent of the U.S. population, they account for more than 20 percent of its suicides.[4] In 2010, on average, twenty-two veterans committed suicide *every day.*[5]

In the last century, human beings have gotten used to some very traumatic things. We routinely scream across the surface of the earth at 75 miles an hour or hurtle through the sky 35,000 feet above it. Some of us even jump out of airplanes or off cliffs and plummet toward the earth at terminal velocity — for *fun!* But shooting someone and watching them die, or witnessing someone getting shot (or hung or stoned to death or decapitated)—things that cause us no *physical* harm—can be so emotionally painful as to be totally debilitating and sometimes, as the Veterans Affairs stats make heartbreakingly clear, unbearable. If in a few dozen years we can get used to high-speed driving and jet travel, why, after *tens of thousands* of years, are we still traumatized by seeing people's limbs ripped from their bodies? It seems an absurd question to ask, but following the events in Costa Rica, I needed to answer it.

Clearly the answer is not because, as a species, we're revolted by the sight of exposed muscle tissue and bone. If we were, every meat counter across the globe would be shut down and we'd all be strict vegetarians. Not only are meat counters still in abundance, here in the United States we have a system, via the U.S. Department of Agriculture, for grading the quality and attractiveness of animal carnage. And even the vegetarians among us—even those who claim to be "revolted" or "disgusted" by the sight of meat —usually manage to walk past displays of beheaded chickens or hanging gutted pigs without fainting or breaking into tears. Nor is carnage traumatic simply because when people are ripped apart they die. Death itself is not necessarily traumatic. Sometimes, when someone is suffering and that suffering cannot be alleviated, it's actually a mercy. We literally pray for it to come. If someone dies after living into her nineties or beyond, we sigh and say, *Well, she had a good life.*

But when the exposed muscle and bone involved is *human* muscle and bone, and the resulting death is seen as premature and cruel—and what violent death is not premature and cruel?—witnessing it is a different experience entirely.

Of course the trauma of inflicting or witnessing carnage is related to our love of human life, to the recognition that we too can suffer such a fate, that we are fragile in the same ways. But why is it that when we read about such a death in the newspaper, or hear about it on the radio or TV, even in great detail, it's not as traumatic as actually seeing it? (Why, for example, was I not plunged into morbidity after reading Homer back in college?) Consider the difference, emotionally speaking, between coming upon a dead body and watching someone die. Perhaps you've never experienced either. If so, consider the difference between coming across a dead animal, a dog or cat on the side of the road, say, and seeing a dog or cat get hit by a car. The former is sad, possibly even depressing; it will likely affect your mood for a few minutes, maybe a few hours. But the latter is horrifying, likely to stay with you for days, if not weeks or months.

Consider another aspect of death. We all have dead loved ones, but unless their deaths were recent or tragic, most of us are not particularly troubled by this. (In other words, if your Aunt Sally died in 1983, you're probably over it by now.) But when someone we love is in the *process* of dying—is fighting cancer, say, or is in surgery following a serious accident—we are generally in terrible shape: stressed, crying, lashing out. (Our "loved" ones, after all, are not only the recipients of love, they are the providers of it.) It seems few of us fear *being* dead but, to a greater or lesser extent, we all fear *dying*.

My own experiences are a case in point. Prior to the horror on the Inter-American Highway, I'd seen four other bodies that had succumbed to fatal violence, each the victim of a vehicle crash. At the age of nine, I was riding in the back seat of the family car heading south on I-5 in San Diego when we came upon two motorcyclists lying dead in the middle lanes, their bikes (and helmets) in the roadway nearby. At twenty-six, I was driving home from work late one night when, a hundred yards ahead of me, a drunk driver lost control of his car and flew off the highway into some trees. The impact of the crash cleaved his skull in two. In my late thirties, a friend and I were traveling on U.S. Route 50, southeast of Great Basin National Park, when we came upon a lone motorcyclist who'd lost control of his bike and ridden straight into a road cut.

Each of these events had been gut-wrenching. (Indeed, the drunk-driving death was nearly as gruesome as the one in Costa Rica: arriving at the crumpled car, I'd reached through the shattered driver's-side window and touched the dead man's shoulder before registering that the spot of lighter color at the top of his head was his exposed brain.) But none of these deaths stayed with me for long; I was rather morose for a day or two afterward but didn't miss any work or sleep. At no point did I shed tears.

Why? The biggest difference between these deaths and the death in Costa Rica was that I never saw any of these people alive. Even though I only saw the victim in Costa Rica for, at most, two seconds before he made his fateful dive, it was enough to register him as a living, breathing human being. The way he stood at the side of the highway—slightly crouched, his posture full of intent

—and the particular way he dove—feebly, like an exhausted traveler flopping onto a hotel bed—said something about him. From the simple circumstances of the scene, I knew he was a man who had the fortitude to stand by the highway and calculate the right moment to carry out his terrible plan. The spot he'd chosen for his death told me something as well: he'd kept himself on the side of the highway away from the houses, a place where he'd be less likely to be stopped. He didn't hang himself or take pills or slit his wrists, methods that would leave his body more or less intact. Instead, he put himself in front of a moving truck, ensuring that his body would be brutally crushed. This carried a message of self-hatred. Even more revealing: he made someone else kill him. He caused an innocent person to experience the pain and trauma of destroying another human being—in one of the most gruesome ways imaginable. And he did so at a location and time that ensured a high number of witnesses. This was an expression of rage.

So the trauma of witnessing his death was, at least in part, associated with witnessing the transition, with seeing a life—whole, animated, vibrant—become broken, still, hopeless. Of seeing someone with the potential to love and feel loved lose the potential to do either.

But it was also due to something else: intentionality. Those other bodies I'd seen were the victims of accidents. They'd wanted to live, but luck (or bad judgment) had conspired against them. The man on the Inter-American Highway had *chosen* to turn his body into carnage. Intentionality, I realized, was the deepest horror of Columbine and 9/11—and Auschwitz and Hiroshima and Jonestown and . . . the list goes on. Accidents happen. But when someone makes the decision to toss life—delicate, precious, the source of love—aside like a piece of trash, the horror cuts us to the bone.

When Elizabeth and I reached our hotel in Alajuela, we walked into the reception area and gave our names to the man at the desk. In a barely audible voice I told him about the accident, that the police might be calling to speak with us.

Nodding, he handed me a piece of paper where he'd written some names and phone numbers. The truck driver had already called. So had the police. They all wanted Elizabeth and me to drive back to the scene and give a statement.

This was not going to happen. It had taken us ninety minutes to get to the hotel from the accident scene. All through San José, traffic had been a mess. When we'd reached Alajuela, the main road through town was under construction, so we, along with the rest of the late-afternoon commuters, had been detoured onto side streets, which were clogged. We'd progressed one or two car lengths at a time, moving slower than the pedestrians on the sidewalks. This invited people to walk through the lanes of traffic and cut between our SUV and the cars in front of us. Normally this is fairly innocuous behavior—anyone who's navigated a jammed parking lot following a concert or sporting event has done it. People who live in New York or other big cities prone to gridlock do it every day. But having seen what we'd seen, it struck us as reckless and terrifying. Each time someone had walked in front of the SUV, I'd pressed harder on the brake pedal. Eventually my leg had cramped.

"No," I said. "We can't. We can talk to them on the phone. If the police want to come here, we're happy to answer any questions they might have. But we're not getting back on the road."

The desk clerk registered how serious I was and nodded. "I'll call the driver back." The driver didn't pick up, so the clerk left a message. I told the clerk I would sit in the lobby until the driver returned the call—I'd already left the driver hanging once, and I was determined not to do it again. I suggested that Elizabeth take the key and go find the room, but she didn't want to separate. Neither did I. We took each other's hand and sat down to wait.

The clerk had someone bring us glasses of water. Knowing that our reservations had been booked by Aratinga Tours, a company that caters to bird-watchers, he tried to take our minds off the situation by asking what birds we'd seen on our trip. We did our best to respond, but our hearts were not in it.

After twenty minutes, the driver called back. To avoid any confusion that might be caused by my less-than-perfect Spanish, I asked the clerk to translate. But the driver was only calling to tell me that my statement was no longer needed. Other witnesses had come forward to say what Elizabeth and I would have said, that the driver had done nothing wrong. A few people who lived in the houses adjacent to the highway had also come forward. Apparently they'd seen the suicidal man standing on the side of the road for some time before he'd made his fatal decision. They said it appeared he'd been "timing cars," waiting for the right vehicle and the right moment to make his move.

Taking the phone, I said to the driver what I'd tried to say when we'd both been standing in front of his truck, that I was sorry for what had happened to him, that he shouldn't blame himself for the man's death. In a quiet, pensive voice, he said, *"Sí. Gracias."*

The call finished, the clerk again tried to cheer us up. "Okay, now you can relax," he said. "Enjoy the hotel. The grounds are filled with many beautiful birds."

Following his earlier tone-deaf attempts at idle chitchat, his advice made me want to snap at him. Had he not heard the tremble in the truck driver's voice? Could he not understand what we'd all just been through?

Months later, as my morbid fascination with death finally began to fade, I realized some obvious things: We're not going to stop dying in horrible accidents or intentionally killing each other anytime soon. Nor are we going to stop witnessing such events. Carnage is here to stay. Since the dawn of time, we've been accommodating it. It circumscribes every aspect of our lives. Indeed, the very reason we organize ourselves into families, tribes, clans, and nations—the reason we create things like the Federal Aviation Administration and the National Highway Traffic Safety Administration, the reason we wear helmets and buckle our seatbelts and lock our doors at night—is to avoid becoming carnage. The clerk was not discounting the horror of it. He was just reminding us that the point is—has always been—to go on living.

Notes

1. Homer, *The Iliad,* trans. Richmond Lattimore (Chicago: University of Chicago Press, 1961), 237.

2. The number of casualties in these conflicts vary somewhat by source, but the numbers here, which include civilian deaths, represent a general consensus.

3. "PTSD: A Growing Epidemic," *NIH MedLinePlus 4,* no. 1 (Winter 2009), http://www.nlm.nih.gov/medlineplus/magazine/issues/winter09/articles/winter09pgl0-14.html.

4. Janet Kemp and Robert Bossarte, "Suicide Data Report, 2012," U.S. Department of Veterans Affairs, http://www.va.gov/opa/docs/Suicide-Data-Report-2012-final.pdf,15.

5. Ibid.

LEE MARTIN

Bastards

FROM *The Georgia Review*

THE SUMMER BEFORE I started high school, my parents said we
were going home. We'd spent the past six years in a suburb of Chicago where my mother had taken a teaching job, but now that she
was retiring, we'd decided to move back downstate. Instead of re-
modeling the house on our farm outside Sumner, we started looking in town. My parents ended up buying a modest frame house
with a front porch and clapboard siding—a well-kept home.

"Now this is all right," my father said. "This is just fine."

He insisted on vigilance, perhaps because when I was barely a
year old his life, and my mother's and mine, irrevocably turned
because of his own carelessness. On a November day in 1956, he
lost both of his hands in a farming accident. He was harvesting
corn when the shucking box on his picker clogged. Instead of taking the time to shut down the power take-off, he tried to clear the
corn from the box while its snapping rollers were still turning. The
rollers caught his hand, and when he tried to free it with his other
one, the rollers took it too. As long as I could remember, he'd
worn prostheses, or as he called them, his "hooks."

Our new house sat on a double lot. My father plowed the second
lot and put in a large vegetable garden, then lined a row of peach
saplings down the center of the backyard. We tilled and hoed and
weeded. We watered and mowed and raked. My mother's flower-
beds were lush with peonies, zinnias, marigolds; she planted iris
bulbs, tulips, daffodils. Our grass might have been full of clover, as
most yards were, but we kept it mowed and trimmed.

A family was known by how well it took care of what it owned,
my father said. On the farm, we could let things slip a bit if we got

too busy to keep it all shipshape. There, our house sat at the end
of a long lane and was invisible from the road.

"That won't fly in town," he said. "Here, people are always
watching." Evenings that summer, he walked through the backyard
to check on the peach saplings and the garden. Then he sat on the
front porch in a lawn chair and watched the night come on. In the
twilight, he must have taken a last survey of our well-tended yard
and felt the pride of having everything in order.

We were making a fresh start after those years in Chicagoland,
where our lives had felt odd to us. My father was no longer a
farmer. He didn't work at all and had a hard time knowing what
to do with his days. My mother, a soft-spoken, timid woman, was
ill-suited for her life among people who were bolder and more as-
sertive; in fact, we'd gone to Chicago because my mother had lost
her teaching job in Sumner when the school board thought she
wasn't a tough enough disciplinarian. I, on the other hand, started
to think too much of myself. I had entered my teenage years head-
strong and ready to test my father's limits. We had raucous fights
during which we shouted and swore and otherwise behaved like
the heathens our neighbors in the apartment building surely believed us to be.

"I'll take you down a notch or two," he often said.

We ended up in confrontations that sometimes turned physical.
We shoved at each other. He whipped my legs with his belt. We
screamed at each other. We said vile things.

"Mercy," my mother sometimes said. "Just listen to you."

My father and I often ended up in tears and then retreated to
the stony silence of our shame.

That was what we were trying to put behind us when we came
back downstate. In our new house, though we never spoke of this,
my father and I promised ourselves we'd be better.

We had a detached garage where he kept his Ford F-100 pickup
truck. One night, someone let himself into the garage under cover
of darkness and walked out with some of my father's tools.

"Thieves," he said. He padlocked the garage doors. "Let 'em
try to get in there now." He banged his hooks together. "The bastards," he said.

This all happened in our small town of Sumner, Illinois. Population: 1,000. A town of working-class people in the southeastern

part of the state, some 250 miles from Chicago. A town that prospered from the sweat of farmers like my father, and oil field roughnecks, and refinery workers, and those who worked in the various factories in neighboring towns. We were blue-collar folks, and we knew the value of hard work and what it took to have something worth having.

The three of us wanted to have kinder lives, and for a time in our new house, we did. Summer nights, my father and I sat at our kitchen table, listening to a Cardinals game on the radio. My mother popped corn and pared apples. We drank Pepsi-Colas and let ourselves imagine that such evenings could become our regular come and go.

My aunt and uncle and cousin paid us frequent visits. We had supper, and then we brought out the cards and played pitch, a bidding game that pitted a pair of partners against another pair. As we played, we engaged in good-humored teasing and taunting, and I reveled in the fact that my father and I could enjoy picking at each other the way family members did who didn't live in anger. A dig here or there surely wouldn't do any harm.

One night I made a bonehead move, leading with the king of hearts before the ace had been played. My father, who was partnered with my cousin, shook his head and said to him, "I can't believe that move. Can you, Phillip? Did someone just open the door and let Stupid walk in?"

Because he couldn't hold the cards in his hook, he kept them laid out and hidden behind the raised cover of a *Look* magazine. My aunt held up the magazine cover so no one else could see them. He would tell her which card to play and she would put it on the table—but when I led that king of hearts, he used the point of his hook to slide out the ace and take the trick.

My uncle tried to ease the sting by saying, "That's just one trick. That's nothing to worry about at all. Let's see what the old man does now. Let's see if he's got the cards."

Maybe everything would have been all right if I'd said, *Yeah, old man. Show us what you've got.* But then my father looked at me and said, "You've got to pay attention. You've got to know what's been played and what hasn't. You don't see Phillip making any goofs like that. Now get with it, or no one will want you as his partner anymore."

My aunt said, "Oh, leave that boy alone." Her defense of me

only called attention to my shame. "I'm sure he's doing the best he can. No need to ride him like that. After all, it's just a game."

But it wasn't just a game. It was another reminder of all that boiled between my father and me, all that we tried to keep locked up on nights like this when we were with people, all that bad blood. My face was hot. An ache came into my throat and I choked back tears. I kept my head lowered and my eyes on my cards. I waited for the game to continue, but for what seemed like the longest time it didn't. The clock on the wall hummed. The refrigerator's compressor kicked on. My uncle cleared his throat.

I realized then that everyone was being cautious about what they said. My aunt and uncle and cousin knew my father's temper. They must have suspected that he and I were in the habit of knocking our heads together, and no one wanted to be the one to say the next thing, the thing that might cause us to explode.

Finally my father returned to the game and pushed a card out into the center of the table. Even he could tell we were on the brink of something dangerous and was trying to get us back on safe ground.

The one thing my father and I shared was shame. I wish I hadn't been so sensitive. I wish he hadn't been so rough. I wish he'd shut down that power take-off and made it impossible for his accident to happen. I wish he'd never had to put on those hooks and the anger that came with them. I wish he hadn't been so stupid in that cornfield. But I never said any of these things to him. I never told him I was sorry for all that he suffered. We never talked about his accident, which was one more thing we tried to contain and put away from us. Not until years later, after my father was dead, did my aunt tell me stories about him and the rage he brought into our home after his accident—stories I couldn't recall because I was so young at the time.

"Oh, it was terrible," she said. "He'd rant and rave. It was like he was out of his head."

I did remember the white packets of phenobarbital tablets, prescribed those days as a sedative, that I found in the medicine chest at our farmhouse years later, when I was still a small boy.

"That accident," my aunt said. "It changed him. It changed his whole life."

*

If it hadn't been for my mother that night around our kitchen table, who knows what might have happened.

What did she do? Nothing dramatic. She came into our kitchen and stood behind me. She laid her hand on my shoulder. She held it there, not saying a word, and finally my uncle took his turn and played a card, and then my cousin, and then I did the same, and the game went on, and all the while my mother was there, her hand the lightest thing I could imagine at that moment, so light that I barely felt her touching me at all, but I knew she was—and that, as it would so many times thereafter, made all the difference.

"Who wants cake and ice cream?" she finally said, and just like that we went on.

A few months later, in the days of short light and icicles hanging from the eaves, my father noticed footprints in the snow around our house—the snow that gave away the voyeur. We tracked him around the perimeter of our house, this man who wore Red Wing boots. We could see the outline of the wing on the heels pressed down into the snow and the blurred letters of words we knew were *Red Wing Shoes*. The man had walked around our house, turning at every window so he could look inside.

My father and I both owned Red Wing boots, as did a number of other boys and men in our town. I wore size ten, my father a size nine; whoever had left the prints in the snow wore a much larger size. How were we ever to know who it was?

"Well, it was someone," my father said, "and he better hope I never find out who he is."

On nights when I didn't have basketball practice—game nights—I came home after school and went to my room, where I stretched out on my bed, a quilt over me, and read until my eyes grew heavy and the blue dusk began to deepen into night. Most of the time I was alone in the house. In her retirement, my mother had taken a job at the local nursing home, where she worked as a housekeeper, a cook, a laundress. My father was usually either doing something at our farm or loafing in the barbershop before making his way home.

One evening shortly after my father had discovered the tracks, the house was, as usual, still. The only sounds were the roof joists popping as the sun went down and the frigid temperatures of night set in, and the wall furnace clicking on and off, the gas jets roaring to life. I made myself cozy in that silence. I didn't have to be on guard, worried over the next thing I might do or say to provoke my father. I was free to settle into a sound and peaceful sleep.

But now I had the eerie feeling of knowing that someone had stood at our windows and looked into our house. I hated thinking of what he must have seen—my fights with my father, my mother kneeling each night before bed to say a silent prayer, the times when my father called upon me to help him with something: to settle his eyeglasses on his face, to hold a drinking glass so he could close his hook around it, to unzip his pants so he could use the bathroom, to zip them back up when he was done.

Those things were the hardest to imagine a stranger seeing, those private times when my mother was at work and my father had needs only I could fulfill. His voice was shy when he made these requests. He became even more timid as he passed into his old age, on the occasions I had to bathe him or clean him after he'd used the toilet. Our eyes would never meet, embarrassed as we both were. We'd be on the other side of our anger by then, but our language would still be the language of old foes, wary and reserved. The language of men who mistrusted our right to this love born from scars, considering it of questionable origin.

I wasn't sure I wanted my father to find out who was watching us. Part of me cringed to think of our privacy violated, but another part of me wondered whether the fact that someone was watching would keep us on the straight and narrow, make us kinder to each other. For several days running, no anger rose up between us. I came home from basketball practice to the supper my mother had kept warm for me, and as I ate, my father sat at the table with me. We talked in normal tones about how the team was playing, the games that were coming up, how I was doing in school. My father had always taken an interest in my athletics and my schoolwork, but now there was no criticism in what he had to offer, no "you can do better." We were just a father and a son chatting on a winter's night, and when I'd finished my supper I went to my room to do my homework and then later came out to watch television. My mother and father watched too, and we were just a family like that, finally switching out our lights and lying down to sleep.

One night the movie *In Cold Blood* was on television. I sat in front of our black-and-white Zenith set, totally immersed in the world of

1950s rural Kansas and the story of the murder of the Clutters on a November night in 1959. They'd been a family—a mother and father and a boy and a girl. They'd been living their lives without a thought that something like this might happen. The mother belonged to the local garden club; the father was a successful farmer. The girl was busy with her boyfriend, the way girls are at that age; the boy played on his high school basketball team just like me. The depiction of the killers moving through the dark house set me on edge, and when they bound and gagged the Clutters and then shot them one by one, I felt that this was all too real, as it had been of course on that November night when Perry Smith and Dick Hickock—not the actors Robert Blake and Scott Wilson, who portrayed them—had committed those brutal killings.

I went to bed that night unable to close my eyes, afraid to sleep. I kept seeing the Clutters, hands and feet tied with rope, tape over their mouths. I kept hearing the shotgun blasts. Then I thought I saw a shadow move across my bedroom curtains. I imagined I heard the squeak of boots on snow. I even swore I heard a faint tapping on the glass.

Who was out there, or wasn't it anyone at all? I was too afraid to lift the edge of the curtain so I could look outside. I didn't sleep at all that night, one of the longest nights of my life, and in the morning there were no fresh prints in the snow.

But something had changed for me. Even now, it's hard for me to say what it was. Something, perhaps, about what it cost to live in fear, to live with the prospect of violence, to always be on guard against it. I'd acquired some knowledge of all that my father gave up when he had his accident: the joy and ease that came from living in the present moment, with no thought about what haunted him from the past, no dread of what might be waiting ahead of him. That's what I'd inherited from him: this unsteady hold on life, this mistrust, this suspicion. Something about watching *In Cold Blood* and then later imagining someone at my bedroom window had made me understand what I'd long felt but always lacked words to call by name. I was imprisoned, locked up inside my father's rage, held in a place I didn't want to be but didn't know how to escape.

On a night soon after my *In Cold Blood* scare, our back door opened. My father and I were in the living room with the television on, but we heard the door, and we both turned toward the kitchen, where my mother was finishing the dishes.

I heard her turn off the water at the sink, and I knew she was gathering up the hem of her apron so she could dry her hands as I'd seen her do so many times. I heard footsteps on the linoleum floor, heavy steps I knew didn't belong to my mother but to who-ever had opened our door and stepped inside—a man, from the sound of those steps, a man who was wearing heavy work boots.

I heard my mother's measured voice. "What is it that you want?"

My father was already pushing himself up from his chair, the evening paper he'd been reading sliding to the floor.

I felt cold air on my legs, and I knew the intruder had left the back door standing open.

"We don't have anything you want," my mother said, her voice rising just a bit. "Are you lost?"

Her question pierced me. *Yes,* I wanted to call out. *Yes, I'm lost.*

But I didn't, of course. I got up from my chair. I followed my father into the kitchen, toward whatever danger might be waiting there.

The intruder was a boy of maybe twenty years of age, a tall, skinny boy with a CPO jacket too short for his long arms. The knobs of his wrists were blanched white from the cold. His face was red and inflamed with acne. He wore a pair of Red Wing boots with stains—oil? blood?—darkening the toes. His wild eyes darted about, first to my mother, then to my father, then over my father's shoulder to me.

"Are you lost?" my mother said again. She actually took a step toward him. "Are you looking for another house?"

The boy swallowed. His Adam's apple slid up and down his gul-let. He held his mouth open, and his thin lips quivered. His long blond hair was in tangles. I saw he had an ugly gash in the meat of his left hand, and just as I noticed it he tried to stanch the blood by wrapping his palm in the hem of his coat.

"Are you hurt?" my mother said. "Let me see."

She reached out her hand to him, and the boy looked at it— veined and wrinkled and chafed raw from the detergents in the laundry at the nursing home. The boy lifted his eyes and looked at my mother with what I believed was yearning, the same desire for her refuge and protection that I had often felt, the same desire to finally be unburdened. I didn't know this boy or what his trouble was, but I knew what it was to want to be free from this life that pressed down on me, this bastard life, a life that was spurious and counterfeit, a poor imitation of the happier one that might have been mine if my father hadn't made a mistake that day in the corn-field, if he hadn't lost his hands and become an angry man.

The boy let his hand come free from the hem of his coat. He studied the cut. Then he looked at my mother again, and in my silence I urged him to go to her, to let her take care of him. I wanted to watch her clean his wound, put ointment on it, bandage it. I wanted her to speak to him in her soft tones, to tell him, *It's fine, it's fine, everything will be just fine.*

The rest of my life was out there waiting for me. I wanted it to be a life of goodness. And I think I wanted to be able to look back at that moment someday and say it made all the difference.

But I can't say that, because just as the boy was about to reach out his cut hand to my mother, my father banged his hooks to-gether.

"Who the hell do you think you are," he said, "to come into my house?"

That's when the boy got spooked. He turned and ran, his boots loud on our floor. He ran out into the cold night, and I felt my heart go with him. I felt something leave our house, some measure of hope. If there had been more room for my mother's kindness that night, there might have been a healing, one that might have saved me.

"You better run," my father said.

I would need years and years to escape the anger of that house, and even now, when I live a more gentle life, I still feel I'm fighting the rage my father left inside me, always trying to tamp it down, always on guard against its return.

I'd lock it up if I could, forget the combination, let the tumblers go to rust, so no one could ever turn them.

"That poor boy," my mother said that night.

I'll always wonder what drew him to our house. Was there a mercy there that my father and I were too blind to see? Was it ours for the claiming, if only we would? Maybe we were too busy feeling hurt to see that we could forgive ourselves; in spite of my mother's influence, we couldn't accept that we, the damaged and the maimed, had a right to a kinder way of living.

My father closed the door that night. He fit the curve of his hook to the underside of the knob and pulled until the door was latched. He opened his hook and concentrated on grasping the tab of the lock inside the knob. He didn't ask for help, and neither my mother nor I offered any. He took awhile, but he kept working at it until, finally, the door was locked.

"That kid was wild," my father said. "He was out of his head." He banged his hooks together again. "To come into our house? What kind of person would do that? What's happened to people? What kind of life does that kid have?"

"He was in trouble," my mother said.

Something in her voice shook me—a note of weariness, a resignation. It was as if she were giving up on my father and me, and maybe she did for that brief moment. Maybe she thought, *God, help them.*

I could tell my father heard the same thing I did: my mother, the eternal believer. His face crumpled with confusion. Had he heard what he thought he did? This was the woman he'd married when he was nearly forty, the woman who'd loved him before the accident and beyond, the woman he'd counted on for so much.

When he finally spoke, his voice quavered. "I know he was," he said. That was as close as he could come to telling my mother he was sorry for all the anger he'd brought into our home. I was ashamed of my own part in that anger. I was ashamed of the two of us.

Although I stayed in the kitchen, some part of me went with my father as he moved on into the living room. I heard his hook scraping at the knob of the front door as he locked it, closing us in, sealing us up.

"You don't have to worry now," he said. In his bluster, I heard what I'd never been able to distinguish in the noise of all our fighting. He was proud. He was watching out for us. This was his secret. His world was always tilting. He was on guard. Let the bastards come. He'd be ready. Wounded, as he was, he knew no other way to speak of love.

LISA NIKOLIDAKIS

Family Tradition

FROM *Southern Indiana Review*

ON MY TWENTY-SEVENTH birthday, in a two-bedroom bunga-
low in New Jersey, my father murdered his live-in girlfriend, her
fifteen-year-old daughter, then shot himself. I never sensed the
shots. I should have felt them in my gut, having been born of the
same blood, the same inheritance, the same home. It should have
been like that feeling one twin gets when the other is in trouble, a
hand burned on the stove matched with the other's intuitive pain.
But the six pints of Guinness I'd slaughtered in celebration of my
birthday kept everything muffled. Instead I felt only the fog of
drunkenness, that genetic trait of its own, and spent the end of
the night passed out in a chair, cocooned in a deep, black silence.

Twenty years earlier, my mother somehow sensed her father's
shot and left her shift at Olga's diner early, certain, never once
doubting herself that it had happened. When she came home, my
father and I were sitting at the kitchen table, the food before us
long grown cold, the news of my grandfather's suicide having quieted any chatter, my younger brother having fortunately spent that
night at a friend's house. My mother took one look at us and threw
her apron down, the smell of it thick with fryer grease, and cried,
her shoulders shaking as she gasped for breath. With an arm's embrace, my father consoled her while she buried her face and wept
into a tuft of chest hair that escaped his shirt. When she raised her
head, my father pressed his forehead to hers in a rare moment so
tender, I knew I was supposed to cry. My first experience with grief.
Instead I sat motionless, a robotic reflexiveness, a brief denial of
my mother's pain as I watched the outpouring; it wasn't until my
father told me to go to my room that I felt anything, my fists curled

into tiny balls. And later, months later, when my mother still cried and, worse, stared vacantly, absently, into nothingness, I began bargaining and making promises to God to make it all stop.

My grandfather's suicide wasn't shocking in the traditional sense. His letters mailed to my mother in New Jersey from the Arizona desert had become increasingly desperate-sounding. He'd been a flyboy in World War II's Air Corps, a fact that made him seem infinitely handsome to me, the pictures of him in uniform epitomizing for my young mind what a man is supposed to look like: broad-jawed, trim, dedicated to his country. I suspect he'd written letters to his first wife, a woman he'd married just months before he left for England, sheltering her from the horrors of war, reassuring her that they would unite again soon, would start their real life. But when the war neared its end and he returned home fifty missions later, he found her pregnant. Within a year he was officially divorced and remarried to my grandmother, who, from what my own mother tells me, looked eerily like his first wife. A ghost of a replacement. Perhaps if the first wife hadn't wronged him, hadn't cuckolded him in front of the neighbors and waged a separate war of infidelity on him, he would've been a good husband and father. Instead he was changed, bitter, violent, and would remain that way for the rest of his life. Years later my grandfather contracted emphysema, a disease that he first tried to pacify by smoking more, and his letters, always handwritten in a scrawling, thoughtful script, revealed his increasing loneliness, isolation, and pain.

I wasn't supposed to read the letters—especially the last one —but I snuck them into the basement when my mother was at work, tried piecing together the parts of her that I knew little about. Their content was considered too adult for me, but even at the age of six or seven, when a vase would shatter against the wall and the chase continued into the bedroom, the thuds and shrieks making it apparent what was going on, I'd slip my feet into my mother's abandoned shoes, tiptoeing through the field of shards, broom in hand. There were hints, clues in the chunky, ambiguous phrases and references to events in the letters, that told me vases were smashed when my mother grew up as well, though she likely held the dustpan back then. Sometimes the letters asked for forgiveness, other times they demanded it, but most often they pointed the finger at my grandmother, accusing her of provoking and prodding and pushing until the violence that he held tight beneath his skin erupted, usually with the assistance of alcohol. And while my mother contends that my grandmother never antagonized, her looking so much like a replica of the woman who initially broke his heart seems to have been enough for him to justify the abuse.

When the war ended and my grandfather returned home, he continued his work with what became the air force, and soon after turned dependently to the bottle, then compulsively to the pen. I imagine him walking toward a bar on Saturday, the sun at its apex, his shadow stacked neatly behind him on the sidewalk, a block of shade, confident in its solidarity. By last call he'd stagger home in the dark with a bottle still swinging from his fist until he hurled it at a cat or a paper bag caught in the wind, the sound of the glass shattering resonating just loudly enough to remind the world that he existed, that he hadn't turned into a shadow himself.

Often I am lumped together with my grandfather in sentences uttered at family reunions, hushed asides of "You know, we had another writer in the family too." The resonance of those whispers appears in my mother's eyes whenever I speak of my habit of writing in a bar. While my laptop seems more evolved than his mass of scribbled-on napkins, I am aware that my pints are made from the same ingredients as the ones he drank alone. Sometimes I wonder when I first walk into a bar which seat he would've chosen if he were there; I wonder if the stool against the wall was his favorite too. I wonder all of this as I light a cigarette and ignore anyone who tries to speak to me, diligent and certain that my one task is simply to write.

In addition to the letters I know about, I assume he wrote stories, though he just as easily could've written rants or essays; I'm only certain he wouldn't have been a poet. I am sure, however, that his work was about the war and his bitter awareness of mankind's absent humanity. I imagine he organized his work geographically, the stories moving through the emptiness of the vast eastern front to the trenched and heavily populated western one; or maybe his thoughts centered around food, his writing recounting memories of home-cooked meals, their spiced aromas filling his boyhood home, pitting them against standard Air Corps rations of tins of bully beef, Diamond Brand tuna, and hardened Arnold's biscuits. He could have put things together according to the seasons, complaining of the bitter German winters, detailing the differences between the rigid expression on a frozen body's face and that of the warm and malleable corpse of spring. Or maybe he scripted his words by recounting his mental stages, remembering the fresh excitement of finally flying into combat coupled with complicated grief for the human beings he shot, those that ran for their lives before collapsing flat into the earth in a plume of dust. His work would have traced his movement, his emotional state from naive young pilot to hardened realist, over the span of many pages, although maybe he was just too horrified to share them with anyone else. But more simply, his writing was likely about how untrustworthy people, especially women, are. Whatever his subject matter, he wrote from the day he got home from the war until he fixed a shotgun between his dry lips and used a makeshift stick his step-nephew crafted for him, supposedly to help him move objects in his room closer to him, to pull his last trigger.

My own father had no war experience or disloyal first wife to justify how a man could carry around so much venom and pain from place to place. Instead my father jumped ship while in the Merchant Marine—a state-imposed military sentence in Greece —which, once he fled, helped perpetuate his paranoia. His fear of government imprisonment for his traitorous rebellion grew so deep that by nineteen he'd made his way to America in search of the kind of freedom that only people from other countries idealize—a belief so deep that it became an innate truth, not just another history-class concept. He embraced America as if the epigraph on the Statue of Liberty were written expressly for him, a solitary huddled mass.

But something about that makes it sound innocent and misrepresented. Yes, he felt that America was the land of opportunity, but not so much for its constitutional guarantees as for its being the perfect place, maybe the only place, for a street-savvy man with infinite charisma to exploit the good-natured and hospitable extensions of the people he needed for survival. My mother was one of the first, a waitress who had long struggled with her weight, self-esteem, and troubled childhood; she served as the perfect person to pitch a campaign of false love on. I'd seen him haggle car salesmen down thousands of dollars on multiple occasions, men trained to be impervious, shaking their heads and my father's hand as he talked them into an undoable deal. I can only imagine that my mother, who had never seriously dated a man, stood no chance against his persuasive platform of bullshit and charm.

Photos of my parents from the early years show them grinning, stuffing clichéd cake into one another's mouths. Smiles all around at taking me to the park for the first time as I fearlessly chased swans deeper into their pond. But the real trouble comes when one knows the end of a story first; now when I look back on those early, gleeful pictures, I see only a ruse. While my mother tells me there were moments of genuine happiness, I can never forget that my father needed a green card more than anything, and my mother, who was subsequently subjected to totalitarian ruling, was ripe for the picking. And like any actor worth his weight, he played the part of the family man convincingly for a time.

Sit-down family meals were stressed as important in my child-hood, always beginning with a prayer and sometimes ending with an Aesop's fable thrown in for good moral measure. But it didn't take long until, even when I was a very young child, I noticed his talking about specific waitresses too often. Casual droppings of Connies and Jennifers at our dinner table, each mention of their names making me more uncomfortable than when a sex scene crept on in a movie we were watching together. Soon after, the blame was placed on conflicting work schedules, and we sat down to eat together as a unit only a few times a week.

"Can I have more potatoes, please?" My father held his plate toward my mother, though he was technically closer to the stove than she. He winked at my brother, Mike, as she rose and took his plate. "Did I tell you kids what Jenny said at work last night?"

Mike and I exchanged a glance, a checks-and-balances system to figure out when things were rhetorical.

"She's so funny," he said and ran his hand through his curls. My mother placed his dish, potatoes piled high, in front of him, and he smacked her ass lightly in appreciation. "She came up and said that there was this old guy at her table who kept pinching her, so she grabbed my arm." He paused to flex his enormous bicep. "She said, 'You're the only real man in this place.'" He laughed proudly, his gold tooth showing, and turned to my brother, six years old at the time, and whispered playfully so we all could hear him, "Jenny's one hot number." He continued at regular volume:

"Man, the other cooks weren't happy after that. Especially Jenny's boyfriend!"

Polite smiles all around, but I kicked Mike under the table.

"Can I have some more chicken?" he asked, and my mother rose to fetch.

My father spoke about Greece with fire, his accent thick as stew, recounting its perfect green sea, plentiful olives, and passionate people, but his descriptions were never concrete. Not really. It was more like listening to the recollections of dreams, that space of bleary disconnect, when he'd recall life in Crete, mixing his fact with fantasy just like they did in Greek school. In fact, until I was about twelve years old, I really believed in the Minotaur and Medusa, though I'd abandoned silly notions of Santa long before. The fiction was so intertwined with the facts that it seemed real. I never questioned it. And a shrine to his island, *his* Crete, hung on my parents' bedroom wall and solidified the truth about the far-off land he called home. A painting proudly displayed the topography of Crete, a cluster of grapes in one corner, a creature with the body of a man and the head of a bull in another. Only recently has it occurred to me that he really could have been from anywhere. I do think of him as quintessentially Greek in almost every way, but he could've just as easily watched three or four Russian movies and sold me on visions of vodka-drenched snow and tall bearskin hats. I rarely saw pictures from his childhood, though I knew he had two sisters, because they visited us in the States when I was a child. I never understood who lived in the house he grew up in—or even if it was a house. I had no idea what his parents did for a living or, for that matter, where my grandfather had disappeared to, since my father spoke only of my *yia-yia*. But more importantly, I never questioned those gaps. He seemed fabricated, a character sprung from the pages of *Bulfinch's Mythology*, and though I've spent most of my life trying to deny the biological fact, he was indeed my father.

When I was fifteen years old, before the divorce was final, before the police had to physically remove him from our home on that last court-sanctioned day, I had it out with him. His demeanor had always been a threatening one—biceps too thick for me to wrap my hands around—but anyone with a history of physical abuse can tell you that the temporary pain of getting hit is nothing; it feels deceptively avoidable and bruises fade. But the emotional and manipulative torture lingers, like an extra ingredient in the body that can never be shaken. Just a couple of months before the final eviction, my father and I, the only two at home, were in his bedroom, that shrine to Crete and Orthodoxy, and with the ruddy icons staring out from behind their encased glass, he threatened me with body blows as I jumped on his bed. When he raised his hand to hit me, a familiar bent elbow, a flash of knuckle, I used the give in the bed to spring into the air and kick him with both feet square in the center of his chest. As he fell back onto the dresser, loose change cascaded to the rug, the wobbling mirrors distorting our confrontation. I told him, yelled at him, for the first time, that I hated him: the first shouted smile of my life. Pure joy in defiance, in the bare truth of the word *hate*. And then, as he attempted to regain his balance, I grabbed my backpack and ran, spending the night in the woods across the street from our home, perched behind a log that allowed me to see my parents' frantic search while it was too dark for them to see me. All fires need time to burn out.

My parents finally divorced when I was sixteen, but it is easily arguable that they should've parted ways far earlier. The horror stories are nothing short of gross, and almost too embarrassing to type: he twice was arrested for indecent exposure, having flashed his genitals to young girls once at the mall, again at a bus stop; he forayed into the world of cocaine with confidence and eagerness; he drank himself into staggering, forgetful, mean oblivions, many ending with him passed out at the wheel in our driveway, waking only when the sun glared too strong. But most importantly, the air in my childhood home was always thick with fear, control, and irrationality. After sixteen years of living with my father, I could barely breathe.

I would love to be the exception in the abuse equation, the girl who tells psychoanalysts where to stick their theories, but I can't. I hated my father, very likely still do in some ways, but I always wanted his love, craved it with the intensity that a stranded wanderer in the desert desires water. So when the bad times subsided, as they always did for periods of remission, and the onslaught of heartfelt-sounding apologies and promises came, I accepted them. The words are clichéd and trite, straight out of Lifetime movies. Barrages of "I'm so sorry" and "You know I'd never hurt you again" are difficult to swallow when they come from the person doing the damage, but though I'm a cynic in most ways, I always subscribed to the hope that people can change—especially my father, who sounded so convincing delivering those lines. And maybe this is why I drink. Constantly repeating a cycle that inevitably fails is enough to drive anyone to seek a happier place to live. My happier place has long since been the bar. Alcohol does not disappoint; it is the perfectly consistent, dependable anesthetic that gets me slightly less in touch with this history but in some ways infinitely more linked to it. The irony is that when I drink, I rarely contemplate the similarities.

The last words I spoke to my father were "Fuck you." At the turn of the millennium. He called the house my brother, Mike, and I shared, and when I answered, he didn't recognize my voice. I tried to convince him that it was me speaking, his only daughter. Thinking it a joke, he argued and insisted I put his daughter on the line. I hung up and he called back. I tried to persuade him again—all three times he called. Finally I decided that if my own father didn't know the sound of my voice, didn't hear in my pleading my desperate need for him to sense that I was his daughter, then fuck him. Tough last words, but I still don't regret them. They'd slowly gathered momentum over my lifetime, formulating stroke by stroke until I had first one letter, then two, then finally two whole, enormous words that summed up what I desperately needed to say.

Mike had called to tell me that he thought our father had been murdered, but it wasn't until hours later, as we watched the eleven o'clock news together at a local Irish pub, that we learned he'd been the gunman who had killed others before taking his own life. Fortunately, it was a Tuesday night, so the bar was slow and we were the only people in the back room with the pool tables and TV. The bartender, who'd known me for years as a regular, helped me double-fist Guinness and Jameson, though none of it seemed to register on my system. We shot a few racks of the game my father had taught me to play when I was far too young to be in bars. I said little and played well—perhaps better than I ever had before. Bent at the waist, positioned at the head of the pool table, the green spreading before me, multiplying, widening, I made my shots, one after the other, my stroke never steadier, the balls sinking with ease. My father taught me those tricks—how to bank, to ride the rail—and I wondered what it meant that I was poised under pressure, that I played his game so well, that my hands were perfectly even. I drank another Jameson, tried to abandon my thoughts.

We played until the news came on. On tiptoe, I reached to turn up the volume and sat back down on the green felt next to my brother, each of us with stick in hand. The Channel 3 chopper-cam zoomed in shakily on my father's house. I couldn't believe how long his grass was; he used to take landscaping seriously. Uniforms—both police and SWAT—swarmed the property, while the perimeter of the yard was spotted with the neighbors who had gathered to watch someone else's tragedy, to have a story to tell over dinner. Mike and I watched in silence as three bagged bodies, one after the other, were wheeled out the front door of my father's small suburban home like some grotesque ballet.

Earlier in the day, the police wouldn't tell us much, so we hadn't called our mother to let her know what was going on; we had decided instead to wait for the facts, to not ruin her workday with ambiguous worrying. In that six-hour span of time from when Mike and I first found out until we saw our father's name printed in fat, bold letters on TV, we hadn't been sure whether he was dead or alive. Too many possible scenarios. A number of them left him alive. We sequestered ourselves in my home first, certain that my father did not know where I lived, and then grew stir-crazy and sure that he wouldn't think to look for us at the Irish pub. My brother had different worries than I did, although he sympathized with mine. My father had embraced him as the firstborn son, the one who would carry on the family name. I was the mistake who, in his Old World estimation, should've been born male, so the abuse tended to land at my feet, not Mike's. If my father were on a killing spree, were, indeed, still at large, I'd surely be at the top of his to-do list. I'm certain my brother felt fear too, but it was likely that of instability. If my father had really snapped, had finally lost it and crossed the proverbial line that he'd always seemed to dance close to but never over, surely anyone, my brother included, could be harmed. Or maybe Mike was just afraid that he'd miss me and hit him by accident.

Two minutes after the story went out on the news, my cell phone rang. I took it out of my pocket, saw that it was my mother, walked out onto the deck, lit a cigarette, and answered with the line "We already know." My mother did not cry then—too much shock and worry to process anything other than maternal instinct. I assured her we were fine; we were at the bar. She wanted us to come over that night, and though Mike did, I couldn't. Instead I stayed until last call, poking at the ice at the bottom of my whiskey until I went home, drank another beer, and curled up on my cold living room floor. I don't remember sleeping or dreaming, but when I awoke, half a Yuengling Lager was still firmly gripped in my right hand, fibers of the carpet pushed deep into my cheek and nostril.

My grandfather's note was eloquent. He didn't want to be a burden any longer and was curious about what happens after death, not at all terrified in the face of that unknown. He begged for those who survived him not to mourn him—he'd been lost years ago. My father, like most suicides, left no note, no closure, no justification. Just a long list of unanswerable questions and confusion.

Ten years earlier, my brother had told me that our father had suffered a mild heart attack. Mike announced this somberly as I shoveled my way through a bowl of Special K. Without lifting my eyes, I asked if he was dead. When my brother said no, I replied, callously, "Bummer." So when the news came and I found what my father had done, my response terrified me. I'd always thought his death would be freeing in some way, a release from the years I'd lived in fear of him and his volatility. I'd believed that I'd managed to forge some sort of peace with my past or had finally drenched myself in enough alcohol to mask the details of my childhood. Maybe it was because, even though he lived two towns over, I'd closed that chapter with those final harsh words. But when I got the news, my entire body convulsed, a pulsing that I'd imagined only people with epilepsy or characters in novels with the DTs got. I felt uncontrolled and spastic, a full-body experience with grief.

I read the police and autopsy reports repeatedly in an effort to understand the literal details of that last evening, but none of that really matters. What does is that all of the history that I'd managed to come to terms with, the years of abuse that I'd crafted into stories and fables, came boiling back to the surface. Had it just been a suicide, like the one my grandfather embraced with his shotgun, I think my reaction would've been different. But this scenario was too reminiscent. My father once held me at gunpoint when I came home from school. A slurred rant about teaching my mother a lesson, a shotgun steadied against the kitchen table to fix its aim. Luckily, his anger morphed into a sobbing grief, and he stumbled down the hallway, gun in hand, and passed out in his bedroom. But over the years, as I abandoned my youthful angst and anger and attempted to embrace a life that actually lets strangers in with a shred of hope, I always, deep down, believed that my father knew how to toe the line between abusive and sociopathic. Yes, he had threatened the lot of us, but he had never crossed over. This time he had.

I'd only met the girl he killed once, on Christmas, just before I told my father off that final time. Like my grandfather, my father shacked up with a replacement family dynamic that mirrored the one he'd lost. The woman was a brunette like my mother—though the similarities between the two stopped there—and the children, an older daughter and younger son, were about as far apart in age as my brother and me. The only reason the son survived the rampage was that he happened to be in juvenile detention at the time.

The girlfriend was troubled, and while I hate to write anything unflattering about the dead, she was an addict. My father told us that he'd had to lock up even cough medicine in his safe because she would drink a full bottle of it in search of a cheap buzz. When I first met her, she was braless in pajamas at four in the afternoon, hair unbrushed, slurring her way through holiday tidings. The son seemed to like my brother, whom he'd met before, but wouldn't say a word to me. Then there was the daughter. She was sweet and introverted and liked to draw—like me in so many ways that watching her draw was like looking into a mirror to my past. Overall she was glum, but she perked up when she told me about her art classes, and when I got a look at her pitiful broken pencils and used paper, I drove back to my house and bagged up charcoals, oils, acrylics, pens, pads—everything I could to make the guilt subside. Jesus, did I feel guilty. I could see in her eyes that same desperation to be saved that I'd felt my whole life, like it was a language only we spoke, and much as I wanted to help her—to grab her hand and tell her we were making a break for it, that I'd never let her suffer through those parents again—I obviously couldn't kidnap her. As I pulled away from my father's house that night, that sinking, guilty feeling gnawed at me so ferociously that the only way I knew how to silence it was with a twelve-pack.

I never went back to my father's house until after the deaths, until it was a crime scene, and I suppose the physical distance helped me repress the memory of the girl that I'd identified with so much that we could've been the same person—we were, in some ways, the same little girl. So later, much later, when I received the phone call and knew people had been killed, part of me hoped it was she who wielded the gun and killed my father like I'd wanted to so many times, but I sensed immediately and innately, directly from my gut, that she was dead.

I went to work tending bar the day after the news. No makeup on, barely functioning, eyes puffed, but I needed the distraction. After a night of describing my father into the phone to coroners and policemen, answering questions like "Did he have any tattoos, birthmarks?" I learned that it was far easier for investigators to throw around words like *estranged* than it is to hear them. I slept in tiny fits that week, passing out for twenty minutes or so at a time, deconstructing the scene, the words, my father, all of it. Estranged. Strange. *Well, he had a gold tooth. No, I don't remember which side.* I tried to picture him smiling. Was it the left? I couldn't be sure. Birthmarks? I considered telling them to shave his head, that surely there'd be a small cluster of sixes under that mass of curly black hair. Estranged. Stranger.

As the oldest surviving child, I became the executrix of his affairs, and spent a week, on and off, in my father's house, Vicks VapoRub dabbed on the divot beneath my nose to mask the smell of decomposition that permeated the carpet, walls, and air. It had taken three days for the bodies to be discovered. My brother helped at first as we went through years of back paperwork in an effort to find something, anything, that would help us legally. A will, an insurance policy, the deed to the house, the titles to the four broken-down cars in the yard. The legal affairs fell into my lap, and it became my duty to sell off his possessions in order to maximize the estate. In retrospect, someone else may have been better suited for the task. I sold his boat at a bar for $500, though it was surely worth more. TVs and audio equipment I gave to friends, and I actually kept a CD player for myself. When I found that it enjoyed making songs skip only during my favorite parts, I took it into the street and smashed it as my neighbors looked on. I also adopted his fish, the only witnesses to the crime, but of course they have no memory. I gave them gangster names and begrudgingly cared for them until, thankfully, one year later, some kind of ichthyosis infected the lot of them and they went belly-up.

Although I did find two insurance policies and the title for a Chevy Blazer in my father's basement, the other discoveries were far worse: dirty letters and sex toys, private fantasies that no one should commit to paper just in case their children one day have to sift through them. Barrels to guns and eleven boxes of ammunition that the police didn't take sat in the open safe, I assume because the mishmash of parts weren't usable without the triggers and grips—though I thought it terribly irresponsible of them to leave that stuff behind. Tax returns from fifteen years earlier. Smutty, bushy, Greek porn. Almost 1,000 empty trash bags on the metal shelves. Burned-out lightbulbs. Receipts of donations to the church. Evidence of bad spelling everywhere. There was a paper I'd written for Greek school on what Easter meant to me that I could no longer translate in its entirety, though I remembered having gotten in trouble for it when I'd gushed about candy and a bunny instead of penitence and Jesus. But the numbness I'd carried with me over the course of that week turned to tears for the first time when I discovered a stained manila folder with my name on it. My father had over fifty pictures of me as a child that I'd never seen—happy, smiling photos that served as evidence of a childhood I simply didn't and don't remember. And while he'd always made sure that I knew that he loved my brother more than me, he had only fourteen pictures of Mike.

Before leaving my father's house for the last time—the last time either of us would set foot indoors, anyhow—my brother and I stood in the living room, scanning the panorama of violence. Just above the couch hung the framed painting of Crete that had been in my parents' bedroom for so many years, and our gazes seemed to stop on it at the same time.

"We should smash that piece of shit," I said.

"Oh, yeah," Mike agreed. "Absolutely."

He hoisted it off the wall and held it between us so that the painting faced us, the end of it resting against the floor.

"Ready?" he asked.

We each lifted a leg and stomped down. To our surprise, our feet returned with a bouncing jerk.

The painting, that embodiment of everything my father stood for, was nothing but a framed beach towel.

"What the fuck?" Mike asked, laughing. "Who frames a towel?"

I laughed too. In the moment it seemed absurdly funny, like a great practical joke from beyond the grave, so we fell into that contagious, ridiculous laughter, cackling until our stomachs cramped and tears crept down our cheeks, but simultaneously we quieted. Our business wasn't finished.

Turn after turn we furiously stomped the cloth, our legs springing back to us repeatedly in failure, so we retaliated with a flurry of stomping, with anger and determination to drive a hole straight through that impossible, goddamned towel. Exhausted, we paused and stared at one another. Finally Mike said, "I got it," and opened the Swiss Army knife on his key ring. He looked at me as though for approval, so I nodded quickly, and he jabbed his stubby knife clean through the towel.

"Oh, you've gotta try this," he said.

And so we stood in that house, the scent of decomposing bodies still thick in the air, taking turns stabbing the beach towel my father had often pointed to when recalling tales of his home. I pierced the Minotaur's forehead, slicing from the tip of one horn down to the center of its dark and broad torso, while Mike took to the lettering, slashing through the words *Crete* and *Greece*, splitting the Hellenic alphabet in two. Had anyone looked in the front door, I'm sure they'd have thought that our mania, our temporary fixedness on destruction and violence, was some depraved family tradition, but we passed the knife back and forth, not speaking a word, carving the faded blue fabric of the Aegean Sea into foamy white shreds until finally there was no decipherable picture left.

JOYCE CAROL OATES

The Lost Sister: An Elegy

FROM *Narrative Magazine*

1.

SHE WAS NOT a planned birth.

She was purely coincidental, accidental. A gift.

Born on June 16, 1956. My eighteenth birthday.

"Help us name your baby sister, Joyce."

We were thrilled, but we were also frightened.

Though my brother, Robin, and I had known for months that our mother was *pregnant,* somehow we had not quite wished to realize that our mother would be *having a baby*.

In the sense in which *having a baby* means a new presence in the household, an entirely new center of gravity. As if a radioactive substance had come to rest in our midst, deceptively small, even miniature, but casting off a powerful light.

At times, a blinding light.

And if light can be deafening, a deafening light.

"Help us name your baby sister, Joyce."

It was a great gift to me, who loved names. I took the responsibility very seriously.

As I was "Joyce Carol," so it was suggested that my baby sister have two names as well.

Names passing through my brain like an incantation.

Names that were fascinating to me, in themselves. Syllables of sound like poetry.

As a young child I had imagined that a name conferred a sort of significance. Power, importance. Mystery. Sometimes when my name was spoken—in certain voices, though not all—I shivered as if my very soul had been touched. I felt that Joyce Carol was a very special name, for it sounded in my ears musical and lithesome; it did not sound heavy, harsh, dull.

I knew that my parents had named me, and that their naming of me was special to them. I think I recall that my mother had seen the name Joyce in a newspaper and had liked the name because it seemed happy-sounding. But both my parents had named me.

My father, who loved music, who played the piano by ear, who often sang, hummed, whistled to himself when he was working or around the house. You could hear Daddy in another room, singing under his breath. The name Carol to my father suggested music, song. Somehow this musical tendency in my father is bound up with my name.

Now it was my responsibility to name my baby sister.

(Did I confer with Robin? I want to think that I did.)

Favorite names were *Valerie, Cynthia, Sylvia, Abigail, Annette, Lynn, Margareta, Violet, Veronica, Rhoda, Rhea, Nedra, Charlotte*—names of girls who'd been or were classmates of mine in Lockport or in Williamsville; girls who were friends of mine, or might have been; girls I admired close up, or at a distance; girls who were clearly special, and special to me.

The writer/poet knows that names confer magic. Or fail to confer magic. The older sister of the newborn baby knew that the baby's name would be crucial throughout her life. *She must not be named carelessly but very carefully. With love.*

My high school friends were nothing short of astonished when I finally told them, as I'd been reluctant to tell them for months, that my mother was going to have a baby in June.

"But your mother is too old!" one of my friends said tactlessly.

In fact, my mother was forty-two years old. I did not want to think that this was *old*.

Having to tell others of my mother's pregnancy made me painfully self-conscious. I felt my face burn unpleasantly as my girlfriends plied me with questions.

"When did you know?"

"Why didn't you tell anyone?"

"Isn't it going to be strange—a baby in the family? So much younger than you?"

With girlish enthusiasm, perhaps not altogether sincere, my friends expressed the wish that there might come to be a baby in their households. In their midst I stood faintly smiling, hoping to change the subject.

Not wanting to think, *Why are you smiling? Why are you so happy on my behalf? The baby is my replacement. I will be forgotten now.*

(Though in 1956, certainly forty-two was considered *old* for childbirth.)

When my parents told Robin and me about the baby expected in June we'd been surprised, and embarrassed. We must have been somewhat dazed, but true to our family reticence, we had not asked many questions. We'd been mildly, moderately happy about the news—I think. At least, we hadn't been unhappy.

Neither of us had exclaimed to the other, *Why are they doing such a thing!*

They don't need a baby in the family, when they have us.

(Indeed, it seemed to me not long ago that my parents told me the astonishing news that I had a "new baby brother" whose name was Robin.

A baby brother! A *baby!*

I'd been five years old. Five and a half. [Such fractions are crucial when you are a child.] I don't recall whether I had known that my mother would be having a baby, or whether I knew anything at all about human babies. Though I would have seen barn cats heavily pregnant, which went on to give birth to litters of kittens, and it could not have been a total mystery to a sharp-eyed child like myself that the kittens had somehow *come out of the momma cat.*

My brother was born at a preposterously inconvenient time, I'd thought: Christmas Day! Was it the baby's *fault*? What could the baby be thinking? Interfering with a five-and-a-half-year-old's long-awaited Christmas Day—December 25, 1943.

His eyes had been robin's-egg blue. A beautiful baby with soft, silky fair-brown hair. How astonished I'd been, and how betrayed I had felt by my parents!

Soon afterward I came to adore my baby brother and was often photographed holding him or playing with him. There is a favorite photograph of us together in which Robin is tugging at one of my long corkscrew curls while I gaze down at him with a kind of prim alarm. But when my father brought my mother home from the Lockport Public Hospital with the *new baby brother named Robin* wrapped in a blanket, my reaction was to run and hide. In a drafty closet of the house I heard my name called—*Joyce? Joyce?*—but I refused to answer. I was determined not to answer for a long time.)

June 16, 1956, which happened to be, purely coincidentally, my eighteenth birthday.

But no one believes in the purely coincidental. There is a predilection in us to believe in symbolism, which is a kind of purposeful meaning.

What did it mean, that my sister was born on *my birthday?*

Apart from the coincidental date, it was natural to surmise that my parents had planned their third child to be born at about the time their oldest child would be leaving home.

So I found myself thinking, though I knew better. As in later years it would be presented to me as meaningful in some benevolent astrological way that I'd been born on Bloomsday—I, who would grow up to admire James Joyce.

(And did my parents name me for the great Irish writer?)

(No, no, and *no*.)

But among the relatives, and among my friends, and among those who thought they knew my parents, it was taken for granted that my mother and father had calculated to have a third child to replace the one to be leaving home. *As if anyone could calculate a pregnancy with such precision!*

The fact was, as my (naturally reticent) parents would indicate, the pregnancy seemed to have been an accident. A surprise, possibly a shock to the middle-aged parents, but an accident with no hidden symbolic significance.

A not-unhappy accident.

As my parents would come to view it, a gift.

"It will be easy to remember your birthdays. We can celebrate them both together."

"Help us name your baby sister, Joyce."

But I was having difficulty choosing. Among so many beautiful names, how to select just two?

I understood, of course—asking me to name my baby sister was a kindly way of involving me in her presence in the family, so that I would not feel slighted, or cast away.

Or perhaps my parents sincerely believed that I was the one in the family who had a way with *words* and was to be entrusted with this responsibility.

Did I love my baby sister? Yes. For I could not help myself, seeing the baby in my mother's arms; seeing how happy my mother was, and my father; feeling my eyes fill with tears.

Was I ever so small? Did they ever love me so much?

It is claimed that the firstborn of a family will always feel, in an essential way, very special, chosen. Yet it seems logical that the firstborn is the one to be displaced, whether graciously or rudely, by the second-born; still more by the third-born.

In a large family each sibling must feel not so very chosen—not likely to feel self-important. Yet, surrounded by brothers and sisters, wonderfully not-alone.

It seemed natural to me that the new baby must nullify the others in my parents' emotions: my brother, myself. The very vulnerability of a new baby is a displacement of the so-much-less-vulnerable older children. This was something to be accepted as inevitable, and desirable.

As if my parents were nudging me to think, sensibly, *You are an adult now, or nearly. You are ready to leave home. And now, you will leave home.*

The name I finally chose for my baby sister was Lynn Ann—for the gliding *n*-sounds.

2.

No. I can't speak of her.
It is not possible. The words are not available.

As she has no speech, so I have no ready speech to present her.
I am not allowed to "imagine"—and so, I am helpless.

*

There is no way. There is no access.
There is only distance, as across a deep chasm.

If there is a way it is oblique, awkward.
It is the way of one foot in front of another, and another—
plodding, cautious of the steep fall.

It is not exactly cowardly—(I suppose: for if I were cowardly
I would never undertake such a hopeless task but flee from it)—
but it is cautious. It is not the sort of pain that becomes pleasurable.

Reckless to press forward when you know you will fail and yet—
you cannot go forward except by this route.

You cannot pretend: your sister was never born.

Spoken quickly and carelessly, *autistic* can sound like *artistic*.

It was not really true that I'd fled to college. More accurately, it was
time for me to depart, and so I departed.

And after I graduated from college, I went to graduate school
at the University of Wisconsin at Madison, where I met, fell in love
with, and married Raymond Smith. And so I never came home
again to live in Millersport.

At the time it wasn't known—it was not yet suspected—that
my sister would have severe "developmental disabilities." For such
suspicions are slow to manifest themselves in even the most alert,
responsible, and loving parents.

After five or six years, when my husband and I were living and
teaching in Detroit, I began to hear that my parents were taking
my sister to doctors in the Buffalo area, having been referred by
her Lockport pediatrician, who understood that there was nothing
he could do, nor even confidently name.

Lynn doesn't look at us. She doesn't talk, or try to talk.
She doesn't seem to recognize us. She will only eat certain foods.
She is getting to have a bad temper.

The term *retarded* might have been suggested. But never did I hear
that word spoken in our household, nor did I ever speak this term
in any way associated with my sister.

There may have been a taboo of sorts, against the articulation of this word with its associations of poverty, ignorance, dementia. A crude word sometimes used as an epithet of particular cruelty.

Eventually, the diagnosis "autistic" came to be spoken. (By my father, gravely. So far as I knew my mother would not ever utter this word, which would have greatly pained her.) Not much was known of autism at this time (in the mid-1960s) but there was a distinction between *autism* and *mental retardation* that seemed crucial to maintain.

For *mental retardation* was not uncommon in the North Country in those years. I have not spoken of the numerous examples of "retarded" persons I'd encountered in the vicinity of Millersport and in Lockport, mostly school-age; how there would seem to have been a disproportionate number, compared to my experience elsewhere, later in my life; so that, when I think of *mental retardation,* immediately I am thinking of certain rural families, and of their offspring, routed into special education classes in school, and generally shunned, avoided, or in some unhappy cases teased and tormented by the presumably normal.

In the Judd family, for instance, there was very likely mental retardation. But I did not want to dwell on this likelihood in writing about my friend Helen Judd, for that was not my subject; that *mental retardation, sexual abuse of children,* and *incest* were related in crucial ways seems to us obvious, but requiring greater length and space to examine.

My grandmother Blanche Morgenstern did not seem to accept the diagnosis of autism, in fact. It seemed to be her (implicit, un-argued) conviction that there was nothing seriously wrong with her younger granddaughter. Year following year she took the Grey-hound bus from Lockport to visit her son's family in Millersport, and with each visit she brought a present for Lynn, as she'd once brought presents for me—coloring books, Crayolas, picture books; each present, as my brother dryly remarked, our sister destroyed within a few minutes, with varying degrees of fury.

What will become of Lynn, do you think?
What will become of Mom and Dad?

It may be difficult for others to understand that very little of this was ever discussed in our family, at least not among my parents and my brother and me. By degrees Lynn Ann became my parents' unique and in a way sacred responsibility, as it is said children afflicted with Down syndrome are particularly loved by their parents; not as a problem but as a sort of gift. You might ask after Lynn in the most casual and sunny of ways—"How's Lynn?"—and the answer was likely to be "Good." But the matter of Lynn Ann Oates was a private one, and such privacy was inviolable.

None of my friends from high school or college would ever meet my sister. My husband would never meet my sister. For nearly fifteen years my parents lived in a kind of quarantine with my sister; few people visited them, for few would feel comfortable in a setting in which a seemingly deranged/retarded girl roamed freely, running in and out of rooms. Or perhaps my parents simply didn't want anyone to visit, which is equally likely.

Until her final illness, my grandmother Blanche continued to visit Millersport bearing her symbolic gifts. My grandmother deeply loved her son and his family, for she had no family otherwise; what we knew of her remarriage, after her young, handsome Irish husband Carleton Oates had abandoned her decades before, did not seem happy, and did not bear examination. (Is it my family's reticence, or is this not-wishing-to-violate-another's-privacy commonplace?) Perhaps it was an expression of love, respect, dignity that you did not ever ask any question that would embarrass another or suggest that a facade of domestic happiness was not altogether sincere.

Certainly no one spoke of Lynn in any way other than casual. In my memory, any discussion of Lynn was not welcomed at all.

What will become of us! We are badly in need of help.

Foolish to have left my paperback copy of Henry James's *The Golden Bowl* on a table in my parents' living room. I'd come home to visit for a few days and, unthinking, left some of my books where Lynn could find them. All the books were destroyed but it's only *The Golden Bowl* I recall, the irony, the pathos, James's great web of words, printed words, as inscrutable to my sister as Sanskrit would be to me, and for that reason richly deserving of destruction.

Or, more plausibly: my rampaging sister destroyed the book not knowing it was a *book* or even that it was *Joyce's book* but only that it was an object new in the household, therefore out of place, offensive to her sense of decorum and order.

It is painful to recall: my sister would tear pages in her fists, she would tear at the pages with her teeth. She would make high-pitched strangulated cries, or she would grunt, in her misery, frustration, desperation. She would not ever—not once—so much as look at me, though she must have sensed my presence.

(Though she could not have known how uncannily she resembled me, and I resembled her. *Like twins separated by eighteen years.*)

It was inanimate objects my sister would attack, generally. She would never attack me.

(And yet—one day she might have attacked me. As a pubescent child, older, taller, stronger, very likely Lynn would have attacked me, as she would one day attack my mother.)

How vivid it is still, the ravaged copy of *The Golden Bowl* with its eloquent, elaborate, and all but impenetrable introduction by R. P. Blackmur. Badly torn, and the lurid imprint of small sharp teeth on what remained of the pages.

"Oh, Lynn! What did you *do.*"

I was acutely aware of my mother in the kitchen doorway a short distance away, who'd come to see what was wrong. If words were exchanged between my mother and me at this time I have forgotten them.

Very likely my mother had suggested that it was my own fault for having left the books in that vulnerable place where Lynn would find them. And of course this was true. If there was *fault* here, it could only be my own.

In the kitchen my excited sister was on her feet but hunched and rocking from side to side making her strangulated *Nyah-nyah-nyah* sound. It was not laughter, and it was not derisive or taunting —it was purely sound, and meaningless. At this time Lynn might have been eight, nine, ten years old—a child who grew physically, but not mentally.

The confrontation with *The Golden Bowl* had been the child's triumph but it had left her dangerously overexcited; there was the danger that she might attack something else now, or someone.

Still, they kept Lynn at home until she was fifteen. And taller and heavier than my mother, and very excitable. And dangerous.

And that would be the last time I saw my sister, at about the age of fifteen.

It was repeatedly said of her, *But Lynn seemed perfectly normal as a baby. She was so beautiful! She gave no sign.*

Was it so, Lynn had given no sign? Who can recall, so many years later?

In retrospect, we see what we are hoping to see. We see what our most flattering narrative will allow us to see. But in medias res we scarcely know what we are seeing, for it happens too swiftly to be processed.

For it came to be a story told and retold—no doubt recounted endlessly by my parents to doctors, therapists, nurses—of how when she'd been very young, two or three years old, Lynn had fallen and fractured or broken her left leg. For many weeks she had to wear a cast. She'd been walking, or trying to walk; now she reverted to crawling, or dragging her leg along the floor. She wept, she rocked her little body from side to side in the very emblem of child misery. Later it was speculated (by my parents, but also by others) that at this crucial time in her development, whatever progress Lynn had been making—learning to walk, to speak, to communicate—was retarded.

It was said of the afflicted child, *She thinks she is being punished. How can we make the poor child understand, she is not being punished? How make her understand, she is loved?*

Possibly the heavy cast on Lynn's leg had something to do with her mental deficiencies, which grew more evident with time. Yet possibly the cast on Lynn's leg had nothing at all to do with her mental development.

Some years later it would be suggested (by one of the numerous specialists to whom Lynn was eventually taken) that autism is a form of schizophrenia caused by bad mothering.

Bad mothering. It is very hard for me to spell out these cruel and ignorant words.

Carolina Oates, the warmest and most loving of mothers, made to feel by (male) "specialists" that she was to blame for her child's mental disability!

For years we were distressed by this crude diagnosis. We knew that it was not true—my mother was not "cold and aloof," as the bad mother is charged—but this pseudoscience was confirmed by the general misogynist bias of Freudian psychoanalytic theory in which the mother (alone) is the fulcrum of harm—the mother who "causes" her son's homosexuality, for instance. (And what of the father's role in a child's development? Has the father no corresponding responsibility, or guilt?) The fraudulent diagnosis hurt my mother terribly, and surely entered her soul. You do not tell a woman who is already distressed by her child's disability that it is her fault.

So many years later I am upset on behalf of my gentle, soft-spoken, and self-effacing mother, who'd given as much as any mother might give in the effort of a futile and protracted maternal task. My mother was not so much upset as crushed, shamed. And this for years.

Blaming the mother for autism, indeed for schizophrenia or homosexuality, would seem no less reprehensible than the popular treatment of the 1940s and early 1950s for bad behavior of another kind, the lobotomy, now thoroughly discredited.

The misogyny of science, particularly psychology! Those many decades, indeed centuries, when the medical norm was the white male specimen and the female a sort of weak aberration from that norm, when not openly assailed, condescended to, pitied, and scorned. Do you know that the much-revered "father of modern gynecology," J. Marion Sims (1813–1884), was a doctor who experimented on his African-American female slaves, without anesthetics, over a period of years; that he performed gynecological operations, without anesthetics, on Irish (i.e., non-"white") women who were too poor and uneducated to protest? By the by, the revered Dr. Sims also experimented on African-American infants. If you know these lurid facts, perhaps you also know that a statue of the father of modern gynecology still stands in Central Park, New York City—indeed, Dr. Sims is the first American physician to have been honored with a statue. And so for me to lament the crude, careless mistreatment of my mother by "specialists" in child development in mid-twentieth-century America in western New York State is surely naive.

Decades later in the twenty-first century a newer, neurophysiological examination of the phenomenon of autism suggests that the condition is caused not by bad parenting of any kind but by congenital brain damage.

Neurochemistry, not bad mothering.

Still, the old misogyny dies hard. You will still find plenty of people, including presumably educated clinicians, who tend to blame the mother for the pathology of the child.

In recent years there has been a populist, antiscientific movement against vaccinations, based on the (erroneous) belief that vaccinations cause autism in young children; more widely, and more convincingly, neuroscientists believe that the causes of autism are manifold: genetics, environment. No single factor will "cause" autism, but there are conditions that are likely to increase the possibility of autism. Yet unaccountably, at the time of this writing, incidents of autism seem to be on the rise in the United States.

Those of us who know autism intimately have long been baffled by high-profile cases of autism in the public eye. Dustin Hoffman in *Rain Man*, Temple Grandin as author, speaker, animal theorist. Such individuals seem very mildly autistic compared to my mute, wholly disengaged sister, who was never to utter a single coherent word, let alone give public lectures and write best-selling books. (But Temple Grandin's ingenious "hug box" to hold her, who shrank from human touch and contact, might have been an excellent device to contain my sister's fits of excitement and distress.)

It is even being proposed, in some quarters, that autism might be celebrated as a kind of neurodiversity. Just as a considerable number of deaf persons do not wish to be made to hear but prefer the silence of sign language to oral speech, so there are those, among them Temple Grandin, who believe that autism should not be eradicated, if any cures might ever be developed.

This is a romantic position, but it is not a very convincing position, for one who knows firsthand what severe autism is. Even if autism could speak, from its claustrophobic chambers, could we believe what it might say? And how responsible would we be, to act on that belief?

3.

In 1971, when Lynn was fifteen years old, my father at last arranged for her to be committed to a therapeutic care facility in the Buffalo area for mentally disabled individuals like herself who had become too difficult to be kept at home. This was a decision very hard for my parents to make, though it would seem, to others in the family, belated by years—long overdue.

One day my sister had turned on my mother in the kitchen. Since neither of my parents wished to speak in any way negative or critical about Lynn, and did not willingly respond to queries about their safety in continuing to keep her at home, I never learned any details of the attack. But I had long worried that something like this might happen, and that my mother, who spent virtually all her waking hours caring for my sister, might be badly injured; or at the very least that my mother would be exhausted and demoralized.

You could not simply say to such devoted parents, *But you have to put Lynn in a home! You are not equipped to take care of her.*

My normally reasonable father was not reasonable when it came to discussing this domestic crisis. It was not advised to bring the subject up, for Daddy would quickly become defensive and incensed. To speak in even a hushed and apologetic voice was to risk being disloyal, intrusive. The strain on my mother, who was Lynn's primary caretaker, day following day and week following week for years, was overwhelming; eventually her health was undermined. I would one day learn that my mother was taking prescription tranquillizers to deal with the stress of taking care of Lynn, and this with my father's approval. My father, of course, spent most of his time at work—out of the house.

By this time my parents were living in a small ranch house they'd had built on the original farm property; the old farmhouse and the farm buildings had been demolished. My Hungarian grandmother, Lena Bush, had died. My brother Robin—that is, Fred Jr.—was in his late twenties, married, and living some miles away in Clarence, New York. The old life of the farm, the life of my childhood, was irrevocably lost, and in its place, it sometimes seemed, was a surreal nightmare of domesticity: my beloved parents, no longer young, in a single-story clapboard ranch house like so many others on Transit Road, obsessively tending to their mentally ravaged daughter who so uncannily resembled the elder daughter whose place she had taken.

It must have been a relief for my parents, particularly my mother, when Lynn was at last committed to a facility—yet at the same time, a kind of defeat. They had tried so hard to keep their daughter at home; they had not wished to concede that something was wrong with her, and that she might be a danger to others as to herself. *They had loved Lynn no less than they'd loved their older daughter and their son, Fred, and this love for Lynn would never abate.*

In this facility near Buffalo, which specialized in the care of autistic and other brain-damaged young people, my sister would receive excellent professional care. Eventually she was placed in a group home with five other patients; all were taken by van to a school for the disabled, five days a week, six hours a day. In these highly structured communities it is said that the mentally disabled are happiest.

It is the exterior world that distresses them, the world inhabited by their "normal" brothers and sisters. For in their confined world they are safe and at peace.

I would think she has a horrible life but she does not seem sad—so my brother has said.

The shiny helmet looks heavy and unwieldy but in fact it is made of a very light plastic. The interior is padded and is (said to be) comfortable, like the interior of a bicycle helmet. The chin straps are easily adjustable and (it is said) not likely to cause strangulation or injury except in the most freakish of circumstances when the afflicted individual is bent on injuring himself.

At some point in adolescence Lynn began to suffer seizures that resembled epileptic seizures. Though these are controlled to a degree by medication, she is obliged to wear a safety helmet at all times except when she is secure in her bed.

Doctors have said, *She isn't angry. As we understand anger.*

Carefully they have said, *Your sister does become frustrated. It is typical of those with her condition, to become frustrated. Her face is sometimes contorted in what appears to be a look of rage or anguish but it is not a psychological or emotional expression of the kind one of us might feel. It is an expression caused by a muscular strain or spasm in the face.*

Do not think that it is hostility directed toward you.

Do not think that she is aware of, or in any way responding to, you.

Across this abyss, there is no possibility of contact.

It is romantic to think so. It is consoling to think so. And so my parents never gave up hoping, and perhaps (they imagined) they were able to bridge that abyss. Certainly they brought Lynn home with them every Sunday without fail until they were too ill and too elderly to do so, even after she began to have seizures occasionally, and had to wear her safety helmet at all times during the day; even when it was clear that she did not know them and that after a while in their house, always kept clean and tidy before her arrival, she began to fret with discomfort, wanting badly to be returned to the facility that was now more familiar to her, and more, if she'd had a word for such a place, her home.

No one would have wished to contest my parents' conviction that they could communicate with their younger daughter. Nor did they speak of it. Their love for this daughter was intensely private, even as it appeared to be, to others in the family, infinite in its patience, generosity, fortitude. This is what is meant by "unqualified love"—that does not diminish over time. It is heartrending to think that my parents loved my brother and me in this way also, not more than they loved our sister but surely not less, and not because of religious conviction, or even ethical principle, but because this was their nature.

A parental love as natural as breathing, or dreaming.

Your sister has never once acknowledged you.

Your sister has never once looked at you.

Your sister has never once glanced at you.

Your sister has no idea who you are, what you are.

That you are, that you exist, your sister has no idea.

No idea that anyone else exists, as she can have no idea that she herself exists.

If there is a riddle, your sister is the riddle.

Here is the *tough nut to crack*. The *koan*.

Disconcerting how with her dark-brown eyes, wavy dark-brown hair, and pale skin, your younger sister so resembles *you*.

Anyone who sees her and sees you—looks from one to the other —feels this frisson of recognition: how your sister who is eighteen years younger than you and who has never uttered a word in her entire life so strikingly resembles *you*.

She will not meet your eye no matter how patiently, or impatiently, you wait. For she is not like *you*.

She is an individual without language. It is not possible for you to imagine what this must be, to be without language.

For nearly sixty years she has lived in silence. She does not hear the voices of others as we hear voices; but she has learned to hear in her therapeutic classes at the facility. Her own speech is grunts, groans, moans, whimpers, and cries of frustration and dismay. She does not laugh; she has not ever learned to laugh.

In the presence of the brain-damaged we find ourselves in the

Uncanny Valley. It is we who are made to feel unease, even terror. I am made to feel guilt—for I have had access to language, to spoken and written speech, and she has not. And this, by an accident of birth.

Not what we deserve, but what is given us.

Not what we are, but what we are made to be.

I have not seen my afflicted sister since 1971, when she was fifteen years old. Tall for her age, wiry-thin, gangling, with pale skin, an expression on her face of anger, anguish—or as easily vacancy and obstinacy. *A mirror-self, just subtly distorted. Sister-twin, separated by eighteen years.* Though I have thought of Lynn often in the intervening years, I have not seen her; initially, because my parents would not have wished this, and eventually, because such a visit would be upsetting to her, as to me. And futile. *She would not know me, nor even glance at me. What I would know of her, I could not bear.*

It is difficult to imagine a mouth that has never uttered a single word, and has never smiled.

Eyes that have never lifted to any face, still less locked with another's gaze.

All literature—all art—springs from the hope of communicating with others. And yet there are others for whom the effort of communication is not possible, or desirable.

Seems like she doesn't know we're here.

What do you think she is thinking?

Perhaps this is the unanswerable question: Does the brain *think*?

If the brain is sufficiently injured, or undeveloped: Can the brain *think*?

In itself, perhaps the brain does not *think*; it is the human agent within the brain, which some have called the soul, that *thinks*. And yet—can a soul, or a mind, be differentiated from its brain? We speak of "our" brain as if we owned it, in a way; as we might speak of "our" ankle, "our" eyes. But such common usage is misguided, perhaps. *We are nothing apart from our brains, thus it is our brains that think. Or fail to think.*

Obviously, our brains generate consciousness—but this is an unconscious process. We are habituated to believe, at least in our Western tradition, that "we" are located somewhere inside our brains, behind our eyes; for it is our eyes "we" see through. When we look into the eyes of others, as we speak to them, we are looking "into" the brain, that is, the core of personality—or so we think. (It is unnerving to think that just as our personalities reside in an organic, perishable brain, in some infinitely vast network of neurons beyond all efforts of tracking, the personalities of others reside in a similar place.) Except, of course, in some individuals, there is no eye contact—the brain refuses to function in accord with our expectations.

In April 2014, fourteen years after our father's death, in response to a query, my brother brings me up-to-date on our sister's condition, which seems unchanged: *Lynn is totally nonverbal and does not talk at all. She has frequent seizures and wears a helmet at all times to protect her when she falls . . . She does not recognize me nor do I think she recognizes anyone at all. She is shy, and does not like it when her routine is changed.*

It would have startled and displeased my parents, if I'd suggested going to visit Lynn in her facility; it would have seemed intrusive to them, for they would have surmised that if I visited my sister, it might be for the purpose of writing about her; and they would not have wanted me to write about her, not then, not ever. And so I had not ever inquired about visiting her—though I had many times fantasized about visiting the now-adult woman who very likely closely resembles me as I would have been if at birth some neurological catastrophe had occurred to render my brain impaired. And after sixty years, as I contemplate visiting Lynn at last, with my brother Fred, I feel faint with dread, and guilt.

For the fact is, the visit would not benefit Lynn, only me. The visit would be intrusive and upsetting to her, who is upset by any break in her routine. Only my brother has visited Lynn, in the years since my parents' deaths. But Lynn does not recognize him, has no awareness of him, and for him too such visits are futile; except as Fred Oates Jr. is Lynn's guardian, he has no role in her life. Yet my brother has (heroically, I think) acquitted himself fully as her guardian, and has borne the responsibility he'd accepted at my father's request.

"Help us name your baby sister, Joyce."

It was a festive time. It was, in fact, my birthday: my eighteenth birthday. I had not been forgotten after all.

My parents smiled with happiness. It was their hope, if I helped to name my sister, that I would love her too.

This was long ago. Yes, it was a happy time.

For so much lay ahead, unanticipated. No reason to anticipate the wholly unexpected of years to come.

After days of deliberation I presented my parents with the name that seemed to me the ideal name — *Lynn Ann Oates.*

A very nice name, they said. "Thank you, Joyce."

MARSHA POMERANTZ

Right/Left: A Triptych

FROM *Raritan*

1. Share/Split

MY FRIEND BOA slithered up the stairs beside me to my room, keeping a lower profile than such well-known confidants as, say, Christopher Robin's bear. Boa was a bootlace strung with red, yellow, blue, and green wooden beads, and as I led him by the knotted nose, I told him how things were in the world. He was always pleased to give my findings independent confirmation.

The facts:

1. *Mothers don't eat.* It had come to my attention that mothers were fueled by something other than food: possibly telephone talk and worry. I wondered how old you had to be to turn into a mother and not have to eat anymore.

At breakfast my mother would hover ominously as I moped over my oatmeal. At lunch she would often be cleaning, exuding busyness and wearing a kerchief that swept her hair up from the nape and tied in a knot above her forehead—like Alice's headgear in *The Honeymooners,* only the Russian-immigrant version, a flower print with strong, blotchy pinks. At dinner, as Lowell Thomas brought the news from North, from South, from East, from West, my mother brought the lamb chops, mashed potatoes, and thoroughly boiled vegetables from the stove to the table. Rarely did she sit down with us and eat them. If she sat, she would jump up to get an extra knife, then to answer the phone, then to put the pots in the sink and fill them with water so they wouldn't dry out and exhaust both her and the metal-scented Brillo pad that already oozed rust.

As I ate I distributed dinner to the four corners of my personal geography, imagining an ingested olive-drab green bean traveling through my middle to my left big toe, a forkful of mashed potatoes dispatched to the right elbow, and so on. I tried to make sure that all parts of me received sufficient supplies.

Despite my best efforts to keep all my regions intact under a centralized administration, I learned that

2. *Halvsies is all.* This finding was made not at the kitchen table but in the car on the way to my grandmother's in the Bronx. It was a Sunday; my father was driving the two-tone '51 Buick, my mother sat next to him, and I was in the backseat. Maybe the Yiddish hour was on WEVD, and maybe my mother was singing along, off-key, to "*Rozhinkes mit mandlen*" ("Raisins and Almonds," which she may or may not have eaten). "So if you're our little girl," my father said, the glance over his shoulder falling short of my eyes, "which half is your mother's and which half is your father's?" They seemed to be waiting for an answer. After due deliberation, I awarded my right side, which I favored, to my mother, whom I loved more that year, the antagonism over oatmeal notwithstanding. Years later I was still assuaging my guilt with the thought that the left side contained my heart, location of loving and thudding, so my father didn't get such a bad deal.

It has been suggested to me that this early split was the forerunner of other geographical divisions in my life, such as the attempt to inhabit both Israel and the United States, journalism and poetry, one man and another. My behavior in a swimming pool is symptomatic. Some people, when lowering themselves into an occupied lane, say, "Do you mind if we share this?" I say, "Do you mind if we split this?" The distinction is obvious only in the American half of my life. In an Israeli swimming lane the word for *share* is the reflexive form of *split*, so I say, if I bother to ask, what amounts to, "Can we split ourselves on this?" Which goes a long way toward explaining Middle East politics.

The principle of halvsies also came into play with the youngest of my three older brothers, the only one close enough in age to share a split with. When our neighbors gave us a chocolate bunny and egg at Easter, the gifts were usually stored on a shelf in the basement, where their existence could be denied until the end of Passover. Finally they were brought upstairs to be divided, and then of course the question was who would get the bigger half. Fairly early I learned the moral advantage of saying I preferred the smaller. It felt less like losing. And it was practice for turning into a mother. At Easter I learned another fact, related to the principle that contiguity implies causality: I learned that

3. *Rabbits lay eggs.* They were everywhere together: plush bunnies and dyed eggs nestled in shredded green cellophane approximating spring. Clearly it was a matter of kinship.

There was an alternative, vegetable theory for the origin of eggs, however: the first book I ever took out of the school library, when I was seven, was called *The Egg Tree*, and it was full of pictures of pastel-painted Easter eggs blooming on bare branches. My mother lifted her head from the gossip columns of the *Daily News* to take a look. "Jewish girls don't read books like that," she said. Although I didn't return this book to the library immediately, I no longer had the heart to pursue my research into rabbit-and-egg relations. My heart, in any case, was in occupied territory.

My father the occupier had yet another theory about eggs, which I discovered inadvertently on the rare occasions when I'd come home from school and find him there. He'd be in the hall near the back door, under a light that I noticed only years later was a bare bulb, checking messages tucked behind the warping plastic switch plate. The ritual went like this:

"Where's Mom?"

"In my back pocket." I'd duly glance into the one where his wallet wasn't. "Not there," I'd say. "What's new?"

"*Ah katz iz geloifen oifn dach und geleikt ahn ei.*" Yiddish for "A cat ran up on the roof and laid an egg."

I thought maybe he was right about a cat being on the roof, but he couldn't be right about a cat laying an egg. Even Hallmark greeting cards reinforced the theory that eggs came from bunnies. Then again, I did know that startling things occurred up there on the shingle slopes. For instance,

4. *People roll snowballs off the roof in the middle of the night.* I had very firm proof of this, having woken up in the dark one winter to the sound of small creaks and large plunks from above. By this time I was about ten, and more scientifically inclined. My confidant Boa, under the bed among the dust bunnies and the mite eggs, heard these sounds with his very own ears. If someone was rolling things

off the roof, I thought, I would see the evidence on the ground.
I looked out the window. Sure enough, indentations in the snow
below the edge of the eaves. I ran and woke my mother.

"Someone's rolling snowballs off the roof."

"Don't be silly."

I coaxed her out of bed and into my room to see the evidence
from my window.

"Icicles dropping off," she said. "Go back to sleep."

"I can't."

"You're not trying hard enough."

I swore I'd never say that to my kids. Better yet, I'd never turn
into a mother at all.

Fortunately, I found more tolerance for truth in other quarters.
One night a few weeks later, when, being the youngest, I'd had to
go to bed while family and guests reveled downstairs, there was a
knock at my door. My cousin Miriam came in and sat on the bed.

"How ya doin', kid?" she inquired, with a little box to the elbow she didn't realize was the locus of potatoes mashed with
chicken fat.

I was pleased to have her company and even more pleased
by the revelation she was about to share, not split, with me and
nobody else: she had been born an Eskimo, named Minigoochi,
kidnapped as a child, forcibly imported to the gray geometry of
Astoria, Queens. She gave me extensive details about life in the
igloo and herring for breakfast; none of that oatmeal. I sensed a
fellow displaced person, another being half elsewhere. Maybe the
snowball rollers had been her long-lost relatives and arrived on the
wrong day, signaling high and low.

Years later, clearing out my parents' home after my mother died, I
found in the heavily varnished credenza (my mother, when enun-
ciating, said *credenzer*) a small clear-plastic box containing wooden
beads colored red, yellow, blue, and green: Boa, deconstructed.
I threw him out, or maybe threw him in as a bonus to the tag-
sale customer who bought the busy flowered kerchief, or the radio
containing Lowell Thomas, or the mattress of my insomnia on a
snowy night.

Recently I had lunch with my cousin Miriam and thanked her
for confiding in me about her Minigoochi life. She had no recollection of either the life or the story, but, patting my potato elbow,

accepted my gratitude with grace. It surprised me at this late date that even she had deserted the cause of truth. But then, only half of what I've written here is true. I won't say which half, and I won't say which half I love more.

2. *Milk/Meat*

I learned to tell my right hand from my left by standing in the kitchen, facing the sink, and thinking about the dishes in the closets. At the time I was still too short to peer over the porcelain rim and learn that in the Northern Hemisphere water swirls down the drain counterclockwise.

Right, I knew, was the closet where the dairy (*milchig*) dishes were stored. They were accompanied by the usual array of implements, such as an eggbeater and a potato masher. We called this the *milchika* side, adding that final *a* for lubrication between consonants, like a pat of butter stirred into noodles to keep them unstuck. Left was the closet where the meat (*fleishig*) dishes, with their respective eggbeater and potato masher, bided their time. We called it the *fleishika* side, the *a* in this case analogous to a dollop of chicken fat averting the clumping of peas. "Right" was associated with milk, crumbly white farmer cheese, and sour cream. "Left" was chicken soup, chopped liver, and hamburgers of a doneness in which what juice remained was as dark as the crust.

There was a color code in the kitchen that prevented the mixing of milk and meat. The *milchika* dish drainer was red; the dish sponge was pink. The *milchika* towels had red stripes down the sides, so that red, and by extension, warm colors, meant dairy; you would not use these towels, during some stove emergency, to lift the lid off overly exuberant chicken soup. To do that you would use the towels with blue stripes down the sides. And by the way, how many times do I have to tell you that's what pot holders are for?

As long as I stayed at home, right and left were relatively uncomplicated. Asked to hold up my right hand, I merely did the preschool version of a thought experiment: planting myself so that the seam of the worn linoleum ran under the arches of my saddle shoes, I conjured up the porcelain of the sink, the glossy white-painted wooden cabinets with chromium pulls beneath it, the glossy white-painted closet doors at each side, and voilà, in less than ten minutes the correct hand would shoot up. If butterscotch pudding (*milchig,* in a dish from the right side) was being proffered as a prize for the right answer, the thought experiment could be accomplished in less than ten seconds.

It was at school, when contemplating a first-grade workbook, that I got my directional signals crossed. As I recall, there were two kinds of black-and-white line drawings, accompanied by two kinds of insidious fill-in-the-blanks. The first was something like: *Look, look, Spot! Dick has a balloon in his* _____ (*right, left*) *hand.*

This question, I began to understand, required a somewhat more sophisticated thought experiment than those of my early career. I had to put myself in Dick's place, i.e., pretend I was in the kitchen, but facing the stove, which was opposite the sink. Or maybe pretend I was the sink, with a right-hand closet and a left-hand closet, facing me. Or was I still me, stepping inside the page and turning around, carrying the kitchen closets with me, the cups swinging riskily on their hooks, the cow-shaped creamer lowing morosely at the disturbance, the carefully hoarded, yellowing, reusable plastic containers rolling with every degree of my rotation? Eventually, I figured out that Dick's left hand was opposite my right hand. This was what it meant to recognize another being; I was mastering the difficult arts of empathy and differentiation.

Then came the second challenge: *Look, look! Dick is on the* _____ (*right, left*). *Jane is on the* _____ (*left, right*). *Spot is in the middle.* There was Dick again, that person-in-reverse. But what degree of empathy was required this time? Whose right? Whose left? Were we still talking about Dick's hands, or were we back to right and left vis-à-vis me?

I lurched through first grade somehow, looking both ways *and* up and down before crossing streets, as the principal, at assemblies, advised. I was pretty good at up and down. But this question of whose right, whose right of way, whose way, has continued to plague me. It was only intensified by my twenty years in Israel, where reading, not to say living, is done from right to left instead of from left to right, though numeration, usually but not always, is left to right.

On a visit to the United States sometime during those twenty years I drove my aging parents to a fish restaurant, got out, and checked the hours on the door before easing them out of the car and propping them up on their varifooted walking equipment. We ambled haltingly over to the restaurant, which, at three o'clock, as it turned out, was not yet open. The hours I'd read as eight to four were in fact four to eight. Some might attribute this confusion to my personal right/left handicap. Others, I hope, will blame the rabbis for determining that fish is *pareve*, considered neither dairy nor meat, and can be associated with either the right-hand, red-towel closet or the left-hand, blue-towel closet, depending on which pot it is cooked in and what accompanies it on the plate. Only recently have I been puzzled by this neutral classification of the finned breed. Hath not a fish eyes? If you prick it, doth it not bleed? Then how could it be served with a dairy meal?

My parents were annoyed and disappointed by our ill-timed foray; so much for my good intentions. But maybe I hadn't really wanted to take them to this restaurant. Maybe I was just getting back at them for having had such unwieldy, old-fashioned, overloaded kitchen closets that made my thinking lumber so.

For an understanding of family vengeance—as well as empathy and fish—we of course look to Shakespeare: of what use a pound of flesh? "To bait fish withal." The Bard, incidentally, was kind enough to minimize his stage directions, so that we are spared the question of whether right and left pertain to the actors or the audience. If Christian Portia were to enter stage right and Jewish Jessica stage left, I, for one, wouldn't know where to put myself.

What directional guidance we do get in *The Merchant of Venice* hardly tells us which end is up. The clown Launcelot Gobbo, Shylock's servant, walks down the street and meets his father, who is looking for him and, being blind, doesn't know he's found him. Young Gobbo, apparently settling some dish-closet accounts of his own, teases his father with these directions to Shylock's:

> Turn up on your right hand at the next turning, but at the next turning of all, on your left; marry, at the very next turning turn of no hand, but turn down indirectly to the Jew's house.

I happened to be puzzling over this scene while standing in line at a U.S. post office one day, holding some letters addressed in Hebrew and some addressed in English. I concluded my business, and, with empathy in my heart and stamps in my purse, walked toward the exit, where I reached for the wooden handle on the glass door. No thought experiments: I just took in the ꓶꓶꓴꓒ sign and pulled. The door went nowhere. Suddenly I noticed Dick, Jane, and Spot all smirking at me from the sidewalk. Now in digital color, Dick sported *fleishika* designer jeans with a *milchika* striped polo. "Oh," he said, "the places you'll go."

"*Exeunt omnes*," I replied.

3. Undo/Redo

During my time in Israel there was a family emergency on Long Island. I got on a plane in Tel Aviv, flew for eleven hours, landed in New York, took a taxi to my parents' house, picked up the car keys, went out, slamming the door, realized I had locked myself out, remembered which basement window might be unlatched, backed myself into it, landing feetfirst in a sink, got the house keys, dashed out the door, drove to the hospital, parked in a garage, entered the lobby, and stood by a potted ficus deciding whether to go first to my mother with heart failure on the seventh floor or my father half-paralyzed by a stroke on the fourth. A dry leaf from the detritus around the basement window apparently still clung to the elbow of my sweater; a man passing plucked it off, smiling, and handed it to me.

My mother, in a frail voice from her bed—I have the impression of pink, but nothing was pink there, only blanched skin and bleached sheets—my mother, whose warnings and interpretations I usually rejected, said, "Go see him but try not to be shocked." I walked slowly down the corridor, over beige linoleum squares, practicing unsurprise.

Where, in the middle of my father, was the dividing line, the hyphen in half-dead? I imagined a column of hyphens, like vertebrae, held in proximity by cartilage and air and the goodwill of some unintentioned Being. Or the same hyphens, each rotated 90 degrees, the way you pivot a gurney to get it through the door, hyphens turned vertical, forming a semi-permeable perforated line, allowing a little life to ooze through, osmotic, from left to right, and a little death from right to left. If you listened closely you could hear the backwash, like blood murmuring around a weakened heart valve.

All this so as not to look at his face, which asked me how much

I was willing to know of who he now was. And what did I know before?

The German artist Hannah Höch made *mischling* photomontages in her series *From an Ethnographic Museum*, showing alien eyes, unpaired, in an unsuspecting face; exposing rough seams between cultures, raveled and frayed. One montage, *Abducted* (1925), shows an African sculpture of four bare people riding the long back of a beast, two women between two men, all facing left. But Höch replaced the head of the first woman with a Western profile facing right: pale skin, bobbed hair, lipstick on an appalled mouth open in protest against this inexorable motion. The hostage has as much chance of reversing her fate as someone sliding backward through a small, low window, trying to get unborn.

Anthropologist Mary Douglas wrote about discreteness of categories as the essence of purity in many faiths and cultures. According to this theory, something is unkosher—unfit, unseemly —if it mixes attributes of two or more categories, as lobsters and shrimp do, for instance: *mischlings* living in the sea but having no fins or scales, not swimming but walking on the seafloor.

All this so as not to look at his face.

Every day for a couple of weeks I exercised my father's dead half, moving the leg out slightly from under the sheet, bending, straightening, bending, straightening skin, bone, and string of muscle. Someone in charge had told me this would help circulation, maybe muscle tone; there was hope of restoring use. I explained to my father what I was doing, but I never knew what he absorbed. Words would come out of him from time to time, but I couldn't tell if those were words he intended. Gradually it became clear that nothing in his leg would change, and one day I gave up. Later I pictured the scene as something from a grade-B cowboy movie: lying on a craggy ledge, I had slowly disengaged my fingers, numbed by his dangling weight, and let him slide over the edge. I wondered if he had felt himself slip. His left hand clutched my right arm against the bed rail.

In the next stage of betrayal I moved him on a gurney through the underground passage from the hospital to the geriatric institute, from the live side to the dead side. He and my mother had been volunteers in "geriatrics," and he had often wheeled patients back and forth through that tunnel for X-rays and tests. I had witnessed his usefulness, his hand on the shoulder of a man in a wheelchair, his nearly nonchalant pressing of the elevator button, his unmindful placing of one foot in front of the other. Did he know now that he was going in the final direction to the last place?

One day I shaved him carefully, crying, and went back to Israel. Years later I saw a 1934 marble sculpture of Giacometti's: half head, half skull, with open mouth and closed jaw. I recognized the cheekbones.

I picture time flowing from left to right, like prevailing winds on a flat map. On my computer screen is a little arrow labeled UNDO, curving back toward the left. REDO curves toward the right. Through the open window above my desk I hear a baby crying. I click UNDO: silence. Unnerved, I click REDO. The baby cries again. I can huff, I can puff, I can blow the winds back.

At the nurses' station on my mother's floor in an old-age home, four years after my father's death, there were signs to help people get their bearings: THE WEATHER IS (CLOUDY, RAINY, SUNNY). Once a sign said TODAY IS TUESDAY on Wednesday. It would be right in another six days, but who had another six days?

On the day that turned out to be my mother's last, bad weather took over her body. She tossed from one side of the bed to the other, her head missing the pillow and thumping against the bars. "Wow," she said, and then: "What's happening?" I was trying not to be shocked and so was she, but I could tell she wasn't trying hard enough. Months later I found a photo of a gargoyle in the newspaper travel section, with the same startled eyes.

When one of my brothers and I were called back later that night, whoever she was had already been abducted. Her jaw was tied up with a towel, in the old-fashioned toothache style, apparently to stop her from asking "What's happening?" wherever she was going, or from saying mean things. When I was a kid she used to say, "Do that again and I'll knock your block off." And one night just a few months earlier, when I was visiting her at home and had tucked her in and put the water glass in its place and the Tylenol in its place so she could find them in the night of her "legal" blindness, she turned toward me and said, "Who's going to do this for you?"

I had cut out the picture of the gargoyle, thinking maybe I'd make a photomontage. I'm still wondering what could share that page.

JILL SISSON QUINN

Big Night

FROM *New England Review*

THE U.S. CONTAINS more species of salamander than any other country, but in an entire lifetime you may never encounter one. Salamanders—secretive, fossorial, nocturnal—exit underground harbors only in darkness. Even those that gather in great masses to breed do so without a sound, moving monklike through the yammering of wood frogs and spring peepers to ephemeral ponds.

In the country's eastern half, many folks would be surprised to find they share their neighborhoods with *Ambystoma maculatum*, the spotted salamander, a creature that looks like it belongs in the Amazon. Two uneven rows of big bright-yellow dots extend from head to tail on its dark, glossy body, a body I have always thought looks purple, though most field guides describe it as steel-gray or black. Spotteds are stout and medium-sized; at four to seven inches long, they look like they'd make a good meal for something. But they're not easy to find. Scientists tracking them with radio telemetry, through tiny transmitters surgically implanted into the salamanders' midsections, discovered one spotted salamander living four feet underground. To find one of these brightly colored animals beneath a rock or within a log feels like hitting the jackpot.

My interest in salamanders renewed with surprising force the same spring my husband and I began the process of adopting a child. I had recently moved away from an area of high salamander density (from New Jersey, which has sixteen species, to Wisconsin, which has only seven) and ceased teaching environmental education; instead I was teaching English and spending my workdays indoors. Nevertheless, I aimed to be present for the annual nocturnal mass breeding of the spotted. There was a chance I would see them and a chance I wouldn't, these creatures that seemed scarce but were relatively numerous, that lived singly all year long but on a single evening gathered in multitudes. It was just this odd combination of uncertainty and possibility that I would need to embrace in my journey to becoming a parent.

What's more, the adoption process seemed at times (excuse the pun) rather cold-blooded. Mechanical. Deliberate. Too conscious. Take, for example, the initial paperwork, a long list of characteristics we had to decide whether we would accept in a child. We had checked "yes" for premature birth and low birth weight, and "maybe" for developmental delays and failure to thrive; "yes" for heart murmur, but "no" for heart defect; "yes" for cleft lip and club foot but "maybe" for epilepsy and microcephalus; "yes" for diabetes but "no" for hemophilia. Under both hearing and vision we'd checked "yes" for partial loss and "no" for total loss. Somewhat contradictorily, we'd checked only "maybe" for tobacco, alcohol, and drug use during pregnancy but "yes" for *no* prenatal care. We'd checked "yes" for criminal history in background, "yes" for mental illness, and "yes" for all the ethnic groups listed. We'd folded the paper into thirds, slid it into an envelope, and mailed it to the adoption agency we had selected, to enter it in the May lottery.

This was in March. As we waited to hear if we'd won, I needed something else to anticipate that, like a child, had as yet eluded me. I needed something to actively look for, something I couldn't be sure I would find.

Many have attributed the "child wish," as it is called rather poetically in the scientific literature, to biology—a yearning innate and necessary for survival. "This gazing at my child," essayist Lia Purpura has written, "is a kind of eating, it is that elementally nourishing." It seems reasonable to assume a species would die out if it did not have an inborn drive to create offspring. But natural selection would hardly hinge a species' survival to a desire for such a delayed effect. And for most of our evolution we didn't even know what act created children. If the biological child wish were true, we would be in peril—ingrained with a strong yearning for a particular end yet lacking any knowledge of how to achieve it; *this* would have caused extinction. By now the truth should be obvious:

what we have an innate biological drive for is the *creating*, not the offspring. It's sex we want, not children.

It appears, though, as if the human desire for children is innate simply because it is so common; most people want to and do have children. According to the U.S. Census Bureau's American Community Survey, in 2008 the number of women who had given birth ranged from 6 percent of teenagers aged fifteen to nineteen to 82 percent of women aged forty to forty-four. So by the end of their childbearing years, most women have borne children—more than three-fourths, a solid majority. Of the 6 percent of married women, per the Centers for Disease Control, who have complete infertility, many seek alternative methods of fulfilling the child wish. More than 1 percent of infants born in 2012 were the result of assisted reproductive technology (ART), a number that does not include the likely high and rarely publicized number of failed ART attempts. In addition, 1 percent of all women aged eighteen to forty-four, about half of whom already have a child through birth, have adopted.

These last two groups clearly want children. They've gone well beyond the mechanisms nature has provided to acquire them: the first may have induced ovulation with drugs and undergone multiple cycles of in vitro fertilization, accepted eggs into their bodies they did not create and sperm from men they've never met; the second has perhaps made uncomfortable decisions about the sort of child they want—its age, ability, race, and, for a little more dough, gender—and spent so much time preparing and signing paperwork that the process may begin to feel more akin to divorce than adoption. Both cases require significant amounts of money and entertainment of the child wish for much, much longer than the year it takes most people to have a child naturally. So when we go to such extremes to have a child, is it really the child wish we're fulfilling, or has the wish taken on some other nature? In other words, what exactly is it we desire when we desire children?

I've always been fascinated by salamanders. Early on, I saw them retreating now and then beneath a ring of pioneer-laid stones around a favorite spring in the woods where I grew up. Later, walking off some adolescent woe, I leaned into a steep hill, brushed away leaves, and found the soil beneath so moist and rich with salamanders I could hardly believe it. (Long before, there would

have been unbelievably more: the nonnative earthworm, brought
to America in European ship ballast, gobbles up the forest's leaf
litter, leaving less to support our native invertebrates and thus
fewer invertebrates to feed our woodland salamanders, then, finally, fewer salamanders.) In my job as an environmental educator
in New Jersey I taught elementary- and middle-school students.
Salamanders, if you knew where and when to look, were often the
easiest thing to conjure up for a hundred city kids who had just
two and a half days to spend in the woods. Salamanders are more
numerous than turtles. They are easier to catch than frogs. You
kneel at a forest seep, fingers numb, lifting and replacing rocks
wrapped in moss, one after another. Most reveal nothing. But then
something happens in the mud beneath an upturned stone: what
looks like just the current of the stream escaping becomes a salamander.

In general, salamanders don't bite, though, surprisingly, most
do have tiny, flexible, cone-shaped teeth used for grasping prey.
They don't pee on you like toads, or musk you like stinkpots or
mink frogs. They don't scare the hell out of you at first like snakes
do. As long as you don't grab them by the tail (which would be
cruel—many detach their tails in self-defense and leave them behind, wriggling wildly for the confused predator while they escape,
then burn precious calories in tail regeneration), they are easy to
handle. They seem relatively untroubled by capture, staring at you
with dare-to-amuse-me eyes. If you want to commune with some
animal, salamanders can be an exquisite choice.

Many species, despite overall general population declines, are
still shockingly numerous. "If you took all the salamanders in the
forest and put them in a sack," I would say to my herpetology students at the environmental education center, "and then put all the
small mammals in that same forest in a second sack, the sack of
salamanders would be larger." Another comparison: salamanders
make up more than 2.6 times the biomass of birds during the peak
breeding season. Once or twice a year, my students didn't need
these thought-experiments; on a warm day after rain, there would
be mass migrations of red efts, the toxic-looking—and, to a blue
jay, toxic-tasting—juvenile, terrestrial stage of the eastern spotted
newt. You couldn't walk without fear of crushing one. Those days
were a great unplanned lesson on fulfillment and desire. With kids
transporting efts by hand across roads and paths, adopting par-

ticularly cute ones as temporary pets, we never got where we were going. Where we were going became where we were. What we unearthed became what we had set out for.

Salamander courtship and breeding offer quite a few zoological surprises. Up to a third of red-backed salamanders are monogamous, a rarity for amphibians—though their monogamy, it turns out, is more social than reproductive. Many terrestrial salamanders guard their eggs, curling body or tail around their clutch in the kind of circumferential hug one might more reasonably expect of a canine or rodent. But perhaps nothing tops the reproductive behavior of the spotted, which once a year holds a bacchanalian nuptial dance that lasts into the wee hours of the morning.

No one is sure what drives the various species of ambystoma, the mole salamanders, out of the networks of small mammal burrows they occupy singly for up to fifty-one weeks of the year, to mate in spring. Because they all appear at the same time, migrating to safe, fishless waters, herpetologists have come to call this event "Big Night." To ambystoma, the essential factors for Big Night must be quite precise. But to us, with our calendars and thermometers and sling psychrometers, it's just another numbers game.

They emerge in the first warm rain after winter. But how warm and how rainy is anybody's guess; different studies conclude different temperatures, and sometimes just fog or sudden snowmelt is enough. The most accurate predictor may have been right under our noses—or our feet—all along: in a ten-year study of mole salamanders in St. Louis County, Missouri, mass migrations started when soil temperatures a foot deep reached at least 40.1 degrees Fahrenheit *and* the thermal profile reversed—meaning it was finally warmer at the surface than underneath.

On that aforementioned first warm, rainy night after winter, spotteds return to the place of their birth, likely aided by the smell of the water and plants of each particular pool. In experiments, blindfolded—yes, blindfolded—salamanders have easily been able to find their pools; intercepted adults preferred home pond odors to those of foreign ponds.

Then, under the water, the dance begins. According to James W. Petranka, in *Salamanders of the United States and Canada* (2010), the male contacts the female with his snout, once, twice, again, and again; she prods him in return each time. He circles her ceaselessly, rocking his head back and forth over her back and beneath her chin. Then, shuffling aside, he deposits several packets of sperm on substrate in the water, or on top of other males' deposits. Called spermatophores, these are six- to eight-millimeter tapering gelatinous stalks with little calderas at the top holding the seminal fluid. The female searches for them, a side step with the back feet, a walk with the front. She chassés across the pond bottom, squatting over spermatophore after spermatophore, taking in seminal fluid with her cloacal lips. The mating occurs in groups of three to fifty or more, and with all that twisting and turning of spots I imagine it must look like a sort of subaquatic Jackson Pollock painting.

Although it is referred to as Big Night, the mating period can actually last from three days to over two months; but even when prolonged, breeding usually occurs in just a few major bouts. The point is not to miss it. Because I couldn't know when it was going to happen, by my logic, I needed to be at the water before it possibly could. So all through March I hiked to frozen pools. I wasn't wearing snowshoes anymore—but only because the trail was so packed I didn't need them; if I stepped off the path, winter was still knee-deep.

Five years ago, after four years of trying unsuccessfully to conceive, my husband and I gathered with several other couples at a local agency for an informational meeting on adoption. It was exactly the opposite of Big Night. There we were: the city's infertile, unfecund, no matter our achievements, unable to create in the most basic, most ancient of ways, in a way some people did by accident. There was no need to meet and greet. We knew all about each other—the baby-name books resignedly shelved amid rows of travel guides, all the insane things we'd considered, like postcoital headstands and egg-white lubricant. But in spite of the air of defeat, the faces of the women looked paradoxically triumphant; their determination to be mothers would not be trounced by this refusal of their unborn children to come into existence, to continuously pass out of them like tears, not solid, but liquid. After receiving a fat folder of handouts, my husband and I paraded to our seats, navigating the circuitous route afforded by round tables butted up against walls in a small room. We sat down and took off our coats. I heard something but didn't move. Then, a voice:

"Your wallet," it said.

I turned and saw the source of the sound I had ignored. My wallet had fallen out of my pocket. It was now lying on the floor in the center of the room. The finger of the man who had seen it fall extended toward it, as if accusing us all of what it seemed we were about to do: buy something. Not a baby, of course. What was it we really wanted?

Although the child wish itself may not be innate, it may still have natural underpinnings. Our biological clock is perhaps not set at "baby" but at more abstract things: security, love, esteem, meaningfulness. Such needs can be met in many ways, including having children. And the child wish, of course, like all human behavior, is heavily influenced by learning and environment. Perhaps no other period in history than the 1950s and 1960s, with its focus on the perfect family—think *Father Knows Best* and *Leave It to Beaver*—has made it seem as if not having children is abnormal, that if you choose to remain childless, you don't know what you are missing.

The child wish can be so strong, sometimes good people who want to be parents do desperate things. A week earlier, I had read a blurb in the U.S. news section of my local paper about a man and woman who traded an exotic bird for two children. The guardian of the children wanted $2,000, originally, for the boy and girl, four and five years old, respectively. But the couple, who had been trying unsuccessfully to get pregnant for years, did not have two grand, so they gave her $175 in cash and their $1,500 pet cockatoo.

The "adoptive" parents, according to the case detective, "had good intentions from what we see." But I had trouble believing this, that to buy a child, even to raise it as one's own, was not tainted with the same unlawfulness as to sell one. An economic transaction seemed no way to start a family. Weren't the buyers as much at fault as the sellers? After all, if there were no demand in the first place, there would be no supply. Isn't that the law of economics?

Dutch philosopher Paul van Tongeren has written that a paradox arises when "the manner in which we want something is in conflict with the nature of the thing we want." Although he seems to be writing primarily about the use of assisted reproductive technology, I can see how adoption also applies. According to van Tongeren, the child wish hinges on elements of surprise combined with unmatched love; we don't choose our children and we love them unconditionally. What we desire when we desire children is actually a wild unbridling from choice and control—the most intense astonishment and rapture the universe can provide. Yvonne Denier, of Belgium's Center for Biomedical Ethics and Law, agrees: when we wish for a child, she notes, we want something that by its very nature escapes us, something we are unable to control attaining. We cannot decide to have a child, she writes, in the same way we might decide on a holiday destination, by weighing pros and cons and choosing the characteristics we do and do not want.

Compared to the heat of passion in which one normally produces children, assisted reproductive technology and adoption can at times feel rather calculated. Beyond sex, fulfilling the child wish naturally is passive, a nine-month unraveling from womb to world governed only by imagination. It takes just two people. ART and adoption, in contrast, usually take much longer and involve crowds of stakeholders. Both feel deliberate, premeditated, a long road of things changing hands. ART can feel like playing God, disrupting natural selection, messing with the rhythm of the universe. We measure adoption's progress not by sonograms and tiny knit caps, but in fits and starts of legalese and paperwork. At times one worries that adopting means participating in a system that exploits the poor. One unhinges at the phrases *child laundering* and *human trafficking*.

My husband and I left that day without filling out any paperwork, unable to pinpoint exactly what it was we wanted or to reconcile that with how we were going to get it. We also never set foot in a fertility clinic. Five years passed. We met a couple who did not want to become parents, a friendship that did not require bracing ourselves for the inevitable phone call or dinner announcement that would change every second spent with them to a reminder of our inadequacies. We took up wine and mojitos and went to Paris. We got advanced degrees. Every month we buried the possibility of a child, until we had no more room for grief.

Once, teaching that herpetology session at the environmental education center, surrounded by fifth-graders, I held a northern red salamander we'd just found. As I relayed some fact or another the salamander began to writhe, opened its mouth, and out popped another, smaller salamander.

"It just had a baby!" one of the children shouted.

"No," I said after a moment, gently correcting him, "I think that was dinner."

Many salamanders, including the northern red, engage in cannibalism. The tiger salamander—the country's most widespread species—actually produces larva that can develop to be either cannibalistic or not. When populations are dense, the cannibalistic morph appears. Through smell, it can tell whom it's related to and how closely they're related, preferring to prey on non-kin.

The fifth-graders and I knew that amphibians don't have live births, and births don't originate from the same place as words. But what had happened seemed perfectly natural, expected even: something smaller had come from something larger. So I have to admit, looking down on what had occurred, feeling topsy-turvy from the moment, birth was also my first thought.

The tendency to see death as birth, or link the two in some way, is not all that unreasonable a leap. For an organism programmed for survival, recognition of mortality results in all kinds of tricks of the mind to reduce our anxiety, including, according to one study, increasing our desire for children. It makes sense: children offer both literal and symbolic immortality. They can carry on one's genes, one's beliefs, one's business, one's memory. Part of our wish for having a child is really about reducing our fear of no longer existing.

Is this why, at age thirty-eight, sitting in an airport waiting for our plane after visiting my family at Christmas, watching worn-out parents trying to corral their spirited children, I turned to my husband, who had over the past five years often brought up adoption, and said, "Let's do it"?

Fear of death is hardly the only motivator for having children, and certainly not a totally conscious one. There are a multiplicity of factors, measured by many tools: the "Reasons for Parenthood Scale," the "Parenthood Motivation Index," and, my favorite mostly because of its title, which sounds like something a six-year-old might create to interview Santa Claus, "The Child Wish Questionnaire." I muddle through the research: a whole host of causes for desiring children exists, ranging from happy early childhood

memories to the influence of organized religion and traditional
female sex roles to the belief that having a child around is "nice,"
makes one happy, and provides a unique relationship. Nothing
is that surprising. What actually surprises is the reality of parenthood, which, most research suggests, decreases happiness. Much
has been written about it. Roy F. Baumeister, in *Meanings of Life*
(1992), called this the "parenthood paradox." Perhaps the most
cited indicator of the lowered sense of well-being felt by parents
is the fact that on one survey, women rated taking care of their
children only slightly more positive than commuting and doing
housework. This makes the great lengths folks using ART or adopting go to even more curious.

By April the snow began to melt. I knew the time was approaching
for Big Night. At work, vernal pools strung through my mind like
the trail of shiny white pebbles laid by Hansel and Gretel. One
night I took the dog to the woods. In the past she had stumbled
upon a spotted salamander or two when we weren't even looking.
But that night, when the beam from my headlamp, aimed at curious holes in the mud—probably openings where squirrels had
buried and dug up nuts, or rained-out tracks from deer hooves
—crossed before her in the dark, in the rain, she just looked confused.

If even the dog was flummoxed, I thought, *what would a baby do?*
We had received a return letter from the adoption agency confirm-
ing our entry in the May lottery, but with no information regarding when or where it would happen, or how they would deliver the
results. I worried a little bit. *Could a baby do this?* I wondered.

Could you bring a baby to the woods in the rain on a cold night?
Sit it on your hat or gloves laid side by side—like you sometimes
do yourself—on top of the wet grass while you moseyed around
looking for amphibians? A fear overtook me. How would I change
as a parent? Would I leave my baby at home with my husband while
I went on amphibian hunts? Would I stop hunting altogether? I
didn't find any salamanders that night, but when I got home and
took off my clothes to shower, I did find the first tick of the season.
Ticks don't faze me. But how would I feel if I found this tick crawling over the pudgy little kneecap of my amphibian-hunt-spectating
baby?

A certain level of ambivalence toward parenthood is common.

A 1997 study in the *Journal of Marriage and the Family* found ambivalence toward childbearing in 20 percent of young couples. A 2010 *Journal of Reproductive and Infant Psychology* article concludes that some ambivalence toward childbearing is "widespread." And the 2012 National Center for Health Statistics reports that 37 percent of U.S. births are unintended, meaning mistimed or unwanted—more than a third. Particularly for women, to whom most childbearing and -rearing responsibilities still fall, and who more accurately anticipate all these responsibilities, whether or not to have a child is a complex issue.

And statistics show the social pressure to have children may be changing. One study followed 12,700 U.K. women born between 1950 and 1960 to their midforties. Seventeen percent are childless. That number was 10 percent for those born in 1946 and rose to 19 percent for those born in 1960. Delaying parenthood has birthrates down in multiple countries: Greece, Switzerland, Britain, Japan, Canada. While delaying parenthood doesn't necessarily mean couples will remain childless, it does alter the idea that childlessness is selfish, shameful, or to be pitied.

A married friend of mine who decidedly does not want children—never has, never will—once asked her mother, who also had two boys and another girl (all healthy, all successful), what she thought about having children. The reply: "If I could do it again, I wouldn't." My friend was pleased with the answer, which vindicated her own feelings. And yet, of course, she would not exist if this very woman had not conceived her.

Chances of becoming pregnant through ART, one cycle of which costs, on average in the U.S., $12,400, an amount rarely covered by health insurance, are 40 percent for women aged thirty-five and under, 32 percent for women aged thirty-five to thirty-seven, 22 percent for women aged thirty-eight to forty, 12 percent for women forty-one to forty-two, 5 percent for women forty-three to forty-four, and 1 percent for women forty-four and older. Despite less than promising odds for even the youngest age bracket, each year more than 85,000 women choose ART, on average requiring three cycles (over $36,000) to have a "live birth," a clinical-sounding term which also includes babies born alive, preterm, who won't survive.

Adoption may seem like less of a gamble: if you have unlimited funds, inconceivable patience, and openness to a child with any type of needs, you will end up a parent. But most people do have boundaries. When I looked at the numbers, I was comfortable with the $3,000 required for a home study and initial fees, even though I knew we might never be chosen by an expectant couple considering adoption; but I worried about the unpredictable amount we might pay for prenatal care, legal fees, and counseling to an expectant mother who could understandably change her mind at some point during the pregnancy or (in Wisconsin) the thirty-day period after birth (called a "false start"—for the majority, 72 percent, false starts costs less than $5,000); the possibility of this happening multiple times (38 percent of adoptive parents have at least one false start); or, in the unlikely chance a birth mother with whom we were matched gave birth to a baby with serious defects (chances: less than 4 percent), that we would make the decision to walk away. If we did this, our losses would be big: the entire cost of the adoption (usually around $25,000), any hope of ever becoming parents, and our own integrity.

I wondered how we would fund an adoption should we win the lottery (pardon that irony). I did some research; one article listed hard-to-get grants, loans, and ideas for saving up this large chunk of money, ending, rather ridiculously, with the idea of garage sales and bake sales. *Leave no stone unturned,* the last line said.

ART and adoption both involve uncertainty, though hardly the type von Tongeren and Denier describe that characterizes the child wish. Any uncertainty involved in ART and adoption clashes with a cavalcade of consciously and carefully considered decisions, procedures, phone calls, and appointments. Often you must move forward deliberately in the face of crushing defeat. The child wish can become a child obsession. Why do people go through with it?

I found more insight into the answer to this question not from studies of the motivations of couples considering IVF or adoption (such studies tend to give results not much different from studies of those trying to conceive naturally), but in studies of problem gambling. Research on gambling addiction gleans insight on how we make decisions, how we respond to personal gains and losses, and why we take risks. Humans seem to be drawn to the astounding occurrence, regardless of its likelihood of happening. We are traditionally bad odds-makers. We believe that a win is likely after a series of losses, just as we expect sun after a week of rain, or, if you are looking for salamanders, vice versa—though here our assumptions may be correct, as weather does follow patterns. We abhor cognitive regret—stopping something too early and missing out on the next big reward—and are driven to recoup our losses. There is always the possibility that, although we never know where or when we'll hit it, a big win is just around the corner. *One more rock overturned*, one of my sources said, *and you'll find dinner.*

The closer it got to the adoption lottery, however, I found myself no more distressed about losing than I was about winning. I began, salamander-style, to get cold feet.

The adoption lottery seemed a bit unconventional, despite its being hosted by a licensed Christian social service organization of Wisconsin and upper Michigan. When my husband and I first heard of it, I imagined that if they drew your application, somewhere, instantaneously, a stork that would soon appear above the thatched roof of your own house was plucking a baby from the pond where all little children lie, according to the Hans Christian Andersen tale, "dreaming more sweetly than they will ever dream in the time to come." It seemed almost too good to be true.

The prize, though, if they drew your application, wouldn't be a baby but acceptance into the agency's domestic infant program, just the start of the sometimes multiple-year process of becoming an adoptive parent. It's a popular agency, probably because of its long, successful history of providing good counsel to birth parents and adoptive families, as well as its reasonable fees. So instead of dealing with a never-ending wait list, they hold a biannual lottery.

At the meeting required to enter the lottery, we were told that on two unspecified dates—one in early May and one in early November—social workers from the organization's various offices throughout the state would gather together, number the applications, put the numbers in a hat, and blindly draw a particular quantity determined by their leader. After we mailed in our application, I wondered often about this event. I imagined tiny slips of paper—the one with my number on it, for instance—blowing off a table when someone exited or entered the room before it made its way into the hat, leaving me with no chance at all of being picked. Was there a lottery witness? Did a senior citizen stand against the wall, hands joined together solemnly as on so many states' televised daily lotto picks, to ensure that everything went fairly and squarely? And if, as the social worker informed us, we would be allowed to reconsider the items we marked on the application again at a later date—whether we could parent a child with microcephalus or one born from a schizophrenic, for instance—why was it even on the lottery application in the first place? Was this really some kind of weeding-out process? I imagined the social workers —all women, most likely mothers themselves—laughing wildly at those whose applications indicated a desire for the perfect child, ripping them up, and trashing them immediately. If this truly was a lottery, why not just have us write our name and number on the back of a raffle ticket and, if our ticket was drawn, consider the hard questions later?

Some psychologists believe gambling mirrors sexual excitement, with its repeated buildup, climax, and release of tension. Maybe this is why the idea of the adoption lottery excited my husband and me so much, why we chose this agency over others where we could have signed a contract and jumped right into the adoption process. It felt natural to begin parenthood this way: to cast our lot, and then wait a month or two to see what happened.

Mid-April rolled around. I still had not seen a single salamander. One weekend the forecast was warm and rainy, but I was busy entertaining a friend who had flown in to visit. On Saturday she slept in, and I grabbed an umbrella to walk the dog and check out an overflow area near our lake, finding two deep open holes: turtle hatchlings must have overwintered in the nest and emerged in the last few days. It was a sign of something—but as of yet, I saw no amphibians.

We stayed indoors all weekend. On Sunday morning we missed a call from my husband's little brother. On Sunday night it was still raining. He called again, and my husband disappeared to talk to him. He returned to announce that his brother's wife was pregnant—twelve weeks pregnant, with identical twins.

I left my husband and guest to hunt for salamanders. Many factors were at work in my decision to go out that night, and I don't deny any of them. The major mistake in psychology may be the belief that awareness changes behavior. It doesn't: we like our social pressure, our sorrow, our envy. I knew I should be overjoyed by the prospect of two new nieces or nephews—and I was—but I admit I was also irritated, as if there were some kind of cosmological math occurring that didn't add up: two babies for them, and zero for us.

I drove the streets past every pond I knew, looking for slick salamander bodies in my headlights, wondering how many I was running over in my desperate quest. But it began to snow. In the morning five inches would cover the ground. I became dizzy from the windy country roads, staring into the oncoming flakes with my brights on. The seasons ran through my mind, lapping one another. They tangled in my brain and I couldn't shake the feeling that I'd missed something, even though I knew it was still early. It felt too late.

A week or so later I bought a pair of boots—no matter that I should be saving money—at the local Fleet Farm, the kind kids wear to jump in puddles (or obstetricians, I recently found out from a friend, whose son's birth proved messy and more difficult than the norm). I couldn't believe I'd been traipsing around the shores of ponds all these years without them. I also couldn't believe I was still traipsing around the shores of ponds at my age, a kitchen strainer in hand. I knew I should be shuttling kids to soccer practice, piano lessons, laundering the clothes of *kids* who do this. Was there something wrong with me? Because I didn't have children I couldn't stop being one? I felt like a ten-year-old boy, not a thirty-eight-year-old woman. In an old army ammunition plant near Madison, Wisconsin, a reservoir contains a population of tiger salamanders that, in adapting to their enclosed environment, have become neotenic, retaining for life their juvenile characteristics—feathery gills, keeled tails. They still reproduce, but along with their young, never leave the water to live on land as do most adult tiger salamanders. Officials want to drain the reservoir, seen as a safety hazard, but locals are working hard to preserve it and its salamander population.

The day before Easter I hiked to a pond a couple miles into the forest. It was dry and warm, so I still didn't find any salamanders. For this reason, I was reluctant to put on my boots, which I had been carrying in a backpack. Finally, since I didn't want to have carried them in vain, I slipped them on and waded into the water. That is when I saw them.

All over the substrate, on submerged sticks and grasses, like a thousand tiny glass slippers, lay the spermatophores of now-vanished male spotted salamanders. I picked up a stick where a salamander had laid three in a row to examine them more closely.

They were translucent, the size of half your pinkie fingertip. You might think they were some kind of tree mold, or something a snail left behind. They littered the bottom of the pond like confetti, evidence of the start of the salamander new year. Upon further inspection, I found floating beneath last year's submerged cattail leaves loose constellations of eggs coalescing into infant galaxies.

I wanted to pick them up, but two feet was as far as I could go. I began to sink a little, and water threatened to deluge my boots. I was in the muck.

Despite knowing that the day-to-day tasks of raising an infant (changing diapers, doing laundry, cleaning up vomit) and raising a teenager (worrying, feeling hated) are unlikely to increase my happiness, and that social pressures to have children and labels of selfishness for the child-free are diminishing, I have not lost my child wish. Perhaps my (and others') child wish is so strong because the paradox of parenthood was nonexistent in the ancestral evolutionary environment. When we lived in small clans and tribes, children weren't such a drain on just two people. The "village" helped to care for the howling, nocturnal infant and adolescence wasn't so trying on parents because children began their own families at puberty.

So say Sonja Lyubomirsky and Julia K. Boehm of the University of California, Riverside, in their 2010 article "Human Motives, Happiness, and the Puzzle of Parenthood" (*Perspectives on Psychological Science*). Furthermore, they point out that studies indicating a correlation between parenthood and decreased well-being have a severe limitation: it may not be possible to measure the kind of joy we receive from hanging out with our kids.

Consider this: When my nephew was a baby (he is eighteen now) I carried him along on a hike with my mother and his two sisters. We jumped over puddles in ATV trails where, annually, American toads laid their jellied egg-strings, and descended to the creek where my father had often taken my sisters and me as children. A soft wind blew aspen leaves from the trees. I took in the whole scene. But then my attention was caught by something I will never forget: my nephew's long moment of focus on a single leaf falling to the creek, from sky to water's surface. It was the first time he had seen the likes of this. He had no room in his head for the big picture, for cycles and seasons and laws of physics. His life thus far was a patchwork of private astonishments. Maybe this is what children give us.

The night of Easter was warm and humid. When I walked the dog, the spring peepers were deafening, like some kind of unoiled mechanism inside my ears. Despite my previous day's discovery of the eggs and spermatophores, I reasoned that maybe a bout of latecomer-breeding would happen again that night.

Back home, sweating, I sat in a chair facing my husband, who was on the couch typing up his doctoral thesis.

"I feel like tonight is the night." I said. "It's foggy. It's still sixty degrees. And it's very humid."

I was surprised when he put his laptop to the side and grabbed his camera to accompany me. We made the brief drive to the pool. Right away, when we exited the car, I saw something dark and glossy in the middle of the road. A salamander. Not the spotted but the blue spotted: slightly smaller and more slender, deep indigo on top, cloud-colored on the bottom, with sky-blue speckles. Blue spotteds also migrate to vernal pools in great masses, though their mating dance is more private as they pair off in the water, spread out, and lay their eggs mostly singly, attached to underwater vegetation.

When we entered the woods, we were in new territory. My husband and I have spent plenty of time outside in daylight hours, and certainly done our share of camping, but this was the first time we'd been out and about together in a dark wood. And it was unexpectedly pleasant. Something rustled, a sound that, we were surprised to find when we shined our lights at the ground, came from leaves lifting over worms pushing out of the soil. For a while we saw nothing, but when we got closer to the water they started appearing, every five feet or so a blue-spotted salamander, same as the one we saw on the road.

"This is a good pool," my husband declared, and I felt a small surge of affirmation. "I wonder if there are any in the frog pond by my work."

"The frog pond?" I asked, curious.

"The overflow area by the lake," he replied.

We went to check out this pond, along with another one nearby. The night was perfect. We labored for hours, covering ground we'd never walked in daylight. Even though we saw no nuptial dancing, it was clearly a Big Night for blue-spotted salamanders. I'd never seen so many. We didn't get home till after midnight, and fell into bed, exhausted.

We did not win the lottery. The news was delivered in the mail along with another child characteristics checklist—blank, to be pondered all over again—and an invitation to enter the next lottery, which would occur in November. Earlier that week we had also received a large manila envelope enclosing a poster-sized drawing of "Quinn County." My niece, for a school assignment on mapping, had named a district after us. I wondered what part of that child's mind, who lives 800 miles distant and whom I hadn't seen for a few months, I occupy. What word ignited her memory of me, brought me into existence in a place I no longer inhabit, to be gifted with a whole province?

We must never balk at unfamiliar territory. The worlds we discover, like those unanticipated red eft migrations that so engrossed my students or the midnight parade of blue-spotted salamanders my husband and I encountered, are often more astounding than what we set out for. For the truth is this: no one is desperate for a child until they can't have one. The child wish is an art. We may entertain it any way we want as long as we know it is not about fulfillment. We must recognize that the laws mothers everywhere lay across the land—the grass is always greener; life is a gamble—were writ by the universe long ago and to live fully we must embrace them.

Finished with lotteries, I picked up the phone and called another adoption agency that had openings. I would, I decided, burrow beneath the bills and contracts, let them occupy a level I was not fully conscious of, as do those fossorial creatures I so admire, surfacing and resurfacing for the false starts. I would invite the ambivalence, the uncertainty that accompanied my original wish for a child, which is what, finally, defines it. Right then all I felt was calm. It was a calm that allowed me to imagine what it would look like if I ever found those spotted salamanders on Big Night in the beam of my flashlight: the yellow spots on their backs a hundred gold coins tossed into a fountain—the child wish, in whatever way it would, unraveling.

JUSTIN PHILLIP REED

Killing Like They Do in the Movies

FROM *Catapult*

1. Digging Beneath My Uncle's Feet

IN 1996, I knew nothing of the word *lynch*, only that it was also the last name of a girl in my grade whom none of us talked to.

They found Uncle Craig hanging from a tree on McKeever Road. I remember that his skin was darker than most of the skin I had seen, remember thinking later that his body and the tree must have shared a darkness. Crooked silhouette of limbs and fingers and trunks, all that Carolina morning burning holes through it. I shouldn't have been able to beautify that image. I want to take to task my mind's archive of envisioned, consumable violence.

At seven, I knew only what it was: a hanging. Not who, not why, and not since when.

A chain of associations drags me out of sleep. I dreamed someone tattooed on my forearm a talismanic pentagram. I somehow surface recalling the gruesome kills of Michael Myers throughout the *Halloween* franchise. All the white teenage girls, strangled or bleeding out, and then Tyra Banks: gutted and hanging by the neck from a wire. I demand a metaphor for how these scenes are imagined—how dust and waste and forgotten things might collect in the bed of a huge river, how I could pick up a small stone formed from centuries of this and wonder about its weight in my palm, the color contrast, and never question the river, what cut across it, sank through it, floated on its surface.

It's not that Michael Myers had never strung up a body before *Halloween: Resurrection* (2002). On the contrary, it was by then the killer's hallmark to suspend his victims, cocking his head in odd curiosity or appraisal of his work. It's that Banks's Blackness, her Black woman body silent in the center of the room, reveals the grotesque as no curio but a well-known wound. I've been failing to write a poem that ends with the lines *this body didn't teach you all / you know about gore, but damn / if it didn't try.*

I haven't thought about Uncle Craig in I don't know how long, had forgotten ever having known someone who was lynched, and this lapse is what troubles me when I throw back the sheets. I ask my mother for details, and she calls from work, and yeah it had to be about '96 because that was the year after Daddy died and left her with two sons and the year my sister was born, and she wants to send me pictures of Craig's daughter's daughter, who is beautiful and in one picture is holding my baby niece, and our girls are always beautiful, but yeah, Momma doesn't think they ever found who did it, doesn't think they were really looking, no use in me being mad about it now, she's gotta go visit Craig's wife Aunt Deborah in Columbia and see the new granddaughter, and she's gonna send me all these pictures of the beautiful girls.

2. *We Live on Elm Street*

Wes Craven died. Brain cancer. Violent, but relatively goreless, considering. Features and images went up online to commemorate what Craven had given us. I wonder if maybe lately I don't have much grief left on reserve for famous white men, or if I have trouble mourning in general, but in a predictable mix of homage and nostalgia, that evening I decided to watch *A Nightmare on Elm Street* (1984), Craven's classic franchise-starter in which razor-fingered Freddy Krueger stalks the dreams of four archetypal suburban kids.

I rarely think of Craven, but I can easily visualize many of the kill scenes that made him famous and his killers infamous. I keep a mental library of the kills. I often call on them while writing poems as though for a diction of fantasized violence, a showcase of its pronunciations. This is what Craven and his counterparts have given me.

A few minutes into the film I began to dread the rest of it. Each scene seemed to climb toward the least red death in the film—

that of Rod, the first victim's dark, "rough-edged," pretty-faced boyfriend, the prime suspect in her death; Rod, whom Freddy— existing somewhere between nightmare and poltergeist—hangs by a bedsheet in what will appear to the always-ain't-seen-nothin' cops to be an otherwise empty jail cell.

It's a bloodless kill. It looks to the adults like a simple guilt-fueled suicide. Meanwhile, I barely register it as the scene of a film. My ears fumble the dialogue. My eyes take in the images from the laptop screen, but my mind is digressing, recycling props kaleidoscopically, replacing Rod with Sandra Bland. That I can color in the glue-and-scissors details around Bland's death with a scene as outrageous and inventive as this one irritates me. The story from the Waller County jail has as many holes, cuts, edits, and special effects as Craven's slasher. Black ghosts dangle in all the corners of my horror flicks lately, even when I am not looking.

Upon discovering Rod's body, the heroine, Nancy, shrieks the beginning of her long frustration. She knows what's killing her friends, what's coming after her. Knowing makes her crazy. Disrupting everyone else's resistance to knowing makes her the problem.

3. Everybody Knows Your Name

When I enter the bar, its walls are talking loudly among themselves, the way a dead woods might always be filled with falling trees regardless of whether an eavesdropping ear would hear. One wall has its mouth full of Josephine Baker and all her feathers. Another holds Miles Davis in the dark throat of its holler, his trumpet paused mid-rapture. There are others, bound in frames, jazzing up the space. All the patrons are white. Their beer voices slap up the Black talent and bounce back. I come like a gap in a white caravan and grit my teeth against the din of it. Down an aisle of stools and minimalist tables, a vintage-looking man plays a vintage-looking piano, grinning at the skinny woman thinly singing another jazz standard, her hair in a vintage-looking bun. A young New Yorker sits across from me and gets bored with my pointing out how white spaces have "this thing" for making ornament of nonwhite strife and achievement—which are often difficult to tell apart. I'm also bored. I'm trying to understand this nearly ubiquitous need for the Negro edge. Bodies dangling like festive decorations, tricking the light. Somehow I've become a conduit for haunting—a needle pushed across the black cut, which spins even when I don't want to lower my nose to it because maybe tonight my spine needs respite from the violent signals of memory and literacy. How hopeful. Not this night. *What happens when I'm not here? What am I assumed to cosign when I am here?* These are two different questions with similar answers. Sometimes when I say I'm bored, I mean bored into. White nostalgia in the age of the hipster bar is a dense sulfuric stink. For one reason or another, I keep inhaling. I order a pizza and neat whiskeys.

4. Who Kills Casey Becker

We are introduced to a blonde, and the plot seems likely to center on her. She is stalked and attacked, but her blondness and surplus lines of dialogue are supposed to save her. She dies around twelve minutes in, murdered in the most violent way. The violent murder of a blonde who spoke frequently suggests that no one is safe. Craven's *Scream,* credited with revitalizing the slasher subgenre in 1996, follows a formula previously deployed in *A Nightmare on Elm Street.* I can trace the tradition back to Hitchcock's *Psycho.*

Some nights, when I want to slip inside the guilty space between guaranteed discomfort and the foreknowledge of it, I turn on the movie just to watch this paradigm-shifting first scene. The killing of Casey Becker in *Scream* was momentous. It marked the end of Craven's hiatus from big-box-office horror. It marked Drew Barrymore's return to prominence. It established the Ghostface Killer —that easily laughable horror symbol—as a significant addition to the lineage of masked murderers. It brought the Michael Myers tradition back to the unsuspecting suburbs, where high school girls are often home alone and anyone, especially their boyfriends, could be the home-invading butcher. It's as if in the imagination of Smalltown, USA, few other perils exist.

The killing of Casey Becker was historic. It's difficult to see the scene—her body disemboweled, dragged, and hanged from a large tree with the rope of a swing—as existing outside of American history, as created anywhere but in the continuum of a societal id that can't forget what it's seen its own hands do, that merely shuffles the moving parts of memory.

There being no Black characters in *Scream* and so few in its contemporaries illustrates a dissonance, the rasp of an unintended truth. These films imagine the extremities of white cultural depravity and brutality but do so in an America where only whiteness factors (and is in fact not "white" but some agreed-upon glare of homogeneity convinced of its comfort). This arrangement falls back quickly on psychosis-as-motive, in which the mysteries of mental disorder and individual deviance are alibis for the whites-only fantasy. The artifice of chance is the drama. In the case of *Scream*, the logic seems presented like so: "These two white teens are psychological anomalies *and* their killing spree of other white teens is an isolated incident *although* all of their parents are always circumstantially absent *and* there will be a sequel in which another white man terrorizes the very same white people . . ."

5. *My Other Education*

I was a queer and skinny child whose dominant emotion was fear. While other boys practiced succeeding at masculinity, thrashing and breaking their bodies in hours of commune, I hung back and cultivated a knowledge of exits, of how to get out alive, how to avoid entry. I was probably sitting on the floor, legs in a bow, safe from my cousins' game of tackle football in the front yard, when my aunt and uncle put a rented copy of *Scream* in the VCR.

When I was a fifth- or sixth-grader in after-school care, Momma had an HBO subscription and I had a habit of unwrapping the aluminum foil from the school's afternoon snacks, folding and shaping it into a hook circa Ben Willis of *I Know What You Did Last Summer*, and smuggling the flimsy prop out of the cafeteria and onto the playground, where I stalked my classmates throughout the plastic fort. I daydreamed of drafting a horror novel but only got as far as the cover image. I filled sketchbooks with color-penciled movie posters for teen slashers that existed and some that I hoped soon would. My drawings were decent. My illustration of the new playground had graced the school yearbook cover. One of my tornado scenes, inspired by Jan de Bont's 1996 special-effects montage *Twister*, had aired on the morning news. In third grade, my post-*Titanic* sketches of nude women had stirred some quiet controversy among the faculty, but in the end the principal was lenient, even impressed, having found the renderings "tasteful." I managed to keep the slasher sketches to myself until middle school, when all the low-boiling parts of me wanted to be acted out. My crosshatched knives stabbed no bodies but hovered in white space, dripping potential.

6. *The Punch Line*

I'm a queer and skinny adult whose flesh has known more blades than fists, whose mind knows the MOs of Bundy, Dahmer, Gacy, Ramirez, and others, who is still a bit bolstered by being able to stomach certain information without a cringe.

One study purports that Black people are believed to feel pain to a lesser degree than whites. Another supports the existence of racial PTSD. Another: the physiological effects of racism can substantially shorten a life. What Black bodies perhaps know: you can spend a long lifetime performing the role of a retort, a punch line. I want to make of this an if-then statement, a colored optimism. My poetry students are optimistic about clichés. They hypothesize that *if* an artist acknowledges the cliché and/or transforms it just enough, *then* an audience can more readily accept the cliché.

In 1997, singer Brandy played the lead role in an updated movie version of Rodgers and Hammerstein's musical *Cinderella*. The cast—portraying mixed-race families, royal and common—still (humorously) perplexes people on IMDb message boards. The year after, Brandy was Karla Wilson in *I Still Know What You Did Last Summer,* a sequel for which the filmmakers seem to have taken a cue from *Scream 2* and included Black characters in the supporting cast *and* allowed them to survive more than half the action.

Scream 2 cast Omar Epps, Jada Pinkett, Elise Neal, and Duane Martin. In the first minute, Pinkett's Maureen delivers the line "All I'm saying is the horror genre's historical for excluding the African-American element," and the sequel laughs loudly at its predecessor. Epps's Phil jokes about "an all-Black movie," and Craven maybe giggles a little at himself. (His directing credit immediately preceding *Scream* had been *Vampire in Brooklyn,* which grossed less than its budget and boasted a predominantly Black cast.) Martin's character, Joel—a source of comic relief—is the only one of the four who survives *Scream 2;* the others suffer together a total of at least thirteen stab wounds, Phil and Maureen having been targeted, it turns out, because their names loosely replicated those of white characters who died in the original *Scream.*

Karla Wilson is the best college friend of *Last Summer* veteran Julie James, played by Jennifer Love Hewitt. Julie runs a lot but lives again, as does her partner, Ray. Unlike her partner, Tyrell, Karla —having fallen backward through the glass ceiling of a bedroom, having fallen backward through the glass roof of a greenhouse, having fallen backward through a glass door and played dead— also lives, limping into the penultimate scene.

7. She Is (Beside) Herself

My first and only real conversation with my great-grandmother, the truest stoic I ever knew, was a warning after she caught wind that I "went around" with white girls. Perhaps she recalled how this would've ended in the early part of the century she had lived, had witnessed. The consistent drama of horror seems to be its nestling inside the trope of preying on and violating innocence, which is the domain ruled by young white women, if ruling is a way of being puppeteered. I wonder if Uncle Craig was somebody's Black friend, or if I should mention that Aunt Deborah could pass as white.

In Sylvia Plath's poem "The Jailer," the speaker declares that the title figure burns holes in her skin with lit cigarettes, *Pretending I am a negress with pink paws. / I am myself. That is not enough.* I hold these lines like a grudge. Plath's speaker wants to level an indictment against the shadowy man who has imprisoned, abused, sedated, and violated her. A numeration of injustices. Here, to be burned with cigarettes is apparently a violence that a Black woman traditionally vests. Unambiguously, "paws" belong to an animal. *I am myself,* as if the rapist's imagining the inhuman Black body in the speaker's stead lubricates his brutality. He is deluded, unappeasable. The poem swells with the desperation of this moment. *I am myself.* For whom is that not enough?

8. Spectacle/Sport

Consider the state-sanctioned hubs of public humiliation and mu-
tilation. Gladiator death matches, Crusades, the Inquisition, the
evolution of legal public execution including lynching, from the
advent of television into continuously looped video clips of police
shootings—all as if there's a consistent desire to access carnage
from the safe distance of a spectator. Less than a century out of
Jim Crow, I doubt it's difficult to argue that a public imagination
lingers with the same appetite for gore that lynchings—their rape,
dragging, shooting, castration, hanging, burning, and displayed
decay—once sated. Now it leaches elsewhere.

The physical kill. The imaginary kill. The execution that is *nigger*. The amateur porn subgenre of race-play. I tell a friend, *No, I
won't let a man call me that, fucking or not,* but I've watched a Black
man enjoy exactly this somewhere on MyVidster, threefourfive
times now. When the white boys slap the hog-tied Rogan Hardy
and call him *nigger,* their jaws glitch over the strange shape of the
word, their faces momentarily funhoused away from human, the
eyelids receding, whites waxing cartoonish. I watch and a heated
radius expands. I've been sweating the matters of agency and impulse. My friend responds *but it's fantasy*—which it is, for everyone
except the actors: the man whose mouth makes the killing and
the one whose body approximates a corpse. But maybe, I concede,
even for them.

9. Unmaking the Monster

I try to elude the burden. Then I attempt to share it. I remember
how I got here, who sent me, the single sentence that propels me.

"What white people have to do is try to find out in their own
hearts why it was necessary to have the nigger in the first place."
James Baldwin poses this challenge on a PBS segment of Henry
Morgenthau III's "The Negro and the American Promise" in 1963.
"Cause I'm not a nigger," he continues. "I'm a man. But if you
think I'm a nigger, it means you need it." Skip to 2011: in Chap-
ter 7 ("Black Is Back!") of *Horror Noire: Blacks in American Horror
Films from the 1890s to Present,* Robin R. Means Coleman analyzes

Craven's 1991 cult favorite *The People Under the Stairs*, "in which the 'hood and the suburbs stood in confrontation against each other ... with the 'hood proving victorious." She writes of the white slumlords in the film:

> The couple, then, represent a bundle of horrible taboos: (1) food (forced cannibalism); (2) death (they murder the two thieves); and (3) incest (among themselves and with their "daughters"). Central to the narrative of their taboos is that these are horrors easily hidden behind wealth and Whiteness; two positions of power which mean one would seldom be suspected of, or can get a pass for, evil.

Coleman has, by this point in the chapter, already made legible a few ills of *Candyman* (1992), a supernatural slasher that is perhaps more candid about its leaning on the myth of Black monstrosity than it means to be, practically in syzygy with *King Kong* and, Coleman argues, *The Birth of a Nation*. But *Candyman*'s eponymous hook-handed haint is only the Vader mask to its messy racial mush-mouth.

The Candyman is the vengeful spirit of a lynched man, Daniel Robitaille, mutilated for his miscegenation. His bloody acts manifest his desire to seduce the live white Helen to her death. His trail of impoverished Black victims from the Cabrini-Green projects seems peripheral to this bizarre infatuation. Helen debuts as a (bored and scorned and) curious grad student in Chicago. After hearing the legend of Candyman, she's taken in by a headline: "Cause of Death, What Killed Ruthie Jean? Life in the Projects." Her arrival in "the 'hood" from the highway's good side, looking for sources to inflate her thesis on urban legends, is cute and exploitative. What killed Ruthie Jean is more enigmatic and enticing than what usually kills the all-Black residents of Cabrini-Green, where, according to Helen and her friend Bernadette, every day a kid gets shot. Around seventeen minutes in:

BERNADETTE: I just want you to think, okay? The gangs hold this whole neighborhood hostage.
HELEN: Okay, let's just turn around then. Let's just go back and we can write a nice little boring thesis regurgitating all the usual crap about urban legends.

In recent months I've been gradually collecting notes for the practice of centering Blackness. The Candyman is a distraction.

Decor. I fold him aside. Helen needs this haunting. Her whiteness and access to a predominantly white institution of higher education have failed to elude the risk of mediocrity. Whatever is lurking in the gutted Cabrini-Green projects, whatever killed Ruthie Jean, can save Helen from disappointing namelessness. In a stasis-intrusion model of plot, little dissimilates the intrusion of Candyman (who appears only to her) into Helen's high-story-condo life from Helen's intrusion into Cabrini-Green—where most of the blood in the film is shed—except that nobody seems to hallucinate Helen, or the corpses made in her presence.

When I view the images of mobs huddled under hanged men, of Michael Brown's half-fetal body four hours facedown and cops at compass points, I want to talk about necessity. I want to ask, *What do you need? Do you know?* What did the landscape of Darlington, South Carolina, need with Craig's darkness? What does the urge toward mass murder need with anomalous madness? It seems that forms of atrocity have no use for the semantics of mental fitness. Darren Wilson hallucinated a demon and a body dropped. What did he need? What does ritual human sacrifice need with a god?

10. *Grace and Mercy*

One of the most insidious facets of Dylann Roof's massacre of the Emanuel AME Church in Charleston, South Carolina, is the matter of setting: the Black church is a testament to and tomb of America's sustained racist violence, a memorial of the pillaged spirit poorly substituted with religion. Its insistence on the power of healing forgiveness is unwavering because what else. There is always something to forgive, to get over.

I was brought up in these places. My grandma can be found in one three or four days a week. Even on the phone she has a suffocating hopefulness. All that she survives she does so "by God's good grace." I'm still not irreverent enough to tell her that her God and our Black lives are irreconcilable to me. I want to call more often. I wish she would just pray at home.

I'm anxious, ambivalent about the representations of daily horrors—man shot down, gun planted; woman pulled from car, her pregnant body slammed—because I neither trust America to live with its own memory nor trust myself not to forget to live. I mean I might try to forget in order to live. I might try. I'm often afraid. I'm not above trying.

There's a scene in *I Still Know What You Did Last Summer,* after a hurricane hits and the body pile first peaks, when Julie—who took this vacation in the Bahamas in an effort to move on from the murders of the previous year—finally reveals to her friends that they're all going to die and the who and the why.

> KARLA: How could you not tell me the whole story? I'm your best friend!
>
> JULIE: I just wanted it to be over. I didn't wanna involve anybody else.
>
> KARLA: Well, it's too late for that now.

They all stand in a downpour, distraught, on a useless pier.

OLIVER SACKS

A General Feeling of Disorder

FROM *The New York Review of Books*

1.

NOTHING IS MORE crucial to the survival and independence
of organisms—be they elephants or protozoa—than the maintenance of a constant internal environment. Claude Bernard, the
great French physiologist, said everything on this matter when,
in the 1850s, he wrote, *"La fixité du milieu intérieur est la condition
de la vie libre."* Maintaining such constancy is called homeostasis.
The basics of homeostasis are relatively simple but miraculously
efficient at the cellular level, where ion pumps in cell membranes
allow the chemical interior of cells to remain constant, whatever
the vicissitudes of the external environment. More complex monitoring systems are demanded when it comes to ensuring homeostasis in multicellular organisms—animals, and human beings, in
particular.

Homeostatic regulation is accomplished by the development of
special nerve cells and nerve nets (plexuses) scattered throughout
our bodies, as well as by direct chemical means (hormones, etc.).
These scattered nerve cells and plexuses become organized into
a system or confederation that is largely autonomous in its functioning; hence its name, the autonomic nervous system (ANS).
The ANS was only recognized and explored in the early part of
the twentieth century, whereas many of the functions of the central nervous system (CNS), especially the brain, had already been
mapped in detail in the nineteenth century. This is something of
a paradox, for the autonomic nervous system evolved long before
the central nervous system.

They were (and to a considerable extent still are) independent evolutions, extremely different in organization, as well as formation. Central nervous systems, along with muscles and sense organs, evolved to allow animals to get around in the world—forage, hunt, seek mates, avoid or fight enemies, etc. The central nervous system, with its sense organs (including those in the joints, the muscles, the movable parts of the body), tells one who one is and what one is doing. The autonomic nervous system, sleeplessly monitoring every organ and tissue in the body, tells one how one is. Curiously, the brain itself has no sense organs, which is why one can have gross disorders here, yet feel no malaise. Thus Ralph Waldo Emerson, who developed Alzheimer's disease in his sixties, would say, "I have lost my mental faculties but am perfectly well."

By the early twentieth century, two general divisions of the autonomic nervous system were recognized: a "sympathetic" part, which, by increasing the heart's output, sharpening the senses, and tensing the muscles, readies an animal for action (in extreme situations, for instance, life-saving fight or flight); and the corresponding opposite—a "parasympathetic" part—which increases activity in the "housekeeping" parts of the body (gut, kidneys, liver, etc.), slowing the heart and promoting relaxation and sleep. These two portions of the ANS work, normally, in a happy reciprocity; thus the delicious postprandial somnolence that follows a heavy meal is not the time to run a race or get into a fight. When the two parts of the ANS are working harmoniously together, one feels "well," or "normal."

No one has written more eloquently about this than Antonio Damasio in his book *The Feeling of What Happens* and many subsequent books and papers. He speaks of a "core consciousness," the basic feeling of *how one is,* which eventually becomes a dim, implicit feeling of consciousness.[1] It is especially when things are going wrong, internally—when homeostasis is not being maintained; when the autonomic balance starts listing heavily to one side or the other—that this core consciousness, the feeling of *how one is,* takes on an intrusive, unpleasant quality, and now one will say, "I feel ill—something is amiss." At such times one no longer *looks* well either.

As an example of this, migraine is a sort of prototype illness, often very unpleasant but transient, and self-limiting; benign in the sense that it does not cause death or serious injury and that it is not associated with any tissue damage or trauma or infection; and occurring only as an often-hereditary disturbance of the nervous system. Migraine provides, in miniature, the essential features of *being ill*—of trouble inside the body—without actual illness.

When I came to New York, nearly fifty years ago, the first patients I saw suffered from attacks of migraine—"common migraine," so called because it attacks at least 10 percent of the population. (I myself have had attacks of them throughout my life.)[2] Seeing such patients, trying to understand or help them, constituted my apprenticeship in medicine—and led to my first book, *Migraine*.

Though there are many (one is tempted to say, innumerable) possible presentations of common migraine—I described nearly a hundred such in my book—its commonest harbinger may be just an indefinable but undeniable feeling of *something amiss*. This is exactly what Emil du Bois-Reymond emphasized when, in 1860, he described his own attacks of migraine: "I wake," he writes, "with a general feeling of disorder."

In his case (he had had migraines every three to four weeks, since his twentieth year), there would be "a slight pain in the region of the right temple which . . . reaches its greatest intensity at midday; towards evening it usually passes off . . . At rest the pain is bearable, but it is increased by motion to a high degree of violence . . . It responds to each beat of the temporal artery." Moreover, du Bois-Reymond *looked* different during his migraines: "The countenance is pale and sunken, the right eye small and reddened." During violent attacks he would experience nausea and "gastric disorder." The "general feeling of disorder" that so often inaugurates migraines may continue, getting more and more severe in the course of an attack; the worst-affected patients may be reduced to lying in a leaden haze, feeling half-dead, or even that death would be preferable.[3]

I cite du Bois-Reymond's self-description, as I do at the very beginning of *Migraine,* partly for its precision and beauty (as are common in nineteenth-century neurological descriptions, but rare now), but above all because it is *exemplary*—all cases of migraine vary, but they are, so to speak, permutations of his.

The vascular and visceral symptoms of migraine are typical of unbridled parasympathetic activity, but they may be preceded by a physiologically opposite state. One may feel full of energy, even a sort of euphoria, for a few hours *before* a migraine—George Eliot would speak of herself as feeling "dangerously well" at such times. There may, similarly, especially if the suffering has been very intense, be a "rebound" *after* a migraine. This was very clear with one of my patients (Case #68 in *Migraine*), a young mathematician with very severe migraines. For him the resolution of a migraine, accompanied by a huge passage of pale urine, was always followed by a burst of original mathematical thinking. "Curing" his migraines, we found, "cured" his mathematical creativity, and he elected, given this strange economy of body and mind, to keep both.

While this is the general pattern of a migraine, there can occur rapidly changing fluctuations and contradictory symptoms—a feeling that patients often call "unsettled." In this unsettled state (I wrote in *Migraine*), "one may feel hot or cold, or both . . . bloated and tight, or loose and queasy; a peculiar tension, or languor, or both . . . sundry strains and discomforts, which come and go."

Indeed, everything comes and goes, and if one could take a scan or inner photograph of the body at such times, one would see vascular beds opening and closing, peristalsis accelerating or stopping, viscera squirming or tightening in spasms, secretions suddenly increasing or decreasing—as if the nervous system itself were in a state of indecision. Instability, fluctuation, and oscillation are of the essence in the unsettled state, this general feeling of disorder. We lose the normal feeling of "wellness," which all of us, and perhaps all animals, have in health.

2.

If new thoughts about illness and recovery—or old thoughts in new form—have been stimulated by thinking back to my first patients, they have been given an unexpected salience by a very different personal experience in recent weeks.

On Monday, February 16, I could say I felt well, in my usual state of health—at least such health and energy as a fairly active eighty-one-year-old can hope to enjoy—and this despite learning, a month earlier, that much of my liver was occupied by metastatic cancer. Various palliative treatments had been suggested—treatments that might reduce the load of metastases in my liver and permit a few extra months of life. The one I opted for, decided to

try first, involved my surgeon, an interventional radiologist, thread-
ing a catheter up to the bifurcation of the hepatic artery, and then
injecting a mass of tiny beads into the right hepatic artery, where
they would be carried to the smallest arterioles, blocking these,
cutting off the blood supply and oxygen needed by the metastases
—in effect, starving and asphyxiating them to death. (My surgeon,
who has a gift for vivid metaphor, compared this to killing rats in
the basement; or, in a pleasanter image, mowing down the dandelions on the back lawn.) If such an embolization proved to be
effective, and tolerated, it could be done on the other side of the
liver (the dandelions on the front lawn) a month or so later.

The procedure, though relatively benign, would lead to the
death of a huge mass of melanoma cells (almost 50 percent of my
liver had been occupied by metastases). These, in dying, would
give off a variety of unpleasant and pain-producing substances,
and would then have to be removed, as all dead material must be
removed from the body. This immense task of garbage disposal
would be undertaken by cells of the immune system—macro-
phages—that are specialized to engulf alien or dead matter in the
body. I might think of them, my surgeon suggested, as tiny spiders,
millions or perhaps billions in number, scurrying inside me, en-
gulfing the melanoma debris. This enormous cellular task would
sap all my energy, and I would feel, in consequence, a tiredness
beyond anything I had ever felt before, to say nothing of pain and
other problems.

I am glad I was forewarned, for the following day (Tuesday, the
seventeenth), soon after waking from the embolization—it was
performed under general anesthesia—I was to be assailed by feelings of excruciating tiredness and paroxysms of sleep so abrupt
they could poleaxe me in the middle of a sentence or a mouthful, or when visiting friends were talking or laughing loudly a yard
away from me. Sometimes too delirium would seize me within seconds, even in the middle of handwriting. I felt extremely weak and
inert—I would sometimes sit motionless until hoisted to my feet
and walked by two helpers. While pain seemed tolerable at rest, an
involuntary movement such as a sneeze or hiccup would produce
an explosion, a sort of negative orgasm of pain, despite my being
maintained, like all post-embolization patients, on a continuous
intravenous infusion of narcotics. This massive infusion of narcot-

ics halted all bowel activity for nearly a week, so that everything I ate—I had no appetite, but had to "take nourishment," as the nursing staff put it—was retained inside me.

Another problem—not uncommon after the embolization of a large part of the liver—was a release of ADH, anti-diuretic hormone, which caused an enormous accumulation of fluid in my body. My feet became so swollen they were almost unrecognizable *as* feet, and I developed a thick tire of edema around my trunk. This "hyperhydration" led to lowered levels of sodium in my blood, which probably contributed to my deliria. With all this, and a variety of other symptoms—temperature regulation was unstable, I would be hot one minute, cold the next—I felt awful. I had "a general feeling of disorder" raised to an almost infinite degree. If I had to feel like this from now on, I kept thinking, I would sooner be dead.

I stayed in the hospital for six days after embolization, and then returned home. Although I still felt worse than I had ever felt in my life, I did in fact feel a little better, minimally better, with each passing day (and everyone told me, as they tend to tell sick people, that I was looking "great"). I still had sudden, overwhelming paroxysms of sleep, but I forced myself to work, correcting the galleys of my autobiography (even though I might fall asleep in midsentence, my head dropping heavily onto the galleys, my hand still clutching a pen). These post-embolization days would have been very difficult to endure without this task (which was also a joy).

On day ten, I turned a corner—I felt awful, as usual, in the morning, but a completely different person in the afternoon. This was delightful, and wholly unexpected: there was no intimation, beforehand, that such a transformation was about to happen. I regained some appetite, my bowels started working again, and on February 28 and March 1, I had a huge and delicious diuresis, losing fifteen pounds over the course of two days. I suddenly found myself full of physical and creative energy and a euphoria almost akin to hypomania. I strode up and down the corridor in my apartment building while exuberant thoughts rushed through my mind.

How much of this was a reestablishment of balance in the body; how much an autonomic rebound after a profound autonomic depression; how much other physiological factors; and how much the sheer joy of writing, I do not know. But my transformed state and feeling were, I suspect, very close to what Nietzsche experienced after a period of illness and expressed so lyrically in *The Gay Science:*

> Gratitude pours forth continually, as if the unexpected had just happened—the gratitude of a convalescent—for *convalescence* was unexpected . . . The rejoicing of strength that is returning, of a reawakened faith in a tomorrow and the day after tomorrow, of a sudden sense and anticipation of a future, of impending adventures, of seas that are open again.

Epilogue

The hepatic artery embolization destroyed 80 percent of the tumors in my liver. Now, three weeks later, I am having the remainder of the metastases embolized. With this, I hope I may feel *really* well for three or four months, in a way that, perhaps, with so many metastases growing inside me and draining my energy for a year or more, would scarcely have been possible before.

Notes

1. Antonio Damasio and Gil B. Carvalho, "The Nature of Feelings: Evolutionary and Neurobiological Origins," *Nature Reviews Neuroscience* 14 (February 2013).

2. I also have attacks of "migraine aura," with scintillating zigzag patterns and other visual phenomena. They for me have no obvious relation to my "common" migraines, but for many others the two are linked, this hybrid attack being called a "classical" migraine.

3. Aretaeus noted in the second century that patients in such a state "are weary of life and wish to die." Such feelings, while they may originate, and be correlated with, autonomic imbalance, must connect with those "central" parts of the ANS in which feeling, mood, sentience, and (core) consciousness are mediated—the brainstem, hypothalamus, amygdala, and other subcortical structures.

KATHERINE E. STANDEFER

In Praise of Contempt

FROM *The Iowa Review*

I BUY THE ice cream cone because I want a cold treat, but by
the time I hit the underpass on my way west out of town the heat
has cracked off the chocolate dip, folding it into my mouth, and
what's left underneath is a white phallus, tongue-slicked into perfect shape. I grin. And deep-throat it. The way I do. The way I always have, since I first did by accident on the train out of Chicago
some time in middle school, heading back to the suburbs, sitting
next to my suited father in the ill green light of the Metra. I slid
the long cone of cream deep into my soft mouth and drew it slowly
out. I licked around and around and around its sides, plunged it
back in. Then my father leaned over to hiss at me, "Stop, the businessmen are staring."

"What," I said. And I meant it, for an instant. Then I felt the
color draw into my cheeks. And looked around. What I was tasting
was so sweet.

West out of town means the Tucson Mountains, parabolas of dust
and cliff. Out here, the warm pavement crumbles to gravel. The
car bends through the last dusty strip malls and pops up over a
ridge of saguaro cacti. White ice cream drips down my hands; I
lick my fingers. I lick at the soft bow of flesh between my fingers;
I lick my sticky palm.

This is what happens when I've just had sex for the first time in
a while: I get lit. My body will not shut up, wants more. I've come
to the desert to concentrate, to read a book I needed to finish
weeks ago. I've got to get out of the house, because we know what
happens when a girl stays in the house.

What always has.

What always has since I became friends with Lexi Alexander in the sixth grade, since we spent summer nights in the air-conditioned cold of her parents' basement office signed into AOL chat rooms. She taught me to "cyber," to type dirty things, to give dirty and get dirty in return, whoever it was out there, who they said they were, or maybe not.

A/S/L? we asked. *Age, sex, location?* Were these really men with pants at their knees, or were they middle-school boys like we were middle-school girls, tittering, crossing our legs?

It was my favorite thing. The guttural clicking and grinding sound of the modem as it struggled to connect. The way we pretended to be just pretending. There was a language I was learning there. Once my parents got a second landline and I had my own AOL account, Aryn sent me a picture of six, seven middle-aged men, their faces red, their dicks out, and one slender woman lying beneath all those hard cocks. Cocks in her hands and mouth and cunt. And after I'd looked and looked and looked, I went downstairs to one of the poles that held up the basement ceiling, and I held myself up by the crossbar and slid myself along the pole until I got *that* feeling. Pumping, my legs wrapped around the concrete.

It was a wildness in me, the way I needed this, the way I went back again and again. There was a magnet in my body that drew pleasure toward it.

But listen, I've lied; this did not start then. This started so early there is no start. I've been humping things as long as I've been conscious.

Yesterday I fucked a married man. Have I graduated? He is a military intelligence officer.

At my favorite trailhead, the mountains round and swoop like a woman lying on her side. Cliffs drop off her back. The only sound is the high-pitched worrying of Gambel's quail in the brush.

I ditch my car, the only one in the lot, and follow the dry wash a few curves into the canyon. There's a shelf in the rock about six feet up that I clamber to, taking out a dewy water bottle. For hours I read, heat radiating up into my belly through the rock. A few people pass with their dogs, paws crashing into the sand. The light shifts, goes warm against the cliff walls. Then the light goes down.

At some point I text the man I have just fucked, who is on a training base two hours away. Yesterday you could not have told me to drive an hour or two for sex. It is the end of the school year, when papers are due and my grading stack piles up, and I'm leaving the country in a week. Yesterday I would have said I was busy. Now I am texting the offer to drive halfway, saying we could get a hotel room or fuck somewhere in public. I take a deep breath, put the phone away.

In the dark, the owls hoot at each other from opposite sides of the canyon. I can see one settle onto the crown of a saguaro, then swoop, big wings outstretched, to the next. A black whoosh. A bulk of a shadow. Backlit by the moon, I can see how she leans forward to hoot, flipping her tail feathers down for balance. Her body rocks when she hoots, *hoo-HOO*. My phone buzzes. The military intelligence officer's wife isn't sure right now, he says. She is in Georgia, the last place they were stationed. She thinks she doesn't want him to have sex with anyone again until she can. I feel myself slump in disappointment, or maybe desperation. Not about him in particular but for the sex, this brief burst of pleasure. The day before, I'd made him come too quickly by bucking.

These hips don't lie, etc.

He sends me a picture of his penis, draped flaccid onto his eased-down athletic shorts: a consolation prize.

"Enjoy that while it's out for me," I tell him.

The thing about this man is, I don't really even like him. At lunch the day before, at a downtown restaurant where we sat by the long glass windows and slowly ate salads, I actually thought I might kill him. He was one of those people who had to be right. He talked a lot. He had a funny half-smile he used when he said inflammatory things, as though his being cute, being gap-toothed, could take me off my intellectual guard. Everything I said he needed to tweak, to correct. The bizarre opinions he held are not of importance here. I became blank and drank a lot of water. I tried to determine whether or not, once he shut up, the sex would be good.

I did not invent the Hate Fuck, which makes me feel better about this.

At that point, it had been just over two months since I'd had sex. This was not the worst sex drought I've experienced. Not by far. Still, I admit an edge of desperation. There is a kind of madness that sweeps over me when I have been celibate between six and eight weeks, an irritating, distracting hunger, a skin need. It becomes nearly impossible to get my work done. I sometimes pay for a massage, just to feel someone's hands on my body. If the buildup reaches five months, I begin to make terrible decisions.

So while a younger, more romantic version of myself might have walked out, I waited. Online, our exchange had been marked by clear communication, the directness I prefer. It seemed entirely possible the sex itself would be good, and that was the point. Not lunch. One's lunch-conversation skills do not appear to be particularly correlated with one's skills in the sack.

Besides, this is how it goes now. The single men my age are picked over. The ones on the websites whom I meet for a drink are disagreeable, unattractive. I wonder if this is how I am viewed too, on the cusp of thirty. I joke with my friends that I won't get to date seriously again until the first round of divorces.

In the meantime, I seem to be star pickings for married men. The ones who've been with their partners ten years or more, who stopped sleeping with each other, or who almost broke up out of infidelity. For these couples—working out their definitions of openness, cracking their relationships to accommodate sex in new ways—I am something of a unicorn. Willing to sleep with men with wives. Willing to step into these secret arrangements, intended to infuse new energy into old patterns. Willing to replace, for all of us, what has quietly slipped away.

Some of my friends give me horrified looks when I say the word *married*.

This particular married man, monitored by no less than the United States government, gave me a fake name online, used a fake town. His picture, though certainly him, looked like a different him. Mildly irritating, but I understood. "If the military finds out you're having extramarital relations, you lose your job," he told me.

"Even consensual?" I said.

"Yeah, they consider everything an affair," he said.

"Like a don't-ask-don't-tell for straight people," I said.

Which is to say that my friends are not the only ones who conceive of marriage as an immutable thing. An immutably *monogamous* thing.

Some of them shake their heads, saying, "I could never." Meaning they could never do what I am doing. Others narrow their eyes and ask how I know, definitively, that the second person in the marriage has really consented to the arrangement. Often the wife's accompanying profile on OkCupid provides reassurance. Sometimes it's the way a man answers these questions—the specificity of his answers.

With the anonymity of the Internet, though, it's frankly more likely a married man simply wouldn't tell me he's married. So in some way, I tell my friends, the fact that he even brings up his wife is a tally in his favor.

Which is all beside the point. What makes people more nervous, I think (even with the wife's consent squared away), is the foundation of such a relationship. To sleep with men already committed to someone else is to affirm our right to sexual pleasure. There can be no other rationale. To fuck a man who cannot vow his emotional support, who will not meet one's family, who may not even be a friend, nods to the primacy of the body. To the body's set of needs beyond our systems of morality. The needs exist whether we are married or not, although I think many of us like to believe that exchanging "I do's" will somehow shift this essential nature. It does not. And if I am not encountering men I want to commit to— if the men before me are simply not those who echo back the life I am building, and if I believe that as a body I need and deserve sex —a married man is no different from any other.

What I did like was his thighs, stocked with muscle, and the light hair barely visible beneath the collar of his shirt. What I liked was that gap in his teeth. He paid the check. And after that, when he caught my hand in a public park on the way back to our cars, when he leaned over and gently kissed me, when he asked me where I would like to go, tilting his head, something trembled inside me. I took him to my house.

Back in the wash, night settles. Owls. The flutish, descending song of canyon wrens. Stars brightening. The rock ledge, radiating heat. Bats flutter over the wash. Some bird makes a kind of vibrating sound, high-pitched, almost electronic. Then my phone buzzes. It is a picture of his erect cock.

There are two stories here, one in which I get wet in a canyon and lie down on the warm rock and slip my fingers into my swollen self, or one in which I watch the owls. Both stories are true, although perhaps both can be exaggerations too—stories I tell to characterize myself for different audiences. For between those afternoons in Lexi's finished basement and this buzzing cell phone, I have been many different people.

The owls, in some way, represent the life I wanted as a young woman, a sort of quiet existence, romantic and velvet-dark, in which sex was a component of love. In which sex was *making love,* unfurling quietly and slowly, with meaning, on thin air mattresses beneath the stars.

How does one go from this sweetness to the woman who fucks married men she does not much like? I can only say that first it went the other way. How did the cybering girl become so sweet, locked down? Culture had its way with me. The girl who loved cybersex did not go anywhere but inside, hidden behind heavy layers. For years I could sense sex moving inside me, giant and hot, pulsing against the gates, and I did my best to put it away— through judgment, through restriction, using *No* as my measure of success. This, I know, is an old story. But what is buried sears its way through. If I go back to the beginning, none of this is surprising.

We assume these things do not go together, the owls and the fingers wandering south, but as Sallie Tisdale writes, "the planet itself is laden with sex, marbled with my physical and psychic responses to its parts, made out of my relationship with its skin." She says, "How we are rooted to the earth through our bodies determines how we see other bodies, and ultimately the earth itself." What I think Tisdale means is that the romantic pleasure I take from this dusk—the depth of my presence, the sharpness of the details I take in—is not at all different from the way I enjoy my own body, the bodies of others. Which is to say, I am no less romantic than I used to be—only more openly other things too.

On the hike out, I walk with my headlamp off, fumbling by starlight. Even with my bad knee I can pick my way through the sand over the rock. In the side pocket of my hiking pack, my phone buzzes. He came.

I was not raised by swingers or prostitutes but by midwestern Methodists sincere in the idea that sex is appropriate only in the context of marriage—or at the very least love. To be fair, my parents, married for more than thirty years, are the kind of couple who make this seem easy. Growing up, my parents kissed in front of us. They spoke gently. They laughed. They compromised, each of their lives fashioned in balance with the other's. As a teenager, a friend of mine—whose parents fought bitterly—confessed that my parents alone were her model for a healthy love.

Still, I have begun to wonder whether my parents' devotion to the sincerity of sex was perhaps just what they believed to be the correct parenting line. No doubt it was an ethics supposed to prevent my own pain and confusion. Perhaps like any good parents, they hoped to usher their daughters, three of them in total, through young adulthood without the kind of mess that sex can inspire—a stew of self-esteem concerns, infection, and potential pregnancy. For this, I cannot fault them.

But as a grown-up I've begun to hear stories, and I'm realizing that even my parents likely diverged from love-based sex at some point. Why, then, steer me so intensely toward the idea of abstinence until marriage? Were their own sexual experiences outside wedlock negative? Have they, afterward, categorized them negatively because they feel like they're supposed to, while attending to the memories privately with nostalgia or a wry amusement? I wonder how many of us are pretending we fit, holding publicly to conventional moral standards while pursuing (or stumbling into) our true interests. As Christopher Ryan and Cacilda Jethá discuss in *Sex at Dawn: How We Mate, Why We Stray, and What It Means for Modern Relationships,* if we all pretend we don't have—or want—sex outside the common narrative, the common narrative remains: as a thick, muscled force that makes people question their desires, their "normalcy." How damaging this is depends on the way someone experiences such secret desires, the way they judge their own ability (or inability) to deny such cravings. Years ago I carried a toxic shame, spitting hot judgment at others out of my anger toward myself. While of course there are those who truly want what's considered "normal," those people are not me. And so it is critical to me that I honor these desires, that I fumble my way toward them. I learn how this works; I find my way into strange spaces with strange men. I set my own boundaries, I check my intuition. And in the end I get myself quite happily fucked.

The wife changes her mind. We meet halfway, at the Shell station beside the main junction of a tiny town. When I pull up next to his red car, he looks over, grins. We meet in the space between our cars and kiss like we love each other. He taps his pelvis into mine.

"There's law enforcement all over this town," he says when he pulls back. "Border patrol, sheriffs . . . could actually be hard to find a spot."

"We could try for a pullout somewhere," I said. "These are rural roads."

"Could," he says. He shrugs. Then he glances into the back of my car. "Oh, your seat's even down," he says. "Your car may be dirty, but it's got more room. You have a blanket."

"I do indeed have a blanket," I say. I grabbed it because I had a feeling this would happen.

"Dirty, but with character," he nods.

We head south in my station wagon, around the bend from the pizza place, through the bulk of the vineyards. The grasslands are shining a sharp white in this dry season, in this late-afternoon light. He's telling me why he's hung over this time. It seems he's always hung over. He tells me about all the military guys razzing this one other guy, who's into Jesus, who's into monogamy. They were telling him he should find some sluts with them tonight, because there's things you can do with those sluts that you wouldn't want to do with your wife because you'd degrade her. They were kidding, he says—they just wanted a rise out of this guy—but I kind of hate him for even joking like this. The words roll a little too easily off his tongue. The Jesus guy, he said, left with two "morbidly obese" women. "Someone's gonna have a guilt hangover tomorrow," he sings. I laugh hollowly. I focus on the road.

If I were true to one part of myself, I couldn't be true to another part. Which is to say, if I want to fuck this man in five minutes, it's a good idea to be amenable.

We turn onto a few dirt roads, thinking we'll pull over, but they deliver us to someone's house. We turn back. We try again. We coast one rise after another, trying to calculate the likelihood of traffic. The car chatters over washboard. The main thing is, we don't want to get arrested.

He is my first married man, or the first I have actually fucked. The others, professors and postdocs in the earth sciences, caught me at a particularly tender time, when I craved partnership and love too much. We went on long, meandering dates, sometimes awkward, in which I drank Irish coffees late at night and tried to decide whether or not there was chemistry as the men scooted closer to me near the bar. And if there was chemistry, I had to ask myself if I could swallow the fact of the wives. Sometimes I could not.

You understand, to connect to them too much was dangerous. They were married men. I build dikes around the edges of my own desire, to direct the waters: these suitable candidates for love, these not. The ideal was always that someone would be Such A Good Friend while also containing some disqualifying factor. Something to steady the heart. The ideal was that once the dynamics were established, I wouldn't have to worry about things growing in the wrong direction.

More often, though, I allowed myself to sleep with men for whom I felt just the right level of contempt. Some combination of flaring arousal and disgust. Men with whom I could chat *enough*, men with whom I could laugh *enough*. Men about whom I could say, "Of course not!" to my friends, and still fuck the shit out of them.

Contempt is not a word we like. Contempt means disregard for, disrespect for. Contempt finds one beneath consideration. Contempt finds one deserving of scorn.

To act out of contempt initially inspired self-loathing, a warm, sickening rush of shame. Even as someone leaned in to kiss me, I was dismissing them, and this seemed unforgivable, I think because I bought into the idea that there are only two kinds of relationships in this world: those grounded in a sort of perfect love and those that are not (that should, accordingly, be disbanded immediately, or hastily cleaned up, atoned for).

Now I see that even my friendships contain moments of distance. I do not mean to say that the contempt we contain, which flares in us, need always be visible to others or acted upon, but I do know that its existence can be of use. The kind of contempt I am praising is but a sliver, a powerful small thing, which holds a space, preventing inappropriate enmeshment. (Too much contempt, of course, and one simply does not call.)

These men too dismiss me. If our relationship is to be just sex, they necessarily must acknowledge what I am not. Contempt is a marker of the kind of situation where such a delicate balance is possible. If not the foggy risk of love, the creeping risk of hate. In a body such as mine—insistent, hungry, clear in its requests—if I am to have sex more than once a year, I will inevitably be confronting one or the other of these potential imbalances.

What is easy to forget is the way bodies grow tenderness. We like to think that humans arrive at a kiss only when tenderness is already present, grown from emotional encounters or situational closeness. But in fact a kiss can grow tenderness, as though from a seed. Do not confuse the presence of contempt with the absence of kindness. With men like this one, especially. The tenderness of the body calms my reactivity toward him. It draws a kind of sweetness out of us, it builds an intimacy from our very tissues. From the touch of mouth to neck, from hand to hip. We lie together afterward, leg over leg, and laugh about small things, relieved, drawn into mutual sweetness.

We fuck with a tender contempt. Or we fuck tenderly, and contempt mediates.

We climb over a rise, and then, what I want to see: a Forest Service sign. I have a right, like any American, to fuck on public land. I pull the car over. Its front faces a ranch with a big two-story cabin-style house. He seems nervous. I am thrilled.

I'd pictured us making out outside the car in the wind, to build more heat, but he wants to get right into the hatchback. I acquiesce, stepping out of my cowboy boots, spreading the blanket onto the scratchy gray floor of the folded-down seats.

I lean down, to slip open his buttons with both hands and mouth.

He fucks me in the hatchback. It has to be a hundred degrees in there, the sun pouring through the windows. Sweat pools in gray drops on his forehead. Only one falls on me before he brushes them away with the back of his hand. Our bodies slide around on each other. I hold his hips against me. Finally his face clenches. It is over. The windows of the car are fogged. "Like *Titanic*," I say, moving like I'll run my hand down the wet window, and he rolls his eyes.

"If you'd said that during, I'd have killed you."

We crack the doors. Fresh, cool wind pours over our bodies. We are dry in moments.

"It's so nice not to have to put in extra effort," he says as we drive back to town. And I laugh.

"Yes," I say. He puts his hand on my thigh.

I could have used an orgasm, but I don't actually care. I'm leaving the country at the end of the week; his training will end, and he'll move to Seattle. I suspect we'll never see each other again. I love that this does not concern me.

On the way home, I buy jalapeño chips at the Shell station and crunch loudly on them while I drive. I lick my fingers and absorb the salt. I feel delicious. I feel amazing. The whole valley is coated in perfect desert light, the high rolling hills covered in a white sheen.

GEORGE STEINER

The Eleventh Commandment

FROM *Salmagundi*

THE EMINENT LOGICIAN W. V. O. Quine invoked "blameless intuitions." Such are the best I can offer.

Hostility to Jews, or Jew-hatred, is as ancient as Judaism itself. The oppression of Jews, attempts to ostracize them from prevailing society long predate the analysis in Josephus's *Contra Apionem*. Contempt, hatred, violence against Jews and Jewish communities never cease. Can we spell out some of their invariants?

The origins of monotheism are manifold and hybrid. They direct us to the solar cult in the Egypt of Akhnaton; to the ironic speculations of Xenophanes (if cattle had a God he would wear horns). Diversities of monotheism can be made out at diverse points and legacies in the ancient Middle East, in Iranian pieties. Within Judaism the adoption of any strict monotheism is gradual and marked by mutinous reversions to archaic pluralities. There are "sons of God" and manifest traces of polytheism in the Psalms. Local, tribal sanctuaries long persist. The Prophets engage them in fierce polemics. Relapse into idol-worship and pagan sacrificial rites is a perennial threat.

Paradoxically, it is with the loss of secular power and the destruction of the Temple that a rigorous monotheism asserts itself. This assertion entails a singular, unsparing exigence of abstraction. It posits a deity which prohibits any iconic figuration. There is to be no imagining of God in any incarnate or mimetic forms. His internalized presence is as blank as the desert air. Ethical imperatives are not conceptualizations of divinity, but footnotes to His inconceivable "thereness." He "is what he is," insubstantial as is the fire in the Bush.

These prescriptions challenge, indeed contradict, deep-lying, as it were, organic impulses and needs in the human psyche. Common man feeds on representations, as Schopenhauer taught; understanding seeks out the concrete. The imperious negations in Jewish monotheism have been known to elicit repulsion, indeed terror, in the gentile. There is something radically human in Pompey's revulsion when he confronts the total emptiness of the Holy of Holies. Christological trinitarianism, the teeming Christian iconographies of the God-family, the legions of saints and graphic relics embody a vehement dissent from authentic monotheism. They people the imagined reaches of eternity. As Nietzsche noted, the pagan world and its Hellenistic-Christian derivatives crowd nature —the nymphs in the brook, the elves in the forest—with benign or demonic presences. These are busy in the everyday. Judaism leaves man almost monstrously alone in the face, not to be imaged or conceived of, of a Deity, of an absent immediacy which has had no personalized meeting with God since Baruch.

One asks: do certain constants in Jewish moral and intellectual history relate to this vexing apprenticeship of abstraction, of abstention from the iconic? These are eminently manifest in Spinoza. In the wholly disproportionate contribution of Jewish thinkers to modern mathematical logic, to set-theory, to mastery in chess. Do they have affinities to the development of atonal and twelve-tone music? Schoenberg's idiom seems peculiarly apposite to the central definition of the Almighty in *Moses und Aron:* "unimaginable, inconceivable, invisible." Consider Kafka's resort to the silence of the sirens or Wittgenstein's celebrated injunction at the close of the *Tractatus* invoking a necessary silence in respect "of that of which one cannot speak."

The hell of the concentration camps defies linguistic means of description and comprehension. The systematic torture and elimination of millions renders somehow obscene the pretense to a verbalized epilogue. Even the mourning which comes closest—that of Paul Celan, of Lanzmann—falls short of the incommensurable. Horror is, or should be, struck speechless. Can one "think" the Shoah, where "thought" inescapably is concomitant with articulation, even entirely inward? There may therefore be contiguities —how could it be otherwise?—between the incommunicable "zero at the bone" which is Auschwitz and the legacy of abstraction, the inspired nihilism at the bitter core of Sinaitic monotheism. Have such contiguities scandalized and provoked?

A second motive of detestation, documented in antiquity, is Judaism's claim, already Abrahamic, to the status of a "chosen people." In the liberal West, Jewish fears and profane ecumenism have queried, debated, attenuated the meaning of such divine predilection. Ought it not to signify "a people chosen to suffer," to be a witness unto God's universal regard for all men and women? But despite such a pacifying gloss and such apologetic good sense, the archaic postulate of uniqueness, of a neighborhood to God more proximate than that allowed to any other ethnic community, persists. It hammers away beneath a rationalist, even humorous surface (Ronald Knox's "How odd of God / To choose the Jews"). The claim has never ceased to infuriate non-Jews. In the genesis of Nazism it triggered homicidal imitation and parody. Today the allegories of election are operative in the aspirations to divinely underwritten promises of homecoming and territorial sovereignty instrumental to Zionism. Add to this the tradition whereby the dying Moses asks God that henceforth the divine epiphany should be granted solely to Israelites. Contested by Amos, this plea for uniqueness is reiterated in such apocrypha as the influential *Testament of Job*. "Let intimacy with transcendence be ours alone." An awesome arrogance can be inferred.

The persona of Judas crystallizes but by no means initiates the millennial association, charged with both panic and contempt, between the Jew and money. The primal ambiguity of money—key to happiness, root of all evil, at once blessed and satanic—is virtually universal in social perceptions and symbolism. Even rationalized, money retains its demonic aura. The sensibility, the history of the Jew are taken to be inextricably inwoven with that of wealth, with Mammon and the Golden Calf, with Shylock and Rothschild. Those thirty pieces of silver, emblematic of Judas's treason, modulate into the Christian enforcement on the Jew of the sin, of the corrosions of usury (so formidably chanted in Ezra Pound's *Usura* canto). The Jew is compelled to "make money," a loaded phrase. The yield is simultaneously precious and excremental, as psychoanalysis seeks to explain. Moneylender and alchemist, the Jew manipulates, masters, fructifies the occult yet also supreme rationale and functions of money as does no other ethnic community. With the instauration of modern capitalism, of investment finance and the money markets, literature will quicken atavistic fears into profane urgency: witness the role of the Jew in Balzac, in Trollope, in

Zola's *L'Argent*. On the analytic front, econometrics, the Nobel in economics are all but a Jewish reserve.

Observe the deranged contradiction: Jew-hatred is directed at both the Bolshevik *and* the capitalist! The Jew is seen (justly) to play a leading part in utopian socialism, in the vengeful rejection of unequal riches and monetary values which gives to Marxism, to Marxism-Leninism their prophetic, messianic charisma. Their promise that "gold will be used for toilet seats." On the other hand, Wall Street, the esoteric juggleries of high finance, the bourse are stigmatized as expressions of Jewish plutocracy. They are distinctive of the Jew as Marx, himself a Jew, proclaimed. How can anti-Semitism have it both ways? No defiance of logic, no schizophrenia takes us nearer the absurd, irrational, but also entrenched, visceral sources and substance of Jew-hatred than does this simultaneous mechanism. In the outpourings of libel and caricature, the Jew is both the "bloodthirsty Red" and the pinstriped mogul.

Dispersed or confined to the ghetto, despised and subject to violent persecution, be it under Domitian, in the medieval Rhineland, in the Spain of the Inquisition, in the Russian pogroms and, apocalyptically, during the Shoah, the Jews have continued to exercise on the gentile world an unsettling, exasperating moral pressure. It is *the blackmail of the ideal*.

I have already adverted to the overwhelming, counterintuitive, perhaps in some sense unnatural exactions which Mosaic monotheism would impose on human reflexes and feelings. Christian polytheism, the compromises engaging the "Son of Man," the Man-God, have never effaced certain deep fissures and tensions within Christianity itself. The reproachful specter of genuine monotheism stalks the canonic multiplicities of Christian doctrine. It surfaces in such hybrids as strict Calvinism, Jansenism, and the Unitarian arrangement. It resounds in Pascal's agonized appeal to "the God of Abraham, Isaac, and Jacob." The refusal of the Jew to participate in such mythologies makes a hostage of Christianity "unto the end of time," for there can be no Second Coming so long as the Jew does not enter *freely* into the *ecclesia*.

Next came the uncompromising imperatives of Sinai and the Decalogue. Commandments out of common reach and the norm of human conduct. We are to cherish our neighbor more than ourselves. Smitten, we are to offer the other cheek. We are to forgive whatever injury is done to us. We must share our portion of worldly goods. Directly inspired by the Mosaic precedent, by the psalms and the prophets, Jesus is no more thoroughly the Jew than in his Sermon on the Mount. He affronts man—this is the right word—with behavioral criteria and ideals far beyond natural instincts and the resources of spirit in everyman. The Galilean propounds axioms of *caritas*, of mutual altruism, of disinterested love and *agape*, the key Pauline rubric, which only the sanctified, the "latter-day saints," can hope to enact. Who can satisfy the Pascalian ordinance that "the self is hateful" rephrased in Levinas's Talmudic exaltation of the primacy of "the other"? But in excess of our means these prescriptions plague us with their unattainable value. Perfection as blackmail. The necessary hypocrisies, the mundane bargains, the gymnastics of absolution and self-forgiveness by which women and men conduct their private and civic affairs are encoded by the most adroit public relations virtuoso in history: by Paul of Tarsus. From whose tactics of grace and dispensation the Jew-hatred in Christianity takes its lasting, theologically buttressed contagion.

I have already referred to the third major indictment of average humanity: that formulated by utopian, messianic modes of socialism, especially Marxist. The abolition of private property, the promise of equality, the exchange not of money but of trust for trust promulgated in Karl Marx's 1843 program are rooted in Judaic aspirations, in what one might call the left wing of the prophetic inheritance. The territorial, proprietary, privately oriented motivations of the "human animal," *la bête humaine,* do not only counteract these Edenic prescriptions. They do not only inspire fear and insurgence. They bequeath a toxic residue of guilt. No one fuels more detestation than one whose exemplary ideals we acknowledge, inwardly, to be justified but feel ourselves incapable of matching. (I *know* that there are spare rooms in my privileged house, but do not share them.)

The Mosaic summons, the witness of the seer from Nazareth, the exigencies of messianic socialism (as codified in certain fundamentalist *kibbutzim*) —three variants on the Judaic demands for perfection. On the didactic absolutism of altruistic merit, our instincts and pragmatic resources are found wanting. Hence millennia of resentment and enmity. All of which Adolf Hitler summarized succinctly in one of his reported table-talks: "The Jew has invented conscience."

*

And yet he endures. There are today more Jews thought to be alive on the planet than there were prior to the Shoah. If this is indeed so, it is a scandal (in the grave sense of Greek *skandalon*), an enormity difficult to grasp. Out of homicidal decimation, like no other in history, out of an explicit, systematic death sentence emerges not only a ghostly remnant of survivors but the contested land of Israel and the good fortune of North American Judaism. Jews have returned to Berlin. There is probably no way of gauging the psychic damage done, the scars left. The Jew, descendant of measureless hurt. He may harbor within him a covert derangement. But he is, and that existential banality defies likelihood and horror.

Allow a simple thought-experiment. Take an ancient people with a complex language; with a coherent social-political fabric; an evolved ritual-religious practice; a favored rural and urban habitat; artifacts and art of high quality. What is left of the Etruscans? A handful of archaeological vestiges and sepulchral sites. Why no modern heirs to the Etruscans?

The same effacement is true of countless historically attested civilizations and ethnic identities. Some, as in Central America, lasted a thousand years and left behind resplendent monuments, alphabets, cosmologies. The utter genius of ancient Greece, the power of imperial Rome, the aesthetic, political constructs of Byzantium enter into eclipse, then persist in the atrophy of the museum. Is there anything more instinct with death than the Elgin marbles?

We bear witness to two exceptions only. To only two lineages of unbroken selfhood over more than 3,000 years. In the case of the Chinese, demography (vast numbers) and the absence of genocidal visitations from abroad have secured continuity.

The case of the Jews is *sui generis*. It is that of a scattered, numerically limited people, victimized by recurrent persecution and, at the last, by a systematic industry of annulment (Stalinism conjoins Nazism). Dying, an American publicist posed the stark question: if you intuit another mass murder, would you choose not to have children or do everything practicable to bring about their exit from Judaism? Each Jewish parent must answer. If she and he reject the alternative, what ontological luxury are they enacting?

Still, the Jew insists on being. With an unexamined, nonnegotiable tactlessness of soul. He is the anti-Hamlet par excellence: "not to be" is not an option. Suicide is a blasphemy inflicted from, as it were, without (in mortal danger as at Masada, in medieval ghettos lit alight by the hounding mob).

Is the ultimate source of Jew-hatred, of the enduring plague of anti-Semitism, the provocative wonder of Judaism's persistence? Of the Jewish refusal of abdication from life? A refusal sustained against monstrous odds, in the face of constant oppression and the seductions of assimilation (precisely at the hour of danger, as for example during the Six-Day War, Jews, comfortably assimilated, have rallied to themselves). Why in God's name—citing that phrase literally—are there still Jews? Is this the maddening anomaly, this thorn in the flesh of time, which many gentiles have found to be outrageous and inexplicable? Is the endeavor to eliminate the Jew, by outright violence or exclusion, an attempt to resolve this enigma? Simply: why is the world not *Judenrein,* a term which appears to date back to the turn of the twentieth century in the Linz bicycle club, "cleansed of Jews"? No Etruscans left, no Mayans.

I have no confident answer. Only a tentative conjecture, an intuition, although perhaps not altogether "blameless."

The nucleus of Judaism is a pact with life, to which the commandment "Thou shalt not kill," a commandment so utterly alien to human nature and human history, is merely an inspired footnote.

What are the origins of this contract—do its gravitational waves pulse in the myth of Genesis, in God's solemn promise of survival to Noah and to Abraham? What negotiation counter to death underlies it? We do not know. How has this accord been transmitted? Modern biology dictates that no such transmission is genetically feasible. Nevertheless, Lamarckian proposals are beginning to reaffirm their pertinence. Sigmund Freud remained a convinced Lamarckian. It is difficult to dismiss the role, the potency of the life-pact in the composition, in the counterfactual destiny, of the Jew. Jewish orthodoxy and scripture remain neutral as to any afterlife. The sacred prevails here and now, the wager is on sunrise. (The primacy of the present tense is unmistakable in Hebrew syntax.)

Only this pact, surpassing common vitality or optimism, can help explain the survival of the Jew across millennia of persecution and repeated decimation. After the purposed finality of the Holocaust. In play was the anomaly of what Ibsen called "the life-lie," of the inextinguishable energies of the Jewish psyche, albeit damaged. How otherwise can we grasp the fact that Jews kept sane, kept resilient after the torment and eradication of millions in the death camps? After the slaughter of their children and the complicity in hatred or indifference of the vast majority of their fellow men? At the moment of his liberation, the radical refusenik, after a decade of incarceration, much of it in solitary, *dances* across the border line, mocking his guards! Dances as did David before the Ark. In celebration of the mystery of indestructible life that is Judaism.

The incensed response to this mystery must have been initiated and deepened in the collective unconscious—an opaque but probably indispensable reality—of the gentile. At times, this unconscious finds manifest expression. For example in the mesmerizing legend of the Wandering Jew. An object of homicidal detestation and pursuit, Ahasverus wanders "like night from land to land." He is untouchable, immune to the privilege of extinction.

It is my conjecture that this immunity both exasperates and subconsciously terrifies non-Jews. The Jew *has been around too long.* Like a reproachful atavism, at once spectral and formidably alive. Alert to incipient disaster, he has learned to breathe underwater. This is not an accomplishment that makes friends.

Is there any realistic "solution" (a word itself scarred, *Endlösung* in the glossary of the butchers)?

An estimated 71 percent of Jews in the U.S.A. enter mixed marriages. It is very difficult to determine how many of such unions comport an abandonment of Jewish practices and remembrance. Obviously crucial is the upbringing of their children. Experts affirm that only 20 percent of the children of mixed marriages will be taught anything of their Jewish heritage. The great majority drift out of any Jewish observance and self-definition. In Israel itself, demography undermines Judaism. Later in our century Palestinian Arabs are expected to outnumber Jews. The format that remains could well be that of a retrenched community in Israel and of Orthodox clusters widely disseminated. Conceivably the future of Judaism now lies with their fanatical fruitfulness (some half-dozen offspring or more) in the paradox of a transnational ghetto. Much speaks against the end-game metamorphosis, including the wondrously renascent dynamics of the Hebrew language. Nonetheless, it is a possible epilogue.

Would it terminate anti-Semitism?

Detestation of the Jew has been of eminent value to Christendom. It has served as a *katharsis* purging Christian dogma and imaginings of otherwise intractable theological and sociological tensions. The obduracy of the Jew compels the adjournment of the Second Coming. Jewish legalism, its servile adherence to the letter, highlights the contrasting Christian commitment to the spirit. At every salient point the Jew is the adversary in a binary dialectic organic to Christianity. Ecumenical touches after genocide, the papal invitation to understanding and conciliation cannot efface the fundamental charge: the Jew is the deicide, the God-killer on Golgotha. He embodies the progeny of Judas. Thus there is in his sufferings a certain logic of retribution. Where would Christian eschatology be without his adverse lastingness? Yet at the same time it is this lastingness which is intolerable.

Might the spread of atheism, notably in the West, inhibit the rejection of the Jew? Rigorous atheism, the discarding of supernaturalism and transcendent hope, are probably rare. They demand a consequent asceticism and self-governance of consciousness. Customarily these shade into innumerable nuances of indifference, of fitful inattention or downright amnesia. They extend from polemic negation, itself dogmatic, to mundane apathy. The anti-Semitism of the atheist is, strictly considered, an absurdity. It lacks all serious logic or resistance to Mosaic encroachments. Its motivations can be those of social snobbery or of political and professional rivalry. This is the Marxist-Leninist construct. It can, as in fascism and Nazism, enlist the idiocies of racism. But it lacks any central logic, any true engagement with the unalterable status of the "chosen" Jew. It is at once visceral and irrelevant. Proust is the unrivaled taxonomist of this complex. Evidence suggests that diverse modes of atheism, of God-boredom, are spreading in the monetary technological fabric of the developed world. As Laplace foretold, the hypothesis of any deity or supreme being is unnecessary in the regime of the exact and the applied sciences. The criteria of the fact, the rules of evidence, now saturate our unexamined private and social proceedings. In a post-theological order anti-Semitism may wither to embarrassing vulgarity, it may fade to mere triviality. Exclusion from the golf club. This, in turn, would chime with the ebbing of defensive apartheid in the assimilated Jew.

The instauration of the State of Israel, that sad miracle, has made it difficult, almost sophistic, to discriminate between anti-

Zionism and anti-Semitism. These meld in the panoply of Islamic hatreds. Islam has no quarrel with the faith of Abraham. The *causus belli* is the Jewish incursion into the Middle East. What, short of the abolition of Israel, could assuage Arab fury? Once again the fate of a Jewish handful endangers peace at large. Armageddon is located in the Holy Land. Orthodox dwellers do not even acknowledge the nation because its secular foundation lacks messianic license. In the diaspora divisions and hypocrisies abound. Numerous enlightened Jews find the chauvinism, the militarism, the humiliation of Palestinians, all of which are said to be essential to Israel's security, repellent. Jewish intellectuals are prominent in attempts to boycott Israel. Others are parlor Zionists publicly and financially supportive but wholly disinclined to settle in Eretz Israel. In turn, the gentile will use anti-Zionism to legitimize, to mask the traditional reflexes and venom of anti-Semitism. The fog of mendacities thickens when Christian fundamentalists such as American Southern Baptists see in Israel a necessary prelude to their own soteriology (it is in Zion that Jesus will again "reveal himself"). None of these strategies looks to be open to rational rebuttal. The mythologies of odium are legion and nonnegotiable.

Add to this the somber footnote of Jewish self-hatred. It obtrudes even on the serenity of Spinoza. The Jew projects on himself the contempt, the misprisions, of the gentile anti-Semite. It is only when he accepts this devaluation, preaches Karl Marx, it is only when he liquidates his heritage, that he will pass out of the nightmare of his condition and blend into normalcy. Pride and self-tormenting ironies alternate in Heine's ambivalence, in the pirouettes in and out of Judaism of Karl Kraus. Echoing Hegel, Wittgenstein denies all Jewish creativity; at best, the Jew is a talented mime, a critic and commentator parasitic in the cultural and aesthetic realms. Biology dooms him to inherent "femininity," according to Weininger. Even circumcision is suspect. Witness the tragicomic turnings and twistings of Philip Roth.

Are we now approaching the (inadmissible) center?

The existence of Judaism is inextricably inwoven with that of Mosaic monotheism. Whether in worship or denial, in exultation or despair, in trust or in repentance, the Jew defines himself to himself and to others in terms of his dialogue with or silence toward (*Entgegen schweigen*) God. This incessant exchange (also silence is exchange) is enshrined in Torah and the Talmud. These are the daily bread of Jewish consciousness, more significant, as many rabbis have insisted, than any ritual. Rescind the God-concept, also where it is agonistic, and the Jew is no longer intelligible. He recedes into the pantheon art gallery of dead creeds (those Aztec divinities). Sever the Jew from Sinai and he is no more. No sociological, no psychological investigation can quantify the spectrum of faith or disbelief, of agnosticism or episodic recall, in individual Jewish men and women. To how many, under what domestic or public circumstance, is the invocation of the "God of Abraham, Isaac, and Jacob" more than automatism or inherited good manners? Impossible to say. Let monotheism decay, make nonsense rhymes of prayer, reduce the rubric of "God's chosen" to an infantile disorder, and the Jew no longer posits a provocation and object of opprobrium. Would the long nightmare then be over? Is such a mutation conceivable? On the geological and zoological time scale, in regard to the evolution and extinction of species, the more than five millennia claimed by the Jewish calendar are not even the blink of an eye. The phenomenology of the dinosaur dwarfs that of Hebraic scripture. Is the credo of Abraham immune to evanescence?

But even if observance withers to a phantom remnant of the Orthodox, even if vague tatters of belief shrink to atrophied metaphors—we refer still to "sunrise" and "sunset"—one tremendous force and *mysterium tremendum* will endure: that of remembrance.

In the sinew of his or her being, in the innermost self of their self, the Jew will carry, encapsulate, conserve the dead God. This *in memoriam* is incommensurably more powerful, heavier, than any presumed or officious presence. The Jew will be remembrancer and death watch. Decease was prolonged and fitful. Death notices were posted decades prior to Nietzsche (cf. Heine, Jean-Paul). Radical elements in surrealism mime ironic funereal rites. For many Jews God's death was certified in the Shoah.

The Shoah is the *unspeakable*. Strictly considered, the avalanche of words it has generated is an obscenity. There is, there should be, nothing to *say* about the torture, humiliation, starvation, incineration of some six million guiltless men, women, and children —those children—in a systematic hell. Here language abandons meaning. This renunciation is no contingent, ancillary catastrophe. It marks, very precisely, the closure of that dialogue, defining, quintessential, between Judaism and its God. Discourse, the force of the spoken and written word (far beyond either music or the fine arts), have structured Judaism's commerce, narrative, liturgical with its transcendent interlocutor. The articulate, the conceptual, are now void. God's silence, His muteness in the torture cellars and death camps, signifies far more than His impotence or inattention. It proclaims His demise. What remains of the burning bush is the ash in the crematoria. Whose weight, whose inhuman nullity, is psychically measureless. (How can it be that Jews after Auschwitz are not *mad,* that they do not transport with them some virus, however covert, of insanity?)

Could man, the Jew in particular, have helped God to survive —*Dieu a besoin des hommes*—professed existentialism: "Pray to us, God," urged Paul Celan. Could we have given Him warning of the gas ovens? What shall we do without Him in the strident desert of rationalist-technological mundanity? Absurd questions, but fiercely nagging and eerily analogous to the famous "What then shall we do?" of Russian revolutionary hopes. To such questioning the Jew will continue to bear ghostly witness. "Lest I forget thee, oh Jerusalem." This refusal of healing amnesia, this Jewish incapacity to forget, will continue to frighten, to exasperate, the non-Jew. At hidden depths it may remind the non-Jew of his role, active or passively indifferent, in the time of bestiality. Memory is not susceptible to amnesty. It is, therefore, possible that novel, commemorative brands of anti-Semitism will develop. Negationism, already virulent in Islam, is a nauseating but highly suggestive version. It has its parodistic rationale: "How could such a monstrosity have been devised and carried out?" The negationist, however abject his motives, is an advocate for normality: "This simply *cannot* have happened." Henceforth the Jew must be denied his totally incredible recall. Without which he will recede into zero. What is there left of the Jew without his *kaddish,* without his lament for a dead God?

Bearing God's coffin on his bent back—Faulkner knew much of such a journey—the Jew and the non-Jewish Jew may still have their function. Israel is not the finale. Should it fail, in many respects an unthinkable eventuality, a post-Abrahamic, post-theological Judaism will surely endure. Why should there not be high finance, scientific eminence, compassionate largesse in Tasmania? Why not found the best newspaper in Lapland? Would the Jew cease to dance in Patagonia?

Homo sapiens risks nuclear folly and no end to the cycle of massacres unless we learn to be each other's guests. As we are guests of life, having chosen neither our place, time, nor social condition of birth. Guests keep their bags packed. They learn languages. They endeavor to leave their host's residence somewhat more comely, humane, and prosperous than they found it. At the same time they must be ready to exit if the city turns despotic or corrupt. These are demanding reflexes of which the Jew has or should have become past master. His departure has often left his sometime hosts lamed. Witness the centuries of near stagnation after the expulsion of the Jews from Spain. Ask yourself whether German creative and scientific dynamism has recovered after the Reich. Concomitantly, hospitality can harvest rich fruit. What would North American economic, scientific, intellectual stature have been without the Jewish refugee? Freud is buried in Hampstead, Einstein in New Jersey, Paul Celan in Paris. Guests.

Unless I am mistaken, only the Jewish liturgy features an especial blessing for parents among whose children there is a scholar. Jews may number as many philistines or fools as any other ethnic group, but a reverence for the life of the mind, for study and the prestige of the intellect, is ingrained in their awareness. Learning, intellectual debate, textual reference are second nature to Jewish sensibility. Political clout, material gain, the glitter of social class may be desirable. But they fall far behind the sanctity of abstract thought. Marxism is bookish, even Talmudic, to the core. The Jewish contribution to scientific theory far exceeds statistical probability. The very term *intelligentsia* is bred out of the Dreyfus trauma. Today populist democracy, the sovereignty of the mass media, egalitarian cant (political correctness), and the naked howl of money constitute a virulent threat to our uncertain chances against barbarism. Persisting ideals arose out of Athens and Jerusalem. It is "Jerusalem" which endures whenever we afford a child the magic of a good book, the music of an equation. The practices of difficulty are the natural piety of the human spirit.

It will be the task of tomorrow's Jew to act as custodian of a defunct Western monotheism. The Holy of Holies is henceforth known to be truly empty, but remembrance stands guard. Memory is possessive beyond presence. We engage future experience by remembering forward. Writ, though no longer holy, will exercise its authority. The Torah will be recognized as God's biography. The

Jew will remain marked by his former intimacies with God, by the shock and letdown of his near extermination. Anti-Semitism has often portrayed the Jew as a fossil, but it will be a fossil tactlessly alive. "I was what I was," ineradicable. Jewish social thought will devise guidebooks, road maps to a post-metaphysical atlas. Freudian psychoanalysis labored to domesticate the incursive thrusts of our imperfectly entombed past. Future Jewish cartography will aim to orient the human enterprise even as we map our cosmologies by the light of stars and nebulae long extinguished. The Jew will seek to be a navigator in the new emptiness.

The dialectical tension between an unalterable commemoration and the exploration of futurities, often bleak, will continue to set the Jew apart. His will be the uninvited specter at the New Age jollities. Within his tribal solidarities, his cherished cult of family, black holes of solitude will persist. Jewish women and men will affront an inward loneliness in that world after God. It chills Jewish thought in Spinoza, in Wittgenstein. It is the solitude of higher mathematics and of Celan. Jews can be strangers to themselves. That aura of apartness will once again elicit disquiet, hostility, and pestilential phobias among non-Jews. So I suppose, though it is idle to play guessing games about political and social circumstances to come. But one constant looks to be lasting: no pardon for the Jew. Let him remember the future and be on his tired guard. No solace there, but a fascinating voyage. God left one posthumous bequest and eleventh commandment to Israel: "Thou shalt not be bored."

Namesake

FROM *Colorado Review*

WHEN I TOLD my uncle Mason that I was gay, my father was back at the house, getting drunk. Earlier that evening I had come out to my parents, and my father didn't take it well. I knew he wouldn't, so I had put this off as long as I could, telling friends and strangers, but not my family. I was operating on a theory a friend shared with me: Come out to people only when you think it will make the relationship better. And don't fool yourself into thinking that coming out to your parents will open up lines of communication long dormant through years spent in the closet. Revelation rarely heals.

But by this time—it was 1996, and I was twenty-eight—I was in a serious relationship with a lovely man named T., and it felt too wrong to keep that a secret. (Never mind that this relationship would end two months later, when T. told me he loved me, and I said, "Thank you.") To lie about myself was one thing; to pretend that someone I cared about didn't exist was another kind of wrong entirely. And so on a hot summer evening in South Carolina, I sat with my parents on the patio of their house and told them I was gay. I remember contorted faces, and a long silence. I remember my mother telling me, in a quavering voice, that she didn't want me to get AIDS. And I remember what my father said, when my mother finally prodded him to say something, "They shoot horses, don't they?" At the time I didn't know the reference to the film in which Michael Sarrazin shoots Jane Fonda because she's too weak to kill herself, but I got the gist.

Later that night, at a restaurant, I told my uncle Mason, my mother's brother. It was just my mother and me, since my father had disappeared into his bedroom shortly after the scene on the patio. And after some halting commiseration, and awkward pledges of continued love, my uncle asked, "So, is it like *The Birdcage?*"

I laughed, for the first time that evening. *The Birdcage*, released a year earlier and based on the fabulously gay *La Cage aux Folles*, features Robin Williams as the gay owner of a drag club in South Beach and Nathan Lane as his queeny companion and the club's drag headliner, Starina. The plot involves this gay couple's straight son bringing home his fiancée, as well as her deeply conservative parents, and for a second I thought my uncle was making a joke about our inverted version of this plot. Well played, I thought. This was something we could work with.

But no, I quickly realized that his reference was less subtle than that. When my uncle thought "gay," he conjured up the homosexual excess of floats in a gay pride parade, of men in dresses. In his fevered imagination, he was casting me as Starina. I loved drag, but I'd never done it. I didn't have the shoulders for it. So I tried to explain to my uncle that my gay world was very different from the one he imagined. It was, in fact, quite boring, if South Beach was your only point of comparison. And as I walked him through the banal particulars of my so-called gay life, I was struck by how absurd this conversation had become.

Because here's the thing about my uncle, my never-married, more-than-a-little-queeny, bachelor uncle: I had long assumed that *he* was gay, that his name wasn't the only thing we had in common. And given that, how could he so fail to understand the story I was telling him? How could he think that, after dinner, perhaps, I would put on pancake makeup and a dress and lip-sync to "Can't Help Lovin' That Man"?

Later that night he asked me another question: "So, would you ever want to bring someone home to meet the family?" And it struck me that this question, more accurately than his first, reflected his great distance from my life and its possibilities. The world of *The Birdcage* was alien and extreme, but at least he had a reference for it, something that helped him to see it. But a world where I would bring a male partner home to meet my family? That was beyond his ability to imagine. And I wondered: Was there longing in his voice when he asked this question? Was there regret? Was there envy?

When my mother and I got back to the house, we discovered

the remnants of my father's evening: a half-empty bottle of bourbon on the counter, leftover roast beef and rice in the microwave,
the microwave door hanging open like an accusation. He had gotten hungry, my father, but rather than face me, he fled back to his
bedroom when he heard our car pull into the driveway.

Being named after my uncle was a gift. My older brother had
scooped up my father's name, the perfectly fine, though ultimately
forgettable, "Doug." So I was left with "Mason," which, in 1967, was
still fresh. This was a name that set me apart, and I was happy to
have it, not least because my uncle was so much fun. He was game
for all the stupid stuff kids want to do, all the stuff that makes
parents rethink the whole parenting thing. Amusement parks, ar-
cades, houses that defy gravity, mile-high grizzly bears—my uncle
could always be counted on to ferry us away to whatever cheesy
attraction the area offered.

He was the life of every party, the big man whose wet laughter
announced the center of whatever was happening at the moment.
My brother and I competed for his time and attention. On family vacations that required two cars, we'd fight to ride with him,
not simply because he had sharper wheels (absent the upkeep of
children, he allowed himself a new Cadillac every few years), but
because he'd sometimes let us steer, well before the legal age of
steering. Whoever didn't get the front seat would sit in back, ready
to supply my uncle with another Budweiser from the cooler. (As
with the steering, this was well before casual drinking and driving
was an unforgivable sin.)

He was a talented musician, and at the piano his big hands
spanned way more than an octave, enabling the kind of boogie-
woogie, left-hand work people demanded if there was a piano
around. His relationship to the piano seemed entirely organic. He
never required sheet music, and you never knew what he was going to play when he sat down, but you knew he was inventing it on
the spot. It was new every time. My uncle at the piano, his left foot
pounding the floor, setting lamps and vases moving, was the closest thing to excess you could find in my family. He played the role
of uncle to the hilt, swooping in for benign subversions of parental
authority, swooping out again when the time came to pick up the
pieces. Had he ever allowed himself his own Starina moment, it
would have been as Auntie Mame.

There were, of course, downsides to being my uncle's namesake, the chief of which was being called, at least within the family, "Little Mason" until I had reached the unseemly age of thirty-seven, the year "Big Mason" died and cleared the field. But mostly carrying my uncle's name was more boon than burden. It created a bond between us, one that was heightened by the other things we shared: an outgoing personality, a slightly ridiculous sense of humor, a musical talent, and something else I lacked a language for: some quiet sense I had that he lived his life outside the laws that governed other people—that he lived outside expectation. This was an example I would need, though I was too young to know it on those summer days at the beach, when I was six, and my parents would find me curled up in a ball outside my uncle's bedroom door, waiting for him to emerge from his afternoon nap so that the fun could start again.

The bachelor—especially the bachelor uncle—was a figure in the South, a recognizable type. A bit dandyish, the bachelor was a trickster figure, someone who hovered outside convention, who discovered loopholes of possibility. As a category, bachelor carried within it a seemingly unresolvable contradiction. On the one hand, the bachelor signified a kind of heterosexual excess, the single man unleashed from marriage and babies, freed from the confines of the domestic. The bachelor could roam the world of heterosexual possibility, more often than not sporting an ascot, and never get caught. On the other hand, bachelor was a knowing, if relatively polite, slur, a euphemism for queer, or unsexed. And yet, ironically, it was a slur that saved men like my uncle from the taint of homosexuality. It both named the possibility of sexual deviance and politely cloaked that possibility in the figure of heterosexual excess, thus leading to that oddest of phrases, the "confirmed" bachelor. What would it take, one wonders, to confirm such a thing? What kind of test would someone have to pass? The confirmed bachelor led a double life: someone who would never marry because he was queer, and someone who would never marry because he was too busy having sex with lots of different women.

This tension played out in my own family in quiet ways. I remember discovering a book tucked away on the shelves of my parents' den with the title *Everything I Know About Sex*. My uncle's name appeared on the spine as the author. It was a thick book, but when I opened it, I found nothing but empty page after empty page, a gag gift, presumably, and one that my uncle must not have appreciated, since the book was on our shelves rather than his.

I also remember my father's many references to a family friend as my uncle's "girlfriend." She was, indeed, my uncle's constant social companion and had been for as long as I could remember. She was with us on holidays and vacations, as much an aunt to me as Mason was an uncle. But there was never, to the extent that I could tell, the slightest romantic spark between the two of them, not a shared room on vacation, never a held hand. Like my uncle, this family friend never married, and as I got older and learned the term *beard,* I assumed that this was what they had been to each other: social partners who disguised their homosexuality through the social fiction of longtime companions.

But when my father called her my uncle's girlfriend, did he believe it? Or was this, like the joke book, a not-so-subtle jab at the confirmed bachelor, someone whose "girlfriend" would always be in quotes?

That halting conversation on the patio, and the one with my uncle at the restaurant, turned out to be the only times my family and I would talk about these things until ten years later, after both my mother and uncle had died. And this silence wasn't our regular kind of silence, the silence of a family that tacitly agrees not to confront difficulty. Rather, it was willed. It was the silence of an explicit prohibition.

Just a couple of months after coming out to my parents, I received a letter, signed by both my mother and father, though written in my father's hand. I was living in Virginia, where I was teaching. My relationship with T., which had inspired my revelation, had just ended.

The letter seemed oddly familiar to me, since I had seen versions of it in various made-for-TV movies about families torn apart by a son's homosexuality. And though my parents never actually said what was always said in those movies—"I would rather you were dead"—they did write that they would prefer anything to my being gay. The work of filling in the blank of that "anything" was left to me.

They asked me never to speak to them again about my romantic life. I wasn't to mention T., nor was I to speak about any of this to my brother or anyone else in the family. I would always be welcome in their home, they wrote, but only if I came alone, and only if I played by the rules concerning what could and couldn't be said.

The irony wasn't lost on me. By refusing to hear any news of T., they missed the biggest news of all: that we were no longer a couple. Had I been able to tell them that I had broken T.'s heart on a beach in Oregon, perhaps they could have escaped whatever depraved visions troubled their sleep.

I kept this letter for almost a decade. I was angry, and whenever I felt the anger fading, I would retrieve the letter from the box on the top shelf of my closet and feed the anger that had become as essential to me as my name. I imagined the letter as a kind of eternal flame, threatening to engulf the closet that hid it, the house, my life. When the house was quiet, I could almost hear the letter crackle and pop, its flicker dancing in the darkness. Fires eventually burn themselves out, people say. They run out of fuel. I wasn't so sure.

My mother died two years after sending that letter. In the aftermath, communication with my father was even more strained, since my mother was the oil that kept a barely functioning machine going. And when my uncle died, six years later, this left just my father and me, with so much to talk about but no ability to do so. Wanting a smaller house, he sold his and bought my uncle's, so on my rare trips home to see him, I found myself in what had been Uncle Mason's house, choking on the silence.

As a diversion, I spent a fair amount of time snooping through my uncle's things. Silence breeds a longing to know, and in an effort to fill in the missing pieces, I had already constructed a story for him, a tragic account of missed opportunities. He was, in this fantasy, the gay man born fifty years too soon, a man whose desires found no home in the world. That thing inside him that made him want the things he shouldn't want: that was sickness. That was the work of the Devil. And it could be resisted only through discipline, denial, and a surrender to God. In shaping his story this way, I was able to cast myself as its hero, the man who had the opportunities my uncle lacked, who could live his gay life—his real life—for him. I would dedicate every kiss, every grope, every exchange of fluids to my uncle's queer memory.

The first thing I discovered in my snooping was a painful reminder of the distance between us. I had hoped to find, of course, a diary, something that laid out, in dishy detail, the love that dare not speak its name. I had come to expect such things of figures from the queer past, who were, according to my research, obsessive diary-keepers. I knew that Arthur Benson, for example, English writer and master of Magdalene College, Cambridge, had filled 180 volumes with over four million words, almost all of them an attempt to understand the unseemly things he felt for the undergraduates in his charge.

My uncle, it turned out, was no Arthur Benson. He left behind no "Dear Diary" recounting of things that couldn't be spoken. He did keep, however, a rather sporadic log, less a diary than a kind of shorthand remembrance of the day's events. There were no secrets here, no revelations. I scanned for any mention of me, but found only one, from the day I had told the truth about myself: "Distressing news from Mason today." There it was, in his beautiful if prissy hand—he had studied calligraphy—proof that I had been the cause of distress. In those five words I learned more about how he truly felt than I had in any conversation. I had hurt him in ways he never let me know.

The transition from this log entry to a photo of my uncle, probably in his seventies, posing in front of the Liberace Museum was both jarring and hopeful. I knew this museum well, having spent a delightful afternoon there once with a boyfriend, both of us eager to escape the Vegas Strip. We marveled at the mirrored piano, the capes, the sequins, the chandeliers, the pink-feathered boas. But mostly we marveled at our fellow visitors, a bimodal mix of queens and grandparents, thirty-something gay men seeking their idol and senior citizens seeking theirs. How to read my uncle's presence there? A whole generation would go to their graves certain that Liberace was the most heterosexual of men. Another would find in him the flamboyance and camp they needed to survive. What did Liberace mean, when he meant so many very different things at once?

In a separate folder I discovered an honorable discharge from the army, evidence of a thing I had never quite believed: that my uncle served in World War II. I had heard his stories of raucous nights in the Officer's Club in London, where he played the piano, but I could never square those stories with my very nonmilitary sense of my uncle. But here it was, dated December 20, 1945, a "testimonial of honest and faithful service to this country." My uncle was twenty-one years old, not even finished growing, since the paper listed his height at five-nine, and I knew that he had six feet in his future. His weight was a scrawny 132 pounds. Under "Battles and Campaigns," the document listed "Northern France FO 105 WD 45," which, for all its gibberish, sounded a far cry from the drunken hijinks of that Officer's Club in London. Under "Wounds Received in Action," thankfully, "none."

But when I discovered an envelope marked "Army Pictures, World War 2," I found a version of my uncle that made more sense to me. The first photo captures a military version of the Island of Misfit Toys, six young men in full dress uniform, my uncle among them, all six radiating an awkwardness—let's put it plainly—a queerness, that I find immediately endearing. Having lived most of my life among boys and men like these, I recognize them immediately. These were not "the guys"; these were, rather, "those guys," men of questionable masculinity who found solace in their collective otherness. Their facial expressions range from pinched to goofy, their height from my uncle's five-nine to something more like the five-two of a man in the first row, who, according to my uncle's writing on the back, went by the nickname "Short Boy." My uncle is the most striking of the pack, his eyes meeting the camera with a quiet confidence. He's beautiful, in his way, and I'm unsettled by my attraction to him. But I'm particularly drawn to a man in the front row, the most misfitted of this misfit group. Bad hair, cheeks with more than a memory of baby fat, an attempt at manly seriousness that doesn't convince. He's adorable, like a teddy bear. His name is included in the caption on the back (I'll call him J.P.), and I wonder what he's thinking, what it feels like for him to be among these men.

Next I find a photo that looks like an outtake from the *Gomer Pyle* show, my uncle and two other men posed with helmets and rifles. They're holding the rifles at a forty-five-degree angle, and the middle man's helmet is askew. Their uniforms are too large, the pants bunching at the ankles. There's an attempt at masculine bravado, but it fails. These men should not have guns. They're not the gun type. There's another of my uncle with three men on a beach, either France or England. They're in bathing suits, shirtless, huddled together for the camera. My uncle's hand rests lightly on the shoulder of the homely man in front of him. There's a woman in the far background, half clad in a towel. The caption on the back reads, in my uncle's writing, "Beautiful, aren't we? Note the lady undressing behind us." And the thing is, they *are* beautiful, all pale, gangly limbs, exposed and vulnerable. And again, the thought hits me that these are my people. If I saw any of them on the street, I would look twice. I would risk a knowing glance.

And then I find the photo I'm looking for: my uncle, embracing another man. It's J.P. from the first picture, tucked under my uncle's arm, and he's wrapped my uncle in a teddy bear hug. My uncle's left arm draws J.P. to him, his right hand clasping J.P.'s wrist. There's no way to describe this other than romantic. This isn't the kind of physical contact that straight men love to perform, their heterosexuality assured and thus unimpeachable. There's no irony here, no self-consciousness. There's only the comfort of the embrace, and a refusal to let go. I turn the picture over, hoping for a caption, but find only my uncle's last name.

The last picture I discover is different. It's of my uncle, shirtless, with another shirtless man in the background. A military tent stands behind them. I'm struck by my uncle's body language, and his facial expression. His head is cocked to the side, like a puzzled dog. And there's something in his face that's not visible in the other pictures, something resistant, something unwelcoming. It's as if he wonders why he's being looked at, and wishes he weren't. I feel him looking back at me, wondering why I have him in my lens. And he's asking, What do you want from me? What is it you hope to find? I turn the photo over and find only the word CENSORED and some illegible scrawl.

We often think of the military as a bastion of antigay hostility, but this doesn't tell the whole story. In fact, as Allan Bérubé documents in *Coming Out Under Fire: The History of Gay Men and Women in World War II,* the war offered gay men and lesbians both a visibility and a community they lacked in civilian life. As Bérubé writes, "The massive mobilization for World War II relaxed social constraints of peacetime that had kept gay men and women unaware of themselves and each other, 'bringing out' many in the process." William Menninger, a psychiatric consultant to the military, called the wartime army "fundamentally a homosexual society," where men were thrown into close and intimate contact with one another in a space almost completely devoid of women. And while the military worked hard, through psychological profiling, to weed out gay enlistees, both the urgency of the need and the crudeness of their instruments led to a massive failure to ensure the military's heterosexuality. In fact, something of the opposite happened. An alertness to homosexual stereotypes led in many cases not to dismissal but to a sort of segregation, where gay men were channeled into so-called appropriate occupations: the steno pool, clerical jobs, and, to a significant extent, musical and entertainment corps. This gender-inverted typecasting had the effect of creating, where none had existed, gay work cultures and communities. One begins to understand those pictures of my uncle with his posse of the slightly "off" men who had found each other and were relieved to have done so.

These newly formed gay cultures spilled into the cities surrounding army bases, where places like the Pepsi-Cola Servicemen's Canteen dormitory in San Francisco and the Seven Seas Locker Club in San Diego, along with YMCA hotels, became hotbeds of gay cruising and only slightly covert sex. Given such opportunities, civilian life began to look much less attractive. As one GI said, "If I go home . . . how can I stay out all night or promote a serious affair? My parents would simply consider me something perverted and keep me in the house."

Of course, all this new freedom would lead to an inevitable backlash. With the return to civilian life of a newly visible gay culture, the genie had to be put back in the bottle. The decade after the war witnessed an increasing focus on sex perverts and deviants, orchestrated through the federal government, the church, and the media. Returning to their small towns, their families, the eyes of their neighbors, what would happen to men like J.P.? What would happen to my uncle?

But then I remembered that my uncle didn't return to South Carolina after the war, but went to Miami instead, to attend college. Had his time in the war taught him the value of port cities with large military populations? Was he looking for a civilian version of the community he had found in the army? A small book of snapshots, dated 1949 and inscribed to my uncle, poked a few holes in this theory. Though there's the occasional photo of an extremely hunky undergrad, in most of these shots my uncle is surrounded by palm trees and bikinied women. The arms that had held J.P. only a year or two before now linger happily over female shoulders, sometimes two and three at a time. Tucked away at the very back, separated from the other photos by several blank sleeves, as though hidden, is a particularly incriminating shot. It's of my uncle and a girl. He has his arm around her shoulder, and he's holding her hand while he looks into her eyes. One wonders if this is the woman who sent him the snapshots, who wrote in the back, "I won't send you the rest of the pictures until I hear from you! So there."

Removed from the all-male context of those war photos, my uncle, in these Miami days, looks decidedly more manly, more heterosexual. If the war photos reveal one face of the confirmed bachelor, these college shots reveal the other: the bachelor as a happy figure of heterosexual excess and possibility.

And I'm reminded of similar photographic evidence from my own past, a picture that once made my parents very happy. I spent my junior year of college abroad, near London, and I was lucky to discover that a second or third cousin by marriage had a five-bedroom condo in Paris. He needed a house sitter for a few weeks around Christmas, and I leapt at the opportunity. Word soon got out that I had commodious digs in the City of Lights, and friends of mine from home and abroad descended, resulting in a Christmas feast of cheap wine and overcooked duck. My guests—some eight or ten—were all female, and when a photo of that Christmas dinner reached my parents, they must have celebrated. And I was happy to let them celebrate. I was still deeply in the closet—scared to death, in fact, of what I knew to be true about myself—and this picture of the promiscuous bachelor abroad was just what I needed to buttress an increasingly shaky heterosexual facade. It was also just what my parents were looking for. They captioned it "Mason and his Harem" and circulated it throughout the neighborhood.

We see in photographs what we want to see. When is a harem —on a beach or in a Parisian condo—the truth? And when is it a cover for a secret that's hiding in plain sight?

I knew my uncle as a deeply religious man. In this he resembled my mother, whose attempts to get me to go to church were heroic, if ultimately doomed to failure. I've never been a believer, and this was the source of great and increasing stress in my family. At some point my mother gave up on getting me to church, having grown tired, I imagine, of my postsermon critiques. (I once caught the minister in a misquotation of James Joyce.) But the concern for my everlasting soul lingered, emerging in quiet, if indirect, ways.

Only a few years before he died, my uncle mailed me a copy of *Left Behind: A Novel of the Earth's Last Days,* the first in the block-buster series by Tim LaHaye and Jerry Jenkins documenting the rapture—that moment when Jesus returns and the saved ascend with him to heaven, leaving nonbelievers, Jews, and Muslims behind to fight various end-time skirmishes. This gift was astute on my uncle's part. He knew that I always had my head in a book, and what better way to save an intellectual's soul than through a novel? I read it immediately. It was fascinating, in the same way that the white supremacist literature I had made the subject of my first scholarly book was fascinating. It was a window into a mind-set that was repugnant to me but that I wanted to understand. Of course, it didn't have the effect my uncle had intended. Instead of pondering the state of my soul, I wondered why, when the be-lievers were raptured, they left their outer garments behind but took their underwear with them. I wondered what it meant for my uncle to believe that when the rapture came, good people of other faiths would suffer the same fate as atheists. That, say, Gandhi and I, were we contemporaries, would both be doomed to hell.

I never spoke with my uncle about this novel, and he never brought it up. This was the way with our family. We preferred in-direction, anything that allowed us to avoid confrontation: a letter mailed rather than a phone called, a novel that appears with no ac-companying message, or, in a more dramatic example, a message from the grave.

Just such a message came three days after my uncle's death—at his funeral service, in fact. I was seated down front in my uncle's church—a country church, farther out of town than the one I had stopped attending so many years back. I was there with my father, my brother and sister-in-law, perhaps my niece and nephew. Half-way through the preacher's sermon, I realized that his words were aimed at me—literally. He had found me in the second row and was looking directly at me. He made eye contact, and held it, as he talked about the tragic fate of the nonbeliever, and how easily that fate could be avoided, if only he surrendered his arrogance, his belief that he could think his way through the world. My uncle had spoken in his last days, the preacher said, of his faith in God, of his certainty of the life everlasting that awaited him. But he had also spoken of a heaviness of heart. He was worried, the preacher said, about those who lacked such certainty. He was distraught over the fate of people who weren't saved, the hellfire that awaited them.

Although the preacher never mentioned my name, I'm sure that my uncle did, that my uncle's last wish was for this man of God to accomplish what all others had failed at: the salvation of his nephew, whom he loved.

And as the preacher was doing this work, his eyes on me and only me, I became angrier and angrier. How dare he use the occasion of my uncle's funeral to proselytize. How dare he intrude upon my grief to alert me to the dire state of my soul. And I worried, in the days that followed, that this anger would seep onto my uncle, that I would always resent him for such a cheap trick, the hijacking of his own funeral for one last attempt at my salvation.

But instead of anger toward my uncle, I felt sorrow, and this was much worse. For the first time, I tried to put myself in my uncle's place. I tried to imagine what it would feel like if you knew—*knew*, not merely *believed*—that someone you truly loved was doomed to the worst fate imaginable, everlasting torment. Because that's what my uncle knew, that someone he had known and loved since his first cry was damned. And knowing this must have killed him, in much crueler fashion than the congestive heart failure that merely took his life.

I looked for solace anywhere I could find it. I latched on to the fact that my uncle had never once said or implied that I was damned because I was gay. I was damned because I didn't accept Jesus Christ as my Lord and Savior. And while this may appear to be a distinction without a difference—I was damned either way —perhaps it meant that, in my uncle's eyes, my homosexuality wouldn't keep me from heaven. Maybe, then, he knew this about himself as well, that, whatever he may once have felt for J.P., this feeling could sit alongside his faith and not trouble it. Maybe he could be himself before the Lord, if not before the rest of us.

Or maybe there was no solace to be found. Maybe he was so worried about my soul because he still worried about his own. Did he carry with him, like a cancer, what he had once felt for that baby-faced soldier? Did my uncle worry that he too had committed crimes that would keep him from the kingdom of God?

In the years since my uncle's death, my life has come more and more to resemble his. And yet the commonality I now feel most urgently isn't the name we share, or even the presumed if unacknowledged bond of our homosexuality. Rather, it's our experience of being single. Like him, I'm a bachelor, and with the birth of my nephew, and then my niece, I became a bachelor uncle as well.

And what I've found is that history repeats itself. The silence of one generation carries over too easily to the next. I finally came out to my brother and sister-in-law ten years after my parents had asked me not to, but the topic has rarely come up again. In an email, my brother wrote that he doesn't approve of my "lifestyle," but he understands it. My sister-in-law has been better, inquiring once or twice over the years about my romantic life. As for my niece and nephew, we've never officially had "the conversation," though surely they know. How could they not, when the signs are so much more legible than they were in my uncle's day?

My niece and I, in particular, seem to have a tacit understanding. In a recent exchange of texts, she mentioned how much she liked Chick-fil-A. I told her I loved their chicken but hated their politics. She wrote, "Oh yeah, the whole homophobic thing. I'm weak, and eat there anyway. The fact that they're closed on Sundays is a bummer. I boycott them on Sundays." She continued, "My gay friends eat there too. I'll just assume it's okay." This casual reference to her gay *friends* from a girl raised in the same religious climate I fled so long ago—that's the most promising bit of indirection my family has ever produced.

But this indirection is possible only because I occupy the same position as my uncle: the mysteriously single adult. Absent the provocation of a shunned partner, why spoil Thanksgiving dinner with explicit declarations, with demands for respect? I dated off and on (more off than on), but I was never very good at it. Maybe I got too late a start, having been closeted in the years when you get your first practice in merging and compromise. Maybe my independence had become too entrenched, my autonomy too comfortable. Or maybe I simply never met the right guy in the right moment. Whatever the reason, the most I was able to muster with someone would be a few weeks, or, in a handful of cases, a few months.

Eventually, though, I came to appreciate the freedom and opportunity that a single life afforded. I could do what I wanted, when I wanted. I loved not being responsible to another person. I came to cherish, even to hoard, my time alone. A friend might ask what I was going to do on the weekend. "Sit quietly," I would say.

And then, just when I had everything figured out, I met R., and everything changed. My much-cherished private time felt like a waste of time. My quiet nights at home felt suddenly lonely. I fell quickly in love with R., and, remarkably, he fell in love with me. We made it almost three years, until a job took him to New York, and our attempts at a commuting relationship failed. He understood this failure sooner than I did, and when he ended things, I was devastated. And in the aftermath, I was adrift. I had forgotten how to be single. I had forgotten how to appreciate the advantages of an uncoupled life, the freedom, the comfort, the ease. And in those difficult days, I turned once again to my uncle's memory.

I remembered that question he had asked: Would you ever want to bring someone home to meet the family? And I heard again the longing in his voice, but now I was sure that the longing was on my behalf. Whatever he had missed, whatever he had given up, this was what he wanted for me. And I had failed him, had squandered the opportunities my proudly gay life afforded. Yes, I had met the person I wanted to bring home. I had met the person I wanted my family to know. But these things never happened, first because of my parents' prohibition against speech and proximity and my cowardly submission to it, and then simply because lost opportunities are lost forever.

After my mother died, and as my father was, some ten years later, making the moves I'm sure he wished he could have made earlier, he said, "Tell me about R." He knew of him only because I had stopped spending Christmas with my family. If R. wasn't welcome, I said, then neither was I. But after a couple of years of this, my father worked up his courage, and he broke his own rule. "Tell me about R." Not exactly an invitation to a homestay, but perhaps a prelude to it. Of course, R. and I had broken up not long before this, and, my heart broken, this was the last thing I wanted to talk about. Doors open, and then they shut again.

But in the years that followed, my father would occasionally summon his courage and ask me if I was seeing anybody. I appreciated his efforts—they had cost him a great deal, and were motivated only by love—but the answer was always no. I had settled back into my singledom, learned again to value its rhythms. I had created a life that felt full, one that could fairly be described as promiscuous, though the promiscuity was more social than sexual. There are the friends I dine with, the friends I vacation with, and, yes, the friends I sleep with. And there are also those friends—a smaller number, surely—who provide that thing we hope to find in a lifelong partner: the ability to be my truest self, with no fear of abandonment. Call it a division of labor if you will, but that makes it sound like more work than it is. Maybe it's a division of love. It's what can happen in that space outside, the space my uncle inhabited.

In that respect, and despite whatever differences he felt between us, my life looks not unlike my uncle's. I've never been to war, and he never marched in a gay pride parade, but we've both been bachelors. In those days after his death, snooping through his photographs, I tried to turn my bachelor uncle into my gay uncle. At the time, that was what I needed: an antecedent, a version of myself that sat securely at the heart of our family. And there's a good chance I found it. I still think that photo of my uncle with J.P. tells the truth—or, at least, *a* truth. And I can't help but mourn the life he couldn't bring himself to live. I mourn his lost opportunities, his lost loves.

But then I catch myself. Would he want my pity any more than I want it from those who view my single life as half a life? Would he even recognize himself in the story I've made for him, the story of a gay man who kept his heart a secret? Would he reach across the silence, and the years, to claim me as one of his own, a queer misfit on that Island of Misfit Toys?

I'll never have the answers to these questions. So, not knowing in what ways he might claim me, I choose to claim him. For however much I needed a gay pride uncle, it was the closeted uncle whose example still guides me—the uncle who had, for over fifty years, and at whatever cost, carved out a space of possibility, carved out a life. In a world where the social pressures toward coupling can feel even greater than the pressures toward heterosexuality, I need his example, and his name, now more than ever.

THOMAS CHATTERTON WILLIAMS

Black and Blue and Blond

FROM *The Virginia Quarterly Review*

In 1517, Fray Bartolomé de las Casas, feeling great pity for the Indians who grew worn and lean in the drudging infernos of the Antillean gold mines, proposed to Emperor Charles V that Negroes be brought to the isles of the Caribbean, so that they might grow worn and lean in the drudging infernos of the Antillean gold mines. To that odd variant on the species philanthropist we owe an infinitude of things.

—Jorge Luis Borges, "The Cruel Redeemer Lazarus Morell"

But any fool can see that the white people are not really white, and that black people are not black.

—Albert Murray, *The Omni-Americans*

Our white is so white you can paint a chunka coal and you'd have to crack it open with a sledge hammer to prove it wasn't white clear through.

—Ralph Ellison, *Invisible Man*

THERE IS A millennia-old philosophical experiment that has perplexed minds as fine and diverse as those of Socrates, Plutarch, and John Locke. It's called Theseus's Paradox (or the Ship of Theseus), and the premise is this: The mythical founding-king of Athens kept a thirty-oar ship docked in the Athenian harbor. The vessel was preserved in a seaworthy state through the continual replacement of old timber planks with new ones, piecemeal, until the question inevitably arose: after all of the original planks have been replaced by new and different planks, is it still, in fact, the *same* ship?

For some time now, a recurring vision has put me in mind of Theseus and those shuffling pieces of wood. Only it's people I see and not boats: a lineage of people distending over time. At the end of the line, there is a teenage boy with fair skin and blond hair and probably light eyes, seated at a café table somewhere in Europe. It is fifty or sixty years into the future. And this boy, gathered with his friends, is glibly remarking—in the dispassionate tone of one of my old white Catholic-school classmates claiming to have Cherokee or Iroquois blood—that as improbable as it would seem to look at him, apparently he had black ancestors once upon a time in America. He says it all so matter-of-factly, with no visceral aspect to the telling. I imagine his friends' vague surprise, perhaps a raised eyebrow or two or perhaps not even that—and if I want to torture myself, I can detect an ironic smirk or giggle. Then, to my horror, I see the conversation grow not ugly or embittered or anything like that but simply pass on, giving way to other lesser matters, plans for the weekend or questions about the menu perhaps. And then it's over. Just like that, in one casual exchange, I see a history, a struggle, a whole vibrant and populated world collapse without a trace. I see an entirely different ship.

I met my wife in a bar off of the Place de la Bataille de Stalingrad, in Paris. That was almost five years ago. At the time I was at the end of my twenties and in the middle of one of the only legitimate bachelor phases I've enjoyed as an adult. Otherwise, there had been a series of more or less monogamous relationships of varying lengths: a frivolous year surfing couches with a Gujarati girl from Toronto; a poignant stint in Buenos Aires with an elegant black girl from Virginia; eight perfect then imperfect and seemingly inexorable years with a Nigerian-Italian chef from uptown Manhattan (with an interlude of six intensely felt months in college with my French TA, an exchange student from Nancy); and four turbulent teenage years with my first love, someone LL Cool J could easily describe as an around-the-way girl, from Plainfield, New Jersey. But on that clear January night, in a warm bar overlooking the frigid canal, there was no one else, and I was accountable solely to myself.

Valentine came with a mutual friend, sat down catty-corner to me, and—who knows how these things actually work—something in her bearing triggered a powerful response. I found her insouciant pout and mane of curls flowing over the old fur coat she was bundled in exotic. We hardly spoke, but before I left, I gave her my email address on the chance she found herself in New York, where I was living at the time. Two months later, while there on a reporting assignment, Valentine wrote me, and we met a few days later for a drink. That was when I discovered that she was funny and not really insouciant at all, just shy about her English. It turned out we had a lot in common. I saw her a second time a month later in New York and then again on a work trip to Paris two months after that. Summer had just begun, and we fell in love extremely fast. When it was time to go home, she asked me to change my itinerary and join her in Corsica for a week. I did, and when it was really time to leave, she promised to visit me that August in New York. A few days after she landed, I proposed on a rooftop in Brooklyn, overlooking the Empire State Building and the orange Manhattan sky.

In retrospect, it had been a very long time by then since I'd thought of myself as having any kind of *type*. It wasn't a conscious decision; it was simply the more I'd studied at large universities, the more I'd traveled and lived in big cities, the more women I'd encountered at home and away—which is just to say the more I'd ventured from my own backyard and projected myself into the world—the more I found myself unwilling to preemptively cordon off any of it. And yet—however naive this could seem now—I had somehow always also taken for granted that when the time came to have them, my children would, like me, be black.

A year ago to the day that I write this, Valentine's water broke after a late dinner. In a daze of elation, we did what we'd planned for weeks and woke our brother-in-law, who gamely drove us from our apartment in the northern ninth arrondissement to the *maternité*, all the way on Paris's southern edge. At two in the morning we had the streets practically to ourselves, and the route he took —down the hill from our apartment, beneath the greened copper and gold of the opera house and through the splendor of the Louvre's courtyard, with its pyramids of glass and meticulous gardens, over the River Seine, with Notre Dame rising in the distance on one side and the Palais Royal and the Eiffel Tower shimmering on the other, and down the wide, leafy Boulevards Saint-Germain and Raspail, into Montparnasse, through that neon intersection of cafés from the pages of *A Moveable Feast*—was unspeakably gorgeous. I am not permanently awake to Paris's beauty or even its strangeness, but that night, watching the city flit by my window, it did strike me that such a place—both glorious and fundamentally not mine—would be my daughter's hometown.

Another twenty-four hours elapsed before Marlow arrived. When Valentine finally went into labor, even I was delirious with fatigue and not so much standing by her side as levitating there, sustained by raw emotion alone and thinking incoherently at best. On the fourth or fifth push, I caught a snippet of the doctor's rapid-fire French: "Something, something, something, *tête dorée. . .*" It took a minute before my sluggish mind registered and sorted the sounds, and then it hit me that she was *looking* at my daughter's head and reporting back that it was *blond*. The rest is the usual blur. I caught sight of a tray of placenta, heard a brand-new scream, and nearly fainted. The nurses whisked away my daughter, the doctor saw to my wife, and I was left to wander the empty corridor until I found the men's room, where I shut myself and wept, like all the other newborns on the floor—a saline cascade of joy and exhaustion, terror and awe mingling together and flooding out of me in unremitting sobs. When, finally, I'd washed my face and returned to meet my beautiful, healthy child, she squinted open a pair of inky-blue irises that I knew even then would lighten considerably but never turn brown. For this precious little being grasping for milk and breath, I felt the first throb of what has been every minute since then the sincerest love I know. An hour or so after that, when Valentine and the baby were back in their room for the night, I fell into a taxi, my own eyes absentmindedly retracing that awfully pretty route. For the first time I can remember, I thought of Theseus's ship.

I realize now that this vision of the boy from the future I've had in my head for the past year traces itself much further back into the past. It must necessarily stretch back at least to 1971, in San Diego, where my father, who was—having been born in 1937 in Jim Crow Texas—the *grandson* of a woman wed to a man born before the Emancipation Proclamation, met my mother, the native-Californian product of European immigrants from places as diverse as Austria-Hungary, Germany, England, and France. This unlikely courtship came all of four years after the *Loving v. Virginia* verdict repealed antimiscegenation laws throughout the country. In ways that are perhaps still impossible for me to fully appreciate, their romance amounted to a radical political act, though now, some four decades on, it seems a lot less like any form of defiance than like what all successful marriages fundamentally must be: the obvious and undeniable joining of two people who love and understand each other enormously.

But that's not the beginning either. This trajectory I now find myself on no more starts in San Diego than in Paris. Not since it is extremely safe to assume that my father, with his freckles, with his mother's Irish maiden name, and with his skin a shade of brown between polished teak and red clay, did not arrive from African shores alone. As James Baldwin, perspicacious as ever, noted of his travels around precisely the kind of segregated southern towns my father would instantly recognize as home, the line between "whites" and "coloreds" in America has always been traversed and logically imprecise: "The prohibition . . . of the social mingling [revealing] the extent of the sexual amalgamation." There were (and still are) "girls the color of honey, men nearly the color of chalk, hair like silk, hair like cotton, hair like wire, eyes blue, gray, green, hazel, black, like the gypsy's, brown like the Arab's, narrow nostrils, thin, wide lips, thin lips, every conceivable variation struck along incredible gamuts." Indeed, to be black (or *white*) for any significant amount of time in America is fundamentally to occupy a position on the mongrel spectrum—strict binaries have always failed spectacularly to contain this elementary truth.

And yet in spite of that, I've spent the past year trying to think my way through the wholly absurd question of what it means for a person to be or not to be black. It's an existential Rubik's Cube I thought I'd solved and put away in childhood. My parents were never less than adamant on the point that both my older brother and I are black. And in the many ways simpler New Jersey world we grew up in—him in the seventies and eighties, me in the eighties and nineties—tended to receive us that way without significant protest, especially when it came to other blacks. This is probably because, on a certain level, *every* black American knows what, again, Baldwin knew: "Whatever he or anyone else may wish to believe . . . his ancestors are both white and black." Still, in the realm of lived experience, race is nothing if not an improvisational feat, and it would be in terribly bad faith to pretend there is not some fine, unspoken, and impossible-to-spell-out balance to all of this. And so I cannot help but wonder if indeed a threshold—the full consequences of which I may or may not even see in my own lifetime—has been crossed. (It's not a wholly academic exercise either, since my father was an only child and in the past year my brother married and had a daughter with a woman from West Siberia.)

"Aw, son," Pappy chuckled warmly when he cradled Marlow in his arms the first time, "she's just a *palomino!*" There was—indeed, there still is—something so comforting to me in his brand of assurance. It's certainly true that in his day and in his fading Texas lexicon, black people could be utterly unflappable when presented with all kinds of improbable mélanges, employing a near infinitude of esoteric terms (not infrequently drawn from the world of horse breeding, which can sound jarring to the contemporary ear) to describe them. I myself had to whip out my iPhone and Google *palomino* ("a pale golden or tan-colored horse with a white mane and tail, originally bred in the southwestern U.S."), but I'd also grown up with other vocabulary, like *high yellow* and *mulatto* and, in my father's house if nowhere else, those now-anachronistic and loaded terms *quadroon* and *octoroon*.

What bizarre words these are. But what a perfectly simple reality they labor to conceal and contain. When you get all the way down to it, what all these elaborate, nebulous descriptors really signify is nothing more complicated than that in the not-so-distant past, if she did not willfully break from her family and try her luck at passing for white (in the fashion of, say, the Creole author of *Kafka Was the Rage*, Anatole Broyard), Marlow, blue eyes and all, would have been disenfranchised and subjugated like all the rest of us —the wisdom, discipline, and brilliant style of American blackness would have been her birthright as well. And so there was for a long time something that could be understood as a more or less genuinely unified experience—not without its terrible hardships but conversely rife with profound satisfactions—which had nothing, or very close to nothing, to do with genetics. Indeed, even though the absurdity of race is always most pellucid at the mar-

gins, my daughter's case wouldn't even have been considered marginal in the former slave states, where theories about hypo-descent
were most strictly observed and a person with as undetectable an
amount as one-thirty-second "black blood" could be "legally" des-
ignated "colored." Which is only to say, despite all of the horrifi-
cally cruel implications of so-called one-drop laws, until relatively
quite recently there was a space reserved for someone like Marlow
fully within the idea of what used to be called the American Negro.

But it is not hard to notice that the impulse toward unquestion-
ing inclusiveness (as a fully justifiable and admirable reaction to
exclusiveness) is going in an increasing number of precincts wherever it is terms like *Negro* go to retire. The reason has less to do
with black people suddenly forgetting their paradoxical origins
than with the idea of whiteness continually growing, however re-
luctantly, less exclusive. With greater than a third of the American
population now reporting at least one family member of a different race, and with, since the year 2000, the option to select any
combination of races on the census form, the very idea of black
Americans as a fundamentally mulatto population is fraying at the
seams.

Perhaps, then, mine is the last American generation for which
the logic—and illogic—of racial classifications could so easily contradict, or just gloss over, the physical protestations and nuances
of the body and face. Which is one of the reasons it did initially
take me by such surprise to find so many recessive traits flourish-
ing in my daughter. I was being forced to confront a truth I had,
if not forgotten, certainly lost sight of for some time: my daughter
does not, as so many well-meaning strangers and friends tend to
put it, just "get those big blue eyes" from her mother. But despite
the length and narrowness of my own nose and the beige hue of
my skin, I've always only been able to see in the mirror a black
man meeting my gaze. One word I have never connected or been
tempted to connect with myself is *biracial*. The same goes for its
updated variant, *multiracial*. Growing up where and as I did, before
the turn of the last century, it simply would not have occurred to
me to refer to myself by either of those designations.

The first time I lived in France, some twelve years ago, to teach
English in a depressed and depressing industrial town along the
northern border with Belgium, I often went to kebab shops late

at night in which I would sometimes be greeted in Arabic. Once the young Algerian behind the counter simply demanded of me, *"Parle arabe! Parle arabe!"* and all I could do was stare at him blankly. "But why did your parents not teach you to speak Arabic!" he implored me, first in a French I hardly followed and then in an exasperated and broken English.

"Because I'm American," I finally replied.

"Yes, but even in America," he pressed on, "why did they not teach you *your* language?"

"Because I'm not an Arab." I laughed uncomprehendingly, and for several beats he just looked at me.

"But your origins, what are your *origins*?"

"Black." I shrugged, and I can still see the look of supreme disbelief unspool on that man's face.

"But *you* are not black," he nearly screamed. *"Michael Jordan* is black!"

It was an astonishingly discomfiting experience, this failure of my identity to register and, once registered, to be accepted, but one I gradually grew used to and now, after half a decade living in France, for better or worse have come to scarcely notice at all. Though it isn't just Arabs who mistake me for one of their own. Whites outside of the States are just as often oblivious to gradations of blackness. On my first trip to Paris as a student in a summer study-abroad program, some classmates and I bought ice cream behind Notre Dame. When we sat at a table on the river, a white American tourist who'd overheard us speaking confessed he was homesick and asked if he could join us. He was very friendly and younger than we were, and I can no longer recall the details of what he'd said, but very quickly he recounted an extremely off-color joke about blacks. When no one laughed and one of my friends explained his error to him, he blushed deeply, and said by way of excuse that he'd simply assumed I was Italian.

What these encounters and many others showed me in my early adulthood is something I should have known already but failed to fully grasp: like the adage about politics, *all* race is local. This makes perfect sense, of course, given the basic biological reality that there is no such thing, on any measurable scientific level, as distinct races of the species *Homo sapiens*. Rather, we all make, according to our own geographical and cultural orientations, inferences about people based on the loose interplay of physical traits, language, custom, and nationality, all of which necessarily lack any fixed or universal meaning. (To be sure, this is not just a black thing—for most of American history it was widely held that northern and southern Europeans constituted entirely separate races.) It is this fungible aspect of personal identity that bestows such a liberating (and at turns oppressive) quality to travel. In the case of coming to France in particular, this very failure to be seen and *interpreted* as one would be back home was, of course, a major selling point in the previous century for a not insignificant number of American blacks, primarily GIs and artists but other types too, who found an incredible degree of freedom from racialized stigma in Paris. For many of these expatriates, it was not that the color of their skin went unnoticed; it didn't. It is instead that it carried a crucially different set of meanings and lacked others still. France long functioned as a haven for American black people—and has never been confused as such for African and Caribbean blacks—precisely because, unlike in the U.S., we've been understood here first and foremost as American and not as black.

In one of the more exceptional meditations on James Baldwin and his European years, "Black Body: Rereading James Baldwin's 'Stranger in the Village,'" the Nigerian-American novelist Teju Cole in *The New Yorker* retraces a 1951 trip the writer made to Leukerbad, Switzerland, a far-flung, then all-white locale in which that very same sense of dignity that Baldwin had discovered in Paris was not always extended to him. Specifically, Cole returns again and again to his essay's true theme, which is an exploration of the various yokes, both visible and unseen, that act upon black-looking "bodies" and therefore an awful lot of black psyches:

> Leukerbad gave Baldwin a way to think about white supremacy from its first principles. It was as though he found it in its simplest form there. The men who suggested that he learn to ski so that they might mock him, the villagers who accused him behind his back of being a firewood thief, the ones who wished to touch his hair and suggested that he grow it out and make himself a winter coat, and the children who "having been taught that the devil is a black man, scream in genuine anguish" as he approached: Baldwin saw these as prototypes (preserved like coelacanths) of attitudes that had evolved into the more intimate, intricate, familiar, and obscene American forms of white supremacy that he already knew so well.

Even as he rejects what he interprets as Baldwin's "self-abnegation" in the face of European high culture—"What he loves does not love him in return . . . This is where I part ways with Baldwin"—and as he evinces a seemingly fuller appreciation of the limitlessness of his own intellectual, artistic, and frankly human birthrights—"I am not an interloper when I look at a Rembrandt portrait"—Cole also repeatedly encases the entirety of the existential experience of blackness in the physical stigmas of an obviously black body. "To be black," he writes, "is to bear the brunt of selective enforcement of the law, and to inhabit a psychic unsteadiness in which there is no guarantee of personal safety. You are a black body first, before you are a kid walking down the street or a Harvard professor who has misplaced his keys."

My father would certainly recognize this feeling of restricted being-in-the-world, and it is what he vigilantly reared me to brace myself for, though it has hardly ever been more than vicariously mine. To my knowledge, I've never been followed in a store, people don't cross the street when I approach, and the sole instance I've ever been pulled over in a car, I was absolutely speeding. But then again there was that time, years ago in Munich, when I was inexplicably not allowed inside that same nightclub my Irish-American friend was made to feel more than welcome to enter. By orders of magnitude, I can grasp what it would mean to endure such slights daily and the doubt and sensitivity they would engender. And so although there has been some ambiguity attached to my own nonwhite body, what I am most certain about in all of this—and perhaps this is a source of paradoxical anxiety for me—is that there will not be any with regard to my daughter's. She will not be turned away from that door or others just like it. And so as she grows and looks at me and smiles, all the while remaining innocent of all of this, I am left with some questions and they are urgent ones: What, exactly, remains of the American Negro in my daughter? Is it nothing but an expression playing around the eyes, the slightest hint of lemon in the epidermis? Is it possible to have black consciousness in a body that does not in any way look *black*?

On this point, not only Cole but also the preponderance of contemporary commentators on the subject, who cloak so much of the messiness and contradiction of lived experience in neat critical-race jargon and theories of the constructed body, do not have answers for me. I find myself looking instead to the unorthodox, self-styled Negro thinkers of the twentieth century and today, whose insights into American life in so many ways remain prescient and unrivaled. I'm thinking specifically of Albert Murray, though I'm also thinking of Ralph Ellison and Stanley Crouch. I find myself returning over and over again, in particular, to Murray's masterpiece, the ingenious and criminally neglected 1970 collection of essays and flat-out good sense, *The Omni-Americans,* and also to Crouch's wonderful commentary on it in his own collection, *Always in Pursuit.* One of Murray's signature issues, which even today too often goes de-emphasized or unsaid, is the simple fact that race—though not racism—is at its core a form of "social science fiction," and that identity, above all, is a matter of culture. For Murray, crucially, what we are really talking about is not even race at all but *ethnicity.* To be black, then, could never be merely a matter of possessing one kind of body versus another (as any Dravidian or Melanesian would know). What Murray understood is "exactly what Ellison had made clear before him," writes Crouch. "Polemical reductions, if believed and acted upon, were capable of draining away all of the human complexities and the cultural facts of American life, which were far different from the patterns and policies of prejudice." In other words, it would be insane to let one's own sense of self and history be determined by a nightclub bouncer or a beat cop.

Nonetheless, it's difficult to shake the sense that I have arrived at a certain bind, in many ways similar to the one familiar to secular Jews. The purpose of all these generations of struggle, I know, has always been the freedom to choose—and yet it is precisely this coveted autonomy that threatens now to annihilate the very identity that won it in the first place.

From time to time, feelings something like panic creep in. On the one hand, there is the acute and very specific panic of wondering if I have indeed permanently altered the culture or "race" or ethnicity or, yes, the very *physiognomy* of an entire line of people, like a freight train slowly but irrevocably switching tracks. On the other, there is the subtler, lower-decibel, gnawing panic, which manifests as a plain awareness of the unearned advantage. It is impossible not to feel that. At a time when, despite all of the tremendous societal progress, blackness—certainly not always but especially at that vexed intersection with poverty or the cultural signifiers of such—is still subject to all manner of violation and disrespect; at a time when blacks continue to be stopped, frisked, stalked, harassed, choked out, and drilled with bullets in broad daylight and left in the street—what does it mean to have escaped a fate? Put baldly, what is proximity to whiteness worth and what does color cost? *And the reverse?*

These are questions I don't yet know how to answer. What I do know is that I used to not just tolerate but submit to and even on some deep level *need* our society's dangerous assumptions about race, even as I suspected them to be irredeemably flawed. It is so much easier to sink deeper into a lukewarm bath than to stand up and walk away. But for my daughter's sake if not my own, I can't afford to linger any longer. Now if I find liberation in moments of doubt, it comes with the one movement I always end up having to make, indeed the only movement I *can* make—away from the abstract, general, and hypothetical and back into the jagged grain of the here and now, into the specificity of my love for my father, mother, brother, wife, and daughter, and into my sheer delight in their existence as distinct and irreplaceable people, not bodies or avatars or sites of racial characteristics and traits. With them, I am left with myself as the same, as a man and a human being who is free to choose and who has made choices and is ultimately fulfilled.

Yet I know that is also not enough. If the point is for everyone to build ships, set sail, and be free, if we are collectively ever going to solve this infinitely trickier paradox of racism in the absence of races, we are, all of us—black, white, and everything in between— going to have to do considerably more than contemplate facades. An entirely new framework must be built. This one's rotten to the core.

Contributors' Notes

FRANCISCO CANTÚ served as a Border Patrol agent for the United States Border Patrol from 2008 to 2012. A former Fulbright Fellow, he now holds an MFA in nonfiction from the University of Arizona. His essays and translations appear frequently in *Guernica,* and his work can also be found in *Ploughshares, Orion,* and *Public Books,* where he serves as a contributing editor. He is currently at work on a book about his time in the borderlands.

ALEXANDER CHEE is the author of the novels *Edinburgh* and *The Queen of the Night,* published by Houghton Mifflin Harcourt. He is a recipient of a 2003 Whiting Award, a 2004 NEA Fellowship in prose, and residency fellowships from the MacDowell Colony, the Virginia Center for the Creative Arts, the Civitella Ranieri Foundation, and Amtrak. His essays and stories have appeared on NPR and in *The New York Times Book Review, Tin House, Slate, Guernica,* and *Out,* among other publications. Currently at work on a collection of essays, he lives in New York City.

CHARLES COMEY is a writer living in a little town in New Hampshire with his wife and two boys. He is a frequent contributor to *The Point.* Currently he is at work on his PhD at the University of Chicago's Committee on Social Thought, where he has been the recipient of a Dolores Zohrab Liebmann Fund Fellowship and the Wayne C. Booth Prize for Teaching. When he's done, he plans to transform his obscure academic labors into not-boring personal-philosophical nonfiction.

PAUL CRENSHAW's stories and essays have appeared or are forth-coming in *The Best American Essays, The Best American Nonrequired Reading, Glimmer Train, Ecotone, North American Review,* and *Brevity,* among others. He teaches writing and literature at Elon University. "Names" is one of a collection of essays on his time in the military in the early 1990s.

JAQUIRA DÍAZ is the recipient of a Kenyon Review Fellowship, a Pushcart Prize, the Carl Djerassi Fiction Fellowship from the Wis-consin Institute for Creative Writing, and an NEA Fellowship to the Hambidge Center for the Creative Arts and Sciences. She has received awards from the MacDowell Colony, the Ragdale Founda-tion, the Virginia Center for Creative Arts, the Elizabeth George Foundation, and the Bread Loaf Writers' Conference. Her work has appeared in *The Guardian, The Sun, The Kenyon Review, The Southern Review, Ninth Letter, Brevity,* and elsewhere.

IRINA DUMITRESCU is a professor of medieval English literature at the University of Bonn. She recently edited a collection of essays on arts and humanities in crisis titled *Rumba Under Fire: The Arts of Survival from West Point to Delhi* (2016). Her essays can be found in *The Yale Review, The Southwest Review, Petits Propos Culinaires,* the *Washington Post,* and *The Manifest-Station.* She was nominated for an MFK Fisher Distinguished Writing Award and has been supported by the Whiting Foundation and the Alexander von Humboldt Foundation.

ELA HARRISON's poetry, essays, and book reviews have appeared in *New England Review, The Georgia Review, Cirque Journal,* and *F Maga-zine.* She also contributes articles on environmental and nutritional issues to online publications, including *BeMore! Magazine.* She holds advanced degrees in classical literature and linguistics (from Oxford, Stanford, and UC Berkeley) and has always studied and worked with herbs. Originally from England and Israel, she has traveled widely and lived in places as diverse as Alaska and Hawaii. Harrison received her MFA from the Rainier Writing Workshop in 2014. Now based in Tucson, Arizona, she translates (includ-ing a German encyclopedia project), writes, edits, provides health coaching, and makes herbal remedies and food for people on heal-ing programs.

SEBASTIAN JUNGER is the *New York Times* best-selling author of *War, The Perfect Storm, Fire,* and *A Death in Belmont.* "The Bonds of

Battle" grew into his most recent book, *Tribe: On Homecoming and Belonging.* Together with Tim Hetherington, he directed the documentary *Restrepo,* which won the Grand Jury Prize at Sundance and was nominated for an Oscar in 2011. He went on to direct *Which Way Is the Front Line from Here?, Korengal,* and *The Last Patrol.* He is a contributing editor to *Vanity Fair* and has been awarded a National Magazine Award and an SAIS-Novartis Prize for Excellence in International Journalism. Junger's essay "The Lion in Winter" was selected by Stephen Jay Gould for *The Best American Essays 2002.* He lives in New York City.

LAURA KIPNIS is a cultural critic and former video artist who writes frequently on sexual politics, aesthetics, emotion, acting out, bad behavior, and various other crevices of the American psyche. She is the author of six books. The latest is *Men: Notes from an Ongoing Investigation;* previous titles include *How to Become a Scandal* and *Against Love: A Polemic.* The next (just finished!) is *Stupid Sex/Higher Ed.* She teaches filmmaking at Northwestern University and lives in New York and Chicago.

JORDAN KISNER has published essays in *n+1, New York Magazine, The American Scholar,* and elsewhere, and she is at work on a book inspired by "Thin Places." She holds an MFA in nonfiction from Columbia University, where she teaches undergraduate writing.

AMITAVA KUMAR is the author of several works of nonfiction, including *Lunch with a Bigot, A Matter of Rats,* and *A Foreigner Carrying in the Crook of His Arm a Tiny Bomb.* He teaches English at Vassar College and is currently writing a book about academic style with the support of a Guggenheim fellowship.

RICHARD M. LANGE's short fiction has appeared in *North American Review, Cimarron Review, Mississippi Review, Ping Pong, Chicago Quarterly Review, Eclipse, Georgetown Review,* and elsewhere, and two of his stories have been nominated for the Pushcart Prize. A former copywriter for a major insurance company, he is working on a novel about the financial crisis. He lives in Santa Cruz, California.

LEE MARTIN has published three memoirs: *From Our House, Turning Bones,* and *Such a Life.* He is also the author of four novels, including *The Bright Forever,* a finalist for the 2006 Pulitzer Prize in Fiction, and, most recently, *Late One Night.* His fiction and nonfiction have appeared in such places as *Harper's Magazine, Ms., Creative*

Nonfiction, The Sun, The Georgia Review, The Kenyon Review, Fourth Genre, River Teeth, The Southern Review, Prairie Schooner, Glimmer Train, and *The Best American Mystery Stories.* He is the winner of the Mary McCarthy Prize in Short Fiction and has been awarded fellowships from the National Endowment for the Arts and the Ohio Arts Council. He teaches in the MFA Program at The Ohio State University.

LISA NIKOLIDAKIS's fiction and nonfiction have appeared in *The Los Angeles Review, Brevity, McSweeney's Internet Tendency, Passages North, Hunger Mountain, The Rumpus, The Greensboro Review,* and elsewhere. She has won an Orlando Prize from the A Room of Her Own Foundation for flash fiction and *The Briar Cliff Review*'s annual contest for nonfiction. She currently teaches creative writing in the Midwest, has just completed a collection of short stories, and is working on an essay collection.

JOYCE CAROL OATES is the author of fiction, poetry, plays, and criticism. Her more than forty novels include *them,* which won the National Book Award in 1970, *Wonderland, You Must Remember This, We Were the Mulvaneys, The Gravedigger's Daughter,* and, in 2016, *The Man Without a Shadow.* She has received the President's Medal in the Humanities, a PEN Lifetime Achievement Award, and, most recently, the A. J. Liebling Award for Outstanding Boxing Writing. She teaches at Princeton University, New York University, and the University of California, Berkeley, and is a founding editor of *Ontario Review.*

MARSHA POMERANTZ is the author of *The Illustrated Edge,* a book of poems (2011). A second manuscript has been a finalist for the National Poetry Series and for the Anthony Hecht Poetry Prize but is still looking for a home. Her poems and essays have been published by *Beloit Poetry Journal, berfrois.com, Boston Review, Harvard Review, Parnassus, PN Review, Raritan, Salamander,* and others, and she has translated a novel, short stories, and poems from the Hebrew. She retired in 2013 as managing editor at the Harvard Art Museums.

JILL SISSON QUINN's essays have appeared in *Orion, Ecotone, OnEarth,* and many other magazines. She has received the Annie Dillard Award in Creative Nonfiction, a John Burroughs Essay Award, and a Rona Jaffe Foundation Writers' Award. Her essay "Sign Here if You Exist" was reprinted in *The Best American Science and Nature Writing 2011.* Her first book, *Deranged,* was published in 2010. A regular commentator for Wisconsin Public Radio's *Wisconsin Life* series, she lives and writes in Scandinavia, Wisconsin.

JUSTIN PHILLIP REED is a South Carolina native and the author of *A History of Flamboyance* (2016). His first full-length book of poetry, *Indecency,* is forthcoming in 2018. His work has appeared—or soon will—in *Boston Review, Callaloo, Catapult, Columbia Poetry Review, Eleven Eleven, The Kenyon Review, Obsidian, PEN American, The Rumpus, Vinyl,* and elsewhere. He received his MFA from Washington University in St. Louis and is the online editor for *Tusculum Review.*

Born in London in 1933, OLIVER SACKS was educated at The Queen's College, Oxford. After receiving his medical degree, Sacks continued his studies in the United States, specializing in neurology and moving to New York City. His first book, *Migraine* (1970), combined an authoritative medical and historical coverage of the condition with the experiences of his suffering patients. Sacks would return again and again to case studies, turning them into a provocative literary form. They provide the basis for two of his best-known books, *Awakenings* (1973) and *The Man Who Mistook His Wife for a Hat* (1985). He wrote two memoirs, *Uncle Tungsten: Memories of a Chemical Boyhood* (2001) and *On the Move: A Life,* which was published shortly before he died in August 2015. "A General Feeling of Disorder" was one of his last essays.

KATHERINE E. STANDEFER won the 2015 Iowa Review Award in Nonfiction. She writes about the body, consent, and medical technology from Tucson, where she teaches intimate creative writing classes that help people engage their experiences of sexuality and illness on the page. She earned her MFA in creative nonfiction at the University of Arizona. A certified sexologist, she also teaches in a pilot narrative medicine program at UA's College of Medicine. Her work has appeared most recently in *Fourth Genre, The Iowa Review, Colorado Review, Indiana Review, Cutbank, Essay Daily,* and *High Country News.*

GEORGE STEINER, the winner of numerous international awards and for many years a book critic at *The New Yorker,* is the author of many books, including *After Babel, Antigones, Language and Silence, Real Presences,* and *Extraterritorial.* His fiction include *Proofs and Three Parables* and *The Portage to San Cristobal of A.H.;* he has also published two memoirs, *Errata: An Examined Life* and *My Unwrit-*

ten Books. A fellow of Churchill College, Cambridge, since 1961, Steiner has taught at a number of universities and was a professor of English and comparative literature at the University of Geneva between 1974 and 1994.

MASON STOKES is a professor of English at Skidmore College in Saratoga Springs, New York, where he teaches courses on African-American literature and queer fiction. He has published widely on race and sexuality in American culture and is also the author of *Saving Julian: A Novel.*

THOMAS CHATTERTON WILLIAMS is the author of a memoir, *Losing My Cool,* and has written for *The New York Times, Harper's Magazine, Smithsonian Journeys, London Review of Books, The New Yorker,* and many other publications. His next book, a reckoning with how we define race in America, will expand his essay "Black and Blue and Blond," published last year in *The Virginia Quarterly Review.* He lives in Paris, where he is an associate editor at *Holiday* and *Purple Fashion Magazine* and a regular book critic for the *San Francisco Chronicle.*

Notable Essays and Literary Nonfiction of 2015

SELECTED BY ROBERT ATWAN

RAYMOND ABBOTT
 Seymour Krim, *Oyez Review,*
 Spring
SUFIYA ABDUR-RAHMAN
 Surrender at the Cinema,
 Ummah Wide, February 15
HANNAH DELA CRUZ ABRAMS
 Dog and Wolf: The Time
 Between, *Southern Humanities
 Review,* vol. 48, no. 3
STEVE ADAMS
 Border Crossing, *Grist,* no. 8
TAMARA ADELMAN
 Rustic Canyon, *Rubbertop Review,*
 no. 7
MARCIA ALDRICH
 The Blue Dress, *Hotel Amerika,*
 Winter
TARIQ AL HAYDAR
 Machine Language, *Crab Orchard
 Review,* Summer/Fall
CYNTHIA ALLEN
 When the Walls Came Down,
 So to Speak, Fall
LAUREN ALWAN
 Eldorado, *ZYZZYVA,* Winter
ZAY AMSBURY
 Immersive Theater, New York:
 A Report from the Field, *The
 Labletter,* no. 17

KATE ANGUS
 My Catalog of Failures,
 The Southeast Review, vol. 33,
 no. 1
KWAME ANTHONY APPIAH
 Race in the Modern World,
 Foreign Affairs, March/April
AARON APPS
 The Formation of This
 Grotesque Fatty Figure, *Passages
 North,* no. 36
AMYE ARCHER
 Slow Motion, *PMS,* no. 14
CHRIS ARTHUR
 Memory Sticks, *The Literary
 Review,* Spring
 Glass, *Tahoma Literary Review,*
 vol. 2, no. 2
RILLA ASKEW
 Trail, *This Land,* Spring
HOWARD AXELROD
 Into the Blind Spot, *The Virginia
 Quarterly Review,* Winter

MATTHEW JAMES BABCOCK
 Boogaloo Too, *Small Print
 Magazine,* Spring/Summer
C. MORGAN BABST
 Death Is a Way to Be, *Guernica,*
 June 15

BLAIR BRAVERMAN
Welcome to Dog World! *The Atavist Magazine,* June

MOLLY BRODAK
Bandit, *Granta,* no. 132

TAFFY BRODESSER-AKNER
Turbulent Calm, *Good,* Spring

MIKE BROIDA
Odysseus at Teleyplos, *The Rumpus,* November 18

VICTOR BROMBERT
Between Two Worlds, *The Hudson Review,* Autumn

NICK BROMELL
Dignity: A Word for Democracy, *Raritan,* Summer

DAVID BROMWICH
Trapped in the Virtual Classroom, *The New York Review of Books,* July 9

VICTORIA BROWN
Nice Girl and Small Man, *Apogee,* no. 6

ROBERT S. BRUNK
We Shall All Be Forgotten, *North Dakota Quarterly,* vol. 80, no. 3

LUCY BRYAN
In Between Places, *Quarterly West,* October 29

CHRISTOPHER BUCKLEY
The Ontology of Hermeneutics, *Catamaran,* Spring

FRANK BURES
Beyond Belief, *The Rotarian,* August

ROSE BURKE
Thirteen Stages of Grief, *The Southampton Review,* Summer/Fall

AMY BUTCHER
A Slow Kind of Unraveling, *Gulf Coast,* Winter/Spring

DAVID BYRNE
A Matter of the Skies, *Boston Review,* January/February

MICHELLE CACHO-NEGRETE
First Husband, *North American Review,* Summer

GARNETTE CADOGAN
Black and Blue, *Freeman's,* no. 1

PABLO CALVI
Secret Reserves, *The Believer,* Fall

SHANNON MICHAEL CANE
Xerox, Paper, Scissors, *Aperture,* Spring

KELLY GREY CARLISLE
Permutations of X, *New England Review,* vol. 35, no. 4

TOM CARSON
Clans of the Cathode, *The Baffler,* no. 29

LIANE KUPFERBERG CARTER
A Room of My Own, *Manifest-Station,* October 28

DOUG PAUL CASE
On Locker Rooms and Looking, *December,* Spring/Summer

CHRISTOPHER CHAMBERS
Amplifier, *The Southern Review,* Summer

J'LYN CHAPMAN
The Good Beast, *Denver Quarterly,* vol. 49, no. 3

WYNN CHAPMAN
The War of the Ashes, *Blackbird,* Fall

JULIE CHINITZ
Sleepless Nights with Khaled El-Masri, *Confrontation,* Fall

ROOHI CHOUDHRY
On Island, *The Butter,* March 2

JILL CHRISTMAN
Going Back to Plum Island, *River Teeth,* Fall

AMY CLARK
The Rocks, *The Chattahoochee Review,* Spring

SUSANNAH CLARK
Signs (2002), *Under the Gum Tree,* April

TA-NEHISI COATES
Letter to My Son, *The Atlantic,* September

ROBERT LONG FOREMAN
Why I Write Nonfiction,
Copper Nickel, no. 20

PATRICIA FOSTER
The Lost Years, *Colorado Review,*
Spring

MATTHEW GAVIN FRANK
Grasshopper Diptych, *Midwestern
Gothic,* Fall

JOEY FRANKLIN
The Full Montaigne, *Ninth Letter,*
Fall/Winter

JONATHAN FRANZEN
Carbon Capture, *The New Yorker,*
April 6

IAN FRAZIER
The Syrian Woman, *Portland,*
Winter

STEVE FRIEDMAN
My Sister, the Runner? *Runner's
World,* January/February

REBEKAH FRUMKIN
Atypical, *Catapult,* December 11

ANDREW FURMAN
Starting from Seed, *The Southern
Review,* Spring

BRENDAN GALVIN
A Few Thousand Walks by the
Little Pamet River: One Poet's
Geography, *Sewanee Review,*
Summer

J. MALCOLM GARCIA
The Feral Children of Kabul,
Tampa Review, no. 50

KENNETH GARCIA
Cattle, Casinos, and Cathouses,
The Southwest Review, vol. 100,
no. 2

EMILY GEMINDER
Coming To: A Lexicology of
Fainting, *Prairie Schooner,* Summer

ELIZABETH GENTRY
The Possum, the Wren, and My
Animal-Soul, *Third Coast,* Fall

PHILIP GERARD
Sherman's Final March, *Our State,*
February

DAVID GESSNER
The Prankster and the Professor,
Tin House, no. 64

ETHAN GILSDORF
The Day My Mother Became a
Stranger, *Boston Magazine,* May

D. GILSON
Michael Jackson & Michel
Foucault Walk into a Bar,
The Threepenny Review, Fall

AMANDA GIRACCA
The Art of Butchery, *Aeon,*
April 24

WILLIAM GIRALDI
Object Lesson, *The New Republic,*
May

AMY GLYNN
Apple, *Literal Latte,* Spring

FLORA GONZALEZ
The Sewing Room, *Solstice,*
Summer

ADAM GOPNIK
The Driver's Seat, *The New Yorker,*
February 2

ALISON GOPNIK
David Hume and the Buddha,
The Atlantic, October

EMILY FOX GORDON
Confessing and Confiding,
The American Scholar, Spring

VIVIAN GORNICK
Why I Live Where I Live, *The New
Republic,* November

MICHAEL GRACEY
My Own Good Daemon, *Ninth
Letter,* Fall/Winter

T. AUSTIN GRAHAM
Songs of the Century, *New Literary
History,* vol. 4, no. 4

SUE GRANZELLA
Andiamo! *Ascent,* May 20

ALLISON GREEN
Twenty Hours and Ten Minutes
of Therapy, *The Gettysburg Review,*
Spring

STEPHEN GREENBLATT
Shakespeare in Tehran, *The New
York Review of Books,* April 2

CHRISTIAN WIMAN
Kill the Creature, *The American Scholar,* Spring

ARIEL WINTER
Tales of Grandma Whittier, *Slice,* no. 17

MELORA WOLFF
Mystery Girls, *Southern Indiana Review,* Fall

LAURA ESTHER WOLFSON
After the Autobiography, *Superstition Review,* July

BARON WORMSER
Harrisong, *Five Points,* vol. 16, no. 3

GREG WRENN
Innocence, *KROnline,* Summer

XU XI
The English of My Story, *Lake Effect,* no. 19

AMY YEE
Exporting Clothes, Importing Safety, *Roads and Kingdoms,* August 27

LEE ZACHARIAS
A Circle, a Line, an Island, *Our State,* May

JESS ZIMMERMAN
A Midlife Crisis, by Any Other Name, *Hazlitt,* July 20

DAVE ZOBY
Hobart Dreams, *The Missouri Review,* Summer

Notable Special Issues of 2015

The Antioch Review, "The Educated
Heart," ed. Robert S. Fogarty,
Fall.

The Baffler, "Venus in Furs," ed.
John Summers, no. 27.

The Chattahoochee Review, "Migration,"
ed. Anna Schachner, Fall/Winter.

Conjunctions, "Natural Causes," ed.
Bradford Morrow, no. 64.

Creative Nonfiction, "The Memoir," ed.
Lee Gutkind, Spring.

Daedalus, "What Is the Brain Good
For?" guest editor, Fred H. Gage,
Winter.

Ecotone, "The Sound Issue," ed.
David Gessner, Fall.

Freeman's, "Arrival," ed.
John Freeman, 2015.

Granta, "India: Another Way of
Seeing," guest editor, Ian Jack,
no. 130.

Harper's Magazine, "How to Be a
Parent," August.

Hayden's Ferry Review, "Borderlands,"
ed. Chelsea Hickok, Fall/Winter.

Hunger Mountain, "The Body Issue,"
ed. Miciah Bay Gault, no. 19.

Image, "Reading from Two
Books: Nature, Scripture, and
Evolution," ed. Gregory Wolfe,
no. 85.

Iron Horse Literary Review, Kirk
Wisland, "Melancholy of Falling
Men" (single-author issue), ed.
Leslie Jill Patterson, vol. 17, no.5.

The Literary Review, "Flight," ed.
Minna Proctor, Fall.

MAKE, "The Value of What's
Forgotten," ed. Jose-Luis
Moctezuma, no. 16.

Midwestern Gothic, nonfiction issue,
ed. Jeff Pfaller and Robert James
Russell, Fall.

The Missouri Review, "Loners," ed.
Speer Morgan, Spring.

n+1, "Conviction," ed. Nikil Saval
and Dayna Tortorici, Spring.

The Nation, 150th anniversary issue,
ed. Katrina Vanden Heuvel and
D. D. Guttenplan, April.

New Literary History, "Song," ed.
Jahan Ramazani and Herbert F.
Tucker, Autumn.

North Dakota Quarterly, "Slow," ed.
Rebecca Rozelle-Stone and
William Caraher, vol. 80, no. 2.

Oregon Humanities, "Safe," ed.
Kathleen Holt, Summer.

Orion, "Writing and Art from
America's Prisons," ed. Richard
Shelton, January/February.

Prairie Schooner, "Sports," guest editor,
Natalie Diaz, Winter.

Room, "Fieldwork," ed. Tayrn
Hubbard, vol. 38, no. 4.

Salmagundi, "The Best of
Salmagundi" (50th anniversary
issue), ed. Robert Boyers and
Peg Boyers, Winter/Spring.

The Sewanee Review, "Folded Sunsets:
At Home and Abroad," ed.
George Core, Summer.

Slice, "Desire," ed. Maria Gagliano,
Celia Blue Johnson, and
Elizabeth Blachman, no. 17.

The Threepenny Review, "A Symposium
on Jokes," ed. Wendy Lesser, Fall.

Tin House, "Theft," ed. Rob Spillman,
no. 65.

Vice, "The Prison Issue," ed. Ellis
Jones, October.

Water-Stone Review, "All We Cannot
Alter," ed. Mary Francois
Rockcastle, no. 18.

Witness, "Trans/lation," ed. Maile
Chapman, Spring.

...

Corrections:

Apologies to Jaquira Díaz, whose "Ordinary Girls" appears in this volume. Because of a printing mishap, the spelling of her last name was mangled in the list of "Notable Essays and Literary Nonfiction of 2014," which included her essay "My Mother and Mercy" from the August issue of *The Sun.*

The following essays should also have appeared in "Notable Essays and Literary Nonfiction of 2014":

ALEXANDER CHEE, Mr. & Mrs. B, *Apology,* Winter

BETTINA DREW, The Great Amnesia, *Southwest Review,* vol. 99, no. 4

SONJA LIVINGSTON, Mock Orange, *Water-Stone Review,* no. 17

JOHN S. O'CONNOR, The Ice House, *Under the Sun,* July 31

NED STUCKEY-FRENCH, Our Queer Little Hybrid Thing, *Assay,* Fall